BETTER TOGETHER

A CHRISTIAN COWBOY ROMANCE

WOLF CREEK RANCH
BOOK FOUR

MANDI BLAKE

Better Together
Wolf Creek Ranch Book 4
By Mandi Blake

Copyright © 2023 Mandi Blake
All Rights Reserved

Published in the United States of America
Cover Designer: Amanda Walker PA & Design Services
Editor: Editing Done Write

CONTENTS

CHAPTER 1

COLT

D ust and dirt settled over the rodeo arena as Colt closed the catch pen. That was the last of the bronc rides. Judging from the cheers, no one seemed to be bothered by the dropping temperature. Wyoming nights were about to hit the unforgiving freeze-your-nose-hairs-off stage.

Colt rolled his right shoulder and felt the pull on the other side. Before tonight, it had been a few years since he'd dislocated a shoulder, and apparently injuries hurt worse in your late twenties. He should have taken better care of his body in his teens.

Adjusting the strap on the shoulder sling, Colt scanned the crowd. He hadn't caught a ride with Ridge this morning, but driving was going to be a killer if he had to use his left arm.

Colt spied a glimpse of his roommate through

the crowd and made a beeline for him. Normally, Colt would work late on Friday nights after the rodeo, but he was useless thanks to the bronc that had bucked him earlier.

"Colt," a woman called as he passed.

"Mrs. Hampton."

The Hamptons had been guests at the ranch all week, and Colt had made fast friends with their son.

Colt swung his good arm out for a side hug. "Did you see Nate's ride?"

The kids practiced riding the horses with Jess and Remi all week and got the chance to show off their new skills for their parents on Friday nights. It was always the highlight of Colt's week.

"I did!" the woman squealed as she wrapped an arm around Colt's waist and squeezed. "He's had a blast. I guarantee he'll be talking about this place for months."

"Good." Wolf Creek Ranch was one of the last dude ranches in the west that hadn't succumbed to the luxury industry. They kept things old-fashioned, just the way Colt liked.

Mrs. Hampton released the hug and stood on her tippy toes to scan the crowd. "Have you seen Jeff?"

Colt looked for Mr. Hampton. He spotted the dark-haired man near the catch pen and pointed. "There."

Mrs. Hampton waved. "Thanks again!"

"Come back next year. We'll get Nate on a trail ride." The eight-year-old was a natural on a horse and loved the outdoors.

"We'll see!" she yelled over her shoulder as she pushed through the crowd toward her husband.

Colt searched again for Ridge and found him not far from where he'd been before. Colt set a course again but stopped to chat with an older couple who hoped to bring their grandkids to the ranch next year.

Jameson Ford, the foreman at Wolf Creek Ranch, announced over the sound system that the show was over, but there were plenty of groups still hanging around chatting by the arena. Colt continued to weave his way through the crowd, trying his best not to bump into anyone with his left side.

"Ridge!"

Colt's roommate—well, housemate—turned and tipped his chin. "Yeah?"

"Can I bum a ride home?" He jerked his head toward the throbbing shoulder.

Ridge rubbed his jaw and scanned the crowd. "Cheyenne's mom is staying with her tonight, and she needs help getting settled in the cabin. You can ride with me, but it'll be a while before I head home."

Ridge and Cheyenne had recently decided to tie the knot, and her mom and sister had just moved here from Tennessee. With her mom still in a wheel-chair after a brutal stroke, she needed all the help she could get.

Colt chanced a roll of his injured shoulder and got nothing but a stab of pain. "Man, I wish I could lend a hand, but I'm no help tonight."

"Don't worry about it. Maybe Paul could give you a ride."

"I'll do it."

Colt's skin tingled at the sound of the sweet feminine voice behind him. Remi had a way of kicking all five of his senses into overdrive whenever she was around.

Always Remi. Only Remi.

Remington Taylor bounded up beside him, and her long ponytail swung from side to side. The arti-ficial lights around the arena lit up her face and fiery-red hair like a flame in the night. That was a good analogy for her role in his life–a light in the darkness.

She was his best friend. Well, she'd decided she was his best friend. He'd decided a long time ago that she was his soul mate, but she hadn't gotten the same memo.

Why couldn't the love score be even, just this once?

She looked up at him with that bright smile that kicked him in the chest like a bucking bronc, and his mouth watered. He had no control whenever Remi came around.

"You sure?" Colt asked.

She grinned and narrowed her eyes at him. "I wouldn't have said I would if I wasn't sure."

Truth. Remi was the quickest decision-maker he'd ever met, but once she made up her mind, she stuck to her guns. Every time.

Colt bumped Remi with his right shoulder and turned to Ridge. "Looks like I found a ride."

Ridge tipped his hat. "See you at the house."

Remi patted Colt's arm. "How's the shoulder?"

"Beat up, but I think I'll survive just one more day."

Remi rolled her eyes and jerked her head toward the path leading back to the hub of the ranch. "Come on. I parked at the stables."

Colt fell into step beside her. "I'm injured. I expected curbside service."

"Did you hit your head when you got bucked?" Remi asked. "You've got two legs."

Colt smiled. "I do. They're good-lookin' legs too. I tried to get Jameson to add shorts to the dress code, but–"

"Have you seen your legs? They're so pale, the moonlight reflecting on your skin might blind someone."

"That's offensive. You'd have more friends if you were nicer," Colt said. Remi was one of the nicest people he'd ever met, but he knew how to look past her sarcasm and playful wit.

"Sorry. I've hit my friend quota. Submissions are closed." Remi bounced a little with each step as the path sloped down toward the stables. The fallen leaves crunched beneath their boots as they walked. "Are you sure you're okay?"

It wasn't like Remi to worry about anything, especially not Colt. "Yeah," he drawled. "Are *you* okay?"

"Of course. I didn't have my shoulder dislocated tonight." She paused for a second, and her whole body shivered. "Well, I think I got a little queasy when they did that thing to put your shoulder back in."

Colt wrapped his good arm around her and pulled her closer to his side. "It's a good thing you didn't get your calling mixed up. You'd have been a terrible nurse passing out in front of the patients."

Remi shoved his arm off her shoulders. "I didn't say I almost passed out. I said... Never mind."

Colt stopped beside the driver's side of Remi's SUV. "You're worried about me."

"I am not. You're a big boy, and you can take care of yourself."

Colt shifted to the side. "You care. You actually have a heart."

Remi pointed the business end of her key at his

face. "Colton Walker, move your skinny butt before I stab you."

"Do you use that language around the kids?" Colt asked.

Remi gasped. She was the kids' activities coordinator, and she took her job way too seriously for someone who chased tiny humans all day. "I am a good role model!"

Shaking his head slowly, he tsked. "The HR department would love to hear about your threats. I think that rusty key would be considered a dangerous weapon."

"We don't even have an HR department. And you've had your tetanus shot. I was with you when you got it last spring."

Colt shivered at the memory of the time he got caught in the barbed wire fence while chasing a foal that was heading toward a ravine. "Why'd you have to bring that up?"

Remi pursed her lips together, and even in the faint light of the moon he could make out her warning expression. She pointed her key to the side, gesturing for him to move it or lose it.

He studied her one last time. Was she worried about him, or was there something else going on with her? "Fine, but I get to choose the radio station." He grabbed the driver's door handle and pulled, but the door didn't budge.

"You have to pull up, then out," Remi explained.

"If you're going to be chivalrous, at least do it with gusto."

Colt did as instructed, and the door opened. He lifted a flimsy piece of tape that hung from the side-view mirror. "Is this duct tape? When are you going to get a vehicle that isn't held together by a hope and a prayer?"

Remi slipped in and reached for the door. "Never."

The metallic screech of her dramatic door slam was loud in the quiet night. Colt slipped into the passenger side and leaned the seat all the way back.

"Jess is going to be mad that you messed up her seat situation," Remi said.

"This is *my* seat."

"I don't know. She's my friend and roommate. I think she trumps you with your measly friend status."

Wow. Words hurt.

"You should promote me then. I think we've been friends long enough that I deserve a raise or something."

"I get mediocre friend benefits from you."

The truth again. And another blatant reminder that Remi would never see him as anything more than a friend.

He'd tried. Given it his best shot. It had been three years and five months since she set the record straight. Friends without a hint of anything more.

Bottom line. Write it in stone. Remi Taylor was off-limits.

There may have been laughing. At his expense. He wasn't sure anymore because that horrible and embarrassing memory was almost one hundred percent suppressed.

The ride to Ridge's house was short, but this was one of those times when Colt wished he still lived on the ranch.

The upside: Ridge used to be a professional football player, and he was ridiculously rich. Therefore, his house was a mega mansion, and Colt got to live there rent free.

The downside: He couldn't walk to his cabin and crash after a long workday.

His shoulder throbbed, and the pain was radiating into his neck and up his jaw.

"Colt, do you want some medicine?" Remi's voice was quiet in the dark cab.

"No. I'm fine."

But even he could hear the bite in his voice. He wasn't fine, but meds weren't an option for him. He could thank his old man for that family curse. Addiction could turn the best man into a devil, and Colt wasn't taking any chances.

Remi reached for the radio dial and skipped through a few stations until she found a Tammy Wynette song. Remi sang along, and her twang matched the country music legend's. There was something about Remi's voice that made his attention perk up like a dog on a trail.

Colt's mom had been a singer. Well, she might be living that dream now for all he knew. She'd been gone for over twenty years, and he'd never gotten the urge to look for her. If she wanted him, she would have come back a long time ago.

Remi turned into the driveway and parked in her usual spot beside the garage. She killed the engine and jumped out. Colt reluctantly sat up and crawled out of the truck. It was going to be a long night, if the pain didn't ease up.

Remi met him at the front of the SUV. "You look awful."

Colt gritted his teeth against the throbbing pain in his arm. "You don't. You always look good."

Sometimes, he could get away with the truth. Only when Remi would assume he was joking. He didn't need a professional to tell him his relationship with Remi was messed up.

"I'm serious, Colt. Are you okay?"

"I'm fine. I just need food and ice."

"Mr. Pizza?" Remi asked.

"Yes. I need comfort food." They were regulars, and Remi only needed to make the call and say hello before Willa at Mr. Pizza knew to put in their usual order.

"You want to add—"

Remi's question was cut off as she gasped and

tumbled off the paved walkway, falling face first into a puddle at the base of the gutter spout.

Clumsiness strikes again. The woman couldn't pass a hole or a small body of water without tumbling into it. She had a gift.

Colt crouched beside her. "You could have just asked me if you wanted to know how cold the water was."

Remi huffed and pushed up onto her hands and knees. "A hand would be nice," she growled.

"You've got two legs."

Remi raised up and lifted her arms. The whole front of her body was wet. "Seriously?"

Colt bent to wrap his good arm around her at the waist, positioning his good shoulder in front of her. Lifting with his legs, he stood with her cold, wet body draped over his shoulder.

"Colt! Put me down!"

"No, I don't trust you to make it inside on your own. You're a danger to yourself."

Remi's voice shook. "Colt, I'm serious."

"You're seriously freezing."

She chuckled, but even that shuttered with cold. "Come on, caveman. I can walk."

"I'm not convinced. I'm not putting you down so you can scar yourself up. It's best if I take care of you." He hefted her higher onto his good shoulder while the other screamed in protest.

"I'm supposed to be taking care of you! Don't get things twisted around here."

Colt stepped up onto the porch and crouched to turn the knob with Remi still dangling over his shoulder. The back door was always unlocked because Colt kept losing the key.

"Says the woman draped over my shoulder because she can't walk inside without kissing the ground."

Remi laughed. A full-belly, melodic laugh that was so contagious that Colt couldn't help but grin at her happiness. That was one thing he loved about Remi: she wasn't afraid to laugh at herself.

Still laughing, Remi sucked in a deep breath and said, "You're going to hurt your shoulder."

Colt stepped inside and kicked the door closed behind him. "It's already hurt, and I only need one good shoulder to carry you around with." The pain in his other shoulder was numbing. That was either a good thing or a bad thing. Joking with Remi was a natural pain reliever, but he'd probably pay for it later.

Which was more dangerous, pills or Remi?

If he had to have a weakness, he was glad it was Remi.

He bent to gently place her feet on the floor, and she immediately crossed her arms over her chest. His wet shoulder and back were thirty-degrees colder without her warmth.

"Freezing," she said through chattering teeth.

"Let's get you into dry clothes." Colt led the way up the stairs to his room and tossed a flannel shirt and sweatpants with a drawstring to her. He pointed to the bathroom connected to the bedroom. "You can take a shower if you want."

Remi turned the clothes over in her shaky hands. "What would I do without you?"

That wasn't the joking thanks he'd expected. The slight sadness in her voice cut him like that rusty barbed wire fence. "You won't ever have to find out."

And just like that, Remi's smile was back as she held up his shirt and pants. "Thanks for the new clothes."

She darted toward the bathroom, but he caught her with his good arm, pulling her back to face him. When he had her full attention, he took the moment to stare into her eyes. They were hazel with dark-brown flecks, and he loved looking at them, dreaming about them, imagining those eyes were his to admire whenever he wanted.

Colt cleared his throat and whispered, "Those are not yours to keep. Stop stealing my clothes."

Remi grinned. It was the same mischievous grin she'd had the time she volunteered him for Christmas caroling at the assisted living center last year. "I'll bring them back...one day."

Colt loosened his hold on her arm, and she

skipped off toward the bathroom. That woman had no idea that she was his world. He'd be revolving around her like a satellite until his dying day, and she'd never be the wiser.

He fisted his left hand and winced. Loving Remi was a lot like an injury that never healed. She said his name, and a bolt of lightning shot through his chest. She smiled up at him, and the urge to wrap her in his arms and kiss her senseless was a fire in his veins.

She reminded him they were just friends, and he died a little inside.

Colt would never claim to know everything, but there was one thing he did know. Remi was going to bring him to his knees one day, and there wasn't anything he could do to stop it.

CHAPTER 2
REMI

Remi slid into the bathroom and locked the door behind her. What had gotten into her? Colt got a bruise, and she turned into a complete sap. He was her friend, that was all, and she didn't want anything else.

But she did get itchy whenever she thought about the inevitable loss of the constant in her life that was Colton Walker.

He wanted a wife and kids and the perfect white picket fence life. He talked about it enough that Remi couldn't forget about it.

She didn't want those things, and that's where the buck stopped. One day, she would lose her best friend, and she wasn't in a hurry to give him away. When that time came, she'd bow out with grace.

But not today. She'd selfishly keep him as long

as she could, even if the version of her he knew was hiding a lot of darkness and mistakes.

Looking around the sleek modern bathroom had her gaping. Colt had been living at Ridge's place for a few months now, but she'd never had a reason to peek into his bedroom or bathroom. Everything was crisp lines and luxury materials. The floor was a faint gray marble and unnaturally warm against her feet. She stepped onto a nearby rug and dug her toes into the softest material she'd ever touched.

Colt was living in some kind of alternate reality. It was great, but Remi would never get used to the finer things in life. She'd grown up in a love-hate relationship with money, and she wanted to talk about it exactly zero percent of the time.

She pulled the wet shirt away from her stomach, but the cold fabric sucked back to her skin as soon as she let it go. Real classy. She wasn't wearing a white T-shirt, but the lines of her figure were too detailed for her liking.

Pulling the shirt over her head, she quickly tossed it into the sink and scrambled for the dry shirt. Colt wasn't one of those bodybuilder types, but he probably had at least a hundred pounds on her. The flannel shirt hung low around her chest and down to the bottom of her thighs.

She snuck a glance at herself in the mirror and chuckled. She looked ridiculous. Colt would get a good laugh when he saw her.

Getting the wet jeans off was probably comical as well, since she ended up lying on the floor and pulling on the hem while bending her leg behind her. Gritting her teeth, she gave the bottom of the jeans one more tug and lost her grip. Both hands flew at her face, knocking her back onto the floor.

"Oof!"

"Remi, are you okay in there?"

Of course, Colt was standing outside the door waiting to save her when she did something stupid.

"I'm fine. Go order the pizza. I'm starving." In truth, the battle with the jeans had worked up her appetite.

She paused and didn't hear him leaving.

"Colt, I can do this myself."

How many times did she hear that from kids' mouths every day? Now she knew how they felt.

"Fine. I'll be downstairs."

This time, she heard his footsteps retreating and the bedroom door close behind him.

Now, she could struggle to dress herself in peace. She tried another stretch and was able to wiggle out of the torture device. She leaned against the cabinets and took a minute to catch her breath. Maybe she should switch to leggings. Or jeggings. Could she get away with jeggings on the ranch? Maybe no one would notice.

Remi slipped on Colt's pants and double knotted them at the waist. Then, she rolled up the bottoms of the legs and propped her hands on her hips. "Job well done."

She waited to hear from Colt on the other side of the door, but there was only silence. Maybe he'd really gone downstairs.

After gathering up her wet clothes, she exited the bathroom with as much grace as she could muster.

Colt's bedroom was basic with only a bed, dresser, nightstand, and chest of drawers. The dark-gray comforter on the bed lay in the general vicinity for the bed to be considered "made" but no corners were lined up or tucked in.

"Amateur," Remi whispered. She'd been making her bed meticulously for as long as she could remember. Making her bed look nice made her feel like she had something of worth. There had been times–times that shall not be named–when she didn't have a bed. Having a comfy place to sleep was a privilege, and she showed her appreciation by making her bed.

Lame but true–however weird it may be.

Remi walked down the stairs, careful to lift the long pants up just a little more so she didn't trip on the hems. She'd done enough of that today, and Colt would probably put her on the prayer list if she fell twice in one day. All of the old ladies in the congregation would be calling and stopping by to wish her well.

The ridiculous vision wasn't imagined. He'd done it before. They'd even brought Remi casseroles all because of a bruise.

At the bottom of the stairs, Remi headed for the laundry room and tossed her wet clothes in the dryer. They'd be dry in an hour, and she would feel like a real person again. Because, no, the all-too-comfy woman wearing Colt's clothes had to be some fictitious joke. Wearing his clothes didn't mean anything. At least, that's the lie she was telling herself today.

She stepped back into the enormous main room of the house. She looked around the kitchen and living room, but there wasn't any sign of Colt. Where did he go? She searched around and found him in the recliner. He was sprawled on his back with an arm draped over his eyes.

He was wearing a different shirt. How did that happen?

He lifted the arm off his eyes and raised his head to look at her. "Took you long enough. The pizza should be here any minute."

"How did you—"

Colt sat up and grunted. His nose scrunched, and his eyes shut tight. "Unlike some of us, I know how to change clothes all by myself."

"How did you do it with one arm?" Remi asked.

He stood and rubbed a hand over his face.

"Carefully. The shirt is made of some stretchy material."

"Colt, I could have helped you." Heat spread up her chest and into her cheeks. That's what friends were for, right? Helping and whatnot. While she was usually willing to lend a hand, helping Colt in and out of his clothes skirted the line.

But Colt wouldn't get the wrong idea if their friendship ever came to that. She'd known some shady men in her life, and Colt wasn't one of them. The guy worried about the bees and turtles when winter came around, for Pete's sake.

His hand dropped from his face lazily. The heaviness in his eyes was new and worrisome. Where was her happy-go-lucky friend?

Then, he looked at her, and all concerns about his wellbeing went up in smoke. His grin broadened, and he looked her over from her head to her feet. "You look good in my clothes, princess."

Remi punched his arm. "Stop it."

Colt jokingly stumbled back, but his gaze didn't waver. That kind of stare from any other man would bring on the harsh tongue she used to fight off her past and anything remotely close to the mistakes she'd made. It was also the same fear that kept her relationship status carefully tucked in the single-hood category.

Most men wouldn't care about her past, but

Colt would. He'd run screaming for the hills if he heard even a whisper of the woman she used to be.

But Colt was still looking at her like he saw more than just his friend standing in front of him when the doorbell rang.

"I'll get it." Remi darted toward the front door and flung it open.

"Hey." The young man shoved the pizzas at her and didn't try to hide the assessing look as his gaze traveled from her head to her feet and back up again.

Remi snatched the pizzas from him. "I fell in a puddle. How much do I owe you?"

"Already paid for." The guy handed over the receipt.

Lucky for him. If she'd been in charge of paying, she wouldn't have left much of a tip after he'd gotten a good look at her in Colt's clothes.

"Thanks. Have a good night." She shut the door with her foot and headed for the kitchen.

"Come and get it!"

Colt walked in and grabbed two cups from the cabinet. "The usual?"

"Yep."

They had a routine. He made the drinks, and she plated the pizza. Tonight, she kept her focus on the pizza instead of Colt. If she could last fifty more minutes in his clothes without things getting weird, she'd be home free.

"Remi, I have to ask you something."

Oh no. Was that hesitation in his voice? "Whatever it is, tread carefully. I'm not in the mood for any jokes about the outfit after the pizza guy gave me the wiggly eyebrows."

When he didn't respond, she stopped pulling the pizza slices apart and looked up at him. Colt was grinning from ear to ear.

"What?" she asked, trying not to worry about whatever had him stifling giggles.

He grabbed the two-liter bottle of orange soda with one hand and held it out to her. "Can you open this for me?"

She took one look at the bottle and his arm in the sling and burst into laughter. She took the drink and opened it. "I guess wearing your pants means I have to do your job."

He poured her Sunkist into a glass with one hand. "This is a one-time thing. I won't be down and out for long, and I'll be back to waiting on you hand and foot."

Remi rolled her eyes. He did treat her like she was incapable of doing anything herself, but truth be told, she liked it a little. Maybe a lot more than she should.

He brought over the glasses and set them on the bar where they always ate. "Your turn. I'm having trouble thinking tonight."

Remi bowed her head and prayed, "Lord, thank You for the food, and thanks for letting Colt hit his shoulder and not his head tonight. Amen."

Colt reached for the first slice of pizza and folded it at the crust. "So, how's Hadley doing?"

Remi had been in charge of the kids' activities at the ranch on her own for years, and as much as she loved it, Hadley's timing couldn't have been more perfect. It was hard to admit, but Remi was getting tired.

"She's great."

Colt stared at her as he chewed.

"What?"

"That's it? She's great?"

Remi shrugged. "Yeah. That's the gist of it."

Colt shook his head. "Okay."

Remi gasped. "Do you like her?"

"What?" Colt mumbled around a huge bite of pizza. "I don't like her. I mean, I like her, but not like that."

"She's really pretty."

"Yeah," Colt agreed.

Drat.

"And nice," Remi added.

"Yeah."

"So, what's not to like?"

What was she doing? Why couldn't she stop her stupid mouth from talking?

"Are you saying I should ask her out?"

Remi's chest tightened. "Why not?"

"No, thanks. I tried that with a woman I work with once. It didn't go so well."

Remi pointed a finger at Colt and mustered her best serious voice. "That didn't happen."

"Pretty sure it did, though you do a really good job of reminding me that it didn't."

Some things were impossible to forget, no matter how much she wanted to erase the memories. The time Colt had asked her out on a date was pretty close to the top of the list.

He'd been at the ranch for two days before he made his move. She'd delivered a hard no along with a stern warning to let it go and move on.

Colt had taken her advice, somewhat. He'd given up on the date, but he hadn't left her alone entirely. Somehow, they'd become friends, and she couldn't even explain how it happened. He'd worked his way into her life in small, unnoticeable ways until he'd attained the title of best friend. She'd meant to keep him and all other men at a distance, but Colt hadn't given up.

He never brought up the time he'd asked her out. Why tonight?

Change the subject. Change the subject. "It might not be the same with Hadley." Heat covered Remi's arms and neck, as soon as the words were out of her mouth.

Colt turned in his chair and faced Remi. "It's fine. I'm not interested in dating her."

Remi narrowed her eyes and assessed him. Something was up. He wasn't interested in Hadley, he brought up the time that shall not be named, and he seemed a lot sadder than usual.

Colt mirrored her appraising look. "What are you doing?"

"Wondering why you're not interested in Hadley."

"I'm just not. Okay?" He turned back to his pizza and stuffed a huge bite into his mouth.

No, not okay. Curiosity killed the cat, and Remi wasn't satisfied with his non-answer. "Is it because she's younger?"

"No."

"Is it because she's a brunette?"

"No."

"Is it because–"

"There's not a reason," Colt said. "I'm not talking about my female interests with you."

"You talk to the guys about your female interests," Remi pointed out.

Colt glanced at her, then looked down at his plate. "You're not the guys."

"So?"

Why did it matter if he saw her as "one of the guys?"

"So, I just don't want to talk about it. Hadley's

nice and all, but she's probably not ready to settle down and have a family. That's where I am right now, and I don't feel like wasting my time dating her just because she's pretty."

Oh no. Their time was coming to an end quicker than she'd realized. She knew he wanted those things, but she didn't know he wanted them right now.

Remi cleared her throat and looked around. "So, did you happen to record the Cardinals game?"

"What is this? Amateur hour? Of course, I recorded it."

"Good 'cause they might make it to the playoffs."

Colt rounded on her with a playful grin. "I knew there was a reason you offered to drive me home. You wanted to watch the game on the big screen."

"Yes. I'm here for the pizza and baseball," Remi deadpanned.

Colt picked up his plate and tossed it in the trash. "Good because I haven't watched it yet."

Remi tossed her own empty plate and grabbed their drinks. "You mean to tell me that game has been recorded on your massive TV for four days, and you didn't watch it?"

"Yep. It's no fun watching it by myself. And Ridge has been busy lately."

"Gee, it's nice to know I'm your backup friend."

Colt wrapped his good arm around her shoulders and herded her toward the living room. "Easy, princess. You know you're my number one."

Remi silently finished that sentence as they walked to the living room.

For now.

CHAPTER 3

REMI

Remi lounged on the plush couch and stared up at the ridiculously high ceiling. "I still can't believe you live here."

Colt was kicked back in the recliner with his good arm resting behind his head. "I know. It's a few steps up from the bunkhouse with Linc."

"You'll be spoiled." Even as she said the words, she knew Colt wasn't the one getting spoiled. She was.

Who wouldn't? She'd lived in basic housing her entire life, and she'd never take a place like this for granted. Just getting to hang out with Colt here was a treat.

"I'm sure things will change soon."

Remi frowned and tuned out the shouts and commentary of the game they were watching. "Why do you say that?"

Colt didn't look away from the TV. "Ridge and Cheyenne are getting married, and I doubt they'll decide to live in the cabin on the ranch."

Remi froze, suddenly hit with the realization that Colt's living situation might change soon. Would he leave Blackwater? He couldn't leave Blackwater, right?

That was something she hadn't thought of until now. While Colt hadn't moved around a lot in his life, Remi was pretty accustomed to packing up on short notice. It was the story of her childhood. Mom got a new boyfriend, and they moved in with him. She got an even newer boyfriend, and they moved in with him. One long string of her mom's boyfriends made up the first thirteen years of her life.

And so began her aversion to dating. She'd known a few people who were or had been in truly healthy relationships, but the statistics didn't lie-- those were rare. The alternative to happily ever after was her mom and the string of toxic relationships she'd dragged Remi through for years.

No, thank you. In fact, Remi had found her own ways to ruin her life starting at a young age. Petty crime, drugs, alcohol. You name it and she'd tried it. If her life was going to suck, she'd wanted to do the damage herself.

It all seemed stupid now. She'd hit rock bottom and decided to set up shop there when Kendra found her. The woman hadn't given Remi much of a choice but to get off her sorry behind and get back on track.

Remi cleared her throat and prayed her words wouldn't shake. "Where will you go?"

Colt seemed unfazed from his hyper-reclined lounger. "I don't know yet. I might ask about one of the new cabins on the ranch. They have two rooms."

"Why do you need two rooms? Are you getting used to the square footage around here?"

Colt waved his good hand in the air. "I know it's not on your agenda, but I want a family at some point. I'm not getting any younger."

There he went with the family talk again. Maybe if he kept bringing it up and reminding her, it wouldn't be such a shock when he dropped the news of his engagement. Well, she'd know he was dating, then getting serious, then thinking about popping the big question, but it would still be a significant change in her life. Colt would have someone else to spend all his time with, and she'd have Jess.

There wasn't anything wrong with Jess. She was a great roommate and a good friend, but she was a little on the abrupt side. No frills or beating around the bush with that one.

"You're not ancient. You're not even thirty."

Sure, their biological clocks were ticking, but Remi wasn't in any hurry to have a family. Well, a family sounded great, but she had enough baggage to tear up anything that resembled a happy family.

There was a natural order to building a legacy. First comes love, second comes marriage...

And that's where it all went sideways. Remi would have to trust in the sanctity of marriage to have a family, and not even Colt could make her believe that any man would put up with her for eternity.

N-O. No.

She was doing everyone a favor, really. She was safer alone where she wouldn't disappoint anyone.

She was safer alone where she couldn't hurt anyone.

Not that it had hurt when her mom left her. It was all she knew, really. Remi could hardly blame the woman.

Remi glanced at Colt where he'd dozed off in the chair. Even in sleep, his brow was furrowed from pain. His dark-brown hair was rumpled from his hat, and a smudge of dirt streaked across his cheek.

She was going to lose him, and there wasn't anything she could do to hang onto her best friend once the right woman came along. The friendship she had with Colt was unparalleled, but the stark reality was that she couldn't keep him forever.

Remi's phone rang, and she scrambled to get it out of her pocket before Colt woke up. She'd just answered the call when Colt sat up.

"Hello."

"Where are you?" Jess asked.

The abrupt greeting wasn't bristly to Remi, though it might seem like it to someone who didn't know Jess. There just wasn't anything extra with her. She said what was on her mind and moved on.

"Colt's place. We're watching the Cardinals game."

Colt stood and stretched one side before walking over to sit on the coffee table in front of her. His dark stare held her paralyzed, and a prickling sensation shot up her spine.

She quickly slapped a hand over her eyes. No, he was not going to start a staring contest and get her all flustered while she was trying to have a semi-normal conversation with Jess.

Colt loved playing games, but his games always left her raw and exposed. It wasn't that way for him, but he always looked at her as if he could read the thoughts in her mind.

The hand over the eyes said she wasn't playing right now. Not that she wouldn't win. She would totally win. She just couldn't focus on her conversation with Jess when Colt was looking at her thoughts like they were swimming in a fish tank.

"Don't wake me up when you come in. I got roped into an early trail ride in the morning," Jess said.

"Night, night, sleeping beauty," Remi crooned.

Jess grumbled and ended the call.

Remi let out a long breath and let her hand fall from her eyes. Was she ready to let down those walls?

Colt leaned forward, propping his good elbow on his knee. Did he have any idea what happened to her carefully constructed fortress when he got close like this?

"Jess and Linc are basically the same person," Colt said.

Normal talk. She could handle that. "You're right. The only difference is I can put up with Jess, and you can't handle Linc."

"I can. He's just too..."

"Unemotional?" Remi finished.

Colt had a lot of feelings for a gruff man in his late twenties. He wasn't a crier, but he felt things more than other men. Maybe all men had feelings, and Colt was just one of the few who expressed them in words. She never had to wonder what Colt was thinking. He always told her.

"Yes! No wonder Jess and Linc work together so well. Neither of them make a fuss about anything."

Remi looked down at the plush rug. If friendship was all about likenesses, where did that leave her and Colt? They were as different as night and day when it came to certain things, but they were determined enough not to let anything get in the way of their friendship.

"Hey," Colt whispered.

Remi looked up and found him staring at her.

Great. He wanted to have a staring contest, and she didn't have the excuse of a phone call this time. The last thing she wanted was to have her soul assessed, but her competitive nature wanted to be the winner.

Thank goodness Colt was lousy at staring contests. His intense stare wouldn't last long.

Ten seconds later, Colt's stare wandered slightly, causing him to blink.

Remi took a deep breath and stood. "Winner, winner."

Staring contests with Colt left her shaken and stirred, mostly because his gaze always wandered to her mouth.

Nope, there would be no introspective assessment about what that might mean.

But Remi never knew how to handle her body's instinctive response. Her stomach flipped, and the air was too thick to breathe. Her heart pounded, and a rush of heat crept up her neck.

Which always left her fleeing the scene.

"You need a refill?" She grabbed his empty water glass and turned toward the kitchen.

Colt reached out and wrapped his hand around her arm. Gently. Colt was a lot bigger than her, but he never exerted any unnecessary strength.

When he didn't let go, she sank back down to the couch.

"Why don't you want a family?" Colt asked. His words were so soft, and the silent plea in his question made sure she couldn't deny him.

But she couldn't tell him. Not the truth. If he or anyone else knew, they wouldn't look at her the same way ever again. They wouldn't be able to see past her mistakes. They couldn't be erased, and once they were out of the bag, there was no stuffing them back into the darkness.

Remi cleared her throat. "I just don't think I would be a good mom."

Colt burst into laughter. Howling, gut-splitting laughter.

Great, the first time he laughed like his usual self tonight, and it was at her expense.

"What's so funny?" She propped her hands on her hips and tried to control her furrowing brow.

Colt shook his head, and the smile on his face didn't waver. "You'd make an amazing mom. And wife."

And there was the real kicker. She wouldn't make an amazing wife because she was not the woman Colt thought she was.

Mistakes, mistakes, mistakes. She had them in spades. Well, in clubs, diamonds, and hearts, too. In both black and red. Yep, she was a full deck of nasty mistakes.

Remi shook her head. "Nope. I don't think I would. There's a difference in playing with kids all day and being a mom. Besides, my therapist and I agree that I'm not marriage material."

Colt's eyes widened. "Your what?"

The garage door opened, and Ridge threw his keys on the counter. "Honey, I'm home!"

Saved by the roommate. Remi jumped to her feet. "Hey, you want some pizza?"

Ridge was already helping himself. "Don't you like regular pizza? Pineapple on one and spinach on the other."

"Take it or leave it."

She'd been defending her pizza topping preferences for years, but Colt hadn't batted an eye when she'd ordered spinach and white sauce on her pizza the first time. It was silly how much that acceptance had meant to her.

Ridge took a bite of the Hawaiian pizza and furrowed his brow at her. "What happened to you?"

Remi looked down. She was still wearing Colt's clothes. "Oh, I fell into a puddle outside."

Ridge glanced at Colt who did nothing to corroborate her story.

"I'm going to get my clothes out of the dryer so I can feel like a real person again instead of a pile of dirty laundry."

"Those clothes are clean!" Colt shouted after her.

She grabbed her warm clothes from the dryer and slipped into them. Colt's clothes were comfy, but spending the evening wearing them was messing with her head. She picked up Colt's shirt and pants and molded the soft fabric in her hands. What was it about Colt's clothes that always ignited the kleptomaniac inside her?

Remi had been tested continuously since coming to Wolf Creek Ranch. First, Mr. Chambers, the owner of the ranch, trusted her to clean the main house. So many shiny things caught her eye, but she was able to dust each and every thing in the house and deposit them right back where they belonged.

Then, she'd been given the housekeeping position for the ranch cabins. It was a test, and she passed when a year had gone by and she hadn't swiped a single thing from a guest. She could resist when her new life and the safety and comfort of it were at stake.

Colt's clothes? Not so easy to resist. It had to be the smell. Colt wasn't an Abercrombie guy, and he didn't smell like a male model. He smelled like dirt and hay and sweat.

What did it say about her that she liked it?

She rolled up the pants and stuffed them under her arm. In the waistband of her pants would be the ideal hiding place, but she was wearing her jeans a little tighter these days. The pizza was to blame.

Back in the kitchen, the men were shoving cold pizza into their mouths.

"I'm heading home." Remi carefully skirted the island with her back to Colt and Ridge, concealing the roll of pants that peeked out from under her arm.

Colt looked up, seeming brighter after his short nap. "Wait. How am I supposed to get ready for bed with one arm?"

Remi pointed to Ridge, careful to keep her left elbow tucked tight to her side. "You're in charge of the patient now."

Ridge looked at Colt, then back to Remi. "Can't you take him with you?"

Remi shook her finger. "Oh no. Mine and Jess's place is a male-free zone. No boys allowed."

"But you're Colt's only friend," Ridge said.

Colt slapped a hand on the counter. "I thought *you* were my friend!"

Ridge looked at the ceiling. "See? Now he thinks I'm his friend, and I have to act like I like him."

"Words hurt!" Colt shouted.

Ridge gave Remi a pitiful, pleading look. "I'm not serving him breakfast in the morning."

Remi headed for the door, angling her body to hide Colt's pants. They'd be her pants soon. She'd be sleeping in them until the smell wore off.

There was nothing wrong with stealing her friend's pants. She'd keep telling herself that when she added the pants to the overflowing drawer in her bedroom she'd filled with Colt's clothes.

She opened the door and positioned her left side safely behind it. "I'll come over and feed the patient."

"I'll miss you! You're my favorite person!" Colt yelled.

He wanted a breakfast sandwich. Thankfully, she spoke Colt's secret language.

She would be back in the morning, and all talk about families would be behind them. Things were great the way they were, and nothing had to change.

CHAPTER 4
COLT

C olt stared at the dangling sleeve of his shirt, working up the nerve to lift his throbbing arm.

The familiar chirp of the door alarm rang through the house. Remi was here. Good. She could help.

"Come and get it!" Remi shouted from downstairs.

"Help!"

Remi grumbled, but the stomping on the stairs told him she was coming to his rescue. Seconds later, she stood in the doorway with her arms crossed over her chest.

What a beautiful sight in the morning. Remi never failed to get his heart racing.

"Do we need to get you one of those Life Alert buttons?"

"Getting old is hard."

"It's a privilege denied to many."

Colt picked up the shirt sleeve and let it fall.

Remi bit back a grin as she approached. "I think you need to put this sleeve on first."

Colt looked from one sleeve to the other. "See? This is why I need you. You got all the brains, and I got all the looks."

"If I got all the brains, we're in trouble." She slid the flannel shirt off his good arm. "You didn't have any problems getting that under shirt on."

"It was touch and go for a minute there."

Remi slid the shirt on his injured arm and then brought the other side around behind him.

"Definitely easier with your help."

"Great. Now let's swallow breakfast." She turned for the door. "I have to get to the ranch early to give Hadley the rundown before the activities start."

"Wait."

Remi turned around, looking like her patience was already running thin.

Colt pointed to the buttons on his shirt. "Please."

Remi rolled her eyes and grunted but started making quick work of the buttons. "You're the slowest human alive."

"I just want you all to myself for a little longer," Colt whispered.

Remi looked up at him, and he took the opportunity. "One, two, three, go," he said quickly.

"Not now," Remi whined.

"Yes now," Colt said, already fully invested in the staring contest.

Staring contests with Remi were his favorite thing. They'd started years ago, and he'd yet to win a game. Remi refused to lose, and Colt got a pass to look at her, uninterrupted, for as long as he could hold his eyes open.

"One day, I'm going to win," he said.

"Not on your life, Walker."

His eyes burned and watered. *Just don't blink. Don't do it.*

He blinked. The loser once again. Same story, different day.

Well, he didn't feel like he'd completely lost. Remi licked her lips every time she won, and that small movement was enough to boost his mood for the entire day.

Remi was the equivalent of thallium poisoning. Killing him slowly.

Colt slid the sling around his neck, and Remi fixed the straps. Then she turned toward the door, dragging him by the collar of his shirt behind her. "Let's go. You can eat in the car."

"What am I going to be able to do today with a useless arm?" It was the question that had been burning in his mind all morning. The ranch foreman, Jameson, had set the dislocated shoulder last night and gave Colt the day off today. But the thought of not being able to work and make a living was one of those fears he kept buried deep in the "Do not enter" section of his mind. He had to find some way to make himself useful.

"You can help Ava in the office. She hasn't been feeling good lately." Remi stopped at the bottom of the stairs and turned on Colt. "Have you heard anything about what's wrong with her?"

Colt shrugged one shoulder. "Jameson just said she's sick. That's all I know. I can help her out today."

Great. Crisis averted. He could be useful, even if it meant checking in guests.

Remi grabbed the brown bag off the counter and headed for the door. "Meet you in the car."

"Do you have a coat? It'll be cold this evening."

Remi looked around the room. "No. I left it at home."

Remi never remembered her coat. It was one of the little things about her that drove him crazy, mostly because he couldn't stand to watch her shiver. She was also the reason he always kept multiple flannel shirts in his truck.

"There's one on the dresser in my room. You can't *have* it, but you can *borrow* it." Colt made sure to emphasize that part, since Remi was a serial clothing stealer. Every once in a while, he stopped by her place to load up all of his stolen clothes. "Run up and grab it while I make coffee."

"No time for coffee!" Remi shouted over her shoulder as she took the stairs two at a time.

Colt huffed. He was getting coffee. And if Remi was driving, they were guaranteed to get to the ranch early anyway. The woman drove like the law was chasing her twenty-four seven.

Remi rushed down the stairs and straight out the door. Colt took his time pouring coffee into two disposable cups and making sure the lids were on tight. With Remi behind the wheel, a coffee spill was inevitable without precautions.

On the way to the ranch, Colt alternated taking bites of his breakfast sandwich with feeding Remi bacon and sausage.

They drove up to the main house with three minutes to spare, but Remi still screeched across the gravel like she needed to come in on two wheels.

"Told you we'd make it on time," Colt said.

"*You* made it on time. I still have to get to the kids' activities center. Get out."

Colt opened the creaky door of the Bronco. "Sheesh. You just lost your tip, princess."

"Out!"

Colt closed the door and turned to wave with a big smile on his face. "Bye. See you at lunch."

Remi rolled down the window. "Will you save me some cobbler?"

"What will you do for me?" Colt asked.

Remi gasped, and the familiar wrinkle between her brows let him know he'd gotten under her skin. "I brought you breakfast!"

"Okay, okay. Cobbler. Got it."

Grinning, Remi shifted into reverse. "I knew there was a reason I kept you around."

"Cobbler and my good looks," Colt said.

She backed out and slung gravel as she headed toward the north path.

Colt walked in the front office and found Stella and Bethany huddled behind the check-in desk. They both stopped whispering and jerked their heads toward him when he entered.

"Don't mind me." He propped his good elbow on the desk. "Who are we talking about?"

Stella had been around the ranch a long time, and she had her nose in everything. Colt liked to know what was going on, but Stella always had the dirt. She brushed a hand over her sweater and raised her eyebrows. "No one."

"Liar," Colt whispered. He turned to Bethany. She had a crush on almost every cowboy on the ranch, and he wasn't above using his charm to get her to spill the beans. "Bethany, what's going on?"

Bethany sat up straighter and cut a glance to Stella. "Nothing."

"Nothing except..." Colt said.

Bethany leaned close and whispered, "We think Ava is pregnant."

Stella huffed and slapped the younger woman's shoulder. "Now everyone will know, and *we* don't even know for sure yet."

Colt straightened with a smile. Mission accomplished. "Don't worry, ladies. Your secret is safe with me."

"Not a chance," Stella said, propping her hands on her hips. "I'm serious, Colt. Keep it under wraps. She hasn't told anyone yet, but we've been suspecting for a while. She's been sick for weeks."

That was the difference between men and women. Colt knew Ava had been sick, but he hadn't put two and two together. "Okay. Okay. I won't say anything."

Well, he wouldn't say anything to anyone except Remi. He didn't keep secrets from her.

Stella pointed a finger at him and narrowed her eyes. "I'll have my eye on you."

"'Cause I'm eye candy?" Colt asked.

Stella smiled and stepped around the desk to wrap him in a hug. "You're my favorite. Don't tell the others."

Colt hugged her back. Stella hadn't ever been a mom, but she would have been a great one. Definitely better than his mom. He didn't remember much about her, but if she'd been anything like

Stella, she wouldn't have left her husband and two sons.

"I can't promise to keep my mouth shut on that one. I'll probably be helping Ava out today, so I'll try to get her to spill the beans about the whole baby thing."

Stella held a finger in front of Colt's lips. "Shut that trap and get to work."

Colt stood tall and gave her a salute. "Yes, ma'am."

Bethany and Stella went back to whispering as Colt headed down the hallway to Ava's office. He knocked on the open door, and Ava looked up from her computer. Her cheeks were paler than usual, and her eyes were dark rimmed.

"Hey. You feeling okay?" she asked.

"I could ask you the same thing." Colt took a seat in the chair across from her desk.

Ava buried her face in her hands. "I haven't had anything to eat in days."

Colt sat forward. Maybe he should have been more concerned with Ava's sickness. "Anything I can do to help?"

A knock on the door turned Colt's attention. Ava's husband, Jameson, stood in the doorway. "Any better?"

Ava shook her head slowly.

Colt stood, looking back and forth between the couple. "Should I come back later?"

Jameson went to Ava's side and wrapped an arm around her. "No, you're fine."

"I actually came by to see if I could help out around here today. I can't do any heavy lifting just yet. I think I'll be good enough to work next week."

Jameson looked down at Ava who kept her face buried in her hands. "She's pregnant. We're planning on telling everyone today."

Colt clapped a hand on Jameson's shoulder. "Congrats, guys. Is this morning sickness? I thought that was...you know, a morning only thing."

Ava shook her head. "Nope. For some, it lasts all day. For weeks."

Jameson's pallor looked a lot like Ava's. "She's been in contact with her doctor a lot. We're hoping it'll ease off soon."

Ava lifted her dark hair off her neck and let out a deep breath. "It's fine. It'll all be worth it in the end."

Colt swallowed a knot in his throat. Seeing Ava sick was causing sympathy pains. He'd never given much thought to the things women had to go through during pregnancy, but he appreciated Ava's attitude about the situation. Everyone on the ranch knew she and Jameson had been hoping to start a family now that their new house was finished.

Colt inched toward the door. Ava didn't seem to be in the mood for company. "Well, since you have me at your beck and call for the day, what can I do for you?"

"Can you take Mr. Chambers to his doctor appointment at 8:30?" Jameson asked. "I have a meeting with a supplier, and I don't think Ava will be feeling better any time soon."

Colt gave two thumbs up. Ava's grandpa owned Wolf Creek Ranch, and he was Colt's favorite old man in the world. "You got it."

"Thanks," Ava whispered. "He could drive himself, but I'd feel better if someone were with him."

"No problem. He knows about the baby, right?" Colt asked.

"We told him earlier this week," Jameson said.

"Good. We'll have something to talk about."

Ava chuckled, but the sound didn't hold much joy. "Since when have you ever worried about having something to talk about?"

"Never. You said you're telling everyone else today?"

"You can tell Remi," Ava said.

Colt grinned. "Thanks. Before I go, I wanted to talk to you about the new cabins."

"You want one?" Jameson asked. "Are things not going well at Ridge's?"

"Things are fine. The place is great. I'm just thinking ahead. I doubt Ridge and Cheyenne will want a housemate after they get married."

Jameson rubbed his jaw. "I hadn't thought about that."

"You've been a little preoccupied," Colt said with a tilt of his head toward Ava.

"You can take your pick," Jameson said. "Just let me know when you want to move in."

"Thanks, man." Giving up his room at Ridge's mansion wasn't as difficult as Colt had expected. Knowing he could settle down on the ranch for a while sounded like paradise.

But that extra room gnawed at him. On one hand, he wanted to fill a house with a wife and kids. On other hand, he just wanted Remi and whatever a life with her would offer. Did she not want kids, or did she just not want to be married? She definitely didn't want to marry *him*.

They'd been talking about it more and more lately, but he still couldn't get a handle on Remi's aversion to marriage. She rarely talked about her parents, but he knew they split up when Remi was young. Had her parents' divorce wrecked her?

He wanted the cabin, but that extra room might be useless. Remi was the deciding factor when it came to a family for him. If she wasn't a part of the equation, he didn't want it. Or he couldn't imagine wanting that life with anyone except her. The thought felt wrong whenever he tried to picture it without Remi.

"We'd love to have you back on the ranch," Jameson said. "Just say the word."

If Colt had to move out eventually, why wait? "Let's do it. I don't care which cabin."

Ava raised her head and grinned. "Is there a reason you want one of the new cabins instead of the old ones?"

There was a reason, but not one he wanted to talk about. He liked to joke around about everything except his unrequited love for Remi. If he told Jameson and Ava he was still holding out hope that Remi would miraculously change her feelings for him, it would be like pouring salt on the wound.

"No reason." Colt stood and headed for the door. "I'd better see if your grandpa is ready to be carted around town. Thanks for the cabin."

Had he just started planning for a future, or had he sealed his fate in loneliness?

CHAPTER 5
REMI

Remi marched over the hill next to the younger kids. To her left, Hadley led the older kids. They could keep the varied ages together for some events, but tug-of-war needed a bit of separation.

"What are we doing next?" Amberly asked. The most chipper in the bunch today, she had a huge smile, a wide imagination, and two and a half teeth in the front of her mouth.

"Tug-of-war. You ever played?"

Amberly's smile fell. "Yeah. We played at my school."

"You don't have to play if you don't want to," Remi added.

Amberly looked back at the other kids in the group. "I might."

Being in charge of kids was a lot of taking cues.

Most kids knew their limits and likes, and Remi tried to offer up a variety of fun things to do.

Tug-of-war wasn't for everyone. It wasn't Remi's favorite. Never had been. But about half the kids got super giddy at the challenge.

When they reached the top of the hill, the two groups lined up in front of the ropes lying on the ground. The younger kids aged from three to six and the older kids were seven to ten.

Remi clapped her hands. "Tug-of-war time. Who wants to play?" She raised a hand, letting them know how to opt in.

The majority of the kids flung their hands in the air.

Remi pointed at the two ropes. "Take your places."

When the kids were evenly divided on each rope, Hadley held the middle tie on one, and Remi held the middle tie on the other.

"One for the money, two for the show, three to get ready, and four to go!"

Remi and Hadley backed up as the teams started to pull. The older kids held a tense back and forth, but the younger kids had a clear winner early on.

Remi helped some of the little kids to their feet. "Was that fun?"

"Yeah! Again!" the kids shouted in unison.

"Whoa! Whoa!" Hadley shouted.

Remi got to her feet and looked to the other

group. Hadley was wedged between two boys who were pushing and shoving at each other. They were around eight or nine, and while they couldn't completely overpower Hadley, their reckless flailing made it hard to wrangle them in.

That escalated quickly.

"Hey, break it up!" Remi shouted as she ran toward them. She pulled one of the boys back and wrapped her arms around him from behind, securing them to his body so he'd stop swinging. He wasn't giving up easily and kept wiggling in her hold.

"Cool it, Grant. We're playing tug-of-war, not battling it out."

She'd barely gotten the words out of her mouth when Grant jerked his head back, nailing Remi in the nose with his thick skull. The bright midday turned dark before the light came back and stars swirled in her vision. The sharp pain pierced to the back of her head and down her spine. Warmth spread down her face as the other kids screamed. She closed her eyes and focused on holding Grant.

"Miss Remi is bleeding!" one of the girls cried.

A few seconds later, Grant started relaxing. He kept squirming, but the fire in him was dying.

Remi blinked through tears. She wasn't sniffling or crying, but the blow to the nose had started up the waterworks.

Hadley was able to get a handle on the other boy, and the rest of the group stepped back.

Remi sank to her knees and whispered to Grant. "Can I let go now?"

He sniffed. "Yeah."

She released her hold on him and wiped a sleeve under her nose. Dark red spread over the brown fabric. It was all over the front of her shirt and the back of Grant's.

"I'm sorry," Grant stuttered through fresh tears.

"Breathe, Grant," Remi said. Her hands shook and her heart pounded.

She'd never get used to handling physical altercations. No matter how many times the kids walked away or made up, it still brought her back to the defenseless kid she'd been. When the kids were out of control, it really shook her to her bones.

Hadley jogged up beside her, wide-eyed and ready to jump into action. "Is it broken?"

Remi wiped her eyes with the other, semi-clean sleeve. "I don't think so." She ran her fingers over the bridge, and it didn't seem knotted or crooked. The pain, however, was a knife in the middle of her face.

"Let's get you back to the main house."

Remi waved her off. "You take the kids to the barn. Jess can give them a horse grooming lesson while I clean up. I'll meet you back there."

Hadley nodded, already switching gears. "You sure you're okay?"

Remi wiped her sleeve under her nose again. Fresh blood was still flowing. "I'm fine. Just need to figure out how to get it to stop bleeding. Jameson will know what to do."

Thankfully, the foreman had spent years as a paramedic before taking the full-time position at the ranch. He gave pretty good advice when it came to handling injuries.

Hadley's brows pinched together. "Right. Call me if you need me."

Someone tugged on Remi's sleeve. Grant and AJ stood beside her with matching pained expressions and red-rimmed eyes.

"We're sorry, Miss Remi."

Remi swallowed past the burning in her throat. Emotions were hard to handle, even for adults. She remembered being their age and stomping down everything she felt. At least these two knew how to offer a genuine apology.

"You're forgiven. Let's remember to have fun and keep our hands to ourselves."

She usually had better wise words, but today, the pain and watery eyes were clouding her thoughts.

"Yes, ma'am," the boys said together before running off to join their friends.

Remi turned to Hadley and sniffed. "I'll have

someone bring Grant a clean shirt from the clothes closet. You think he wears a ten?"

Hadley studied the boy as he ran from two other kids. "Sounds about right. It'll at least get him through the day. I think his parents are on a trail ride."

Remi waved a lazy hand. "I'll be back as soon as I can."

She pulled out her phone and called Ava. The boss might need an incident report too.

"Hello." The greeting was flat, and fresh worry over Ava's sickness clouded Remi's already swirling thoughts.

"Hey, is Jameson with you?"

"He's in his office. You need him?"

"I'm on my way. I got pegged in the nose, and it's still bleeding."

Ava's tone was stronger this time. "You need me to come get you?"

Remi sniffed and stuck the back of her arm under her nose. "I'll make it to the main house. Do you have someone who could grab a size ten boys shirt and take it to the barn? My nose bled all over one of the kids."

"I'll have Colt do it," Ava said.

Not Colt. He'd make a big fuss when he found out about her bloody nose, but beggars couldn't be choosers. "Thanks."

"Do you need new clothes?"

"I have an extra outfit in my truck." She'd wised up after she fell in the puddle yesterday.

"Okay. I'll head out to the barn to help Hadley and Jess with the kids."

Remi pinched her nose and tilted her head back, hoping there weren't any surprises on the trail. "Thanks. I'll be there as soon as this nose stops bleeding."

"Don't rush. Just take care of yourself."

"Thanks. See you soon."

Remi hung up the call and checked the screen. Blood was smeared over the phone, and she wiped it on her jeans. Stupid nose didn't know when to quit.

She made it to her truck just as the phone rang. She slipped into the cab and answered it.

"Hello."

"Are you okay? What do you need?" Colt asked quickly.

Just as she'd suspected, Colt was going to over-react. She hated to cause a fuss, but it was nice to know someone cared enough to seek her out and make sure she was okay.

"I'm fine, and I just need you to get a shirt to Hadley at the barn. The kid wears a size ten. There are lots of options in the closet in the kids' activities center."

"I'm on it. What about you? Ice? Water?"

Remi smiled, and the expression caused a new

wave of tears. These new tears weren't the effect of the blow. They were the emotional kind that pulled in her chest and constricted her throat. "Ice would be great."

"I'll meet you in Jameson's office as soon as I get back from the barn."

Remi hung up without a good-bye. If she said one more word, the silent tears would turn into sobs. She rarely got emotional, but it was hard to act like the kindness of her friends wasn't stitching up the heart that had been broken all her life.

Remi slid into the driver's seat of the Bronco and sighed. "I'm exhausted."

Colt fastened his belt in the passenger seat and tossed his hat onto the dash. "You're exhausted? You have no idea how tiring it is worrying about you all day every day. You're a walking recipe for disaster. I sit on pins and needles waiting to hear about the next way you'll stub your toe."

Remi scoffed and started the engine. "You gotta stop worrying about me, Walker. I've made it this far on my own."

"Not a chance, princess. You're stuck with me and my neurotic worrying. How's the sniffer?"

Remi ran her fingertip over the bridge of her nose again. There was a little bump, but it might just be swelling from the hit. She still didn't think it was truly broken. "It still works, so it's all good."

She backed out and headed toward the road leading out of the ranch. When Colt didn't say anything, she glanced over to find him watching her.

"What? What's wrong with you?"

Colt was never quiet, and his silence was a big red flag.

"Nothing." He sat back against the seat and turned his attention to the road ahead. "Did you hear the news about Ava?"

Remi's grip tightened on the wheel. They'd have a baby on the ranch soon, and while she was full of excitement for Jameson and Ava, the nagging reminder that other people her age were starting families hit a sore spot. "Yeah. That's good news for them, but I hope the morning sickness wears off soon."

"Me too. She looks miserable. It's great that we'll have a kid around the ranch soon. Mr. Chambers is excited to be a great-grandpa."

"I bet. That's wild."

Remi cleared her throat and hoped Colt would change the subject. It was difficult for her to relate to that kind of exciting news. They were surrounded by family who loved them. The new baby would have a grandma, grandpa, and a great-grandpa. Remi had never even known her grandparents. She hadn't seen her dad since she was three. The family she did know was the exact opposite of the healthy, happy family heading up Wolf Creek Ranch.

"I asked for a cabin today."

Remi jerked her head toward Colt, causing a throbbing behind her eyes. Why did he have to sneak in big blows like that? "You did. Why? Why?" she asked quickly.

Colt shrugged his uninjured shoulder. "I'll have to move out sometime. Why not now?"

"But you have time. Ridge hasn't asked you to move out yet."

"He probably won't. He's a good friend, and Cheyenne probably wouldn't want to kick me out either. But they deserve their time together. Plus, I can get started on fixing it up."

Remi's blood ran cold. "Fixing it up?"

Colt rested his head against the seat and didn't answer her question. Maybe he was as unnerved by the subject as she was.

She wanted good for other people. She wasn't a selfish, unhappy person. But seeing Colt get excited about having a family made her heart hurt. He deserved all that and more, and she didn't.

They both stayed quiet all the way to Colt's place. It was probably the longest stretch they'd ever gone without speaking while they were together, and it marked one step closer to that change that was coming to rock her happy world.

She pulled up in front of the house and shifted into park. Colt opened the door and was half out of the truck before he realized she wasn't moving.

"You coming in?"

Remi shook her head. "Nah. I've got a headache from the whole..." She waved a hand in front of her face.

"Stay for a little bit," Colt pleaded. "Cheyenne can drive you home when she leaves later. I don't like the idea of you driving while you have a headache."

"I'm fine. Just need some rest." What she really needed was some time to have a private pity party. She didn't need an audience for the whining.

This was one of those times when she needed a friend–a shoulder to cry on. Colt was the obvious choice for that assignment, but he was the one she'd be losing. He would ask her what was wrong, and she'd have to lie or tell the truth.

Lie: She was fine.

Truth: Things were starting to change between them, and the fear of losing her best friend was throwing her emotions into overdrive.

Another truth: Colt meant a lot to her, but she didn't know how to explain his role in her life. He was her best friend, but friends came and went. If Jess went off and got married, Remi would be happy for her and they would stay friends. If Colt got married, she would lose him. End of story.

Was that really the only reason she was worried about Colt getting married one day? That was a dangerous question and one she wasn't willing to investigate.

Colt stood next to the open door of her beat-up truck, and the look he was giving her said he didn't believe a word that was coming out of her mouth.

"I'm okay. Really. I'm going to go home, ice my face, and watch the Braves game."

Normal. Totally normal.

Colt looked her up and down, searching for cracks in her mask. "Fine. Call me and let me know you made it home okay."

Remi rolled her eyes. "You're worse than a mother hen."

Colt leveled her with a serious look. "I don't care what you call me, as long as you call me."

He could be so infuriating and so sweet at the same time. "Fine. I'll call you."

"And you'll pick me up for church in the morning? I think Ridge and Cheyenne are getting her mom settled into a new place, or I would ride with them."

"Fine. I'll come get you, but I'm teaching the three- to five-year-olds and have to be there early."

"Perfect. Be here even earlier, and I'll make you an omelet."

"With one hand?" Remi pointed to his useless arm.

"Oh, ye of little faith," Colt said.

"Fine. I'll be here extra, extra early to help you make omelets." It seemed she was trading solitude tonight for a full-time Sunday with Colt.

"It's a date. Thanks for the ride." Colt shut the door and walked toward the house.

She knew the words didn't hold the meaning she could easily assign to them, but the word "date" had her palms itching. She'd gotten good at avoiding anything that might resemble a date or any meeting that might result in an invitation. She never dated.

But if spending time with Colt was a date, she might be persuaded to accept the offer.

And that was a big problem. Their paths didn't align, and he'd gotten the wild hair to ask her out on a date once. They didn't need a repeat of that fiasco. She wasn't ready. She probably wouldn't ever be ready.

But Colt was ready to move on, and a good friend wouldn't stop him.

CHAPTER 6
COLT

Colt pushed the flannel shirts in his closet from one side to the other. The only ones left were worn out. Remi had officially moved the majority of his closet to her place. Why should he care? He only needed one shirt a day.

He pulled out one of the new flannels he hid in the back and slid his bad arm into the sleeve. It wasn't as tight this morning. Maybe he'd be back in action at the ranch tomorrow. He'd rest after church and keep an ice pack on it while he watched Sunday night football with Remi, Ridge, and Blake.

Grabbing his phone off the bed, he dialed Remi's number.

"This better be good, Walker."

A wide smile spread over Colt's face. Something was wrong with him. Getting scolded by Remi first thing in the morning was enough to keep his spirits up all day.

"Bring some of my shirts back. Especially the dark-green one. It's my favorite."

"I don't know what you're talking about. It's not my fault you can't keep up with your shirts."

"It's your fault if you're the thief."

Remi was quiet for a moment, and Colt pulled the phone away from his ear. They hadn't been disconnected. "Remi?"

"I'm here. Just busy getting ready."

"And bring back my pants. The ones you stole Friday night."

"What are you talking about? I didn't take your pants."

"I watched you walk out the door with them stuffed under your arm. I love those pants."

The truth was he loved those pants on her, but that was a problem for another day.

There was shuffling on Remi's side of the line. "I didn't take them."

Colt scoffed. "You did, too."

More silence. Something was off with Remi, and he was too concerned about her nose and the awkward gaps in their conversation to care about the pants.

"I plead the fifth," Remi said resolutely.

"You don't have to say anything. I know you have it. Bring them back."

"I don't have them."

Colt grinned. Why did it put an extra pep in his step to know Remi didn't want to give his pants back? "You probably slept in them last night."

"I did no such thing. I wouldn't want my sheets to smell like hay and horses."

"My clothes are clean. They don't smell."

"Hay and horses, Colt," Remi repeated. "Sometimes, you even smell like a wet dog."

"Hey, dogs are man's best friend."

"Guess you don't need me then. Or your shirts."

"Now there are multiple shirts." He was finally getting somewhere. How many had she hoarded?

"I don't have the shirts. That's my story, and I'm sticking to it."

Colt rummaged in his sock drawer for a pair of boot socks. He really needed to do laundry. "You know what? Keep them. My clothes look better on you anyway."

There was another pause on the line, and Colt looked up. Had he crossed the line? He danced around the line all the time, but slipping up and taking it too far was a real fear. "Remi?"

"I've got to go if I'm going to make it in time for omelets."

"Be careful."

"Always."

Colt tossed his phone back onto the bed and sighed. He was bound to screw up one day, and

Remi's reactions to his playful comments were getting stronger by the day.

Grabbing a pair of socks, he sat on the edge of the bed and stretched his sore arm to his foot. The pull in his shoulder was barely a dull ache until he actually had to use it to do some daily task, like putting on socks. Did he really need them today? He could get through a church service without them, right?

After a long-fought battle with the socks, he made it to the kitchen just as Ridge was emerging from his bedroom.

"How's the shoulder?" Ridge asked.

Colt pulled out the tub of coffee grounds. "Still useless. Be glad you can still dress yourself."

"Yeah, I thank the Lord for that every day. I'm guessing I have maybe thirty years before this beat-up body breaks down."

Colt shuddered. He'd been rough on his body his whole life, but he hadn't subjected himself to professional tacklers on the football field the way Ridge had. "Does Cheyenne know what she has to look forward to?"

Ridge sighed as he pulled a bottle of water from the fridge. "Taking care of her mom right now is probably good practice. Maybe I should ask her if she's still sure about marrying a man who's bound to fall apart before their kids get married."

"Nah, Cheyenne's in it for the long haul," Colt said.

The garage door opened, and Cheyenne stepped in. "Are you two talking about me?"

Cheyenne had come to the ranch to dig up dirt on Ridge, but thankfully, she had a swift change of heart and confessed. She might have meant to stir up dust, but stepping up and owning mistakes wasn't for the faint of heart. It took guts, and Colt respected her for telling Ridge about the plot against him.

Colt started the coffee brewing. "You'll be happy to know that I try to trick him into talking smack about you all the time, and he never gives in."

Cheyenne raised up onto her toes and pressed a kiss to Ridge's cheek. "Good to know."

Colt pulled the eggs out of the fridge. "I'm making omelets. Who wants one?"

"Not us," Cheyenne said. "We're having break-fast with Mom and Hadley."

Colt pulled the spatula out of the utensil holder and wielded it like a sword. "I need to talk to you two about something. I know you're getting married soon, so I went ahead and asked Jameson and Ava for one of the wranglers' cabins on the ranch."

Cheyenne's shoulders sank. "What? You don't have to do that."

Colt held up the spatula. "I knew you'd say that,

but I need to get out of here before I get used to the life of luxury."

"She's right," Ridge said. "You don't have to go."

"Thanks, man, but I think it's time." At least, he hoped it was time. He'd been praying about the decision to move out, but it was hard to tell the difference in his own hopes and dreams and what the Lord really wanted him to do. Part of him wanted to just accept the future he couldn't have. Remi didn't want him in the same way he wanted her. He was selfish. He was asking for too much.

Another part of him wanted to start planning for the future he might have. Then he realized that would include a woman other than Remi. Did he even want a family if Remi wasn't part of the equation?

Cheyenne picked at her fingernails and shifted her attention from one side of the kitchen to the other. "Um, has Remi said anything?"

Colt stood straighter. "What? What would she say?"

"I just meant...I don't know what I mean. You two just seem a little close but not close enough."

"Oh, you've noticed," Colt said. "A little close but not close enough is a good way to describe us."

Ridge swiped his hand under his chin, signaling for Cheyenne to cut it out.

"It's fine. I'm fine. It's totally fine," Colt said quickly. It was not fine, but whatever.

"I don't know. You might need to say it three more times before I believe you," Ridge joked.

Cheyenne slapped Ridge's chest. "I think you two are so sweet together. What's the deal? You want to be together, but she doesn't?"

"Yep." Colt banged the egg against the counter, and the whole thing shattered into a pile of goo and shells.

"Easy on the eggs. What did they ever do to you?" Ridge asked.

Colt propped his hand on the counter and hung his head. "I can't change her mind. She doesn't like me as anything other than a friend. I'm still trying to accept it."

Cheyenne rubbed a hand on Colt's back. "I'm sorry. I didn't realize it was like that between you two."

"Yes, it's very much like that." Ridge checked his watch. "We need to go if we're going to meet your mom and Hadley in fifteen minutes."

Cheyenne looked back and forth between Colt and Ridge.

"I'm a big boy," Colt said. He slapped a hand on her shoulder. "But thanks for your concern. Maybe getting a place that'll be big enough for a family will help me get it through my thick head that I just need to move on."

"Maybe you don't need to move on just–"

"We need to go!" Ridge shouted, waving his

hands in the air like distracting Cheyenne might save Colt's life.

Colt gave Cheyenne a thankful grin. "I appreciate your optimism, but I'll be fine."

Fine again. No one was ever going to believe him if he said the word fine one more time.

Three hard knocks reverberated through the house.

Colt turned to answer the back door. "That's Remi. See you guys later."

"I want to say hey to Remi," Cheyenne said.

Ridge grabbed her hand and pulled her toward the door leading to the garage. "If you say hey, we'll never get out of here."

"Okay, fine. Tell her I'll call her later," Cheyenne said as she disappeared into the garage with Ridge.

The back door was unlocked, and Remi never knocked. Maybe it wasn't Remi.

He opened the door to find her standing on the front entryway holding a big brown box.

"You wanted clothes." Remi shoved the box at him. "Here you go."

"You had all of these?" The box was full. He'd known she took his clothes, but this was more than he thought she'd snatched.

"Don't say I never gave you anything," she said as she pushed past him into the house. "I don't smell eggs."

Colt put the box down on the counter in the kitchen. "There was an incident with the eggs."

Remi grabbed a paper towel and started cleaning up the gooey mess. "You should have waited on me. Just hand me the ingredients, and I'll take care of the rest."

Grabbing the cheese and ham cubes from the fridge, Colt did everything Remi asked. This was how he wanted to start every day of his life–doing basic things with Remi like they were a team. Two parts of a whole.

Why didn't she want the same? Why did he have to want things he couldn't have? It was selfish, but Remi made him want the best in life. He'd seen how great things could be with her beside him, and now, everything else was colorless and bland.

Remi had the omelets made within minutes. She had him shoving food in his mouth like someone might steal it from him if he didn't eat it fast enough.

When the plates were cleared, she pushed him toward the door. "Move it or lose it. I can't be late."

"I'm moving, but I don't know what exactly I would be losing. Can you explain–"

She pushed his back. "Colt, go!"

"Can we take my truck? Yours might decide today is a good day to die."

Remi huffed and changed course. "Fine, but I'm driving."

Colt reached in his pocket and tossed the key to her. His shoulder was screaming from getting dressed, and they'd get to church a lot faster if the speed racer was behind the wheel.

The phone in his other pocket rang as he slid into the passenger side of the truck. It was an unknown number, but he quickly answered. "Hello."

"Hi, this is Officer Mary Gentry with the Weston County Police Department. Is this Mr. Colton Walker?"

The breath in Colt's lungs turned to ice. A call from a police department was never a good sign. "It is."

Remi didn't start the truck, and he was barely aware of her watching him as the woman on the phone relayed the information. He heard everything through a fog like he was underwater.

Accident.

Trauma.

Emergency contact.

He couldn't be sure how long the call lasted, but as soon as Officer Gentry ended the call, Colt lowered the phone to his lap and stared at it.

What did she say? It didn't make sense. He was watching all of this happen from a distance, like in a dream.

"Colt!"

Remi's scream beside him barely brought him

out of the darkness. He turned to find her staring at him with wide eyes. Her hand gripped his arm. How had he not noticed the contact?

Remi's words were slow and barely controlled. "What happened?"

Colt looked at the phone again, numb and afraid to say the words he thought he'd heard. He swallowed what seemed like a handful of razor blades and stared at the phone, praying the truth was a lie.

"My brother was in a car accident. He didn't make it."

CHAPTER 7

REMI

Remi's heart sank in her chest, pulling down her shoulders. The pressing weight appeared in an instant. She wanted to push against it, but the gutting sadness kept her down.

"Are you serious? Mark?"

She'd heard about Colt's brother. They'd always had a fragile relationship. Mark struggled with the addictive tendencies passed down from their dad much more than Colt, and the ongoing battle with Mark's sobriety took an unspoken toll. Colt loved his brother, but it was human nature to shy away from something–or someone–who caused repetitive pain.

The blank look on Colt's face as he stared down at his phone as if he'd never seen the thing before had Remi screaming on the inside. It killed her to see her happy friend hurting like this.

Colt lifted his head and cleared his throat. "Brittany was with him. She didn't make it either."

Remi covered her mouth with her hand. She'd heard of some terrible car wrecks, but two deaths meant it must have been brutal. "Were there any other—"

"I don't know," Colt said quickly. "She said it was a single vehicle accident."

Colt jolted in his seat, sitting up ramrod straight and grabbing the door handle. "The kids!"

"Kids?"

Oh, no. Colt's niece and nephew!

Colt scrambled for his phone that had slid from his lap when he'd jumped in his seat. "She didn't say anything about the kids. Surely, she would have said something. Right? Remi, she would have said something."

Remi's stomach rolled and bubbled as her skin flashed hot and clammy. "I—I don't know." She had no idea what the woman on the phone had said, but she prayed Colt was right.

With shaky hands, Colt found the phone and pressed the button to call the woman back. He tapped his boot on the floorboard and stared out the windshield at the driveway.

Remi's hand rested on Colt's arm, and the muscles were tense beneath her sweaty palm. Remi wiped her hand down her jeans, but something told her she needed to hold onto Colt. She slid her hand over his, fisted and resting taut on the console. As soon as her fingertips touched him, his hand opened. He threaded his fingers through hers and squeezed. His grip conveyed a strength he always kept hidden from her, even with his injured shoulder that probably protested with every movement.

"This is Colt Walker. I just spoke with a woman. Officer... Okay. I'll hold."

Colt turned to Remi, and the small wrinkle between his brows was something she'd never seen on him before. Was it fear or pain? Either way, it kicked her in the gut. Sure, Remi was scared and sad to hear about Mark and Brittany, but it was Colt's agony that was wreaking the biggest havoc on her heart.

Colt jolted upright again, keeping his tight hold on her hand. "Yes! This is Colt Walker. You didn't say anything about Mark and Brittany's kids, Ben and Abby. Ben is maybe seven, and Abby is four."

Remi closed her eyes and prayed. She didn't want to see Colt's face if he got more bad news.

Lord, please. Please not the kids, too.

Colt's grip tightened on her hand until the bones rubbed against each other. She gritted her teeth and squeezed her eyes closed.

"I'm coming to get them," Colt said resolutely.

Remi sucked in a shaky breath. *Thank you, Lord.*

Colt stuck the phone between his ear and

shoulder and released her hand. Grabbing a pen in the console, he jotted down a phone number on his palm. "Thank you. Thank you."

Colt ended the call and turned to Remi with wide eyes. "They were placed with a foster family this morning. They were with a babysitter when the wreck happened, and she stayed with them until she had to go to work this morning."

"Where are they? Where do they live?"

"Newcastle. It's about five hours away."

"And you're going to get them? Then what?" She hated to be the one to deliver the reality of tough decisions, but what would happen after he got there?

"I'll bring them home with me. They don't have anyone else. Brittany doesn't have any family. Our dad is probably drinking his breakfast this morning, and who knows where Mom is." Colt flung his good arm in the air like the woman who'd given birth to him and then abandoned him was nothing more than the wind in the Wyoming evergreens.

"You're going to keep the kids?" It was a life-changing decision. It was huge. He'd be responsible for two little humans from now on.

He held up his palm with the numbers scrawled on it. "This is the number of the caseworker that was assigned to them. I'm going to get the kids. I can't leave them. They just lost their parents."

Colt's voice broke on the last word. This was all

so much so fast. How could life change course in a matter of minutes?

"I'm coming with you." The words were out before she'd thought about them, but she didn't want to take them back. If Colt was going to get his niece and nephew, she was going too.

Colt stared at her like he'd never seen her before in his life. It was a gaping, confused look that would have been funny under different circumstances. "You are? Are you sure?"

"Of course, I'm sure. You can't do much with a bum shoulder. How are you going to take care of kids and do whatever needs to be done with your brother's..."

She couldn't finish the thought. Mark's things? Mark's estate? Whatever was left of Mark's home where those kids had been born and raised? It was all crashing down on Colt's shoulders at once, and she would never leave him to handle all of that alone.

"You don't have to come with me."

Remi opened the door and slid out of the truck. "I said I would. Now get to it. We have to pack."

Colt got out and headed toward the house, but the stern look on his face said he was running on autopilot. Making quick decisions wasn't something Colt was good at. Unfortunately, quick–and sometimes life-changing–decisions had been a part of Remi's world since day one. Lift your chin and face the music was her theme song.

She reached for Colt's hand as they walked back inside. "Hey."

Colt accepted her hand, gripping it with a little too much force. "Yeah."

"Everything will be okay. We'll get them." After that, she had no idea what they were going to do, but they'd figure it out together.

"Thanks." He released her hand and wrapped his arm around her shoulders. He pulled her into his side and pressed a kiss to her hair before releasing her.

Colt had never kissed her before. Ever. But the touch of his lips on her hair had the skin on the back of her neck tingling.

He was bounding up the stairs now, taking them two and three at a time, leaving her in the dust.

Whatever that was, Colt didn't seem to think it was a big deal, so she wouldn't either. He was probably just grateful she was sticking around to help.

By the time Remi caught up to him, he was already in his room throwing clothes in a brown duffel bag. "How long do you think we'll have to stay?"

"Three days? I don't know. How long do you think it'll take to get everything settled with the kids?"

Colt pushed a hand through his dark hair. "And

getting everything cleaned out in the house. I'll have to sell it. And everything in it."

"Easy, tiger. We don't have to do everything in the first trip. We'll do what we can with two grieving kids and your bum shoulder."

"Right." Colt tossed a pair of jeans and a few shirts into the bag. "We can probably stay at Mark's place while we're there."

Remi was the one who rolled with the punches, but Colt was doing a very good impression of an impulsive person right now. "I don't see why not. Then you won't need toiletries and all that stuff."

Colt zipped the bag and tossed it over his good shoulder. "Then let's hit the road."

Remi fell into step beside him as they descended the stairs. "I'll grab us some snacks and drinks, so we won't have to stop for food."

"We'll need to run by your place. Too bad I'm not in the habit of stealing your clothes. You could just pack from here."

Remi whipped her head around to glare at him. "You think you're so funny."

In truth, that was just the kind of light-hearted joke they both needed.

"Let's bring that tub of chicken salad in the fridge and a couple of plastic forks. Cheyenne brought it over last night, and it's amazing."

Remi grabbed the chicken salad and the bowl of raspberries beside it. Colt hated raspberries, but at least she'd have something to stress eat for the next five hours.

Colt stepped into the kitchen and set a small cooler on the counter. "Water, Sunkist, and Dr Pepper. Anything else we need?"

Remi tossed the fridge items into the top of the cooler. "Nope. Let's go."

Minutes later, they pulled up at Remi's place. Jess's car was still in the driveway, which meant she was going to be late for church as usual.

Remi jumped out of the truck, leaving the engine running. Colt followed her inside.

"Jess!" Remi shouted as they walked in.

"Bedroom!"

Colt cleared his throat behind her. "I'll wait here. Let me know if you need help carrying anything."

Remi headed for Jess's room. Colt had been to her place dozens of times, and he never tried to venture past the hallway. It was like the narrow passageway might lead to a swamp or a dump. Either way, he avoided that area of her house like the plague.

Knocking on Jess's open bedroom door, Remi got straight to business. "Hey, can you help with the kids today at church? I have to go to Newcastle with Colt. His brother died in a car wreck."

Jess stopped slipping her feet into a pair of boots

to look up. "What? That was way too much info at once."

"Colt's brother died last night. His wife too." Remi pushed down the knot of dread that rose in her throat. "They had two kids."

Jess shook her head slowly. "Wow. That's a lot."

"Yeah. We're going to get the kids."

Jess's eyes widened. "Really? Then what are you going to do with them?"

Remi tried not to panic at the question she'd been asking herself since she heard the news. Colt wanted a family, but she was pretty sure he wanted the whole package. With two kids, the wife part of the equation might be even harder to come by than he thought.

"I guess Colt will be their new guardian. He seems sure about it."

Jess nodded as if that settled the matter. "You sure you know what you're doing?"

Of course, she didn't. But that was the way she lived her life. Make a decision and stick with it, hoping the Lord was leading her in those moments. "No, but Colt has a niece and nephew out there who just lost their parents, and I can't stomach the thought of them being alone right now."

Jess stuffed her foot into the boot and stood. "I get it. Call me if you need anything. I'll handle the kids today."

"And we need to find someone to help Hadley with the kids tomorrow."

"I bet Cheyenne can help. The youth program is finished for the year."

"Right. I'll call her and ask her."

Jess waved a hand in the air. "I'll tell her what's going on at church. You just focus on getting to those kids."

Remi bit her lips between her teeth. She wasn't a crier, and she'd make her lips bleed before she let a tear fall. When the sadness and fear mixed and grew into something ugly and heavy, she reached for her friend, pulling Jess close in a tight hug.

"Thank you," Remi whispered.

Jess gave her a tight squeeze. "Don't mention it. I'm here if you need me."

Remi pulled back and pushed out a deep breath. "I need to get packed, and you need to get to church."

"Right. I just inherited about a dozen little screaming things for the next hour and a half."

There it was. The fear was back when she thought about the two kids they were headed to get. Ben and Abby. They would be a constant in her life now, if she was going to stay friends with Colt. Remi knew a lot about kids after working with them six days a week for the last three years, but Colt was going to have kids that were his. Like, for life.

Jess shoved Remi's shoulder. "Hey, don't worry. You're great with kids."

"Right. I'll be fine." She peeked toward the living room where Colt was probably pacing. "Colt..."

"He'll be fine too. I'll be praying."

Those small words seemed to ease the anxiety swirling in her middle. "Thanks. That's what we need."

"And I'll put you and Colt on the prayer list. You're going to want those casseroles when you get back."

CHAPTER 8

COLT

C olt stared at his phone as he paced. So many thoughts were fighting for attention right now. His brother was gone. The kids were with strangers. Remi was packing for a trip across the state that had an indefinite end date.

It was just like Remi to jump in headfirst when things got tough. That's what she did, and the self-less act secured another part of his heart for her. She'd own the whole thing pretty soon, and there wasn't anything he could do to stop it.

He didn't want to stop it. Remi could have his heart, lungs, and mind. She could even have his liver if she wanted it.

Would she help him with the kids when they got back to the ranch? The thought of raising his niece and nephew sounded like fun, aside from the crippling grief and the fear of messing up. There were so many things he'd have to learn. They'd have to get enrolled in school in Blackwater. At least Ben would. Abby wasn't old enough.

That meant he'd need a babysitter. He'd planned on sticking around through the winter to help with repairs, but would that still be an option if he couldn't find a babysitter? He couldn't bring Abby out on the ranch in three feet of snow while he mended fences and winterproofed permanent campsites and mountain cabins.

His job. He loved working at the ranch, but would having kids require him to change to something different? He technically had set work hours, but he never minded heading out after dark when things popped up unannounced. At least that would have to change now.

He turned the phone over in his hands and pressed the button to make the call to his boss before he lost his nerve.

Mr. Chambers answered on the third ring. His deep, raspy voice was calming, despite the problems Colt had on his mind. "Hello."

"Hey, boss. I know you're probably getting ready for church, but something came up that I need to talk to you about."

"Go on. I'm just having breakfast with Jameson and Ava."

Great. Colt was intruding on the man's Sunday

and his family time. "My brother and his wife were in a car accident last night. Neither of them made it."

There was a scratching on the other end of the line before Mr. Chambers said, "I put you on speakerphone so Jameson and Ava can hear."

"Hey. What's up?" Ava asked cheerfully. She seemed more upbeat than she'd been in the last few weeks.

"My brother and his wife were in a car accident last night. Neither of them made it."

Ava gasped, and Jameson groaned.

"I'm sorry, man. That's awful," Jameson said low.

Colt rubbed the back of his neck where the hairs were standing on end. It still didn't seem real. Mark couldn't really be gone. They hadn't spoken in a few weeks, but Colt was planning to visit for Thanksgiving.

"They had two kids."

There was the scratching of a chair across the floor before Ava whimpered. He'd forgotten about the extra hormones that came with pregnancy.

"What do you need to do? What do you need from us?" Jameson asked.

"I'm going to get the kids. That's all I know. I really have no idea what I'm doing, but Remi is planning on coming with me."

"Do whatever you need to do. We'll take care of things around here," Mr. Chambers said.

"Right. We expected you to be out a little while longer while that shoulder heals," Jameson added.

The shoulder was the least of Colt's worries, but the throbbing pain was back again.

"I know you have a lot to sort out, but let me know if you're still planning to stick around through the off-season," Mr. Chambers said.

"I was, but I really don't know how much I'll be able to do. The youngest isn't in school yet, and–"

"I'll help take care of her," Ava interjected with a sniffle.

Colt had assumed she'd left the room, but her quick willingness to help was like salve on a wound. "Thanks. I'll do whatever I can for the ranch. I love working here, and I don't want to let you down."

"Ach. It'll all work out. You always have a place here," Mr. Chambers said.

Colt sat down on the couch and glanced at the hallway. Remi would be finished packing any minute now, and they would be on their way. Was he ready for this?

"The cabin!" Ava shouted. "Do you still want to move in?"

"Yeah. I guess I'll need a place for all of us." It was too much to ask of Ridge, but the small fee for the cabin rental would come out of Colt's check every week. He could manage the pay cut since he'd been saving every penny he could while living at Ridge's place.

"We'll have it ready for you when you get back," Jameson said. "I can start on it this afternoon."

"I'll help too," Ava said. "Don't worry. We'll take care of everything here. You just get those kids."

Jess stepped out of the hallway and gave Colt a squinted look. She raised her hands together and made the prayer gesture as she mouthed, "Sorry."

Colt gave her an acknowledging nod as she walked out the door. Thankfully, the call with his employers was winding down. "Thanks. I'll keep you posted."

Ava sniffled again. "I'm so glad there are going to be more kids around here. Our little one will have friends to grow up with."

"Speaking of the little one, is it a boy or a girl?" Colt asked. Families were growing everywhere at the ranch, and maybe they'd have the winter to get used to the changes before the busy season started up again.

"We don't know yet, but we don't plan on keeping it a secret once we find out," Jameson said.

Remi stepped into the living room stuffing the sleeve of a shirt into a duffel bag that hung over her shoulder. She had one of Colt's flannel shirts draped over her other arm.

Colt stood and reached to take the bag from Remi. "Good. I want to be the first to know. We're about to get on the road."

"Let us know you make it there," Ava said.

"Will do." Colt wasn't used to checking in with someone who cared if he made it from point A to point B safely, but the gesture proved that Ava would be a great mom.

They ended the call, and Remi handed over the bag. She looked around as if searching for a way out.

"You don't have to do this," Colt reminded her, even though he knew the sting of losing her would be sharp if she backed out.

"No. I want to. I just hope I'm not forgetting anything."

Colt started ticking off things on his fingers. "Socks, underwear, jammies, sleep mask–"

Remi pushed past him with a chuckle. "If you ever see a sleep mask on my face, it's a cry for help. Let's go."

Colt followed Remi to the truck and tossed her bag in the back of the extended cab. The floorboard was covered in tools and shop rags. Thankfully, he'd cleaned it out recently, and there wasn't anything to stain her things.

Remi settled in behind the wheel and popped her knuckles one by one–a sign she was nervous. "Okay, trusty co-pilot, where to?"

Colt plugged his brother's address into the GPS

on his phone, and the female artificial intelligence voice filled the cab. "Starting route to Mark's house."

Remi looked over her shoulder as she backed out of the short driveway. "Anything you need to catch me up on while we drive?"

"I called Mr. Chambers. He knows what's going on. Jameson and Ava too. They'll try to help however they can. Ava said she'd help out with the kids so I can stay on through the winter."

"I'll help too," Remi added.

"You don't have to do that. Weren't you planning to work this winter too?"

Wolf Creek Ranch was closed to visitors from December through February, and while most of the wranglers headed south to Texas or New Mexico, some agreed to stick around and help with general repairs.

Remi shrugged. "I was, but I can ask for limited hours so you can work. You'll need the money more than I will."

Colt knew next to nothing about Remi's money situation. She changed the subject faster than she swiped his clothes whenever he brought it up, which meant he was insanely curious as to whether or not she had money troubles. He tried to discreetly pay for things when they were together in a no-big-deal kind of way, and she hardly ever fought back.

A rush of heat snaked up his back. What was

happening? He opened and closed his hands. The palms were clammy and cold. It was all happening so fast. Mark. Remi. The kids.

"Colt, you okay?"

Remi's question was casual, but she'd probably picked up on the panic he was trying to shake off. "Yeah." His throat was dry and burning, despite the cold bite of the Wyoming fall. "I'll be better when we get there."

He wasn't exactly sure things were going to get better after they arrived in Newcastle, but at least he'd be doing something instead of playing the hurry up and wait game for five hours.

"Tell me about them," Remi said.

"Who?" He wasn't sure he could talk, much less convey accurate information.

"Ben and Abby."

A wave of nausea rose in his throat. Ben and Abby. How were they taking the bad news?

"Ben is smart and funny. Not your typical stand-up comedy. He's sly and sarcastic, which I love. He's just like Mark."

Colt let his head fall back against the seat, closed his eyes, and pounded the side of his fist against his forehead. "This is gonna be tough."

Remi reached for the hand banging against his forehead and pushed it back down into his lap. "Easy, tiger. We don't need a head injury to match that shoulder."

Colt took a deep breath and kept his eyes closed. The searing of his skin eased when Remi touched him. He wanted to grab onto that relief and hold tight, but the last thing he wanted to do was scare her off right now. Maybe if he stayed still, she would leave her hand resting on his. His breaths came slower with each passing second.

"Abby is the sweetest kid. She likes to make bracelets and necklaces out of flowers. Daisies are her favorite." Colt turned his head to look out the window. Snow would cover the ground soon, and there wouldn't be any flowers or sunshine to chase away the sadness for Abby.

Remi let out a deep sigh and moved her hand back to the steering wheel. "Listen, I know this is going to be tough. It'll probably be the toughest thing you have to do in your life."

Colt rolled his head to face her. "Gee. You really know how to cheer a guy up."

Shaking her head, she went on. "It's true, but you're not doing anything alone. I'll be here, and Ava said she would help. I guarantee everyone at the ranch will help." She twisted the worn steering wheel under her palms as she stared out at the road leading them toward Newcastle. "But Ben and Abby are so lucky to have you. You wanted a family. Maybe this is your chance."

Colt's heart sank into the pit of his stomach. The family he imagined didn't look anything like this.

And just like that, the dream was completely gone. "They should have their parents," Colt whispered.

"You're right, but if they can't have their mom and dad, you're the best person to raise them. You love them. I know it."

"Dang straight!"

"See!" Remi shouted back, fueled by his determined affirmation. "You're doing the right thing."

"I couldn't leave them. I just can't. It's not an option." There was one thing he knew for sure–he would do anything for those kids.

"Good, because the foster system can be ugly sometimes."

Colt slowly sat up straighter, careful not to scare Remi out of the conversation that might reveal something about who she'd been before they met. "How do you know?"

Remi glanced at him, then back at the road. "I've heard some things. You know, people don't always foster for the right reasons. I'm sure some of them are good. At least, that's what I've been praying about today."

Nothing in her expression told him she was telling the truth. But there was also no indication of a lie. She'd played it vague enough that he still knew nothing about her childhood.

More than once, he'd convinced himself she'd grown up in the foster system. She never talked about her parents, she never mentioned siblings, and she never talked about a home. She either didn't have those things or they were so bad she didn't want to remember them. Both options made Colt want to punch the dash.

Remi turned on the radio, and an old John Anderson song played a twangy tune. After a minute, she started singing along, and Colt could almost imagine they were just two friends setting out on a road trip without a care in the world.

When the song faded out, Colt remembered the number written on his palm. He'd have to call the caseworker and find out where the kids were, but having that conversation would solidify the truth he was still struggling to accept.

"Thanks for coming," he said quietly in the lull before the next song began.

"What?" Remi asked, much louder than necessary since there wasn't any music to drown out his words.

"I don't know what I would do without you." It was a truth that was almost too scary to put into words. He'd never lost someone he loved. Well, he'd probably loved his mom at some point, but he couldn't remember a single thing about her. His dad had done enough to make sure he was completely unlovable, so there weren't any missed signals there. The man didn't care about anything except his next beer.

But Remi, Colt wasn't sure what his life would

be like without her in it, and he couldn't sit around wondering. It would crush him.

"You'd be fine."

"I'm serious. My happy world just turned into a tornado, and you're still hanging on. You're my ride or die."

Remi held up a finger, pointing it menacingly at the ceiling. "Don't get sappy and start waxing poetic, cowboy."

The wildfire in Colt's chest waned at her slight jab. "But you're my best friend in the whole wide world," he crooned.

"Wow. You need to meet new people if I'm the best you got."

Remi gasped and bolted ramrod straight in her seat. "Speaking of meeting people, I met Camille Harding at the Blackwater Fall Festival last year."

Colt scratched his chin, trying to piece together why that bit of info was so important. "Okay... I've met her before too."

Remi waved one hand in the air. "She said she's an attorney. A family law attorney."

Colt nodded. "Ohh. I forgot about that."

Bouncing in her seat, Remi swatted at his arm. "We have to get her to help us. We have no idea what we're doing."

"You think we need legal help? Do you think they won't let me have Ben and Abby?" The thought had his stomach turning like rocks in a tumbler.

"I have no idea. I hope they will, but maybe we need to call Camille and find out what we can expect when we get to Newcastle."

"That sounds like a great idea, but there's no way I'm calling a stranger on a Sunday to ask for legal help. Plus, I have no idea what she charges."

Remi gripped his arm as her attention wavered from the road to him and back to the road. "We might only get one shot at this, and I'm not a fan of losing."

"You can say that again. You broke my favorite mug after you lost the fantasy football season last year."

"The handle was weak. I barely placed it on the table and the thing just fell off in my hand."

"Whatever you need to tell yourself, princess."

Remi picked up his phone from the console and tossed it at his chest. "Call around until you find Camille's phone number."

"I'm not calling her on a Sunday."

"Who do you think is driving this mayday parade?" Remi shouted. "We'll call her in the morning, but you can find her number now because you're gonna want it after you talk to that caseworker."

Remi was right. The thought of talking to the caseworker on his own and somehow messing everything up before he secured custody of the kids was terrifying.

"Okay, you win. Now, will you please ease up on the gas? This truck isn't built for the wrong side of ninety."

CHAPTER 9

REMI

Remi whistled as they walked up onto the porch of Mark and Brittany's house. The two-story farmhouse boasted tall columns in the front, a three-car garage, and what looked to be dozens of acres stretching for miles around them.

"You didn't tell me your brother was..."

"He's not. Mark and Brittany lived on credit, which I'm sure will be a nightmare for me to clean up."

"Oh, lovely." If only she could send sarcastic thank you cards to the departed. Mark would be getting an earful from her when they met at the pearly gates.

Colt lifted a planter that contained a fake fern and swiped a key from underneath.

"How did you know where the key would be?"

He unlocked the door and waved Remi inside.

"We always hid the key under a pot growing up. Mark isn't creative enough to think of another hiding place on his own."

Remi stepped inside and flipped on a light switch, opting not to correct Colt on his use of the present tense when referring to his brother. He hadn't wanted to talk much about Mark on the long drive, and she would rather jump in a pit of snakes than push him to chat about his feelings when he didn't want to. She'd sat silent through enough therapy sessions in the last few years to know that people talked when they wanted to and when they felt safe.

Colt stopped in the doorway and looked around the living room. Toys were scattered on the floor, blankets lay in heaps on the couch, and cups of juice sat on the coffee table as if a kid might run by at any moment and steal a sip.

Remi propped her hands on her hips. "Well, we have three hours before we can pick up the kids. What should we do first?"

Hopefully, getting Colt into action mode would wash away that weathered look in his eyes.

He rubbed the back of his neck. "I guess we should start cleaning out the fridge. We can leave the things we might eat while we're still here, but everything that could rot needs to go. I don't know when I'll get a chance to come back."

With a salute, Remi headed toward a doorway

that most likely led to a kitchen. "I'm glad the family took the kids to church today."

Colt followed her into the kitchen and opened the cabinets underneath the sink. "Me too. Mark and I didn't go to church when we were young. No one took us. We both went a few times with friends in junior high and high school, and it stuck better for me than it did Mark. I know they went to a service on Easter and Christmas, but beyond that, I bet the kids haven't spent much time in church."

"That'll change now. They'll love our church in Blackwater. The ladies will have a fit over them."

Colt pulled a box of new trash bags out of the cabinet and set it on the counter. "I know. That's one thing I've been thinking about. They won't just have me. I've heard it takes a village to raise kids–"

"And they'll definitely have a whole town looking after them."

Remi opened the fridge and groaned. "This might not take long."

Colt stepped up beside her and his shoulders sagged as he took in the mostly empty fridge. "The police officer didn't say Mark was drunk when the accident happened, but I'd bet my bank account he was."

Pushing his fingers into his hair, Colt turned to pace the kitchen. "I didn't know it was happening again. He seemed fine the last time we talked."

"Colt–"

"Brittany was an alcoholic too, but she liked it all. Drugs, cigarettes, liquor, whatever she could get her hands on." Colt slammed a fist down on the countertop. "Mark finally had a good job. Finally! He was thirty-three years old, and finally got his act together."

The sting of sadness tingled behind the bridge of her nose. Remi knew what addiction could do to families. It had wrecked her own. Knowing Colt had spent his entire life trying to hold up a crumbling family was breaking her heart.

"Colt, I'm—"

"Can we order Chinese? I'm starving."

Remi nodded and pulled her phone from her pocket. Colt had a handful of comfort foods, and Chinese was one of them. She searched for the nearest takeout and placed their usual order. By the time she ended the call, Colt had emptied the contents of the fridge into a trash bag, leaving only a couple of juice drinks and a jar of pickles.

She shoved the phone back into her pocket. "We need to pick up some boxes when we go get the food."

Colt leaned back against the counter and hugged his left elbow close to his side. He hadn't worn the sling, and he'd probably used it too much already today. "Right. I'll have to wait until the kids are with us to pack their things. I don't know what they really need to bring and what can be donated."

"Let's go now. We can hit up a few grocery stores and see how many boxes we can round up before the food is ready."

Remi drove into town, scanning the darkening streets. The sun had gone down, and the orange-tinted streetlights cast shadows over the shops.

They stopped at two stores and gathered enough boxes to fill the bed of Colt's truck, then they stopped by a hardware store and bought a tarp to cover the load on the way back to Blackwater. With warm Chinese food in tow, they headed back out of town to Colt's brother's place.

Colt carried the bags to the kitchen where they realized the small table was covered in papers and toys.

Remi ushered Colt toward the bar. "Let's tackle that after dinner." The defeat in Colt's shoulders was getting worse, and she was running out of ways to protect him from the mountain of responsibilities that had just landed in his lap.

Locating a stack of paper plates, Remi filled their plates while Colt grabbed drinks. One scoop of Mongolian chicken and one scoop of sweet and sour chicken for her. Three large scoops of Mongolian chicken and an egg roll for Colt.

When he took his seat at the bar, he launched into the blessing. "Thank You for the food, Lord. And please help me to know what to do. Tonight with the kids and everything else. Amen."

Remi rubbed a hand over his broad back. She loved that Colt spoke his mind and didn't even hide his fears from the Lord. She never had to wonder what he was thinking or feeling because he told her. There weren't any smoke and mirrors where Colt was concerned.

Colt stabbed a few pieces of chicken with a fork and looked around the room. "Mark and I used to eat a lot of Chinese food."

Remi mumbled around a mouthful of food. She'd been hungry too, and she might have succumbed to a hangry temper if they'd waited any longer. "Hm?"

"We ordered Chinese delivery a lot when Dad was too drunk to make us anything to eat."

Remi swallowed the lump of half-chewed food and wanted to hurl. Her mom hadn't cared much about her, but at least she'd been fed. "I'm sorry."

"Don't be. Mark helped one of our neighbors mow her grass in the summer, and she gave him a few bucks. It was enough to get us by. Dad never ate. I think he drank his calories."

Colt huffed and dug into the food. After a few silent minutes, Colt's plate was clean, and he pushed it away.

Remi was still stuffing her face. "You eat so fast. I can't keep up."

Colt chuckled. "I had an older brother. If I didn't eat fast, he would steal it."

Remi coughed and tried to keep the food in her mouth from spewing out. She covered her mouth and grabbed for a paper towel. "Are you serious?"

"Yep. Especially when we got older."

Remi wiped her mouth and hands on the towel and looked at Colt. The things they'd had to endure growing up weren't so different. "Are you okay?" she asked softly.

He rested his head in his hands and let out a shaky breath. Colt was hurting, and Remi had never cared so much about another person's pain as she did right now.

She pushed her plate away and rested her hands in her lap. "I lost someone once."

Colt raised his head and looked at her with bloodshot eyes. "Who?"

"My cousin, Kylie." It had been years since she'd said the name out loud, and the memory brought with it a fresh stab of regret. "We were inseparable when we were kids. Her mom was better to us than mine was, so we spent a lot of time at her place." Remi shrugged and picked at her fingernail. "We were best friends."

"What happened?"

"I don't know. She ran away when we were young. Granted, I ran away too, but she stayed gone. I haven't seen her since. I looked for her, but I've been afraid to keep looking." Remi pinched her cuticle until the skin broke and a slit of red appeared underneath her nail. "I'm afraid she's dead," she whispered.

Colt stood, pushing the stool back and reaching for Remi's hand. "Stop."

She let herself be pulled into his embrace. The warmth of his chest and the comfort of the arms around her was a haven she'd never known. "Stop what?"

"Picking at your nails," Colt whispered.

Remi wanted to laugh. She wanted to cry and scream and throw her fists in the air. But more than that, she wanted Colt. Her heart wanted to give in, but her head was running away screaming and terrified of what could be between them. Well, what could have been between them if Remi wasn't a scaredy cat and Colt didn't have a family to think about now.

He wouldn't be dating now. He would be caring for his niece and nephew, and Remi had no doubts he would be great for those kids.

Now, he would finally give up on her, and it would be the best decision he ever made. He'd be safe from the fire she brought with her–the wreckage that was catastrophic and left nothing standing.

She'd done the right thing all those years ago when she pushed him away. He needed someone better. Someone without another addictive gene he could pass on to his kids. Someone who understood love and peace and home.

She didn't know about any of those things except what she received from the Lord. But the Lord wasn't going to hurt her. People hurt her, and she'd done a bang-up job of throwing that anger right back at them.

Colt lifted his hands and cupped her jaw, tilting it up so she was looking at him. His thumbs brushed the dry skin of her cheeks. She wasn't crying. At least not where he could see. Her heart knew how to cry on the inside.

"I'm sorry you lost her."

Remi gave a little shrug and tilted her head. "I'm fine."

But as she looked up into Colt's eyes, she wasn't fine. She was silently kicking and screaming and throwing the biggest tantrum. This was about Colt, and she didn't want to make it about her. She wanted to show him a piece of her he'd been asking about for years.

"Thank you for telling me," he said.

His thumb brushed over her jaw again, but his gaze stayed locked on her. Not a staring contest. Not right now. Not when she wanted him–more of him. Not when she was wallowing in the bed she'd made. She'd turned him down for years, and now, she didn't have a choice. She would never have the man she should have said yes to three and a half years ago.

But the look in his eyes said he still wanted her. Did it matter what they wanted anymore? They were picking up the kids in less than an hour, and their lives were changing starting now.

Remi sniffed and took a step back. "Would it make you feel better to watch me belly flop into the pool?"

Colt let his hands fall from her face, and his smile was immediate. "It's thirty degrees outside."

Remi shrugged. "The pool is heated. I snuck back there to check it out before we left for town."

Colt pinched the bridge of his nose, but the smile didn't fade. "Only Mark would have no money, a nice house, and a heated pool."

Remi propped her hands on her hips, feeling triumphant for reversing Colt's sad mood. "I have time for a jump before we have to leave."

Shaking his head, Colt took a step toward her. "No, I don't think seeing you in a swimsuit will do me a lot of good right now."

Remi stiffened. She hadn't mentioned a swimsuit, and her cheeks heated. She'd planned to jump in wearing the clothes she had on. She had four other outfits packed in her duffel bag. "Don't want to have nightmares?"

Colt shook his head. "You're the opposite of a nightmare."

Her breath caught in her lungs. He wouldn't think that if he knew all of the terrible things she'd done.

The phone in Colt's pocket rang, and he read the number on the screen. "It's the caseworker."

"It's probably time to pick up the kids."

He answered the call, and Remi slipped out of the kitchen. Her bag was still by the door, and she slung it over her shoulder. She'd give him some privacy while she found a bedroom. The house looked big enough that she might not have to sleep on the couch.

She passed a room that had to be Abby's and another that was Ben's without a doubt. The next one had an unmade bed and various bottles of medicine and drinks on the nightstand. She'd clean that up before Colt saw it.

The next bedroom was sparse with a made bed. She'd be safe to claim a guest room. She'd let Colt have it if there wasn't another one. He wouldn't want to sleep in his brother's bed.

She tossed the bag onto the bed and checked the time on the clock. Hadley should be home from church, and Remi might not get another chance to call and make sure her fill-in had everything she needed for the coming week.

Remi sat on the edge of the bed and called Hadley.

"Hey! Are you okay? I heard you went to

Newcastle with Colt because..." Hadley's quick greeting trailed off as if she were unwilling to say the bad news.

"Yeah. Are you going to be okay on your own this week?"

"No problem at all. Cheyenne said she would help me."

"Good. I haven't even had a chance to call her, but I'm glad she agreed to help." Cheyenne and her fiancé, Ridge, started a youth learning program at the ranch over the summer, and they'd dealt with kids of all ages in the last few months. Cheyenne would at least know where they could get anything they needed, and Remi had made a detailed schedule before she left.

"So, have you met the kids yet?" Hadley asked.

"Not yet. We're probably about to leave to meet with the caseworker and get them." She rubbed a sweaty palm down the side of her jeans.

Something shuffled on Hadley's end of the call. "Are you ready for this?"

Remi huffed. "Isn't that the question of the day? I guess I am. I'm just here to help Colt."

But that wasn't the whole truth. Ben and Abby would be a big part of Remi's life now too, and she wanted to help them any way she could. If Colt cared about them, she cared too.

There was a quiet knock on the door, and Colt

stood just outside in the hallway. He gave a thumbs up, letting her know they were good to go.

"Colt just told me it's time to leave. I'll try to call you tomorrow to see how things go."

"Don't worry about us. We'll be fine. Bye."

Remi hung up the phone and stood. She said a quick prayer that all went well at the meeting and that they could get the kids without any trouble.

CHAPTER 10

COLT

Colt sat in the waiting room at the Department of Human Resources. The caseworker, Janet Brighton, was finishing up another meeting, and the minutes were ticking by slower than a turtle with a broken leg.

Remi rested her hand on his knee. He hadn't realized he'd been bouncing it until she touched him. "It should be our turn soon. Are you sure you want me to come with you?"

"Positive. What if I say something stupid?"

"Well, I can't stop you from saying things. I'll just do damage control when you do."

Colt groaned and rested his head in his hands. "I'm going to screw up."

"Colton Walker," the receptionist called.

He was on his feet in an instant, scrambling for anything to relieve the nervous energy. "That's me."

The old lady manning the welcome desk pointed toward a hallway on her right. "Miss Brighton will see you now. Third door on the left."

Remi walked close beside him down the hallway, and her nearness was both a balm and an itch. She was going to witness his screw-up, and she'd probably run for the hills when he flubbed this up.

Miss Brighton sat behind a black desk in a small office. The walls were off-white, and there wasn't a single thing hanging on them except what looked like a schedule with lots of numbers.

"Mr. Walker. It's nice to meet you. I'm Janet."

Colt extended a hand and tried to look casual. Janet's hair was tall and seemed to be reinforced by something like rebar. How did it stay up in those big poofs? He'd seen the style in photos from the eighties but never in real life.

"This is Remi Taylor." He laid a hand on Remi's back, coaxing her forward. The tense grin on her face was a mask. She was trying to hold in laughter, and Colt said a silent prayer that Remi could restrain her comments about the larger-than-life hairdo until they were out of the building.

"Nice to meet you, Janet," Remi crooned. Even her voice was altered as she tried not to break.

Janet gestured to the two chairs in front of her desk. "Have a seat. Ben and Abby will be here soon, but we have some things to go over before they arrive. I'm glad your employer was able to send over so many of the documents earlier today. That definitely sped things up."

Good. Colt wanted to be out of here as fast as possible. The white-on-white walls, ceiling, doors, and carpet were giving him a headache.

Janet tapped a stack of papers together on her desk as she sat. "We got the results of your background check just an hour ago. Everything looks fine." She turned to Remi with a slight tilt of her head, which didn't wobble the towering hair even a millimeter. "Are you living in the home with Colt?"

Remi's eyes widened. "Me? No. I'm just here for support. We don't live together."

Janet grinned and turned back to the paperwork. "Oh, okay. Well, let's go over a few things. Ben and Abby will need to be enrolled in the Blackwater School system as soon as you get there. We have assigned a local caseworker to them who will be your contact until the guardianship is finalized."

After being bombarded with questions and information for half an hour, Colt's head was spinning. Hopefully, Remi was remembering all of this too because he was bound to forget half of it.

"One more thing. Brittany has a sister named Tasha White."

Colt's blood froze in his veins. Tasha. How could he have forgotten about Tasha? Colt cleared his throat. "Yes, I met her years ago."

"Met her" was a polite term for wanted to pluck

her eyes out with hot pokers. The woman was a walking snake, and if he never saw her again, it would be too soon.

"Really?" Janet seemed to perk up. "We need to get in touch with her and confirm she isn't interested in custody of the children. Also, Mark and Brittany's estate will be on hold until she can waive rights if she so chooses. Do you know how we can contact her?"

Colt forced his lungs to push air in and out. Tasha wouldn't have any love for the kids, but she would want everything and every penny Mark and Brittany might have had to their names. For all he cared, Tasha could have the debt and anything left, but he'd go down kicking and screaming before she'd get anywhere near Ben and Abby.

"No, I haven't heard anything about her in years." That was the truth. Even Brittany didn't like her sister, especially after the lunatic got drunk at Mark and Brittany's wedding and broke a bottle over the DJ's head. The guy had suffered a skull fracture, and Tasha had been wasted through all of it.

He needed Tasha crashing this party like he needed gum on the bottom of his boot.

"Oh, well. We'll keep looking for her."

The phone buzzed beside Janet. "The Walker kids are here."

Colt bolted out of his seat, but Remi's calming hand rested on his arm.

Janet twirled her chair to the side and primly stood. "Ah, thank you." She looked up at Colt with what might be considered a grin. "Let's go to the meeting room."

Colt and Remi followed Janet down the white-on-white hallway. When Janet rounded a corner, Remi took the opportunity to get Colt's attention and wave her hand over her head in the shape of Janet's mane. Remi mouthed, "Did you see that hair?"

Colt bumped her with his elbow and pinched his lips together. He would not start laughing now because he wouldn't be able to contain it when he was face-to-face with Janet the lion.

Janet opened the door to a room and stepped to the side. Colt followed Remi inside, but the room was empty.

"I'll bring the kids in just a sec," Janet said as she closed the door.

Colt quickly turned to Remi. "Tasha is bad news. Like, we will have a tornado full of rusty nails on our hands if they bring her into this."

Remi's eyes widened. "Are you serious?"

Colt pushed his fingers through his hair. "She's a nightmare wrapped in poison. Brittany didn't even speak to her."

Remi rested a hand on her forehead. "Maybe they won't find her," she whispered.

"Pray. Pray they don't find her," Colt pleaded.

"Okay. I'll pray."

"What if they find her and then they won't let me have the kids? Surely, they wouldn't give Ben and Abby to her just because she's a woman and I'm a man, right?"

Remi swallowed, but she stayed silent.

"Remi!"

"I don't know. I really want to say they would be stupid to give the kids to anyone but you. But I also know that women are seen as better caretakers in the grand scheme of things. We definitely need to call Camille in the morning."

Colt covered his eyes with his hands. "I'm going to puke."

At that moment, the door opened, and Abby bolted toward him. "Uncle Colt!"

Colt knelt and opened his arms, all worries about crazy Tasha gone as Abby wrapped her tiny arms around his neck.

"Abby bug!"

Ben stepped into the doorway with his hands in his pockets. When he locked eyes with Colt, Ben ducked his head and fell into Colt's open arms.

Abby was jumping up and down, jostling his injured arm, but Colt couldn't bring himself to care even a little. Ben and Abby were safe in his arms, and he finally felt like everything would be okay.

Abby pulled away and looked up at Remi. Her

long dark hair fell over her shoulder. "Who are you? I'm Abby."

"I'm Remi, Uncle Colt's friend."

Abby smiled up at Remi, showing all of her tiny baby teeth. "You're pretty."

Colt wholeheartedly agreed. Remi was gorgeous, though she'd pinch the skin on the back of his arm if he ever said as much.

Remi knelt in front of little Abby. "Thank you! And have you looked in a mirror lately? You're gorgeous too."

Abby wrapped her arms around Remi's neck, and Remi returned the hug. "I think we're gonna be best friends," Abby whispered.

Keeping his hold on Ben, Colt slid a hand around Remi's back. Abby effectively took his place as Remi's best friend, and he wasn't the least bit upset.

And when Remi winked at him over Abby's head, he gave every bit of his heart to the three people in his arms.

CHAPTER 11

REMI

R emi dragged a brush through Abby's hair, letting her fingers play in the dark waves. "I think that'll work."

Abby turned on her heels and looked up at Remi. "How do you know how to brush my hair without getting stuck in the knots? Mom always pulls, and it hurts."

It wasn't the first time Abby had casually mentioned her mom, and the single word stabbed Remi's chest each time. Was she supposed to acknowledge the mom who wouldn't be coming back or move on like she'd never been mentioned at all? "There are two secrets." She ticked off the short list on her fingers. "First, use a little bit of water or detangling spray. Second, brush from the bottom up."

Abby tilted her head and scrunched her cute nose. "How do you brush from the bottom up?"

Colt stepped into the bathroom doorway. "You two ready?"

"We were born ready," Remi said, propping her hands on her hips.

Abby put a tiny hand over her mouth and giggled.

Colt rolled his eyes and jerked his head toward the stairs. "Good, 'cause the train's about to leave the station."

Abby gasped. "We're riding in a train!"

"No, no. Not a train. Just Uncle Colt's truck again. He seems to think his truck is cooler than it really is."

Abby laughed again. The kid was a true morning person, and Remi was glad to have another bright smile to accompany the beginning of her day. She held out an open hand, and Abby took it immediately. She was definitely a toucher, and she'd clung to Remi every chance she got.

Making their way down the stairs took a while when Abby's legs were short and she insisted on taking them in half steps, getting a solid footing with both feet on each step.

"Remi, did your hair come like that?" Abby asked as she held tight to the railing.

"It did. I was born with red hair. Actually, it was lighter when I was your age." Remi hadn't spent much time fussing over her natural copper color. There wasn't much she could do to change it, considering she'd never had the extra funds to afford hair dye.

"Did your hair come like that too?" Remi asked back.

"Yeah. Mom said hers used to be dark like mine, but now it's yellow like the sun."

Another mention of the absent mom. Remi made a mental note to check the library for books on helping kids deal with loss. Surely, some expert had written a how-to book about coping.

At the bottom of the stairs, Colt waved his arms toward the door like a crossing guard. "Move those feet, Abby bug. We're going to be late."

"Relax. I'll get us there in time," Remi promised.

Colt shook a finger at her face. "No, you're not driving. My shoulder is fine now, and you drive like the Dukes of Hazzard."

"What's that?" Ben asked.

Colt's eyes widened. He'd warned her last night about Ben's penchant for daredevil tricks. The kid had more medical records than Remi, despite his few years. "Nothing. That just means Remi doesn't follow the rules of the road very well."

"That's not true!" How dare he accuse her of being a bad driver!

Ushering everyone toward the door, Colt sighed.

"Can we please continue this conversation in the truck?"

Remi held up a scolding finger as she passed. "You'll regret that one, Walker."

"I have no doubt."

When everyone was securely fastened in their respective seats, Colt headed toward town. The kids were bickering one minute and playing together like little angels the next, and Remi couldn't hear herself think over the constant chatter.

She glanced at Colt who held the wheel a little too tightly as he stared out at the road ahead. They hadn't gotten a chance to talk this morning, but the events of yesterday had emotionally wiped them both out. He'd seemed happier once they got back to Mark and Brittany's house with the kids the night before, but a cloud of tension strained his shoulders now.

"Don't be nervous," Remi whispered.

"Sure. I'll just stop breathing while I'm at it."

She rested a hand on his arm and gave it a small squeeze. "You're doing a great job. So far, so good."

"Right. What if Janet decided overnight that she doesn't think I'll be a good guardian? What if the judge thinks that too?"

"Stop it. You're spiraling," Remi said. "They don't have anyone else, except–"

"Don't say it," Colt interrupted.

They'd also had a little chat about Tasha after

the kids fell asleep, and everything he'd said about the kids' volatile aunt had kept Remi up until well after midnight. She said another prayer thanking the Lord that the kids had Colt in their lives.

The gentle tugging of her heart she'd felt toward Colt for years was now more like an intense magnetic attraction. His willingness to step up and take care of Ben and Abby was the most selfless act Remi had ever witnessed. How many people would give up their own dreams and the future they'd hoped for to take on children? It was a life-changing decision that Colt had made in an instant.

Because it was the right thing to do, and Colt was a good man.

"Uncle Colt! Ben took my fuzzy pen!"

Remi turned around and plucked the pen from Ben's fingers and handed it back to Abby. "You each have your own pens for a reason."

"But she–"

"Cool it, guys," Colt demanded as he parked in front of the drab building they'd visited the evening before. "Please act like normal kids while we're here."

Abby laughed. "We *are* normal kids!"

"I'm not so sure. Normal kids eat strawberry oatmeal."

Remi laughed at Colt's reference to the breakfast battle. Apparently, Ben only ate freezer waffles, and Abby only ate cereal–Lucky Charms, to be exact.

Inside the building that reminded Remi of a criminal institution, they checked in at the front desk, and the kids were escorted to a playroom. Colt and Remi took their seats in the waiting room. It wasn't exactly a place that allowed for private conversations.

Remi leaned over and whispered, "You okay?"

Colt tapped the heel of his boot in a quick rhythm. "I think I'm gonna hurl."

"Lean that way if you get the urge," she said.

"I don't know if I'm doing and saying the right things." Colt rubbed the back of his neck and tilted his head from side to side.

What could she say that would help? She was just as nervous, and she wasn't the one petitioning for guardianship of her niece and nephew. "You've got this. You'll do fine."

He turned to her, shaking his head. "No, I won't. I'm terrified. I don't know how to care for kids. What if they get hurt? What if—"

Remi slapped a hand over his mouth, halting his doubts. "Stop right there. You can do this. Get it together, Walker."

Colt nodded, and she slowly removed her hand. He let out a defeated sigh. The guy was eaten up with worry.

"Let's pray. I think you need it," Remi said.

Colt nodded and bowed his head as she began.

"Father, Colt is losing his mind, and he could

really use some assurance right now. I keep telling him he can do this, but he's not listening."

Colt cleared his throat, silently asking that she quit poking at him and get on with the prayer he really needed.

"Please go with us into the meeting. Help him to know what to say, and allow Janet to see his heart. Amen."

Colt blew out a breath. "Thanks. If I could just calm down, I'd be fine."

"I know. It'll be over soon, and we can take the kids out for ice cream." A double scoop of Rocky Road sounded amazing. She also needed to figure out Ben and Abby's favorite flavors.

"Mr. Walker."

Janet stood in the entrance to the hallway, beckoning them toward her office.

"It's good to see you again too, Miss Taylor."

"It's good to see you too, Miss Brighton." Though Remi was already struggling to hold back chuckles. Was there a chance Janet's hair was taller this morning than it had been yesterday evening?

They followed Janet into her office and sat in the same seats as before.

"Good news. I've already heard from Judge Weathington, and he'll hear your case tomorrow morning."

Colt sat forward in his chair. "That soon?"

"The court has seventy-two hours to set hearings for guardianship cases. It's important to get these things settled quickly so the children will have an adult to make decisions on their behalf."

"Right. That makes sense. So, they'll legally be mine by tomorrow?"

"For now. Guardianship is a quick process, but if you choose to adopt, those proceedings take much longer."

Remi looked at Colt who looked back at her. Guardianship and adoption sounded to her like they could be interchangeable, but apparently there was a difference. She'd ask Camille when she arrived later today. They'd called her first thing this morning, and she'd agreed to represent Colt and the kids.

Remi placed her hand on Janet's desk. "A friend of ours has agreed to represent Colt in the custody suit."

"That's good. I always recommend hiring an attorney. They're more versed in the process. Can you give me their contact information? I'll let them know about the hearing."

Colt read off the phone number, and Janet keyed it into her electronic file. "That should be all I need. Now, tell me about your living situation."

Colt rubbed his palms over his jeans. "Well, I work at Wolf Creek Ranch. I'm a wrangler."

"Are your hours full-time or part-time?" Janet asked.

"Full-time. We're about to come into the off-season, so my hours won't be as long as in the tourist season."

"Right. Have you thought about childcare?"

Colt tensed beside her. "My boss has agreed to help out with that."

"So, your employer will babysit? Or will work around your childcare needs?"

"Um, both?" Colt wiggled in his seat, and urgency rose in Remi's middle. These were all the things Colt was struggling to get lined up, and she could feel his anxiety climbing.

Help. Help him. He needs help. Do something!

The thoughts bombarded her. Over and over, she listened as Colt struggled to answer the questions.

Lord, what can I do? How can I help him?

A silent peace released the tension from her neck to her feet as the idea dawned.

"I'll be helping," Remi said. "Between the two of us, the kids will always have someone to look after them. I'll be dropping Ben off at school and picking him up in the evenings."

"That's good to know." Janet made more notes with the clicking of her fingernails on the keys. "And your job?"

"I work at the ranch too, but I'll be off during the winter months."

"Oh, well, I guess that settles the childcare concerns, at least for now."

Remi reached for Colt's hand and threaded her fingers with his. "Actually, Colt and I will be getting married soon."

Colt coughed and tried to release her hand to cover his mouth, but she held firm. With no time to chat about her decision, she hoped Colt would play along.

"We've been talking about tying the knot for a while, and this seems like as good a time as any. Right, sweetie?"

Colt stared at her, completely paralyzed by her revelation. She pulled her smile tighter and gave him a slight nod.

Catch on, Walker. We don't have all day.

"Um, yeah...sweetie."

Her shoulders relaxed as she accepted her new role. She could do this for him. She could help. They'd be better together, right?

Her head and heart were in agreement. She knew exactly what the Lord was telling her to do—stop fighting it and show Colt they could be a good team.

Granted, he might not want this. He might still want that family he'd been dreaming about. She couldn't give him that, could she? He was her best friend, and she cared about him, but would he even be able to care about her when he found out about all the awful things she'd done in her life?

Twenty-six years had given her time to dabble

in all of the drugs, drink through all of the liquor, and commit all of the crimes. Granted, her criminal record was clean. She'd somehow avoided the authorities each time she'd bent the rules. She'd robbed, lied, cheated, and scammed, but God was the only witness.

No, maybe she was being stupid. What had seemed like a perfect idea moments ago felt like she'd just slapped Colt with a life sentence.

"Congratulations," Janet said, though her excitement seemed oddly dim. "We can go ahead and get started on your background check as well then."

Oh no. While she didn't have a rap sheet, she did have medical records documenting her overdose. That one last time the drugs had almost taken everything from her. And while she had tons of regrets, she could see the bright side of that dark moment. She'd met Kendra, who had led her to her new life at Wolf Creek Ranch and gave her a fresh start—one she never took for granted.

It had been years since she'd even thought about drugs or alcohol, but would those mistakes come back to rear their ugly heads now?

Remi kept a firm hold on Colt's hand and tried to ignore his stare that tickled her neck. "Right. What do you need from me?"

CHAPTER 12

COLT

C olt clenched and stretched his hands as he walked out of Janet's office. Remi fell into step beside him like she hadn't just thrown a hand grenade into his already jumbled day.

Getting married? Was that some kind of cry for help? There was no way on God's green earth that Remi Taylor had willingly said she was going to marry him.

When they were a safe distance from Janet's office, Colt rounded on Remi and whisper-screamed, "Have you lost your mind?"

Remi had the nerve to roll her eyes. "Don't panic. You said I'd make a good wife."

"How can you be joking right now?" Colt's sense of humor was thoroughly sealed in a concrete box at the moment, and he couldn't reason out Remi's plan in all this.

"I'm not joking. Let's get married," she said in the same tone she'd used when she'd promised ice cream earlier.

Colt rubbed his hands up and down his face. "Please stop playing around and tell me why you've suddenly changed your outlook on marriage."

She sighed and tilted her head back and forth. "Because I think you need help."

"Oh, I'm definitely going to need help. I just inherited two kids and got a wife in the span of twenty-four hours."

Remi chuckled. "I mean, I'll help with the kids."

"You can help with the kids without marrying me."

Why in the world was he trying to give her a reason to back out? Marrying Remi had been his dream for years, and now, it might just be within reach. Whatever the reason behind the change, he wanted to marry Remi.

But the stark reminder that she had some aversion to marriage rang in the back of his mind. She didn't love him, at least not in the same way he loved her. They'd never even kissed! He definitely wanted to kiss her, but...

Oh, and they had two kids. Somehow, they'd gone about the whole making a family timeline all wrong.

Remi put her hands together and leveled him with her most serious expression. "Listen, we don't have to do this if you don't want to. I just had a feeling during the meeting that we should be doing this together. Plus, if Brittany's crazy sister shows up, she won't have a chance of even making waves if we're a united front and providing a good home for Ben and Abby."

Colt's throat constricted as he stared at Remi. She was willing to get married–the one thing she'd always swore to avoid–to help him secure a happy home for his niece and nephew.

She looked at the ground and fiddled with her fingers. "I remember what it was like to be a kid. It was terrifying. I can't let those kids grow up like that."

He reached for Remi's hand and brushed his thumb over the skin. He'd meant to stop her fidgeting, but now, he just wanted to link himself to her. He didn't know much about her childhood, but hearing that the strong and capable Remington Taylor had once been a scared kid tore him up inside.

If she'd let him, he'd spend the rest of his life giving her enough love to erase all those hurts.

Remi stared up at him. "Well, what do you think?"

"I think this has got to be a dream because–"

"Come on, Walker. Cut the dramatic indecision. You're making me sweat."

"You didn't make me sweat at all when you–"

"Let's not bring that up right now," she interrupted. "I have a feeling this is what we're supposed to do, but we don't have to if you don't want to."

Colt rubbed his neck. "I mean, we're not even dating."

Remi paused for a minute, and there was a ghost of sadness in her eyes. "I know you want a marriage like that. And you deserve a partner who... I care about you. I care about you a lot. I've always been afraid of marriage because... I— I bring a lot of baggage to the table. None of it is good. I know it's stupid and selfish, but I wouldn't want to marry a bad man, but I don't think I deserve a good man like you. There. I said it." She threw her hands out to her sides, then let them fall against her thighs.

Colt stared at her, shocked by her openness. "Are you kidding me? I'm not sure I'm a good man, but I can guarantee I won't be a bad man. What are you even talking about?"

"I wasn't always a Christian, and I lived a selfish and reckless life. I did terrible things. I've been with men. I broke the law. Lots of times. Though they won't find it on my record because I never got caught. I took things from good people. I let people down. I lied a lot. I did drugs. I drank. I–"

Colt clapped his hand over her mouth. "Please stop."

Remi's shoulders sank as if the weight of all of those words hung heavy on her small frame.

He wasn't going to say he'd expected any of those things because wow. But he'd never had the impression that Remi was perfect. He only knew that she was perfect for him.

"Stop talking about all those things. I don't care about your past. This is about our future."

Our future. Those small words had big meaning, and the impact of this decision was settling in. Remi had offered to marry him. Granted, not because she expressly wanted to, but because she had a huge heart whether she realized it or not.

She might not ever love him the way he loved her, but he would keep reminding her that she was infinitely important, if only to him and the Lord.

Because the Lord could make something beautiful out of ashes. Remi was a living, breathing example of how He could change a person's heart. She called herself a thief and a liar, but Colt saw a beautiful daughter of the King.

"How can you say that? I just told you I–"

Colt stopped her. "I said what I said. Are we getting hitched or not?"

She stared at him as if daring him to back out. Colt crossed his arms and stared back. "This is one contest I'll win, princess. I'm in. What about you?"

Remi's eyes narrowed a little but didn't blink. "I'm not giving in."

Colt wrapped a hand around her arm and pulled

her down the hallway. "That's what I needed to hear. Let's get married."

Remi laughed behind him. She was actually laughing, and Colt's heart was lighter than ever. There was no doubt, no worry, no stress over the unknown they were walking into.

"Let's tell the kids first," Remi said.

"Right. I guess we have a few details to work out."

They reached the room where the kids were playing, and Colt stopped with his hand on the knob. "Last chance to back out."

Remi pushed past him and opened the door herself.

It seemed Remi was sure of her decision. Was he? He took a second to himself before following Remi.

Lord, is this what You want? Are we supposed to do this together?

At that moment, Abby's high-pitched squeal filled the air. "Ahh! You're getting married!"

That seemed to be the divine answer he'd requested, and he tried to temper his ridiculous smile as he walked in.

"What's this about getting married?" he asked.

Abby launched herself toward him with her arms out. "You and Remi! Can I be the flower girl?"

Colt wrapped Abby in his arms and lifted her off

her feet. "Sure you can. I guess you'll want a pretty dress, too."

Abby gasped.

Remi held up a finger. "Um, Abby, I don't think this is going to be the big wedding you're expecting."

"Do you have a dress?" Abby asked.

Remi looked at Colt as if asking for backup, but he wasn't about to save her from a little girl's over-reaction. He was just as excited as Abby, and nothing was going to rain on their parade.

"I don't. Maybe you could help me pick out something *reasonable*."

Abby gasped again. At this rate, she was in danger of hyperventilation.

Colt turned to Ben and crouched beside him, keeping his hold on Abby. "Ben, what do you say to being my best man?"

Ben shrugged one shoulder, trying to exude a calm and cool reaction. "That would be cool, I guess."

Colt clapped his nephew on the back and stood. "That settles it then. We've got some shopping to do."

Abby threw her hands in the air. "Yay!"

At least the kids were happy and not tragically grieving. Maybe they all needed a happy celebration right now. He had a meeting at the funeral home in five hours to plan the private ceremony for Mark and Brittany, but they could enjoy some time planning a wedding together before the sad reality showed up later.

At the mall, Ben bought a gray suit, Abby found a frilly purple dress, and Remi decided on a simple white dress that looked like it had lace flowers on it. Remi had wanted something sleeker, but Abby insisted on the flowers. Colt picked up two new suits, knowing he'd need one for the wedding and one for the court hearing.

With bags in tow, Remi pointed out a local diner across the street from the strip mall. "You guys hungry?"

"Yes!" Ben shouted.

"Remi, where's your ring?" Abby asked.

Remi looked down at the hand Abby held. "Um, well, I don't have one yet."

Colt hefted the bags higher on his wrists and turned around. "Can't leave without rings."

Ben whined, but Abby cheered.

Remi was beside Colt in an instant. "I don't need a fancy ring. Let's go get something cheap."

"I'm not buying my wife a cheap ring." How could she even think he'd do that?

"I'm not your wife yet, and this is turning into an expensive outing," she whispered.

"Don't worry about it. I know how to save money. I literally only need a bed and pizza to survive, so I put a lot back."

"But this was all my idea," Remi argued.

"Stop your griping and help me find a jewelry store."

Remi gasped. "How dare you talk to your wife like that."

"You're not my wife yet," he said, looking up at the mall directory.

With a growl, Remi pointed to a store on the map. They spent half an hour browsing while Ben grumbled about his hunger. Finally, Remi and Abby had decided on a simple solitaire for her and a small gold band for him, and Colt walked out of the store fifteen hundred dollars lighter.

Remi looked both ways down the sidewalk. "Now, lunch, then ice cream."

Colt piled the contents of their shopping spree on a bench and rummaged in the little bag for Remi's ring.

"Walker, we don't have time for a rest break. Ben's stomach is eating itself."

When Remi turned around, the wrinkle between her brows disappeared. Colt rested on one knee, holding the ring up between them.

Abby squealed and jumped up and down. "I saw this on TV before!"

Remi shook her head, and a whisper of a grin spread over her face. "What are you doing?"

"Proposing to you."

"You've got to be kidding me."

"I'm not. Let me have this moment."

Remi rolled her eyes as Abby tugged on her hand. "Say yes. Say yes!"

Colt cleared his throat, pausing for dramatic effect. "Remington Michelle Taylor—"

"That's not my middle name," Remi said low.

"Whatever. I'm improvising. Remington Louisa Taylor, will you make me the happiest man in the world and do me the honor of becoming my wife?"

Abby and Ben both laughed, and Remi tapped a fingertip on her chin as if considering her options.

This wasn't the first time Remi had made Colt want to hit his knees, but just like in his dreams, this time she would say yes. They could start a life together the way he'd always wanted.

Remi let her arms fall to her sides. "I guess I can marry you, since you asked so nicely."

"Yay!" Abby barreled into Colt, and he wrapped one arm around her, keeping the other holding the ring.

When he stood, Remi held out her left hand, and he took his time placing the simple ring on her finger.

"You ready for this?" Colt whispered.

Remi grinned up at him. "Yeah, I guess I am."

CHAPTER 13

REMI

R emi stood beside Abby in the middle of the Weston County Courthouse. She gripped the small bouquet of roses they'd picked up at the grocery store on the way into town. A few of the petals were wilted over, and a touch of brown lined a few of them.

"Is it my turn yet?" Abby asked.

Remi glanced to her left where briefcase-carrying attorneys rushed toward courtrooms. Then she looked to her right where the long counter ran the length of the room. Three lines for probate, one for marriage licenses, one for driver's license renewal, one for boating and hunting licenses, and one for business licenses. On the back wall, there were five dedicated to vehicle registrations.

Yep, the romance was in full force on the

morning of her wedding. Surely, this was punishment for vowing never to tie the knot.

"Remi." Abby tugged on the side of Remi's white dress.

"Oh, yeah. It's your turn. You look beautiful. Thanks for being my flower girl."

Abby's chubby cheeks lifted around her smile, and she wrapped her arms around Remi's legs. "Thanks. You're pretty too."

Remi wasn't so sure she agreed, but there was no way she would deny Abby anything on this day. The ceremony was purely for the little girl, and it was worth every penny. Abby hadn't cried for her mom or dad once since hearing the news of the wedding.

But the excitement would soon fade, and Remi would be responsible for helping both of the kids cope with losing their parents. She'd lost hers a long time ago, but abandonment wasn't the same as death. Both ways left vicious wounds, but they healed differently, if at all.

Abby released Remi's legs and stepped up to the brown door. The whole courthouse was an homage to the seventies, and there were worn marks around the outer edges of the door. Remi turned the gold knob and stepped back so Abby could enter the judge's office. The little girl held her chin high.

Remi closed the door and left her hand on the knob. Alone in the middle of a bustling courthouse, she rested her head against the door and let her eyes drift closed.

"Father, I want Abby's chin to stay high. Help me to lift her up when she feels alone and scared. Show me how to raise Ben to be a God-fearing man like Colt. And...and help me to be the wife Colt deserves. I have no idea what I'm doing. I want to help, but I'm afraid I'll just make things worse."

That familiar knot of shame clogged her throat. What did she have to offer Colt and the kids? What if she couldn't be what they needed?

What if she relapsed? That was a question she hadn't thought about in almost two years. Getting clean had been the hardest thing she'd ever done, but life had been a bed of roses on the downhill side. Could she know for sure that she'd never think about another hit? Another buzz?

A silent peace released the squeezing in her chest. She could do it. She had people who cared about her now, a job that she loved, and a family who would be counting on her. After knowing what life was like without those things, she couldn't sacrifice those blessings for a hit. Never.

Remi raised her head and whispered, "Amen." She could do this. She could be brave for the people who relied on her. Plus, she had the Lord on her side now, and that made all the difference.

She opened the door to face the music, or at least her new family. The lighting in the office was dimmer than the main lobby of the courthouse, but the smiles on Colt's, Abby's, and Ben's faces made up for the lack of light. Half of Abby's rose petals were scattered on the floor at her feet, Ben fidgeted in his suit, and Colt's smile beamed like he'd just won the lottery.

The happiness was infectious. Despite knowing the whole thing was born from necessity, her stupid girlish heart wanted to believe the life presented before her was real.

Colt met her halfway down the makeshift aisle and reached for her hand. He pulled her close and whispered tickling words against her ear. "You're beautiful. I told you you'd make a great wife."

Remi huffed. "Yeah, right. Sorry you're settling."

Colt leaned back and looked into her eyes. The serious expression on his face stopped her mid-breath. "I'm not settling."

The intensity in his eyes made her want to believe the words, but he was settling. Colt was a good man. Like, he'd probably never had a traffic ticket. Her list of infractions was a mile long, and his was probably limited to instances when his bill payment had gotten lost in the mail.

"Okay, let's just do this. I'm starting to sweat," Remi whispered. The sweating part was true, and there was no telling if her perspiration would ruin the silky fabric of the dress she wore.

Colt led her to the side of the small room where

the judge waited. He was a portly guy with a white mustache and an amazing combover. Kudos to him for keeping his shoulders up with those wisps of hair covering his bald head.

The judge cleared his throat. Oh no, she'd missed something.

"Miss Taylor, are you ready to proceed?"

"Yes. Yes, please."

"You'll need to give your bouquet to your flower girl and take Mr. Walker's hands."

Remi did as she was told and shook her head to push her hair over her shoulders. There. She was ready to declare her undying loyalty. What a surprise on a random Tuesday.

The judge pushed his glasses up onto the bridge of his nose and looked down at the Bible he held. "Dearly beloved, we are gathered here today."

Remi made the mistake of looking up at Colt. The moment their gazes locked, the game began.

She narrowed her eyes and stared back. *I won't lose this time, Walker.*

The seconds ticked by as the judge spoke, but Remi only had eyes for Colt. If he wanted to test the strength of her determination, she'd show him how immovable she could be—in a staring contest and in the decision she'd made to spend the rest of her life with him. Who wouldn't want to spend the rest of her life with her best friend?

"Now, it's my understanding that you would like to recite your own vows."

"What?" Remi's eyes widened.

Colt blinked as he chuckled, declaring her the winner of the staring contest. "I have vows. Or something I'd like to say."

Well, this was news. She should be scared or at least wary. Colt was known to say things that riled up her urge to run, and now was not the time for sprinting. The short heels were the first shoes with height she'd worn since Blake and Everly's wedding, and she'd kicked those off at the beginning of the reception.

Colt cleared his throat and rubbed his thumbs over the backs of her hands. "Remington Taylor, there are a few things I want to get out in the open. This is real for me. I'll be your best friend, your biggest supporter, and your family until the day I die, and I'll never ask for more than you're willing to give."

Oh no. This was worse than she'd expected. Colt was waxing poetic, and she was wilting under the harsh fluorescent lights. Sweat slid down her back as the true impact of Colt's words hit home. He would be the best husband, and she would be a pitiful excuse of a partner.

But what was she willing to give? That was the question. Could she give him her heart? Could she trust him to stand beside her when the extent of her mistakes were laid out on the table? Could she cut the chain on her feelings for him? Could she love him without limits that were dictated by her shame?

Colt squeezed her hands, and she looked back up at him. Could he tell she was panicking on the inside?

"You're it for me, Remi. I'm sold. I'm all in. And I love you. I always have, and I always will."

Air. Water. A hole she could hide in. She needed something, but her brain was shutting down in the middle of the onslaught.

Her feet tingled, and every muscle in her body tensed. It was the fight-or-flight instinct kicking in, and the fast feet were winning.

There was a tug on Remi's dress, and she turned to look down at Abby's dark eyes. "Say something," Abby whispered.

A soft chuckle broke the tension in the room, and Remi relaxed a fraction of an inch as she turned her attention back to Colt. The little girl had pulled her out of the freak-out, and she was back in the here and now where her husband-to-be waited patiently for her eloquently worded vows.

Swallowing what felt like razor blades, Remi croaked out a quick, "Thank you."

The small room was silent, waiting for whatever came next, but there wasn't more. That was all her jumbled mind could come up with in the moment.

"Is that it?" Abby shouted.

Everyone fell into a fit of laughter. Even Remi chuckled as the hold her anxiety had on her heart eased.

Colt's eyes were bright with happiness. He didn't seem the least bit ruffled by her lack of vows.

The judge cleared his throat. "Is that all you'd like to say?"

Remi nodded with much more vigor than the situation required. "Uh-huh."

Thankfully, the judge moved quickly into the part where she and Colt repeated the promises. Those she could handle, and none of the things asked of her were more than she was willing to give. In all truth, she'd been following most of them already when it came to Colt.

In sickness and in health. In the good times and the bad.

Well, Colt didn't know the half of the bad she'd been carrying. She'd given him the CliffsNotes version after her quick decision to announce their fake engagement, but there was no way he understood the things she'd done and the regret she carried.

Colt held her gaze as he repeated the words and slipped the ring onto her finger. She'd never worn a ring in her life, and the band would take some getting used to.

When it was her turn, she vowed to devote her

life to him without so much as a blink. Whatever doubts she'd had before were gone. Maybe this was God's way of showing her she'd made the right decision.

"You may now kiss the bride."

Remi's eyes widened. How in God's green earth had she forgotten there was a kiss at the end of all this? If she'd been hoping things would just stay the same between them after this, all of those hopes hopped out the window, pointing and laughing as they went.

While she stood paralyzed in shock, Colt took a slow step toward her. There wasn't a trace of nervousness in his expression. Maybe she'd gotten all the unease about the kiss.

Colt's left hand gently brushed her jaw, and the calluses reminded her that this was her Colt–the man she'd spent almost every day hanging out with for years. But everything changed when his right hand gripped her waist, pulling her close enough to eliminate the space between them.

Colt leaned down to brush his lips against hers, and Remi stopped breathing. The soft movement awakened a buzzing inside her that drowned out everything else in the world except the man holding her. After a tense second, she inhaled a deep, freeing breath. Having him this close had all of her cylinders firing at once. Inch by inch, she melted into his arms. The gentle hand on her jaw promised to adore her, while the powerful hand gripping her waist swore to protect her.

When Colt pulled back, Remi swayed, knocked off-kilter by the loss of his support. Was she drooling?

"I'm proud to present to you, Mr. and Mrs. Colton Walker."

Abby jumped and cheered, sending petals floating to the ground around her. Ben's scrunched nose said exactly what he'd thought about the kissy time.

Colt shook the judge's hand and thanked him for his service. Remi looked down at her ring–her wedding ring–and tried to make sense of what just happened.

"Can I throw the bouquet?" Abby shouted.

Remi turned, but she wasn't fast enough. Both bouquets were already sailing straight up in the air. Ben darted toward one of them just in time to catch it, but the other landed on the Judge's desk, spraying red and white petals over half a dozen stacks of papers and folders.

Remi and Colt looked back and forth between the two bouquets that had managed to give the drab office a semi romantic vibe despite the outdated design. The judge huffed, jiggling his round belly.

"We'll clean that up," Colt promised.

The judge reached behind his desk and pulled

out a black wastebasket. Shoving it toward Remi, he waddled out of the room.

Abby sniffed. "He is *not* as jolly as Santa Claus."

Colt laughed and started raking petals from the desk into his hand. "I was starting to think he was Santa too, but you're right. Not enough Christmas cheer for sure."

They had the small office free of petals within five minutes, and they all waved good-bye to the judge's white-haired assistant. At least she smiled. The judge had washed his hands of them before the ink was dry on the marriage license.

Abby skipped ahead as they headed out of the courthouse, swishing the skirt of her dress from side to side. Ben jogged after her, shouting for her to wait up.

Remi looked up at Colt walking beside her. He looked like the same man she'd always known, but they were both different now. Could they handle the change? Were they going to be able to handle a new marriage and raising kids?

"Colt, about—"

"We don't have to talk about it," he interrupted.

Well, she hadn't expected that. Colt always wanted to talk about what he thought or felt. She'd always appreciated his candor, but apparently he'd been keeping more bottled up than she realized. He'd confessed to loving her. Did he mean friendly love or romantic love? One she could handle. The other...

"Really? But I just didn't know..."

Colt stopped and took her by the shoulders, turning her to face him. "I said the things I wanted to say, and you said thank you. We don't have to change. We don't have to talk about it. We don't have to do anything different. You're still my best friend, and you always will be."

Looking up into Colt's honest eyes, she could almost believe they could continue on with life as they knew it. But she remembered the kids and turned to make sure they were still in her sights. When she looked back at Colt, he was smiling.

"I said I wouldn't ask for more than you were willing to give. That promise stands forever."

He'd also said he loved her. That he'd always loved her. Those weren't confessions that could be swept under the rug.

And why did her heart swell knowing he'd loved her all this time and hadn't once pressured her for more? He'd asked her once, and when she declined, he'd relented. Or at least, she thought he had.

Why did that patience mean so much to her? Why did it make her almost want to turn her heart over to him?

Almost.

Then there was that kiss. Wowza. Who knew kissing her best friend would rock her world? Why did he have to be a great guy and a great kisser? It was unfair that he had her melting like butter while he still looked cool, calm, and collected as if he'd just dropped off a package at the post office instead of marrying her.

She brushed a hand over the waist of her dress and looked everywhere but at Colt. "Okay. We don't have to talk about it. At least not now, anyway."

Seeming satisfied with her decision to let the matter lie for the time being, Colt took her hand in his and started toward the exit. "We have a few hours before the hearing. Want to get a bite to eat?"

Through all the excitement, she'd completely forgotten she'd skipped breakfast. "For sure. I'm starving."

CHAPTER 14

COLT

Colt stepped out of the courtroom and took a deep breath. "Whew! Glad that's over."

Remi adjusted a sleeping Abby over her shoulder. The kid was half Remi's size, but Abby had snuggled up to Remi during the hearing when nap time rolled around. Apparently, nothing was going to stop the determined little girl from getting her Zs.

Ben looked up at Colt. "Can we get ice cream now?"

"You bet. I'm having a double scoop," Remi said.

Ben looked back and forth between Colt and Remi as they walked out of the courthouse for the second time that day. "So, what happened in there?"

Colt laid a hand on Ben's shoulder and squeezed. The kid was only seven. Young enough to still love hanging out with his Uncle Colt and almost old enough to understand he'd just lost his parents forever.

"The judge said you get to stick with me. I know I'm not your dad, but I've been loving you since you were the size of a peanut. Your dad and I have that in common."

Ben nodded, but who knew how much understanding was really there. "That'll be cool, right? You live on a farm."

"A ranch. You'll love it. Remi does fun stuff all day long. It's her job, but I'm not sure she thinks of it as work."

"And you'd be right," Remi added. "You get to stick with me too. Trust me, we'll have tons of fun."

"But I'll have to go to a new school," Ben said, almost asking a question.

"Yeah. You'll have to change schools. I'm sorry, bud."

Remi had brought up the option to move to Newcastle, but they'd decided together that they'd be able to raise the kids better with the help of their friends on the ranch.

"Remi said you got horses there," Abby said as she raised her head from Remi's shoulder and rubbed her tired eyes.

"Yep. Lots of horses," Colt confirmed. He opened his arms to Remi, silently asking if she wanted to pass Abby to him. She had to be heavy, but Remi shook her head.

As soon as they stepped out into the afternoon sun, Ben took off. He bolted to the side of the stone stairs and climbed up onto the side.

"Benjamin Walker, don't you–"

Remi's warning fell on deaf ears as Ben hopped over the side and disappeared.

Colt shrugged. "He's always been a daredevil. You'll get used to it."

"I'm not sure I will," Remi whispered.

"We'll just have to keep our eyes on him. I'm guessing he's an expert by now and knows his limits."

Remi looked up at him with a quirked brow. "Sounds like he tests the limits on a daily basis. I'm going to need more therapy."

Another comment about therapy. Colt had no idea what kind of things Remi could be working through with a professional, but the mystery had been nagging at him for days. Maybe she'd know whether or not they needed to seek help for the kids while they were dealing with losing their parents. Colt sure wasn't equipped to help, but Remi had stepped up like a champ.

He looked down at his ring and fisted his left hand. He was married to Remi. She was his wife. Forever. No take backsies. It was what he'd always wanted, but the circumstances were all wrong. He'd spilled his guts during the ceremony, and he'd gotten the response he'd expected. Thank you.

Remi wasn't going to confess her undying love. He knew it. But a small part of him held onto the hope that one day she would love him. One thing was for sure—he'd be good to her. Whatever her life had been like before coming to the ranch was history. They were starting a new chapter of a new book, and he was determined to make it an epic adventure.

Ben met them at the bottom of the steps and pointed to the ice cream shop across the street. "There it is!"

"Does everyone know their favorite flavor?" Remi asked.

"I want something pretty with lots of colors," Abby said.

Ben shrugged. "We've never had ice cream twice this close together before."

Colt and Remi were still finding their way around town, but the ice cream shop was right in the town square. Colt narrowed his eyes. "Really?"

Ben swung his arms back and forth. "We've had ice cream at home a few times."

"You don't have an allergy, or...does it hurt your tummy to eat ice cream?" Colt asked.

"No."

Abby shook her head quickly. "Nope. It's yummy."

Remi looked up at Colt with a questioning

expression. Judging from the typical sugary break-fast norms for the kids, it didn't seem like Mark and Brittany were against sweets.

If only he could ask Mark. Colt and Remi had been relying on the kids' knowledge of their own typical days, but they were kids and couldn't always be trusted to tell the truth, especially when ice cream was on the line.

The tests kept coming, and he had no idea if he was passing or failing. He was a dad now, and the learning curve was apparently steep.

Oh, and he was a husband—to a wife who didn't love him or else she was keeping that tidbit under wraps. Who was he kidding? Remi might not ever love him the way he loved her. He kept telling himself he could live with that, but could he really?

"Hey!"

Colt and Remi turned to see Camille Harding making her way down the stone steps. Dressed in a black suit with shiny black heels, their attorney looked the part of a courtroom ringleader. After seeing her in her element during the hearing, he was certain calling her had been one of the best decisions he'd made this week.

"You did great in there," Camille said with a smile as she approached.

"What about you? You were on fire," Remi said. "I have a new hero."

Camille chuckled and gathered her dark hair as the wind tried to blow it around. "Thanks. I know this whole situation isn't ideal, but I have no doubt the two of you will be great parents."

"I sure hope so," Colt said as he extended a hand to her. "Thanks for your help."

Camille shook his hand. "The pleasure is mine. My job comes with lots of battles, but today was a huge victory."

Remi wrapped Abby up tight in her arms. "We can't thank you enough."

"We should get the kids together to play. My nephew, Levi, is around Ben's age."

"Does he live on the ranch too?" Ben asked.

"Not the same ranch that you'll be living on, but it's close by."

Ben pumped a fist in the air. "Yes!"

Camille looked at her watch. "I need to run. I promised Noah I'd try to make it home before bedtime."

"Safe travels," Remi said.

Abby waved one hand frantically. "Yeah, be safe."

Camille waved back. "Bye!"

As soon as she turned toward her car, Ben shouted, "Ice cream!"

"Okay, okay. I heard you loud and clear," Colt said as he ushered them toward the crosswalk.

His phone buzzed in his back pocket, and he pulled it out. "This is Brett."

"You answer that, and I'll take the kids. You want anything?"

"Nah. Thanks though."

Remi reached for Ben's hand as they crossed the street. Colt answered the call but kept staring after Remi and the kids. "Hello."

"Hey, man. Did you place an order for the cabin roofing supplies? I was thinking it might take a while to get them in."

"I ordered everything from Grady a week ago." Colt rubbed the back of his neck, missing his cowboy hat in the bright afternoon sun. Colt was supposed to lead the crew replacing the cabin roofs during the off-season, but what would he do with Abby?

He'd almost forgotten he had Remi's help in all this. If she couldn't keep Abby with her during the days they were working on the roofing, they'd be able to figure out a solution together.

"How are the kids? You heading back this way soon?"

Colt sat on a bench in front of a water fountain in the center of the square. "Hopefully, we'll be on our way back by this weekend. We have to go through all of the kids' clothes and make sure we're bringing everything they need with us."

"How's Remi? She keeping the kids entertained?" Brett asked.

"She's great. She knows more about what they need than I do." Colt looked at his ring again, still shocked by its presence. "Did you hear we got married?"

Brett let out a whooping laugh with a loud snort at the end. "You're kidding!"

"Nope. And would you believe it was her idea?" That part still gave Colt a little thrill.

Brett made a dramatic show of trying to catch his breath. "It's not nice to play tricks like that."

"I'm glad it's not a trick because she's officially mine."

Boy, did it feel good to say that.

"What did you do? Show her your winning lottery ticket?"

Colt huffed. "You know I'm not a gambling man."

"Except when it comes to Remi. Dude, you have kids now, and suddenly you're a catch?"

"I think that was part of the draw, yes."

"I can't believe everyone is getting hitched. My only single friend now is Linc, and he's a terrible wingman."

"You'd be a good catch if you'd shut your mouth for a few minutes."

"That's the pot calling the kettle black if I ever heard it!"

Colt chuckled. "Maybe so, but my long game with Remi wasn't a flirting game. It was..." What was it? Sit tight and have patience?

"Is it so bad that I tell a woman she looks nice when the thought comes to me? Heaven forbid I speak the truth."

"The truth is good, but if you're hitting on every woman under the age of forty, they're all in the know about it. Blackwater is a small town."

"Tell me about it. Blackwater is getting smaller by the minute."

Blackwater, Wyoming wasn't much bigger than the town where Colt and Mark had grown up, and the memories of the metaphorical walls closing in on Colt in his late teen years was particularly vivid.

The thought of his hometown brought with it the reminder of his dad. He hadn't heard from the old guy in months, and he hadn't reached out since Mark's death. Colt had been putting it off for a reason, but his time was running out with the memorial service happening in the next couple of days.

"You'll find someone. Probably before Linc, so don't stress about it."

"Well, that's a comforting thought. Linc will be an old lonely grouch until the day he dies."

"All is not lost, man. Getting married to Remi was a curveball I didn't see coming. Maybe your future wife will fall into your life out of the blue clear sky one day."

"Did you just use a George Strait song to impart wisdom?" Brett asked.

"Maybe. Listen, I need to go."

"All right, but I'm going to need a written explanation as to why I wasn't asked to be your best man."

"I'll get right on that. See ya."

Colt ended the call and stared at his phone. Maybe he needed an ice cream pick-me-up before laying out the bad news for his old man.

No. If he put it off any longer, he'd never make the call. He said a quick prayer for guidance before pressing the button.

"Hello."

It had been months since Colt had heard that voice, but nothing had changed. The first eighteen years of his life came flooding back in an instant. "It's Colt."

"Long time no talk," Jeffrey Walker said.

Colt propped his elbows on his knees and stared at a crack in the brick at his feet. "Yep. And I don't have good news."

"I figured as much."

Spit it out and get it over with. "Mark was in a car wreck. Brittany was with him. They didn't make it."

His dad swore, then huffed a long sigh. "I figured the devil would get him too."

The devil. That was a good label for the addiction that had a tight hold on his dad and brother.

"I don't know if that was the cause. Since it was a one vehicle wreck, they might not have even tested them. The police officer I spoke with didn't mention it to me. Listen, we're having a small service for them on Thursday. It's at Henderson Funeral Home in Newcastle at ten in the morning."

"Ah, okay." His dad's breathing was ragged and hard. It was just before three in the afternoon, and the old man had probably been drinking since the sun came up. When the conversation was over, Jeffrey Walker would drink until he passed out and forget all about his dead son.

For that, Colt could hardly blame him.

"Ben and Abby are with me. We just got out of the guardianship hearing."

"Oh, man. I forgot about Ben and Abby."

Yeah, he would easily forget his grandkids if he barely called to check up on them. Colt would bet his last paycheck that the kids hadn't seen their grandpa more than twice in their lives.

Best to get all the information out at once. "And I got married. In case you cared to know."

"Congrats. I hope she's nothing like your mother."

That did it. Colt had gotten his fill of family bonding time, and the urge to mend old hurts had passed for the moment. "Thanks. Since she agreed to love Ben and Abby like they were her own, I'm guessing she won't be leaving them like Mom left us."

"Good," his dad said resolutely. "Thanks for calling."

The guy had to already be on his way to comatose to have zero reaction to the news of Mark's death. "Talk to you later."

Colt tossed the phone down on the bench beside him and rested his forehead in his hands. He would bet on a meteor hitting him in this very spot before he'd expect to see his dad later this week at the service.

"Colt!"

He looked up to see Abby running toward him, holding a dripping ice cream cone high above her head.

"I got rainbow!"

Colt stood and met her in front of the fountain, sweeping her into his arms and holding her tight against him. "It looks magically delicious."

"It looks like a sugar coma waiting to happen," Remi said as she walked up holding her signature Rocky Road cone.

"Look at this!" Ben said, holding up what looked like chocolate chip cookie dough.

"They all look good. Who's gonna give me a bite?"

Abby and Ben pulled their cones away at the

same time, and Remi burst into an awkward laugh with a mouthful of ice cream.

The tension from the phone call with his dad was gone. It was okay to move on if his dad didn't care about them. The family he was born into was gone, but he had a new family now. One he planned to cherish for the rest of his life.

CHAPTER 15

REMI

A dull pain ached on the side of Remi's head. She lifted her head and blinked rapidly. She'd fallen asleep against the side of Abby's car seat where the little girl still snoozed. Ben was slumped against Remi's other side, breathing in a quiet rhythm of sleep.

Remi craned her neck to see out the window of the back of Colt's truck. They were on the road leading to the ranch, and she'd never seen a better sight in her life. After a week in Newcastle, the homesickness had taken root.

Home. That was something she'd never really had before, but Wolf Creek Ranch fit the bill. Funny it had taken her over twenty years to find it.

"Rise and shine, Sleeping Beauty," Colt whispered from the driver's seat.

Yeah, she probably looked the part of Sleeping

Beauty. Her ponytail was skewed, there was bound to be a red spot on the side of her face where she'd leaned against the car seat, and there may have been drooling going on.

The five-hour drive back to the ranch had taken more like seven with all the stops along the way. Abby needed a bathroom break every hour and a half, and Ben complained of hunger in between Abby's potty emergencies. After the last stop, Remi decided to move to the middle back seat to break up the kids from bickering.

"Morning," Remi said as she stretched her neck.

"It's afternoon."

"Well, you drive like a grandma," Remi said. Aside from the frequent stops, Colt was the slowest driver in existence.

"I'm transporting precious cargo. I have no regrets."

Why did he have to be so sweet? Between the two of them, Colt definitely got the bigger helping of consideration. He never thought about himself first, and it was unsettling. She'd never met anyone so selfless, and the stark contrast between Colt and ninety-nine percent of the world population threw her off. No one was really that good.

Except Colt, apparently.

Colt turned onto the drive leading to the ranch entrance. "You want to wake them up so they can see the ranch?"

Remi brushed a hand over Ben's hair. "Hey, bud. We're home."

Ben inhaled a deep breath and raised his head. With narrowed eyes, he looked around. "Where?"

"The ranch." Remi pointed out the window.

Ben sat up, plastering both hands against the window. "This is it?"

The tree-lined path opened to the hub of the ranch. The main house sat stately on the hill, surrounded by the dining hall, the dance hall, the stables, and cabins behind it.

Abby stretched her arms and legs straight out in front of her. "Are we there yet?"

"We sure are," Remi whispered. "Take a look."

The kids started spouting out everything they saw.

"The horses are over here!" Ben said.

"What's that?" Abby asked.

Colt chuckled. "Don't worry. We'll show you around, as soon as we get settled in the house. Maybe tomorrow we can pack a picnic and make a day of it."

"All of it?" Abby asked.

"Not all of it. The whole ranch is miles and miles, and some of it is in the woods or the mountains where we can't go," Colt explained.

"So, there are unexplored places here?" Ben asked.

Remi raised a finger to Ben. "Don't even think

about running off. I will find you and tie you to the porch until you're old and gray."

Ben actually chuckled at her imagery. The kid had no fear, and that unbridled adventurousness scared her the most these days.

Remi pointed out the main places as they passed, but her own excitement grew as Colt turned the truck toward the cabins on the west side of the ranch. Their friends had been getting the cabin ready for them all week, and the truth hadn't really sunk in for her. She was going to be living on the ranch, with Colt and the kids. It was like God had gifted her a dream come true that she hadn't known to ask for.

Colt parked next to a cabin with a few other trucks parked outside. She recognized Ridge's, Brett's, and Jess's.

"We're here," Colt said as he unfastened his seatbelt.

"I want to get out!" Abby shouted as she pulled on the straps of her car seat.

Remi loosened the buckles as Ben jumped out the other side. "Are you excited?"

"Yes!" Abby screamed.

At least the kids were happy for the moment. It had taken six days for them to start really missing their parents as the loss settled in, and they'd both cried multiple times within the last twenty-four hours. She'd done more hugging and snuggling this week than in all of the years of her life combined, and there would probably be plenty more on the way.

Colt and Ben jogged toward the cabin and bounded up the stairs before rushing inside. Remi helped Abby out and followed.

The inside was better than she'd imagined. With the mix of her things and Colt's, the place actually looked like a home.

Ridge, Brett, and Jess greeted Colt and Ben in the kitchen. They introduced themselves to Ben before Jess took his hand. "Let me show you your bedroom."

"Yeah!" Ben ran off with Jess toward the back of the cabin.

"I want to see too!" Abby released Remi's hand to follow her brother.

Remi shrugged. "Well, I guess we'll finish the introductions later."

The kids shouted in the bedroom, clearly excited about the new space.

"Wait until they get their stuff in there," Colt said.

Jess joined them in the kitchen. "Sounds like we did a good job." She raised a hand for her brother, Brett, to high five.

"You bet we did."

Ben ran out of the bedroom with Abby trailing behind. "Can we please go out on the ranch today?"

Colt looked at Remi. "What do you think?"

"Why don't you take them, and I'll move their stuff in," Remi said.

Ridge raised a hand. "I'll go with Colt and the kids."

"And I'll help out here," Jess said.

Colt chuckled. "Divide and conquer. I guess that's a yes, guys."

Ben and Abby shouted together and ran toward the door.

"Coats!" Remi shouted. "They're in the truck. Wear them!"

Colt stepped up to her and leaned in. How could he make it seem like they were the only people in the room when their friends were three feet away?

"I'll bring the stuff in before we leave. And you don't have to work all day. It's been a long week. You deserve a break."

Remi rolled her eyes, but she couldn't hide a grin. "You're such a dork acting like I'm delicate. Have I ever needed a break?"

"No, but it doesn't mean you won't need a break at some point. Things are about to get crazy."

Boy, did she know it. Every second was touch and go now that they were basically parents. "I'll let you know if I need a break."

Colt leaned down another inch. "Promise?"

Close. Too close. This position was reminiscent

of the wedding kiss that she'd been replaying all week. "Promise," she whispered.

"Okay. We'll be back in time for supper."

Jess pointed to the fridge. "The church made sure you had dinner covered for the rest of the week, and there are four casseroles in the freezer."

Colt whooped. "That's what I'm talkin' 'bout. Those women know how to cook."

Remi checked her watch. "You have two hours, then. Get going."

Colt clapped a hand on her shoulder. "It's a date."

He walked around her and out the door, leaving her stunned and ridiculously shaken by a shoulder slap. Friends did that! So, why was she all tingly from a friend gesture?

"Well, things just got real," Jess said.

"Tell me about it. I'm a mom!"

"And a wife. Can't forget that."

Remi pushed a hand over her hair, remembering her messy ponytail. "I won't be getting any awards in that department."

"You know, marriage gives you a free pass to change things between you and Colt. If that's what you want."

Remi sighed and looked down at the ring on her finger. What did their marriage really mean? Would they move from friends to lovers and live happily ever after? Or would she sabotage everything?

Would he resent her if she couldn't give him her heart the way he wanted?

"I don't know how to love," Remi said.

"It's no wonder. Your parents were whack jobs."

Remi laughed at Jess's lack of filter. "Well, I don't know my dad, but mom was... She just wasn't the nurturing kind."

Jess propped a hand on her hip. "If you had to drive yourself to school at eleven years old, I think your mom should have seen that call from child protective services coming."

"Or the other calls. I can't let Ben and Abby go through that."

"And they won't," Jess said quickly. "Surely, you and Colt can do a little better than your lame excuse for a mama."

"It wouldn't take much," Remi mumbled. "I want to do this right, but I'm gonna mess up. More than once. Probably more than once an hour."

"With that kind of thinking, I might have to agree with you," Jess said.

"Gee, thanks."

"I'm just saying you're setting yourself up to fail."

Remi rested her head back and sighed. "I'm terrified. I think I want things with Colt to be different, but I don't know how a real loving family works. I didn't grow up with that."

"Neither did he."

Jess was right. Colt's mom had left them, his dad was a worthless drunk, and now his brother was gone. She and Colt were in the same boat. They only had each other.

"I don't know if I can do this right."

"You can, but you won't. Now, let's get to work." Jess walked out of the kitchen, leaving Remi feeling more scared than before.

Jess shouted from the next room, "Oh, and there's only one bed. Have fun with that!"

Ben chased Abby around the small living room as the darkness outside covered the open windows. When Ben changed direction and doubled back on Abby, she screamed.

Remi shushed them. "Guys, you're loud enough to scare the wolves and bears."

"Those aren't around here," Ben said.

Remi propped her hands on her hips. "Then where do you think they are?"

"In the wild."

"Good answer. Guess where you are now?"

Ben's eyes widened. "They're not really out there."

"They certainly are," Colt said as he walked out of the bathroom rubbing a towel over his wet hair.

Remi swallowed hard. Colt wore a white T-shirt

and gray sweatpants, but the heat creeping up her neck seemed to think he was scantily clad. It wasn't the clothes. It was the proximity. The later the evening crept on, the more aware she was of the impending single bed situation.

Stop thinking about it. Stop thinking about it.

"But they won't hurt us," Ben said.

"Maybe. But it's always a good idea to be smart out on the ranch." He ticked off a list on his fingers. "First, always stick with one of us or another adult we trust. Number two, don't go out at night unless you have to. And thirdly, we'll be going over some wild animal confrontation tips starting tomorrow."

"Tomorrow? What about tonight?" Ben asked.

Remi stood from the living room floor where she'd been arranging the kids' toys on a small shelf. "The only thing we're doing tonight is catching Zs. It's time for bed."

"Not yet!" Abby whined. "We just got here."

"That was like five hours ago. And you'll still be here tomorrow when you wake up."

"What are we doing tomorrow?" Ben asked.

Colt ticked off another list. "Church. Lunch at the main house. Meeting everyone in the office. School shopping for Ben. And buying groceries."

Abby scrunched up her nose. "I don't want to do some of that stuff."

Remi whisked the little girl into her arms.

"You're with me for your nap and grocery shopping while Colt and Ben school shop."

"Oh, good." Abby wrapped her arms around Remi's neck and squeezed.

It was unnerving how quickly Abby had warmed up to Remi. Every time the little girl reached for her, she was reminded of the missing mother. Remi wasn't a good replacement for a mom, and it seemed Abby needed extra helpings of snuggles and cuddles to make up for the loss.

"Bathroom and bed," Colt said, punctuating each order with claps.

When the kids were tucked into bed, Colt sat on the side of Ben's bed, and Remi sat on Abby's.

"It's my turn to pick," Abby said.

Colt and Remi had added nightly prayers to the kids' routine back in Newcastle, but Abby had also requested a song. They'd fallen into taking turns choosing the song that Colt and Remi would perform.

"Okay, cutie. What'll it be?" Remi asked.

"You know that song on *Shrek*?"

"The *Shrek* movie with the ogre?" Remi asked.

"Oh, yeah. You mean the one at the end?" Colt asked.

Abby shook her head. "The one at the very start."

Remi bit her lips between her teeth to hide the laugh that threatened to escape and looked at Colt.

Were they really about to make "All Star" by Smash-mouth into a bedtime song?

He rubbed his hands together and grinned. "You got it, cupcake." Colt took a deep breath and burst into the upbeat song, and Remi joined in. By the second verse, they were on their feet dancing. Abby and Ben sat up in bed, laughing.

The dancing was easy as Remi played off Colt's moves. The back-and-forth duet was a breeze, and Remi's heart grew lighter with each line. Soon, her smile resisted giving way even enough to sing the words.

By the end, Colt leaned over the end of Ben's bed, laughing and breathless. Remi fell onto Abby's bed on her back and held her middle. The muscles were starting to ache from the laughing.

"Again!" Abby shouted.

Remi waved her hands in the air. "Not tonight. I can't."

"I'm asking for that one again tomorrow," Ben said.

Colt stood to his full height and clapped. "Deal. Now, prayers."

Abby put her hands together and closed her eyes. Mark and Brittany hadn't taken the kids to church a lot–mostly on holidays–so the kids didn't know much about Jesus or praying, but Abby had taken to it like a champ. She knew when it was her turn, and she didn't waste any time jumping into it.

"God, thank you for our new house. Thank you for that song and Colt and Remi. Please take care of Mommy and Daddy. And please let the bears and stuff stay away. They scare me. Amen."

Colt leaned down over Abby and kissed her forehead. "Don't worry about the bears. We'll protect you," he whispered.

Remi nodded. "It's true. You're safe with us."

Ben pulled up the covers and rolled over. "Okay. Good night."

Remi brushed a hand over Ben's hair and kissed his head. "Good night."

Remi followed Colt out of the room and closed the door behind her. She took a deep breath and slumped with her back against the door. "Whew."

"Tell me about it. It's been a long day," Colt whispered.

She looked around the living room. "This place is nice."

"It doesn't even have a TV," Colt said, his mouth turning up on the ends.

Remi smiled too. She'd spent many hours with Colt alone, but there was something about being alone with him in what was now their shared home that had her skin prickling with nervousness. "How will we watch sports?"

"Maybe Jameson will let us record the games on the TV in the dance hall during the off-season."

Remi stuffed her hands into the pockets of her ratty pajama pants. "I guess we should talk?"

Colt rolled his eyes. "You act like we don't talk all day every day."

"You know what I mean. About..." Her gaze darted to the bedroom. The only remaining bedroom in their new home.

"I figured you'd have something to say." He rubbed the back of his neck. "Listen, I know a lot of this is going to be uncomfortable, but it doesn't have to be. I could share a bed with you, but I can't share a bed with you if you don't want to."

Remi chewed on the inside of her cheek and stared at Colt's socked feet. "It's a lot," she whispered.

"Too much too soon?"

She looked up just as Colt nodded. "Okay. I'll sleep on the couch."

"Colt–"

"Don't worry about it. You know I don't expect anything like that from you. I'll never be that guy."

"I know," she whispered. Everything was backward, and Remi didn't know which way was up. She'd shared a bed with men before, and maybe that was her hang-up. Sex had always been a selfish, sinful act, but with Colt–her husband and best friend–it was special and right. She didn't deserve Colt, and he deserved better than her.

Colt took a step toward her and wrapped his

arms around her. She sank into the warmth of his chest and inhaled deep, pushing back against the sadness and shame.

"I hate that this is so tough on you. I just want you to be yourself. I want you to be happy. That's how you've always been, and I don't want that to change."

Remi laughed. "I have *not* always been happy."

Colt hugged her tighter. "You don't have to tell me about that. Unless you want to."

"I want to tell you a lot of things," Remi whispered. "But I–"

"Just wait then. We have a lifetime to talk about everything."

"I'm sorry." The words were so soft, she wasn't sure he'd heard.

"Don't be. Don't ever be."

Colt released her but kept his hands on her shoulders. "You okay now?"

No, she was not okay, but Colt seemed fine, and that was enough. She nodded and grinned.

"Good. I'm stealing a pillow from the bed." He stalked off toward the bedroom but stopped in the doorway. He turned around and stopped for a second.

"What's wrong?"

He shrugged. "It's kind of a bummer that you can't steal my clothes anymore."

Of all the things he could have said, that kicked

her bleeding heart the most. "What's mine is yours, right?"

"And what's mine is yours," Colt said before disappearing into the room.

Remi bolted for the bathroom and locked herself in. In the quiet solitude, she covered her mouth and rested back against the door. The things they'd brought into the marriage were uneven. She'd gotten all of the benefits, and Colt had gotten a wife who couldn't give him the life he'd always wanted.

CHAPTER 16

COLT

A soft poke at Colt's shoulder woke him from the edges of sleep. Blinking back the heaviness, he stared up at Ben.

Great. Colt had done a good job of waking up before the kids the day before, but the craziness of the past week was catching up to him.

Colt stretched his arms over his head. "Morning."

"Why are you sleeping on the couch instead of the bed?"

Well, the kid didn't waste any time getting down to business.

"Just testing out the new furniture."

"Did you have a fight? Mom sleeps in the guest room when she's mad at Dad."

And that was not the information Colt wanted within the first ten seconds of his day. How often had Mark and Brittany fought? What did they consider a fight?

Colt sat up and stretched his neck from one side to the other. "No fights around here. I'm too scared of Remi. Have you seen her 'I dare you' face?"

Ben gave a single chuckle. "Yeah. She's scary."

"Who's scary?" Remi asked as she stepped out of the bedroom. Colt's gray long-sleeve T-shirt hung to the middle of her thighs, covering part of her red pajama pants. Her fiery hair bunched on one side, and she smoothed it with her hands.

Man, it was good to see her face and crazy hair first thing in the morning. "No one. Good morning, princess. We were definitely not talking about you."

Remi narrowed her eyes at him. "I believe you about as far as I can throw you."

Colt leaned over and whispered to Ben, "That's not far."

Ben chuckled, and Remi rolled her eyes. "Ben, go get dressed, and I'll make you something for breakfast."

"Waffles?" Ben asked.

"Real waffles. Not the hockey pucks from the freezer. Clothes!" Remi pointed toward Ben's room.

He ran off to get ready, and Colt stared at Remi, marveling in the ease in which she'd transitioned into mom mode.

"You want waffles too?" she asked.

Colt picked up his blanket and started folding it. "I'll take a couple."

Remi grabbed the pillow and tucked it under her arm. "How did you sleep?"

"Like a log. I only have two sleep modes—comatose and 'what was that?'"

Remi laughed and shoved the pillow at him. "Wake Abby up, and find out if she'll eat a waffle, please."

"Yes, your majesty."

Colt stored the blanket and pillow in the coat closet. It looked like he'd be needing them every night for the foreseeable future. Then he tiptoed into the kids' room. "Abby?"

No answer from the lump on the bed.

He walked to her bedside and pulled the covers from around her neck. "Rise and shine, beautiful."

Abby stirred, inhaling a deep breath as she rolled onto her back. "Is it morning?"

"Yep. Brother is getting ready for school, and Remi is making waffles."

"Oh, okay." Abby stretched out her arms and legs. "Remi said I could go to work with her today."

"You bet, but she has to take Ben to school first. You'll be with me at the stables this morning."

Abby sat up quickly. "I get to see the horses!"

"Horses first thing this morning," Colt confirmed.

Abby threw off the covers and darted out of the room with her tousled hair streaming behind her.

Colt chuckled and followed her. The kids were liking their new home, so far, and Colt was too. If only he knew if Remi was just as content. After the talk about the single bed situation, he'd let a little bit of doubt settle in. Had she really thought he'd force her to sleep in the bed with him, much less do anything physical? If that side of their marriage ever developed, it would be on her terms.

Colt made his way to the kitchen where Ben sat at the table with his head propped in his hands. Remi moved around, grabbing ingredients and things she'd need to whip up breakfast.

"Can I go to school too?" Abby asked as she climbed into a chair at the table.

"Not yet," Remi said without turning around.

"Can you at least teach me my ABCs?"

Remi turned, holding the fork she used to pull waffles from the maker in the air. "You don't know your ABCs?"

"Mommy always said I would learn that when I went to school."

Colt's eyes widened. Remi was not going to like this. Her lips thinned for a second before she turned back to the waffle. "Sounds like we have work to do."

"Yay!" Abby shouted.

"What's your teacher's name?" Remi asked Ben.

Ben raised his head. "Mrs. Carmichael. Can we not talk anymore? I'm sleepy."

Remi opened a few cabinets before finding the platter she was searching for. "Fine, but we're singing with Patsy and Dolly on the way to school."

"Who's Patsy and Dolly? Are those your dolls?" Abby asked. "I have some dolls." She gasped. "Did you bring them?"

"We have every doll," Remi confirmed. "We'll unpack the rest of your stuff this evening and put them in your room where you want them."

"I can't believe I have to share a room with her," Ben grumbled.

Remi stirred more of the mix and pulled the spoon out, testing the consistency. "Maybe one day we'll get a bigger place."

Well, that comment had Colt's back straightening. He looked at Remi, but she turned to pour the mix into the waffle maker. That had to be a good sign, right? Or maybe she was saying she didn't like the cabin. Though, it didn't sound like Remi to be unhappy here. Sure, she'd liked Ridge's place, but she'd lived with Jess in a small two-bedroom house outside of town. It wasn't much to write home about, but she'd never complained to him.

Colt filled two cups with coffee and handed one to Remi. He'd picked out her Dolly Parton tumbler.

Remi took it from him and showed it to Abby.

"This is Dolly. She's a singer. Don't worry. I'll introduce you to the legends."

"Dad liked to sing," Ben whispered.

The use of the past tense was new. The kids had been talking about their parents as if they still did the things they were used to. It was also the first time the kids had mentioned their parents so early in the day.

Grief was closing in on Colt too, and if the kids were feeling half of what he was, they were in for a long and bumpy ride.

Colt squeezed Ben's shoulder. "I know all your dad's favorites. How about I break out the guitar tonight, and we can have a jam session."

Ben sat up straighter. "Really?"

"Really." Colt opened the freezer, pulled out his Atlanta Braves ball cap, and stuck it on his head.

By the time he sat down at the table, Remi, Ben, and Abby were all staring at him.

"What?"

"Did you just get your hat from the freezer?" Abby asked.

The cold against his scalp was already doing its job. "Yep. It helps me wake up."

Remi stared at him with a mixing spoon suspended in the air. "I knew you were weird, but..."

"I'm not weird! I said it helps me wake up."

Remi shook her head. "I'll never understand you."

"I'll never understand you either," Abby said.

Colt winked at little Abby. "You don't have to."

Remi plopped a waffle onto Ben's plate and handed him a bottle of syrup. "You're gonna put your best foot forward today, right?"

"I said I'll think about it," Ben grumbled.

"Well, think hard while you eat. I know it's tough going into a new school in the middle of the year, but I know the other kids will love you."

Ben slathered his waffle with syrup. "Love is a strong word."

Boy, didn't Colt know that. He had a lot more love than most men, and he wasn't quiet about it. Maybe that's what scared Remi so much. She kept her emotions close, and subtle seemed to be the way to go with her. He could find other ways to show her he cared.

"Abby, your waffle is up next. Why don't you get your hair brushed while you wait?" Remi said.

Colt stood. "I'll help with that." He'd been taking lessons from Remi and Abby about how to brush Abby's hair, and he was eager to show off this new skill.

The hair brushing went over well. No tears. The rest of the morning was a shuffle of one kid or the other until they were both ready for the day.

Remi grabbed both of the kids' coats off the rack by the door. "Coats on and cabooses in the trucks."

"What's a caboose?" Abby asked as she slipped her arms into her coat.

"A behind. A booty," Remi said.

Abby laughed. "We don't call it that!"

"I don't care what you call it, but for Pete's sake get a move on it."

"What's a sake?" Abby asked.

Colt looked to Remi, and his blank expression probably matched hers. "Um..."

"We'll have to look that up after I drop Ben off," Remi said, ushering the kids toward the door.

"Bye," Ben said with a wave.

Colt caught him and ruffled his hair. "Bye, bud."

"Bye, Colt!" Abby shouted.

Colt took her by the shoulders and steered her to the side. "You're with me, sweet cheeks."

"Oh," Abby said with a chuckle.

Remi stopped in front of Colt in her rush toward the door. What was the proper good-bye between a husband and wife?

"Have a good day." Colt leaned over and pressed his lips to her cheek. "For the kids," he whispered.

Lies. The kiss was for him. It was innocent enough that Remi might not get spooked, but forward enough that Remi would know he wanted to kiss her.

Remi nodded quickly. "Right." She pushed up onto her toes and laid a kiss on his cheek. The warmth of her lips on his skin was a bigger wakeup call than the frozen hat.

Remi followed Ben out the door, kissing Abby on the way out.

Colt shouted after her. "Have a good day, princess! Make good choices, Ben!"

Remi and Ben gave him matching eye rolls. It was a job well done.

Abby giggled beside him and bounced on the balls of her feet. "Can we go to the horses now?"

Colt knelt in front of her. "Hop on."

Abby climbed onto his back and shouted, "Giddy up!"

C olt led the trail ride group back to the dining hall and doubled back to the stables. He'd missed a week of work, which meant his regular workload had fallen on the shoulders of his friends during that time. Now, it was his turn to double up so they could have a break.

The crunch of dead leaves made it impossible to sneak up on anyone, and Brett was waiting, propped on a barrel, when Colt walked in.

"Morning, hubby," Brett sang.

"It's afternoon."

"What's it like waking up next to your wife?" Brett asked, sounding oddly serious.

"Surreal." Colt grabbed a packing list from the news wall by the barn office and headed toward the packing shed. He wasn't about to tell Brett that there hadn't been any waking up next to Remi yet.

Brett's quick footsteps sounded behind Colt.

"I need to know exactly why Remi decided to marry you," Brett said.

"I have no idea. If you figure it out, let me know." He furrowed his brow and turned to his friend. "Have you heard anything about her past?"

Colt had never pried for info on Remi before, but curiosity was killing this cat.

"No, why?"

"I'm wondering if she was in the foster system. Maybe that's why she wanted to give the kids a good family."

"Sounds plausible, but I can't say for sure."

"And she never talks about her parents. They must not be close, but why?"

"You're telling me she never talks to you about this? I thought you two knew each other inside and out."

Colt pushed into the pack room to find Paul already packing the loads. His wolf-dog, Thane, raised his head from the wooden floor where he'd been resting. The older wrangler acknowledged them with a lift of his chin before getting back to work.

Colt studied the list before handing it to Brett.

"I'm telling you she doesn't want to talk about it, so we don't." Not knowing Remi's whole story left him antsy, but there wasn't anything he could do about it.

Brett shrugged. "I guess that's your answer."

"Yeah." That was the response he'd expected–the one he'd been accepting for years. But he told Remi everything, and it bothered him a little bit that she kept that part of her life from him. Why? Knowing would only help him understand.

"I'm just saying, Remi gets hit on by men all the time, and she never takes the guys up on a date. Why'd she all of a sudden decide to elope with you and ride off into the sunset?"

Colt frowned and stared at his friend. "Do you have a filter?"

"No. Take it or leave it."

"Thanks for reminding me that I'm one little fish in a big ocean." How could he ever think he had a chance to be the one man who reached Remi? The Lord knew he wanted to be, but she'd always been unattainable. It had been a little easier to accept when they were not talking about that one time he'd made a fool of himself. Now, they were not talking about the vows they'd made to stick together, till death do they part.

"So, you figured out how to be a married man over your honeymoon vacation?"

Colt grabbed a bag and started packing. "Not in

the slightest. I love the kids, but I wish I already knew how to be a good parent for them. Like, they have expectations, and I'm afraid I won't measure up. I feel like I got dumped into a race in the middle."

"I felt that way when I found out about Ava," Paul said.

Colt and Brett exchanged a glance. Paul was pretty tight-lipped, and any input from him was typically something to perk up and listen to. He'd only found out a couple of years ago that Ava, the granddaughter of the owner of Wolf Creek Ranch, was his daughter.

Paul snapped a pack and set it to the side. "When I found out Ava was mine, I was happy, but I'd missed so much that it was tough not to think about what I'd lost. Over twenty years of her life. Once I got to know how great she was, I realized how important every second is when you have someone to love in your life."

"Right. I know I was there for Ben and Abby when they were babies, but I had no idea what all I'd missed until now."

Paul nodded. "I wish I could say it gets better, but try to focus on getting to be a part of their lives now."

"You're right. I should look on the bright side."

Brett shoved Colt's shoulder. "Yeah, how ungrateful of you."

"Trust me. I'm plenty grateful. I'm married to my dream woman, and I just got two kids that I already love."

"Stop bragging and get to work," Brett scoffed. "Nobody wants to hear about how all of your dreams came true."

Colt continued to pack, torn between having his prayers answered and not knowing what to do with the gift now that he had it.

After a stretch of silence too long for Brett to handle, he finally huffed. "Dude, why are you so glum? I thought you wanted this."

Colt chuckled. "I do. I was just thinking about how much I miss Remi and the kids."

Brett threw his pack down in dramatic fashion and turned toward the door. "I can't work like this. Paul, he's all yours."

When Colt and Paul were the only ones left in the pack shed, Paul sighed. "I wish he'd find a woman so I wouldn't have to listen to him chatter on anymore."

"Best get to prayin'. He'll need all he can get."

CHAPTER 17
REMI

Remi pulled up in front of Ben's school and parked her beat-up Bronco. Only a few cars remained in the parking lot of the small school after hours, and she stopped to say a quick prayer before walking in.

"Lord, help me to know what's right. I don't know what Ben needs, but I need to figure it out."

She looked up at the sign on the front door.

Buzz, and we'll let you in.

It reminded her of a verse. Knock and the door will be opened to you. She was definitely knocking, but He hadn't answered the door yet.

She pressed the button, and a sharp buzz sounded. A second later, the lock on the door gave way.

Inside, the administrator's office was on the left, and a woman with graying curly hair waved her in.

"Hey! It's good to see you again."

"You too, Mrs. Petty." Everyone at the school had welcomed them with open arms during their meetings and phone calls before Ben started earlier this week. Mrs. Petty was excellent at her job, and the kids seemed to love her too.

"Mrs. Hanes told me to expect you. Her office is down that way on the left. There's a sign out front."

"Thanks. Is Ben already there?"

"He should be in the library. It's right before you get to Mrs. Carmichael's room. You'll see it."

"Thanks again." Remi picked at her fingernails as she walked down the silent hallways. It looked like so many of the schools she'd attended when she was young, but this place had more happiness, even without the kids laughing in the hallways.

She'd been in dozens of meetings like this one, but familiarity didn't make it any easier. Her neck tightened, and her skin prickled as she fought the urge to turn around and run away from the meeting with the school counselor.

Stopping at the door marked as the library, Remi peeked inside. Half a dozen kids were scattered over the small round tables, and Ben sat at the one nearest the door.

"Hey, bud."

Ben looked up from the homework sheet, and he gave her a small smile. A second later, recognition dawned, and the smile faded.

"You ready for the meeting?" she asked.

Ben gathered his books and papers into his backpack. "Yeah. Let's go."

Remi signed Ben out on an old-fashioned clipboard at the librarian's desk and opened her hand to him. He looked at the hand for a few seconds before she pulled it back. She'd been holding the kids' hands every chance possible over the last week, but the circumstances were different when Ben was at school around his friends. He was old enough not to need an assuring handhold, but she'd offered it anyway.

Out in the hallway, they turned toward the counselor's office. "How was your day?"

Ben stared at the floor as he walked. "Do I have to go?"

Remi stopped and squatted beside him. The sadness in his tired eyes and the slump of his shoulders was enough to choke her up. She wrapped her hand around his upper arm and rubbed her thumb over his thin shirt. "I know this is scary, but I've met Mrs. Hanes, and she really wants to help you. I want to help you too, but I'm afraid I won't know how."

Ben looked up at her, and his chin quivered. "I don't know her."

She could have pointed out that he hadn't known her ten days ago, but that wasn't the answer he was looking for right now. "I don't know her either. You don't have to do anything you don't want to do, but I would like it if you just went in this time. We don't have to do this ever again, and if you want, we can let her do all the talking."

Ben stared at his feet but nodded.

Remi opened her arms, and Ben wrapped his arms around her neck. She squeezed, wishing she could absorb his sadness and lift it from his shoulders. Burrowing her face in his neck, she sank into the hug. Apparently, she'd needed the comfort too because every worry and sadness fell away in those quiet seconds with Ben.

"I was sad a lot when I was a kid," Remi whispered.

Ben pulled away and wiped at his face. "Really?"

"Yeah. I didn't have anybody to talk to, so I didn't talk."

"At all?"

"At all. I don't think I talked more than one-word answers until I was about twelve."

"What made you start talking then?" Ben asked.

Now she'd backed herself into a corner. The truth wouldn't help him. She'd finally started talking because she'd needed to defend herself. Bullies, her mom, even the people she'd thought were her friends had tried to break her down. In short, she'd started talking when she'd had enough and needed to stand her ground.

"I finally found someone I could trust." That was the truth. The guidance counselor appointed to her by child services had been patient and understanding, as well as helpful. Mrs. Monk had been the person she needed when the anger and insecurity was at an all-time high. Without that woman, Remi figured she wouldn't have made it out of her teen years.

"Can I trust you?" Ben asked quietly.

Remi's breath hitched, and she squeezed Ben's arm just enough to accentuate her answer. "Yes. I'll always be here for you, and I'll give you the truth. Colt too. He's a good man, and I trust him more than anyone in this world."

"Yeah. I'm glad we get to live with you and Uncle Colt."

"Me too, buddy. We're so glad you and Abby are here." She looked up at the door and back at Ben. "You want to go in?"

"I'll give her a chance, but I really just want you and Uncle Colt."

"I bet Uncle Colt could tell you stories about your dad if you wanted."

Ben's eyes widened. "That would be cool."

"Right. And we can talk about your mom and dad as much or as little as you want. If we talk about them, you'll never forget them."

"I like that. I don't want to forget them."

Remi hugged Ben again. "You promise you'll tell us what you need? We're here for you."

"Promise."

Remi tossed a handful of clothes into the washing machine. The new cabins on the ranch had a washer, a dryer, and a dishwasher, which were the biggest selling points in her opinion. She didn't need a TV. She needed to be able to wash clothes without hauling them to a laundromat twice a week. Between Colt and Ben, the laundry basket stayed full.

Colt stepped into the laundry room doorway and slumped against the wall. "That was the longest, most plot twisting bedtime story I've ever told in my life."

"Did the bears and kittens stop the alien invaders?"

"Of course. They hurled meatballs at the spaceship until the windshield busted. Then they gunked up the control panel with lasagna. The aliens surrendered, and the bears and kittens introduced them to lasagna."

Remi looked up at Colt. "I'm sorry. What?"

"And they lived happily ever after."

"Fine, but be prepared for Abby's nightmares tonight."

"Nah. The aliens only wanted to steal our belts and beef jerky. Abby said we should have just let them have what they wanted so they would go away."

"I'm tempted to agree with her." Remi stood and closed the washing machine. "Did Ben say anything about the song?"

Colt crossed his arms over his chest. "He said Mark sang that one a few times, but Ben had forgotten all the words."

"Did he seem happy to talk about his dad?"

"A little. How did things go with the counselor today?"

Remi started the machine and waved Colt out of the small room. She sat on the end of the couch and tucked her feet under her. "He didn't want to do it. I told him he didn't have to, but he agreed to sit through the first meeting. I doubt he'll want to go back."

Colt plopped down in the middle of the couch beside her and rested his arm on the back. "Was it that bad?"

"No, but even if he does want to talk about it, talking to a stranger is tough. It takes getting used to, and you have to want to be there."

Colt brushed a thumb over her shoulder. "Is that how it was for you?"

She'd been expecting him to ask, but there never seemed to be a good time to talk about everything that had led to her therapy. It worked for some and not others. For her, it hadn't really worked until she was mature enough to respect the people who were trying to help her.

"Yeah. I didn't start until I was eleven, and it was pointless. I went to the meetings, but I was completely shut off."

"Do you still go now?" Colt asked.

"I actually stopped going about a year ago. Mostly because I didn't have anything else I felt like I needed to work through. I've been screwed up for a long time, but I'm starting to figure out how to live with myself."

Colt's thumb brushed over her shoulder and into the crook of her neck, and his gaze followed the path. "You're pretty easy to live with," he whispered.

"You've been living with me for five days. I don't think you're qualified to make that assumption yet."

"I've been living with you in my life for years. Moving in with you hasn't been much of a change. I already knew we would be good at this."

"Oh, really? I'm glad you have it all figured out."

"You don't?"

The drop in Colt's last word was heavy with hurt.

"I didn't mean it like that. I'm just trying to find out what all of this means for us."

"Me, you, and the kids?"

Remi picked at her fingernails. The uncertainty had been eating at her lately. "That, yes. But just me and you too."

Colt sat up and turned his body to face her

completely. "It means what you want it to mean. I told you I wouldn't ask for more than you were willing to give."

"I don't think you're going to force yourself on me. You're not like that."

"Then what are you worried about? I'm happy to share my life with you. My home, my family, my money, my successes, all of it."

Remi looked down at her ring. Colt was willing to give her so much, but what was she willing to give him?

"I told Ben something today that I haven't told to anyone else here."

Colt didn't say anything at first. Would he be hurt by her trust in someone else?

"Do you want to tell me? You still don't have to. I'm glad you're opening up to Ben. He needs someone who might understand what he's going through."

Remi twisted her ring around her finger. "There's a lot you don't know because I try not to talk about it unless I have to. Mostly, I've moved on and accepted the past for what it is—the past. When I decided to leave my therapist indefinitely, one of the things she encouraged me to do was to think of others. I had to focus on myself first, but once I could cope better on my own, she promised I'd be able to open up more of myself to the people I trusted. I wasn't sure it would ever happen, but it *did* happen. In that office with Janet. I knew it was time to devote more of myself to someone else, and it was you. You and the kids."

Colt twirled a string of her hair around his finger. "You don't know how much that means to me."

And there it was. It had taken years to understand what it meant to put someone else first, and now she knew why God called us to love our neighbors. Sure, her therapist wanted Remi to love herself first, but Colt showed her that. The way he dropped everything when she needed a hand. The way he checked on her when she was having a tough time. The way he put her and the kids first.

He taught her how to love herself.

She'd been amazed when she learned that the Lord loved her despite her sins, but that awe had dwindled over the years and she'd forgotten about the power of love.

Remi leaned her head against the back of the couch. "I'm tired."

Colt reached for her hand and stood, pulling her to her feet. "Go to bed."

"I have to wait for the dryer to finish. The pants Ben wants to wear tomorrow are in that load."

"I'll take care of it. Get some rest."

Remi swallowed. Was this what marriage was like? Or was this what marriage to Colt was like? She'd been on her own her whole life, but despite the added responsibility, her life was getting easier in some ways.

Colt smiled down at her, and the glimmer of mischief in his eyes had Remi's pulse racing.

"You're kidding." A staring contest. It had been almost a week since they'd faced off. They'd been distracted by the changes going on in their life and had forgotten the games that used to take up their time.

The seconds passed, but Colt didn't break. Was he getting better at this, or was she getting worse? The warmth of his hand in hers anchored her attention to the spot where they connected.

Colt took a small step toward her, and heat spread up her neck. Staring into his eyes, she was comforted by his nearness, but panic boiled in the back of her mind. Would he kiss her?

The second the thought sprang to her mind, Colt stepped back, breaking the stare and ending the contest. "Sleep tight, princess."

What was happening? She'd wanted him to break the stare, hadn't she? She'd drawn the lines, and he had respected them.

Did she want him to cross those lines?

Colt wouldn't do that. He would patiently wait for her signal, and she loved him for that.

Love. The mere thought had her head spinning. She wasn't sure what it meant. The whole idea was obscure and unattainable. A trophy on a pedestal.

If things were going to change between them, she would have to make the move. Was that what she wanted? A part of her wanted Colt to bulldoze over her insecurities and promise to love her no matter how messed up and broken she was. Another part of her pushed those thoughts back into a cage. They were dangerous and shouldn't be trusted.

"Good night," she whispered as she turned and headed toward the bedroom–the one where she would sleep alone.

CHAPTER 18

COLT

Colt stepped up onto the front porch and toed off his boots. A loud thump sounded from inside the cabin, and he stopped to listen for a few seconds. Laughter. Apparently, everything was fine. He pulled off his hat and walked in.

Abby darted across the living room, screaming at the top of her lungs and wearing nothing but a pair of pink sparkly panties and a hooded towel on her head. Remi chased her with her arms out, reaching for the running kid. Ben climbed onto the back of the couch and jumped off, blazing a hot trail toward the kitchen. He was also only half-clothed, wearing a long-sleeve pajama shirt and Spiderman briefs.

Colt paused in the doorway. After the day he'd had chasing a runaway horse on the Little Canyon

Trail, wrangling kids sounded like the straw that would break the camel's back. After a moment of contemplation, he turned and headed back out the door.

"Don't you dare! Don't you dare leave me!" Remi shouted.

Colt bit his lips to hide the grin. Oh, how he'd wanted to hear those words from her. He just never expected it to be like this.

"Um, I forgot my hat."

"Colt Walker, get back in here!"

Lifting the hat, he hung it on the hook by the door. "Found it."

Remi pointed to Ben as the kid twirled his pajama pants over his head. "Grab that one."

Colt locked his target on Ben who darted toward his bedroom. A few quick steps had Ben in his grasp. Colt tossed his nephew over his shoulder. Screams pierced his ears, no doubt catching the attention of every nocturnal animal within half a mile of the cabin.

Remi grabbed Abby and shoved a nightgown over her head. "You can't run around naked all the time."

"Why not?" Abby asked, laughing.

"Because nakedness is frowned upon in society."

"What's society?"

Remi looked to Colt who hefted Ben higher onto

his shoulder. "Sorry, I have a kid to toss into bed." Why did kids have to ask questions that he didn't have an answer for? That was probably the murkiest part of parenting he'd come across so far.

Colt flipped Ben onto his bed and tickled his neck. "It's bedtime, Ben. Stop playing around."

Ben laughed and squirmed. "I'm not doing it. You are!"

"Tickle me!" Abby shouted as she dove onto the bed, spreading her arms for tickles.

Colt tickled both of them, moving back and forth whenever one seemed close to escaping.

Remi turned on the night-light and let the games continue for a few minutes. Finally, she clapped her hands. "Okay, folks. Bedtime."

Abby whined. "Not yet."

"I'm not tired," Ben said.

Colt tossed the blanket over the kids' heads. "Hold on. I have an idea." He stalked out of the room and searched until he found two small flashlights in the bathroom closet. Not where he'd have picked to store them, but beggars couldn't be choosers when his friends stocked the cabin.

He held up a flashlight for each of the kids. "When your dad and I were kids, we'd stay up flashing signals to each other on the ceiling."

Remi threw her head back and groaned. "Way to teach the kids how to stay up past their bedtime."

Colt leaned over and whispered to her, "Just go

with it. Trust me, it gets boring quickly, and they'll fall asleep." He handed them the flashlights. "Use them wisely."

Ben clicked it on and off. "What's the code?"

"I'm not sharing the secret code. You'll have to make your own."

Abby flopped down onto her back on the bed and pointed the light at the ceiling. "I'm going to draw pictures."

"Can we have a song?" Ben asked.

Colt grabbed his guitar from the corner and sat on the end of Ben's bed. "Whose turn is it?"

"Mine!" Abby shouted. "The one about the snow and the snow and the snow."

Colt looked at Remi, silently asking for help. She had her hand over her mouth, and the tilt in her eyes said she was fighting back a laughing attack.

"Um, I don't know that one," Colt said.

Abby flung her hand in the air. "You know. No place to go. Snow, snow, snow."

"'Let it Snow.' I gotcha." Colt played that one every Christmas in the church choir performance. "Only if Remi will sing the words."

Abby and Ben placed their hands together in front of their faces. "Please," they drawled in unison.

Remi settled onto the end of Abby's bed and gestured for Colt to play. He played the chords, but she gave it a voice—a beautiful voice that captivated him, as well as the kids.

When the song ended, Abby yawned and said, "Again."

"Tomorrow," Remi promised as she pulled the covers over Abby. "Whose turn is it to lead the prayer?"

"Mine," Colt said before bowing his head. "Father, we thank You for the day of happiness You gave us. We thank You for this home and everyone in it. I pray that You would continue to guide us and give us wisdom. And please help me answer Abby's questions. They're so tough, and I know nothing."

That got him a few laughs from the kids, but it was the truth. Abby kept him on his toes with her quest to understand everything, and he hardly ever knew how to answer her questions. "In Jesus's name we pray. Amen."

"Okay, kids. Flash your lights for a few minutes, then go to bed," Remi said.

Abby grabbed her light. "Okay." She popped back up. "Wait. What does insinuate mean?"

Remi threw her hands in the air. "Looks like we need a dictionary."

Colt snapped his fingers. "Christmas present!"

Remi propped her hands on her hips. "What kid wants a dictionary for Christmas?"

"No, I meant me. You're getting me a present, right?"

"It's September! Why are you thinking about Christmas presents?"

Abby snickered and flicked her light on and off.

"Well, I already got yours," Colt said.

Remi gaped. "You did not."

"I did too."

"Did you get me one?" Abby asked.

"Don't worry. You'll have more than one." Colt kissed her forehead and turned to kiss Ben, who rolled over and threw the covers over his head.

"Good night, kids."

"Night!" they shouted together.

Colt followed Remi out of the room and closed the door. "What does insinuate mean? And where did she hear that?"

Remi rounded on him and put her hands on both sides of her head. "I have no idea where she heard it, but I also don't know what insinuate means."

Colt tried to hold back his grin, but Remi was already swatting at his arm.

"I'm serious. I'm so dumb when it comes to vocabulary."

Colt took her by the shoulders and turned her toward the living room. "You're not dumb. You're just not as smart as others."

She pretended to whine as she sank onto the couch. "They'll know more than me in a few years, and they'll stay up late at night laughing about the stupid things I say."

Colt took his spot on the couch next to her. "Probably, but don't let it bother you. At least you're pretty."

Remi laughed, and it was followed by a snort. "That's not funny."

"Sounds like it's funny. You snorted like a pig."

Remi wiped her eyes and sagged into the couch. "This thing is pretty comfortable. I want to fall asleep every time I sit down."

"It's not so bad. I've slept in worse places."

When Remi's eyes closed, Colt took in the peace in her stature. Slumped against the couch, she looked comfortable.

"I miss making music with you," he said. They used to perform on weeknights in the dance hall, but they hadn't started the gig back up since bringing the kids to the ranch. The evenings were spent at home, and there wasn't anywhere he'd rather be.

"Me too," Remi whispered, but she didn't open her eyes.

He pulled his phone out of his pocket. "I have a surprise for you."

That woke her up. "What is it?"

He turned the phone to show her. "Ava downloaded a streaming app on my phone. We can watch sports."

Remi gasped and sat up, clutching the phone in both hands. "Are you serious? I don't know any of the standings anymore. We missed a whole week."

"We can catch up," he said, clicking on the button Ava had shown him.

"You're my favorite," Remi said as she settled up against his side.

Colt ignored the urge to read too much into that statement. He wanted to be her favorite. She'd been his since the day he met her. "Where do we start?"

"The SEC?"

"Alabama played Texas A&M last weekend."

"Perfect."

He started the game and propped the phone on his knees. He rested his arm on the back of the couch, and Remi snuggled closer.

The game was a blowout, but not much could have held his attention when Remi was this close. She gave her heated two cents through the first two quarters, but her comments waned in the third hour. Soon, her soft snores were rhythmic against his shoulder.

He paused the game and tossed the phone onto the couch. Wiggling his arms under her, he lifted Remi and cradled her against his chest. She didn't weigh much more than the kids, and he laid her gently on top of the made bed. He ducked back into the main room and grabbed the blanket he'd been using on the couch every night out of the closet.

Remi's breaths were deep and even as he draped the blanket over her. She slept so soundly to be such a wildfire whenever she was awake.

"Good night, princess." Colt bent to kiss her hair and brushed a hand over the softness. With a whispered, "I love you," he left the room, closing the door behind him.

CHAPTER 19

REMI

R emi focused on the quilt square in her hands. It had been over a month since she'd been to one of the Tuesday night quilting get-togethers at Stella and Vera's place, and apparently, quilting wasn't like riding a bike. It was more like being thrown back into high school five years after graduating.

Stella leaned over and whispered, "How's she doing?"

Vera had disappeared with Abby into the kitchen with the promise of hot chocolate, but the little girl had been guarded all evening. She was usually so friendly. Maybe it was the lack of sleep. Abby's nightmares had doubled up this week, and Remi was starting to feel the exhaustion too.

"She's okay. It's been a hard week. Probably the hardest yet."

"Bring her to me tomorrow. She can help out in the gift shop, and she'll be a friendly face for all the kids at check-in."

Stella manned the gift shop at the ranch, and the job was perfect for her. She loved talking to strangers and helping them get the most out of their vacations. It was no wonder she'd become fast friends with Abby.

"I'll do that. Most of the kids in my group this week are older, and I can tell she's getting left out."

"Remi!"

Abby speed-walked into the living room carrying a lidded mason jar with a straw sticking out of the top with both hands. "Miss Vera gave me *white* hot chocolate. See?"

Remi studied the white liquid in the clear glass. "Is it just warm milk?"

"No! It tastes like white chocolate. It's super sweet."

Glancing at Vera, Remi ignored the warning in the back of her mind. Super sweet within an hour of bedtime sounded like a sign. There wouldn't be any sleep tonight. "I bet it's yummy."

Abby lowered her bottom onto the edge of the couch cushion and gently wiggled herself back onto the seat.

"What's your favorite thing to do here?" Ava asked.

Abby swallowed a big gulp of her drink. "I like

playing. I get to run, and play hide-and-seek, and feed the horses, and roast marshmallows, and swing, and–"

"Wow," Jess said. "So, you get to do everything fun?"

"Yep." Abby went back to drinking herself into a sugar coma.

"How are things with you and Colt?" Stella asked with a wink.

Remi looked down at the stitch, but there was no way she could focus. "Good. Things are good."

"Good? That's it?" Jess asked.

Remi nodded. "Yep. Just good."

And things were good. Probably closer to great, but saying it would invite questions that she couldn't answer. Living with Colt was easy. Probably easier than living with Jess.

But it was also thrilling and exciting. She looked forward to the evenings when they spent time with the kids and tucked them into bed, but the best part of the days was the time she got to spend with Colt alone at night. They watched sports, did chores together, and talked about the kids. It sounded so mundane, but time spent with Colt was never boring. Every look, every selfless act, every small touch bumped her excitement into overdrive like a jolt to the heart.

Things were changing, and she liked it, but there was no way on God's green earth she was admitting that to these women. Her friends were the best, but nothing stayed secret between them. If one knew it, they all knew it, which wasn't so bad, until the married ones told their husbands, and the husbands told Colt.

"I like Uncle Colt," Abby said. "He sings for me every night, and he flips me in the air whenever I want."

Jess choked on the mouthful of water she'd just chugged. "He flips you?"

Remi covered her face with a hand. The flips had been giving her minor heart attacks for weeks, but Colt assured her it was safe.

"Yeah," Abby scooted off the couch, handing her cup to Remi. "I put my hands between my legs like this, and Colt does that too. Then, he pulls my hands, and I flip, flip, flip through his legs!"

Remi held up a finger. "There's only one flip. Let's be clear about that."

"Sounds fun. I want to flip," Jess said.

"Uncle Colt could flip you. He does it to Ben too."

Jess propped an elbow on her knee and rested her chin in her hand. "That's interesting. I'd like to see him try to flip me."

The rumble of a diesel engine sounded over the chuckles, and quick footfalls bounded on the porch. When the door opened, half of the women in the room stood.

Paul burst into the living area and scanned the room. His attention landed on Vera. "I need some towels and your first aid kit."

Vera was on her feet in an instant, rushing to a room in the back of the cabin.

Remi stood. "Who is it?" The shake in her voice couldn't be hidden. Injuries were bound to happen on the ranch, but the knowing did nothing to temper the fear.

"Lincoln."

Remi released a heavy breath. She cared that Linc was injured, but knowing it wasn't Colt or Ben almost brought relieved tears to her eyes.

One look at Jess erased all of the relief. Jess's hard heart had a soft spot for Linc, and all the blood had drained out of her friend's face as she stood and followed Vera.

Stella opened a closet in the corner and reached inside. "Take these blankets."

Vera and Jess hurried back into the room carrying towels and a big kit.

With a determined expression and a tense jaw, Jess walked right past Paul toward the door. "Let's go."

The older cowboy followed, closing the door behind him.

In their absence, the silence lingered. Remi clutched the quilt square in her hand and focused on breathing in and out.

Abby pressed herself against Remi's side and whimpered. Remi scooped the little girl into her arms.

"Sweetie, it's okay. He'll be all right." Was it okay to say things you hoped were true without knowing for sure? It was what she was telling herself, so maybe that honesty counted for something.

"It scared me. I thought it was Ben or Uncle Colt," Abby said through sobs.

Remi hugged her tight. "I thought so too, but they're fine. I don't think they were supposed to be in the same place as Linc tonight."

Abby continued to cry, and Remi looked over the girl's shoulder to her friends. Vera rubbed a hand over Abby's back, and Ava whispered soothing words.

"Let's call Uncle Colt. Maybe hearing his voice will make you feel better."

Abby nodded and wiped her eyes.

Remi sat down with Abby in her lap and called Colt, putting the call on speakerphone and praying he would answer.

"Hello, princess."

Abby perked up. "Are you okay?" she said in a shaky voice.

"I'm great. Fantastic. Wonderful."

"What about Ben?"

"Ben, are you okay?" Colt asked.

Ben's voice was far off, but they could hear his answer. "Yep."

"Okay," Abby said as she wiped her eyes on the backs of her sleeves. "Are you at home?"

"I'm at Jameson's office."

"Can we go home? And you too?" Abby asked.

"Sure, we'll head that way."

When the call ended, Abby stood from Remi's lap. "I'm glad they're okay."

"Me too, sweetie."

They hadn't talked about how the kids had been given the news about their parents, but something in the tense news tonight had triggered something in little Abby.

When Abby had her coat on, she hugged the ladies and gave a round of night-night kisses. Remi carried her out into the dark night and strapped her into her car seat. They were unlikely to encounter any danger on the drive across the ranch, but better safe than sorry was Remi's motto these days.

The back seat was quiet as Remi parked in front of the cabin. A peek in the rear-view mirror revealed a sleeping Abby. It seemed the shock of the evening had been an emotional overload.

She fired off a text to Jess asking about Linc's condition and walked around the truck to get Abby. The little girl wasn't heavy, but getting her out of her car seat was like hefting around a potato sack. With Abby finally resting with her weight against her chest and shoulder, she trudged inside. They'd beaten the guys home, and she prayed they wouldn't storm in like a traveling circus.

With Abby tucked into bed, Remi snuck out of the room and back onto the front porch. The guys arrived a minute later, and she shushed them as they raced toward the front door.

"Shh. Abby is asleep."

"I just talked to her on the phone," Colt said.

Remi shrugged. "When she's done, she's done."

Colt ruffled Ben's hair. "Get ready for bed and sneak in quietly."

"I wanted a song tonight," Ben whined.

"Tomorrow. Think about which one you want."

Ben huffed but got started brushing his teeth and changing into PJs. A few minutes later, he whispered good night on his way into the bedroom.

Remi arranged the kids' shoes by the front door. "How did Ben do?"

"He liked the horses, but he's still not talking much."

"Did you try talking about cars?"

Colt leaned against the back of the couch and crossed his arms over his chest. "I know way more about cars than I ever wanted to know."

Remi nodded. Colt's patience was much better than hers on the quiet rides to school in the mornings. Sometimes, the only words she could get out of him were about cars. "Was there dirt to be played in?"

"Yes, and you'll be glad to know we changed into his extra outfit before going to dinner."

Remi stepped closer to Colt, and his arms fell to the back of the couch. "So, you fed him?"

Colt's gaze didn't leave hers, and he wasn't blinking. Did the nearness affect him these days in the same way it affected her?

"Yes."

She stepped up beside him and propped her hip against the couch. "Did you let him figure things out on his own?"

Colt swallowed. "I think so. Is this a test?"

She playfully patted his cheek. "Yes, and you passed." She rested her head on his shoulder. "You're doing great. Just give him time."

Colt's strong arm wrapped around her shoulders, pulling her in. "I can be patient. I just want him to know he can come to me if he ever has something to talk about."

"He will."

She knew that Colt was the person she could go to with almost everything. It had taken her a while to figure it out, but her heart was softening.

But there were things she still hadn't told him—mistakes she still hated. Shame kept them locked up tight in the hopes they would disappear given enough time.

"Are you still okay with all of this? I haven't asked you this week."

That she could answer. She nodded and looked up at him. "I am. We make a good team." She nudged him with her shoulder. "I knew you were a catch."

Colt pulled her close and pressed a kiss to the top of her head. "Same, princess."

Warmth and comfort spread from her head to her toes, and the urge to flinch away from the contact was gone. When she gave in to the pull, her heart shifted. She'd been distancing herself from Colt's goodness, but the chains holding her back loosened. Colt was going to break down her guilt and shame, and she only hoped he was strong enough to survive the fallout.

CHAPTER 20
COLT

Colt looked over his shoulder where Ben sat atop Burgundy. "We need to turn."

Ben tugged on the right side of the reins. "I got this."

For a kid with endless energy, Ben somehow managed to wrangle some focus when it came time for riding lessons. They'd only squeezed in a handful of sessions so far, but Ben was determined to make the most of his time with the horses.

"One more round, then we need to get home."

"Not yet," Ben whined. "We just got started."

"We've been here for an hour and a half."

"But we had to do all the grooming stuff, and I didn't get to ride a lot."

"The most important part of riding is taking care of the horse."

He could argue that the most important part of

having kids was taking care of them, but he could also see the importance of nurturing adventure and creativity.

Ben didn't need any help in that department. He was just like Mark when it came to getting into trouble. Not in the sense of doing bad things, but he made his own fun. Fun followed him, not the other way around.

When Ben dismounted, they led Burgundy around the small walking yard next to the barn. "Why does he need to stand around after we ride?"

"He needs to cool down."

"Why does it take so long?"

Colt sat on a cement block and patted the one next to him. "He's a big animal. That's a lot of muscle. You'd probably need time to cool off if you were that heavy too."

Ben tilted his head, studying Burgundy. "I have lots of muscle too, but I don't need to cool down."

Colt rubbed a hand over his mouth to hide the grin. "You're just like your dad."

Ben sat beside him and turned to face Colt. "Really?"

"Really, really. Did I ever tell you about the time your dad tried to ride a horse?" The memory brought on a tingle of warmth, but also an ache. Grief was a funny thing.

"He did? I didn't know Dad could ride."

"No, no, no. Your dad definitely couldn't ride a horse. I said he *tried*."

Ben scooted closer. "What happened?"

"Our neighbors a little down the road had a couple of horses in a pasture by the road. Mark got it in his head that he could ride one. I bet he was about eight."

"I'm almost eight," Ben added.

Colt's mouth went dry. The thought of Mark being only a few months older than Ben was right now put the memory into a different perspective. "Yeah. Please don't get any ideas from this story. I'm not sure..."

Not sure how Mark lived as long as he did. But it wouldn't be a good idea to say that out loud.

"Anyway, your dad climbed up on the side of the fence by the road and coaxed a horse over with an apple. While the horse was munching and I was reciting a list of all the ways this could go terribly wrong, your dad hopped on the horse's back."

Ben stood and stepped up on the block he'd been sitting on. "He did?"

Uh-oh. Those wide eyes held pride, not fear.

"Yeah, and the horse promptly bolted, leaving your dad in the dust. He flipped right off the back and landed on his right wrist." Colt showed Ben the odd angle of Mark's arm.

"He never told me that!"

"He probably didn't want you repeating all of his mistakes. Ever think about that, bud?"

"I wouldn't do that." Ben tilted his head from side to side. "Well, not just like that. I would do it better."

Colt rested his head in his hands. "What have I done?"

"I can already ride better than that."

Colt raised his head. "True. Let's keep it that way."

Ben sat back down and watched Burgundy grazing. The crunch of leaves beneath her hooves and the chatter of the people gathering up the hill at the dining hall drifted on the autumn wind.

Ben wiped the palms of his hands over his jeans. "I'll be a good rider. I want to work here someday."

"What are you talking about? You already work here."

"Not really."

"You've got the hat." Colt tipped the brim of the brown hat they'd picked up at the feed and seed a few weeks ago. "And with those boots, everyone would think you work here."

"I mean, I could be a cowboy," Ben said. The wistful note in his words was the mark of a boy dreaming of being a man.

Colt chose this job because it suited him. He loved the rodeo circuit, but settling down here was what he wanted. Most cowboys moved on every few years, but leaving people and places behind wasn't in his nature.

"You're young. You might find something else you want to do for the rest of your life."

"Nope. I want to be a cowboy. I'm gonna be a cowboy."

"It's hard work." Colt propped his elbows on his knees and opened his hands, showing the scars, calluses, and dirt of a long day's work.

"I know." Ben had been helping out on the ranch for over a month, and not once had he complained.

Mark had always gravitated toward desk jobs. He'd wanted the comforts of an office and the assurances of a 401K. Too bad he'd also been unreliable and prone to boredom. Would Ben be the same? When the winter nights grew longer, would Ben get restless?

"But it's the best job," Colt said. "I can't imagine doing anything else."

"Does Remi like it?"

"She loves it." That was an easy answer. Remi wasn't a wrangler, but she spent enough time around the horses to train them to play the games with the kids. She had a heart for innocence–kids and horses.

They'd been silent for a few minutes, watching Burgundy and the purples and pinks of the sunset when Ben said, "Uncle Colt?"

"Yeah?"

"You think Remi loves us too?"

And just like that, Ben had taken an invisible pin and burst the bubble that protected his heart. Everything inside him wanted to scream that Remi loved them, but love was different for everyone. How did Remi see love?

Maybe it wasn't about how she perceived love. Maybe she'd been saying she loved them all along. She'd bound her life to them, left her home, and promised to care for them until her last day.

All those things said she loved them, right?

"I think she does," Colt finally said.

"Yeah, me too."

Colt slapped a hand on Ben's shoulder. "Let's go see what Remi and Abby are up to."

"We have to wash and brush Burgundy first," Ben said.

Yeah, Ben would make a good cowboy. "You get the brushes. I'll bring her in."

Colt let Ben lead the grooming, and he only needed to remind him of two things. Ben even said good night to Burgundy and the other horses, and they left with a promise from Jess to take Ben on a short trail ride on Sunday afternoon.

Ben yawned three times on the way back to the cabin. Colt followed suit each time, and the heaviness settled in his eyes.

"Don't give up just yet. Bath before bed is a must tonight."

Ben groaned. "Are you sure?"

"What's that on your arm?" Colt pointed to the brown stain on Ben's sleeve.

He tugged at his hoodie. "I think it's the ointment stuff we put on Burgundy's hoof."

"Yeah. Bath is definitely happening tonight." Colt parked beside Remi's truck and grabbed his hat off the dash. "Toss your backpack in your room and straight to the bathroom."

Ben didn't grumble as they tromped through the dark. He toed off his boots and hung his hat on the hook by the door.

Inside, the cabin was quiet–too quiet for Remi and Abby to be here. Their shoes were lined up by the door, and a half-eaten plate of scrambled eggs lay abandoned on the table in the kitchen.

Colt stepped up to the bathroom door and listened. No sound.

He knocked. "Remi?"

A splash and Abby's loud laugh came from inside. Found them.

Remi laughed too, and the sound sent a tingle from Colt's head to his toes.

He leaned closer to the door. "What's going on in there?"

"Come back with a warrant!" Remi shouted.

"Yeah! Come back later!" Abby shouted. In a quieter voice, she asked, "What's a warrant?"

Ben darted out of his bedroom and looked from the door to Colt. "What's up?"

"Abby's still in the bathtub."

"So, I don't have to take a bath?"

"You're not getting out of it. You smell like a foot."

Ben threw his head back. "Can I at least have a snack?"

Colt shooed him toward the kitchen. "Whatever keeps you awake until the mermaid gets out of the bathtub."

Remi's and Abby's laughs echoed in the closed room, and Colt looked at his dirty wedding band. A month ago, he'd been praying for this life, but even his dreams paled in comparison to this.

CHAPTER 21

REMI

A frigid chill raced down Remi's back as she zipped Abby's coat up to her neck. "Keep the hood on, please."

"Okay." Abby patted her ears through the hood. Little pink mittens covered her hands.

The first snow of the season had come softly–just enough to cover the leaves on the ground in a thin layer of white–but the bite in the wind promised more to come. Despite the harsh weather, the kids begged to see the creek. They'd brought an afternoon picnic to the clearing on the bank last week when the weather had still been tolerable, but today, they might not last more than a few minutes in the clearing without trees to break the sting of the wind.

"Race you," Ben called over his shoulder as he darted toward the water.

"Wait!" Abby wiggled out of Remi's grasp and shot off after her brother.

Colt cupped his hands around his mouth. "Both of you, slow it down."

Remi slipped on her gloves and tightened her coat around her neck. "I don't want them getting to the creek before us either."

"Yeah, Ben will be in it if we're not careful. That kid thinks he's indestructible."

The kids slowed to a walk, but neither of them were headed in a straight line. The anticipation of getting there had them both running in circles and doubling back just to be able to move faster.

Remi tucked her hands into her coat pockets. "I should have put two layers of pants on them."

Colt chuckled and pointed to the kids on the trail ahead. "I don't think they're bothered by the cold."

"Well, I am." She shivered, and her teeth chattered. "This is my least favorite time of the year."

"Why don't you ever head south for the winter?"

Lots of the ranch workers in Wyoming took seasonal jobs in Texas in the off-season. Half of the horses would take a ride down south, and with no guests to accommodate in the harsh winters, the cowboys went too.

"I thought about it a couple of times, but I... I didn't want to mess up what I have going here."

She didn't want to lose her progress. At least,

that was the reasoning in the beginning. She'd done well in her recovery here, and she wasn't sure if the friends or the ranch itself was to thank. Whatever it was, nothing in Texas was worth a relapse.

"Same for me. I like it here. Why would I leave? Plus, the view is nice."

Remi looked up at him, and he gave her one of those heart-stopping winks. It was ridiculous how charming he could be, and as much as she wanted to act like a full-grown adult, his powers held full sway over her at this point.

Colt picked up his pace as he watched the path ahead. "Abby, where are you going?"

Sure enough, the kid was veering into a side path with her chin tucked to her chest. "I'm just going wherever my little feet takes me."

Remi covered her mouth and chuckled. "Ain't that the truth."

"It's her world. We just live in it," Colt said with such affection that Remi's whole body warmed.

"I wish I could see the world the way she sees it," Remi admitted. Her childhood wonder hadn't been the same as Abby's. Was it coveting for Remi to wish for a peace that wasn't meant for her?

"I wish you could see the world the way I see it."

Her attention jerked to Colt. He looked at her the same way he looked at Abby and Ben. If she could see his devotion to the kids, why was it so hard to believe he held the same fondness for her?

Because she wasn't an innocent child. Never had been. Her childhood was survival, and her adolescence was wreckage. There hadn't existed an in between until recently, and even now, it felt unstable and likely to be ripped away from her in an instant.

Colt's gaze held firm as his pinky brushed against hers. When their hands passed close to each other again, he linked his finger with hers, connecting them by the smallest, yet strongest link. That single touch held the power to kickstart her heart, and in that moment, it was alive and as bright as the sun.

They reached the creek, and Ben jogged toward them. Colt released her finger and held out his hands for whatever Ben carried.

"What ya got?"

Ben opened the pouch he'd made with the bottom of his coat. "Rocks. Which ones of these will skip?"

Leaning down, Colt pulled out a few more jagged rocks and tossed them out of the pile. "You want the flat ones."

Abby crouched near the creek, and Remi walked over to check on her. "What are you doing?"

"Looking for the perfect rock. I need the bestest one."

Remi picked up a dark stone that was flat and oval. "For skipping?"

"No. For wishing." Abby reached for one with layers of light and dark brown. "This one."

"Wishing," Remi whispered to no one. Apparently, Wolf Creek was now a wishing well or a fountain. She looked back at Colt who was making his way down to the bank with Ben.

Abby squared her shoulders and closed her eyes. "I wish Miss Stella would teach me how to sew. And I wish Miss Vera would make me that blackberry cobber I like."

"Cobbler," Remi whispered.

"And please let me ride a pony soon, and I want to go to school. I'm just as big as Ben, and I can learn too."

Colt halted Ben before any of the stones were tossed, and they waited while Abby continued her laundry list of a wish that had morphed into a prayer.

"And please, God, let Mommy and Daddy be okay. And I want a kitty for Christmas. Amen."

Remi covered her mouth and glanced at Colt who was smiling at Abby. Neither of them knew what to make of Abby's list of wishes, but she seemed to know what she wanted.

Abby gripped the rock in her fist and threw it as hard as she could. It sailed into the air and landed with a soft thump on the other side of the creek bank. Her little body sagged into a heap in the grass, and she hung her head. "My wishes never come true."

Remi had Abby in her arms in an instant, hugging her tight enough to feel the little girl's heartbeat against her own. "Sweetie, it's okay."

Colt settled beside them and brushed a hand over Abby's head. Soft whimpers drifted up as she buried her face in Remi's neck. If only she could take the sadness away. She'd gladly carry it herself to save Abby from the heartache.

Colt whispered, "It sounded more like a prayer than a wish."

"It was, but no one ever hears me," she said through sniffles.

"I promise you God hears your prayers. Your wishes might not always come true in the way you wanted, but God has a plan for all of us. Sometimes, He answers your prayer in a better way."

Colt glanced at Remi, and her body warmed from the inside out. Maybe the heat was coming from Abby. She was wearing multiple layers, and so was Remi.

No, the heat was familiar. Her body had an instinctual response whenever Colt was around, and when he looked at her as if she were an answered prayer, there was no fighting the reaction.

She certainly hadn't expected their marriage or the happiness she'd found since accepting this path for her life. Even in the beginning, she hadn't known what would come next. If she'd known this was the life she could have with Colt, would she have married him sooner?

No, they'd come together at the right time–God's time. If that was true, could she embrace the path God was leading her on?

Colt wiped a tear from Abby's face. "I bet Miss Stella would love to teach you how to sew, and I know Miss Vera would make you the best blackberry cobbler. I'll tell you that for free."

Abby chuckled and wiped her face some more. "I know." Then her smile fell again. "I miss Mommy."

Remi pulled Abby close and took deep breaths. *Do not cry. Do not cry.*

"It's okay to miss your mommy and daddy. You should miss them. The more we talk about them and remember them, the closer they'll be to us."

Abby pulled away. "What do you mean?"

Remi laid a hand on Abby's chest. "In our hearts."

"Mommy and Daddy are definitely there," Abby said.

Ben hugged up to Colt's side and snuggled close as the wind picked up speed. "It's cold."

"Let's try the creek again another day," Colt said as he stood. "We can feed the horses if we leave now."

Abby wiggled out of Remi's hold. "Horses!"

She took off up the path toward the truck, and

Ben followed close behind her, hugging his coat tighter around his neck.

Abby turned around and bounced on her toes, hugging her arms around her middle. "This wind will take your underwear off!"

"Don't take your underwear off!" Colt shouted.

Abby ran off toward the truck laughing. Ben had passed her, and they wound around a small curve.

"I'm going to die young, and she'll be the death of me," Colt said.

Remi leaned close to him, and he wrapped his arm around her shoulders. The warmth of his body next to hers had her inching closer. "You really think this is God's better plan for us?"

"I know it is. We're better together. I tried to tell you before, but you wouldn't listen."

"What are you talking about?" She wasn't about to admit she'd been wrong to turn him down years ago, though her own heart was starting to sway that direction. "You're just glad to have someone to help with the kids."

Colt stopped and turned her shoulders until she faced him. It had been days since they'd had a chance to talk one-on-one like this, and the tug of actual longing urged her toward him.

Ugh. She'd officially transformed into one of those vapid women who chased men for attention. But there was no denying she wanted Colt's attention. Now and any other time when the kids were content or sawing logs at the end of a long day.

Colt held tight to her shoulders and leaned in. If he moved just five more inches, they'd be repeating that marital kiss she'd been dreaming about for a month and a half.

"That's not true at all." His deep, stern voice reverberated in her chest.

A small crease appeared between Colt's brows, and the implied frown was unwelcome. Colt wasn't a frowning man, and she didn't want to be the reason for his irritation.

Instead of leaning down to her, the grip on her shoulders tightened as he pulled her closer. She rested her hands on his chest but didn't push away.

No, she wasn't pushing him away anymore.

"I wanted you before the kids, and this" –he waved his hands around them before returning them to her shoulders– "is better than I could have imagined."

Oh, no. Walls were crumbling. Fears she'd so carefully cradled shattered. Chaos and wreckage raged in her heart. Would there be room for new beginnings and a fresh start when the war was over? Her hair whipped in the wind, blowing in all directions like her thoughts.

Uncertainty clawed at her chest. She didn't know how to be the woman he wanted–the one he needed.

"I never learned how to love," she whispered.

He leaned closer, but only by an inch. "Me either. I was thinking we could learn together."

Yes. That was exactly what she wanted. Her fists tightened against his coat, gripping the thick material and pulling him closer. She wanted–

"Ahhh!"

Abby's scream pierced the air, ebbing and rising with the wind.

They took off in an instant, bolting up the path toward the continued scream.

CHAPTER 22

COLT

"Help!"

Colt pushed the run harder as he rounded the curve. Ben was calling for help, but the first scream had been Abby's. A small trail veered off the main path about halfway up the hill, and Colt didn't have to question where the kids had gone. The wranglers used the spot as a drop-off when they needed to lessen the load on the horses on the way back from a long trail ride.

Remi's footfalls pounded behind him. "The crevice."

Pulling extra lungfuls of air in through his nose, Colt pushed toward the path. Which one of the kids had fallen into the crevice? He'd given the jagged, rocky drop a wide berth every time he had to go near it, but the kids didn't know to watch out for it.

He cut the corner sharp, slashing the side of his

face and neck with bare branches. Abby was still screaming, and Ben was still calling for help.

When the small clearing came into view, Colt slid to a stop on the rocky ledge. Ben had a double hold on Abby's wrist, straining to pull her up.

Colt reached down and looped an arm around Abby's middle, hoisting her up in one quick motion. With her safe in his arms, he settled onto his knees and clung to her. His eyes closed, blocking out the view of the rocky crevice's deep bottom.

Abby wailed next to his ear as he said a silent prayer. It gutted him to hear her cry in fear, but he'd take the crying over silence any day.

"Mommy!" Abby's hold on him loosened, and Remi was beside him, pulling Abby into her arms.

Remi's gaze met his over Abby's shoulder. Her face was pale, and the mix of fear and relief was a haunting expression he hoped to never see again. Crying out for Mommy was normal for scared kids, but reaching for Remi had been intentional.

Abby's cries settled into a softer cry, but every muscle in Colt's body remained taut. Ben sat panting by the drop-off, and Colt pulled the kid into his arms.

"You okay, bud?" The shake in Colt's voice would probably stick around a while.

"Yeah." Ben's grip on Colt's neck tightened, and the racing of their hearts pounded in unison. "I was afraid she was gonna fall."

"Me too, but you kept a hold on her. Good job, kid."

"Are you okay? Does anything hurt?" Remi asked.

Abby pulled out of the embrace and pointed to her side. "I hit right here."

Remi tugged Abby's coat and shirt up to reveal a new bruise. The color was still mostly red, but it spread wide over the little ribs.

"Let's get you back to the house. It's freezing out here. Then, we'll get some ice for that."

"I don't think anything is broken. It would hurt a lot more to cry." He'd broken ribs more than once, and the memory of that pain made his stomach roll when he thought about Abby.

Abby wiped her eyes and grabbed for Remi's neck again. "I thought I was a goner."

Colt rubbed a hand over his mouth. Any other time, he would have laughed at Abby's recounting. Today, the fear was still too thick in his throat. Crouching in front of Ben, Colt jerked his chin over his shoulder. "Hop on."

Ben climbed onto Colt's back and wrapped a death-grip on his neck. He didn't try to loosen the hold. He didn't need to breathe right now as much as he needed that assurance of Ben's safety.

Back at the cabin, Remi helped Abby into a warm bath, and Colt directed Ben to change into pajamas. The hero of the day had earned a night without a bath.

Colt gathered Ben's clothes. A rip in the knee of the small jeans caught Colt's breath again. Fear had never ruled his life, but it had set up shop and consumed him today. He'd done some stupid things in his day, but Abby had effectively scared the life out of him.

He tossed the dirty clothes into the hamper and rested his hands on the washing machine. The cold of the metal zinged up his arms, proving that he hadn't been wandering some nightmare.

Was this what it felt like to be a dad? Was it constant fear and worry? How did Mark handle it?

Colt closed his eyes and bowed his head. "Lord, I can't live with fear like this. I'm not supposed to worry, but right now, that's all I can think about. How do I do it? How do I trust that the kids and Remi won't be ripped away from me?" He swallowed hard and rapped his knuckles against the machine. "I can't live like this."

The first full breath he'd taken all afternoon slowly filled his chest. He didn't have to live like this. The Lord never promised an easy path, but He promised to always be near.

Colt straightened as a surge of strength lifted his shoulders. It might only last for a minute, but it was the push he needed to put on a brave face for the kids and Remi.

"Uncle Colt! I can't find any tall socks!" Ben yelled from the other side of the cabin.

A hamper of folded clothes sat on the dryer, and he grabbed a pair of Ben's boot socks. "Got them."

Tossing Ben the socks, Colt turned toward the kitchen. "The hero gets to choose dinner."

"Spaghetti!" Ben shouted as he bounced into the room.

Colt pulled a pot and pan out of the bottom cabinet. "Remi's spaghetti is better, but maybe I can get it started and she can jump in when Abby gets out of the bath."

The kitchen was oddly quiet as Colt started pulling out ingredients. Ben sat at the table looking down at his hands.

"What's up, bud?"

Ben shrugged but didn't look up. "I wasn't a hero. I couldn't pull her up."

Colt wielded the large pan, pointing it at Ben. "You kept her from falling, and that was huge. I don't know if I could have held onto her when I was your age."

"Really?"

"I'm not just saying that. She was squirming around too, which made keeping your hold on her even harder." All of the things Colt hadn't wanted to think about came flooding in at once. Ben had really done something big today. "If she'd fallen, she probably would have broken something–a foot or an arm. She might have hit her head. It's all jagged rock at the bottom of that crevice."

Colt put the pan down and rounded on Ben, wrapping him up in a strong hug. "I'm proud of you."

The bathroom door swung open, banging against the wall. "I'm hungry!"

Colt released the hug and grabbed the meat out of the fridge. "Sorry, your sister is fierce when she gets hangry."

"I'm hungry too. Can we have that buttery bread like we had last time?"

Colt flung open the freezer and pulled out a bag of pre-made garlic bread. "You're in luck."

Abby barreled into the kitchen and jumped toward Colt. He threw out his arms, one holding the meat and the other holding the bread. When she hugged her little arms around his neck, she started peppering him with kisses. They were all over his face, and he closed his eyes against the onslaught and prayed it wouldn't end.

"Thank you for pulling me up," Abby said.

"I'll always be here to pull you up."

She pressed her tiny hands to his cheeks and held him immovable. Her cheeks were pink, and her eyes were dark like her dad's. A punch hit Colt square in the gut. He'd lost his brother, but he couldn't lose anyone else.

Abby kissed his nose and smiled. "I love you."

Colt wrapped her up and threw her over his shoulder. "I love you too."

She screamed and laughed as Colt walked out of the kitchen. Remi stood in the doorway with her arms crossed over her chest. She hadn't lost the haunted look yet.

He set Abby on her feet, and she darted into the living room. Leaning close to Remi, he rubbed a hand up and down her arm. "Hey, she's okay."

"I know."

"It doesn't sound like it. She's really okay."

Remi covered her face. "I know, but I can't stop thinking about what could have happened."

Colt wrapped her up, and she buried her face in his chest. "I get it. I was scared too."

She slung her hands around, shaking them out. "I need to do something."

"You want to finish cooking the spaghetti?"

Peeking around him, she looked around the kitchen. "Finish? Did you start?"

"Um, no. I was getting there, but there isn't any actual fire yet."

Remi patted his chest and stepped into the kitchen. "I'll take care of it."

Colt slapped a hand on Ben's shoulder. "Go play. I'm gonna help Remi cook dinner."

Ben didn't waste a second before running into the living room.

Colt leaned against the counter beside the stove

where Remi worked. The tension in her shoulders and the wrinkle between her brows brought back that helpless feeling from earlier. "What do you need?"

She looked up at him, then back at the meat browning in the pan. "I need to be close. To you, to the kids. I just want to hang out here together tonight."

"I figured. That's why I didn't suggest going to the dining hall tonight." He stepped up behind her and massaged the tight muscles in her shoulders, pressing his thumbs over her shoulder blades and back. "Why don't we take some blankets and pillows out on the porch and look at the stars tonight? It's supposed to be a clear sky."

"It's freezing."

"I'll set up a heater. We'll snuggle up and keep warm."

Remi nodded, then turned around and hugged his neck. Pressing her face into the crook of his shoulder, her soft sobs jerked against him.

Wrapping his arms around her, he whispered softly in her ear. "It's okay. Let it out."

She cried for a few more minutes before wiping her face on the back of her sleeve. "If she'd fallen–"

"Don't say it. I know."

Brushing at her eyes, she sniffed and turned back to the stove. "Great. Now the meat is burnt."

"I don't think anyone will care."

Remi chuckled and glanced at him over her shoulder. "You're probably right. Those kids will eat anything."

He stepped up behind her and braced his hands on the counter on both sides of her. "So, stargazing? Cuddling?" If he leaned down one more inch, he could brush his lips against her hair.

She turned and looked up at him and nodded before her gaze drifted down to his mouth, then his chest, then jumped back to the meat burning on the stove. "That sounds good."

Colt counted to three and pushed away from her. If he didn't put space between them, he'd give in to that urge to confess everything. Instead of pulling her into his arms and kissing her senseless the way he wanted to, he focused on gathering blankets. Who could care about the stars when the best thing in the universe was right here with him?

CHAPTER 23

REMI

Abby wiggled close and rested her head on Remi's chest. "I love snuggling."

"Me too," Colt said, pulling Ben close. The four of them were wrapped up in blankets and resting on pillows on the front porch, and the stars were showing off in the dark sky.

Ben pushed away and huffed. "I don't. I'm too old for snuggling."

"Well, I'm not." Colt turned onto his side and laid an arm over Abby and Remi. The weight on her middle grounded her to reality.

Abby shivered. "Can we sleep out here?"

Remi could agree that Colt's idea to hang out on the porch and watch the stars was a good idea, but the hard porch floor against her back promised at least a few aches in the morning.

"Maybe in the summer," Colt said. "It's supposed to stay below freezing all night."

"But we have the heater. It's warm. And I have Bun Bun." Abby poked the head of her stuffed bunny out from beneath the blankets.

"I want to go camping," Ben said. "Are the stars like this in the summer too?"

Remi looked up at the dark sky. She hadn't appreciated the show God put on every night until she came to the ranch. In fact, she'd been here six months before her therapist had suggested looking for happiness in nature. Until that point, she'd been too focused on making it through each day without relapsing to notice anything at all.

"The stars are like this all the time, but we can't always see them. Sometimes, the clouds get in the way."

"I don't think the stars were like this back home," Ben said.

Colt rolled onto his back and inched Ben closer to his side. "They were. You just didn't notice."

"We didn't go outside a lot." Ben's confession was a whisper, but Remi heard it loud and clear. Missing someone brought up a mix of good and bad memories, and guilt was usually close behind.

"Your mommy and daddy worked a lot," Remi said. At least, Colt said Mark and Brittany were often looking for jobs, and that was a full-time job in itself.

"You work a lot too, but you still let us have fun," Ben said.

Remi turned her head, letting her chin rest on top of Abby's head. Colt was looking back at her. Hurt and indecision colored his shadowed expression. It wasn't the first time the kids had opened up about their homelife before their parents died. They remembered a lot of good times, but they also wondered why their parents had done things the way they had.

She and Colt weren't perfect. They'd forgotten lunchboxes, Ben had been late for school, and they'd fielded cries and complaints when they forced the kids to take baths or eat the dinner they'd made. As fun and challenging as parenting was, finding the balance was something they hadn't mastered, and it seemed Mark and Brittany hadn't either.

Abby let out a contented sigh. "I'm glad we get to live here, even if Mommy and Daddy can't. I wish they could see the stars."

Colt's hand slipped into Remi's that wrapped around Abby, threading their fingers together. A sharp buzz tingled over the skin where they touched and rivaled the chill of any Wyoming winter night.

"I bet your mom and dad saw the stars. I used to camp in the backyard with your dad when we were little."

Remi squeezed Colt's hand. She'd slept outside a

few times when she was young, but she wouldn't call it camping. It was easier to drag her blanket and pillow out onto the back porch when her mom had a fight with whichever boyfriend was her flavor of the week. They never looked for her out there, and her mother usually yelled for her when the fighting was over. They'd pack up and leave, usually ending up at the closest cheap motel.

Had Colt used camping to get away from his dad? The man had a problem with alcohol, but had Colt and Mark ever been in danger of abuse?

Remi had lived that life, and she bore the scars. Not on the outside, but there were times when a quick movement had her jerking back. Then came the memories. They were attached to those instincts. The searing pain after a grown man's knuckles collided with her cheek. The sting in her scalp after getting jerked to the ground by her hair. She couldn't predict which of the painful memories would follow the fear, but the hits always hollowed out her chest.

That couldn't have happened to Colt. Even the thought made her stomach turn.

"Did you live somewhere cool like this when you and Daddy were little?" Abby asked.

"Nah. Nothing as cool as this." Colt's answer was barely a whisper.

"Me either," Remi said after a big swallow. Funny how she and Colt had grown up with nothing but were desperately trying to break the curse.

"Why not?" Ben asked.

Colt ruffled Ben's hair. "We didn't have mommies and daddies who loved us. Or even an aunt and uncle. I think that makes all the difference."

"What about you?" Abby asked, tilting her chin up to Remi.

"Same. I had a mom, but she wasn't a very good mom. And we moved around a lot, so I don't even think I had a real home until I came here."

Ben sat up and turned to Remi. "When did you come here?"

"I think I was twenty-one. The years run together when you pass twenty."

Abby pushed up and looked at Remi. "How did you not have a home?"

Remi brushed a hand over Abby's soft hair. "Home isn't just wherever you're living. Home is where you feel safe and happy. For me, that's here."

"Me too," Abby said. "I like it here."

"Good, because I like it here too," Colt said.

Ben laid back, resting his hands behind his head. "If you could change anything about your life so far, what would it have been?"

"That's deep stuff, bud," Colt said with a chuckle. "Where to start?"

The words were out of Remi's mouth before she

had time to think. "I wish I'd had more people who loved me when I was little. I would have been much happier if I'd had a Miss Stella and a Miss Vera in my life."

"I love them," Abby said wistfully. "It makes me sad you didn't have them when you were little."

Remi cupped Abby's face and pressed a kiss to her forehead. "It's all good. I have more good people in my life than I can count now. I'm especially grateful for you three."

Colt stared up at the stars. "I wish I'd been there more when you were little."

"What do you mean? You were there," Ben said.

"I was there when you were born, and I visited. But I've only seen a small part of your lives. Now I realize just how many awesome times I missed."

Remi bit the inside of her cheek and turned away from Colt. He could have wished he'd had a mother who loved him. He could have wished for a dad who hadn't been a slave to a drink. But she understood his wish. She'd missed more than Colt had, and it didn't matter that the kids weren't hers from birth. She still wanted the things she'd missed. In a way, she considered those years to be stolen.

Abby rolled over and hugged up to Colt. "We'll be here if you want to keep watching us grow up. I'll be five soon."

"You think this is what Heaven is like?" Ben asked.

It was a valid question. Remi had no idea what Heaven would be like, but if she got to choose, it would be a little cabin in the foothills of the Big Horn Mountains.

"I think Heaven is too perfect for us to understand," Colt said. "But I bet it's a lot like this."

Remi turned onto her side and wrapped an arm around Abby. "I can't wait to see it."

"What? You'd have to die first." Ben's high pitch threatened to catch the attention of the animals that roamed the ranch at night.

Colt chuckled. "I'm not afraid of dying, and I imagine your parents weren't either."

Ben wiggled before asking, "Why not?"

"They're with Jesus," Colt explained. "I know your mom and dad knew Jesus, so they're in Heaven now."

"I love Jesus," Abby said. "What does he look like?"

Colt turned his head to look at Remi, and she shrugged. "Don't look at me. I have no idea."

"I don't think anybody knows," Colt added.

"But Mommy and Daddy know now," Abby said.

"Yep. I think you're right." Colt yawned. "I think it's time for bed."

"No! I wanna sleep out here," Ben whined.

"Not tonight. Wait till it gets warmer. I promise to take you out on a trail ride in the summer."

Ben shot up, eyes wide enough to reflect the moonlight. "Really?"

"Really, really. Now, go brush your teeth. We're gonna fold up the blankets, and we'll meet you in the bedroom."

Ben ran off to do as he'd been told, but Abby snuggled deeper into Colt's side. "I like it right here. I think I'll just sleep here."

Colt wrapped his arms around her and cradled her to his chest. "Not today."

She stretched in his arms before he set her on her feet just inside the door. "I'll be checking teeth," Colt said as she ran to the bathroom.

Remi did some stretching of her own as she got to her feet. "I think we made it too comfy out here."

"Tell me about it. If Ben didn't have school in the morning and the wolves weren't out, I'd say we do the whole sleeping outside thing."

Remi picked up the first blanket, and Colt grabbed the other end. She'd never been fond of sleeping in a bed with someone else, but Abby had climbed in beside her a number of times now, and she hadn't minded. In fact, she slept better with Abby beside her.

Lying this close to Colt had one question knocking on the recesses of Remi's mind.

What would it be like to sleep next to him?

She folded the blankets and gathered the

pillows. She knew what it would be like. Safety. Peace.

Home.

Good grief. Why did Colt have to be so good and so tempting?

She chuckled, and Colt looked up with a smile. "What?"

"Nothing." She wasn't about to tell him that most women had a weakness for bad boys, but she had fallen for the good guy, and it was throwing her world into a tailspin.

The words were on the tip of her tongue. *You can sleep in the bed.* It would be easy to speak the words, but they meant so much that the action itself was terrifying. She could do it, but that was a step in their relationship that would change things forever.

So would opening up to him about the things she'd done. The war raging inside her was at an impasse. She wanted to show him she trusted him, but she couldn't expect the street to go both ways until she laid it all on the line for him.

"Colt! Remi! We're ready!" Abby yelled from inside.

Colt picked up the pillows. "Her majesty beckons."

Remi walked into the kids' room and put her hands on her hips. "Teeth brushed?"

"Yes," the kids said in unison.

"Whose turn is it?"

"Mine," Abby said, sitting up in bed. "I want 'Froggy Went a Courtin'.'"

Colt walked in and sat on the end of Ben's bed. "Only if it's a duet."

Remi rolled her eyes. "Fine. I'll sing too." She'd never heard of "Froggy Went a Courtin'" until Colt taught her the words to the old folk song. The kids loved it, and they always had fun singing.

Abby clapped along to the beat, while Ben covered his mouth with two hands to contain his laughter. When the song was over, Abby went straight into leading the prayer.

In the same breath as Amen, she asked, "Do elephants taste boogers when they drink out of their noses?"

Remi flopped back onto Abby's bed. "Sweetie, I have no idea. If I ever meet an elephant, I'll ask."

Abby laughed and rolled over in the bed, tucking the covers beneath her chin. "Good night. Sleep tight."

Remi and Colt took turns kissing the kids' foreheads and saying their own good nights. Abby laughed about who knew what as Remi and Colt snuck out of the room.

"I love that laugh," Remi whispered as they headed for the couch.

Colt flopped down beside her and rested his arm

on the back of the couch. "Me too. Thanks for making the kids so happy. I think the laughing has saved them from a lot of grief."

She rested her head against his arm. "I think you're responsible for the laughs."

"Nah. You make this place a home. I just get to live here." He picked up her left hand and brushed his thumb over her wedding band. She hadn't taken it off since their wedding day. Not once. And despite the messes she often got into, the gold was still as shiny as a new penny.

Colt rested their hands on their legs. "I'm a lucky man to get to have you by my side."

"Ha! I'm far from a good wife." The number-one reason being Colt was getting zero physical benefits from his fairly new bride. Most men at least got to factor that into the happiness of their relationship.

Now. She should say it now, but as much as she wanted to tell him to come to bed with her, the words stuck in her throat.

Colt sighed and released her hand. "I hate to kill the mood, but I heard from Camille today."

Remi sat up straighter. Things were moving slow on the adoption front, and news about probate for Mark and Brittany's estate had been dead silent. "What did she say?"

"They set up a hearing in the family court case, and she has a few things ready to file in probate court. They either have to be mailed or hand delivered, so I think it's time for a trip to Newcastle."

"Okay. When?" They'd been expecting this to happen at some point, but the dates had always been indefinite. Colt had been getting things ready to put the house on the market as much as he could from the other side of the state, but the place needed to be cleaned out before photos could be taken for the real estate listing.

"I need to go this weekend. I got approval from Jameson to have next week off."

Remi bit her lip. A week. She hadn't spent a week without Colt in all the years they'd known each other, but Ben was in school, and they still had two weeks left in the regular tourist season.

She couldn't go with him, and she'd have to manage things here on her own. She'd taken care of herself since before she turned seven, but taking care of two kids alone had a sweat breaking out on her back.

"Are you gonna be okay here? I can wait until the Christmas break so we can all go. I'll just need to see if the hearing can be pushed back."

"No. You need to go. I'll be fine here. We shouldn't put this off any longer. We need that house to sell."

He rested his cheek against her head. "I wish you were going with me."

"Me too, but I'll keep things moving around here. Plus, we have plenty of help."

"Call me if you need anything. I'll answer, as long as I'm not in the courtroom."

Of course, he would. Colt was as reliable as the sun rising in the east and setting in the west. Another reason he was too good for her.

The indecision gnawed at her. She wanted his comfort more than anything, but the fear of never measuring up kept her from opening her mouth and asking for the thing she wanted.

She wanted him, but she had no right to ask it. Married or not, she would always be the kid who adults never wanted to deal with, always the troubled teen who couldn't be trusted, and always the druggy who would rather lie than finish a rehab stint. Saying time had passed didn't change it. She didn't get a do-over because she did it wrong in the first half.

And opening up her heart to him right before he left was only going to make the leaving harder to bear. It wasn't the time to speak up, but would it ever be?

Colt slapped a hand on her knee and pushed to his feet. "I'm gonna get a shower, then I'll clean up the kitchen. You get some rest."

Before heading off to shower, he bent down and kissed her head. It was the sweetest gesture–something he'd do to the kids. She wasn't innocent and worthy like they were, but Colt adored her anyway.

When Colt left her on the couch, drowning in her pity party, she stalked to the bedroom and closed the door. If she waited in the living room, she would be tempted to ask for more than she deserved.

CHAPTER 24

COLT

C olt steadied the flowers in the passenger seat of his truck. No one told him buying a woman flowers also required the skill to transport them. The two vases swayed in the seat, threatening to topple at every bump on the path.

Parking at the south barn, he reached for the seat belt and buckled the vases in. "Stay right there." The flower arrangements were worse at minding than the kids.

Jumping out, he jogged to the new barn. Ridge and Cheyenne had started up a youth learning program over the summer, and construction on a new facility was well underway. The old barn had seen its better days in the nineteen fifties and needed help holding itself up.

Two portable lights lit the inside of the new

construction. The walls and roof were up but not much else.

"Uncle Colt!" Abby shouted as she ran down the breezeway with her arms open.

Colt met her halfway and twirled her in his arms. "Hey, sweetie. Did you have a good day with Ridge and Cheyenne?"

Abby grabbed the collar of Colt's coat. "I did! Miss Cheyenne's mommy has a cool carriage."

Colt chuckled. "A wheelchair."

"Yes. She let me put stickers on it. And Mr. Ridge let me use a hammer with some nails and some wood!"

Oh, boy. The thought of Abby with a weapon was going to cause some nightmares. "Sounds like fun. Did he put you to work?"

"No, silly. I put nails in the wood. Come on. I show you."

"Quick because we need to find your brother and get going. I have a surprise in the truck."

"A surprise! Ben! Hurry!"

That was one way to speed things up. Abby waddled off in her puffy coat.

Ben darted out of a room that would probably one day be an office. "What's the surprise?"

Colt held out a hand for Ben to slap. "Does that question ever work?"

Ben shrugged. "It's worth a shot."

Ridge stepped out of the room and wiped his forehead with a rag. "Don't forget your drinks."

The kids ran off, and Colt greeted his old roommate with a firm handshake. "Were they good?"

"They were great, but does Abby ever stop talking?"

Colt laughed. "Only when she sleeps."

Ben and Abby reappeared with juice pouches and zipped right past Colt toward the truck.

"Race you," Ben said as he picked up speed.

"It's not a race!" Abby yelled.

"Everything is a competition," Ridge whispered.

"Tell me about it. I have a long-running losing streak. Thanks for letting the kids hang out this afternoon."

"No problem. I've missed having kids around."

"They'll be back before you know it." Colt slapped a hand on Ridge's shoulder. "See you next week."

"Tell Remi to call me or Cheyenne if she needs anything while you're gone next week."

"Will do."

Colt turned and headed toward the truck where the kids were bouncing in the thin layer of snow.

"I see flowers!" Abby shouted.

Colt unlocked the door and opened the back seat for the kids to climb in. "Surprise! Flowers for Abby and Remi and a sweet treat for Ben." Colt held up a finger. "Not to be consumed until after dinner."

"What does consumed mean?" Abby asked.

He should have seen that one coming. "Eaten. Find your seats and plant your behinds in them."

When everyone was settled, Ben leaned forward, looking in the front seat. "Where's mine?"

Colt handed a box over the seat. "No touchy until after dinner. And they're to share."

"Whoa. Cupcakes!"

Abby named off every color in the flower arrangements on the way home, and Colt tried his best to recall the flower names. The only ones he was sure of were roses and tulips.

Colt parked in front of the cabin and killed the engine. "Nobody move. We have to have a chat first. Remi isn't home yet, but let's surprise her with the flowers." He held up a finger in front of his lips. "No telling until the big reveal."

Abby bounced in her seat and laughed. Ben nodded, agreeing to aid in the surprise.

Ben jumped out of the truck and made a beeline for the door. Abby scrambled out and did her best to keep up. Carrying both vases and the tray of cupcakes, Colt was slow getting to the porch. He set the gifts down and checked his pockets for the house key. He patted one pocket, then the other. No key.

"Hold up. I've gotta find the key." He went back to the truck and rummaged in the console. Nothing in the cupholder. He stopped and tried to think back over his day. Slapping a hand to his forehead, he remembered giving the set of keys that included his house key and the storage shed key to Brett.

Closing up the truck, he fired off a text to Brett. He was probably still out on a trail ride.

"Looks like we're locked out, kids."

"Oh no! How are we gonna get in?" Abby asked.

Colt rubbed his chin and looked around. "Do either of you remember if Remi opened the bathroom window last night?" She had a habit of cracking the window to let out the steam, since the small bathroom didn't have a vent.

"She did," Abby confirmed.

"Good. How do you feel about sliding in through the window?"

Abby's mouth dropped open. "Really? I can?"

"I'm asking you to do it. Take one for the team."

"What does that mean?" Abby asked with a scrunched nose.

"It means you'll be the hero today. Or heroine. Whatever."

With fists lifted above her head, Abby darted off the porch and around the side of the cabin. "Yes!"

The back of the cabin didn't have a porch, and the bathroom window was up higher than Colt had expected. "Do you think you can do it? I'll keep my hands on you until you get in."

Abby looked up at the window and shrank the slightest bit. "It's high."

Colt opened the window and squatted in front of her. "You don't have to do it. We can hang out at the main house until Brett gets back."

"No, I want to climb in the window. You'll hold me, right?"

"The whole time." Colt offered her his pinky, and she wrapped hers around it. "Pinky promise."

Colt turned Abby around and grabbed her tiny waist. She giggled when he hoisted her into the air. "Now, straighten your legs out. I've got you."

Abby did as he said, holding onto his shoulders with a mighty grip in the process.

"Okay. The toilet is right under the window. So I'll slide you in, feet first. Let me know when you feel the top of the toilet with your feet."

"Got it!"

Ben chanted behind him, "You can do it. You can do it."

"Don't put your foot *in* the toilet." He'd have a tough time explaining that one to Remi.

With most of her body in the window, Abby finally relaxed in his arms. "I found it!"

Colt released her and rested his hands on the windowsill. "Good. Now, can you go unlock the front door?"

"Got it!" Her thumping footfalls traveled across the cabin.

Colt and Ben raced to the front where Abby

waited on the porch. With her hands in the air, she smiled and shouted, "I did it!"

Colt grabbed her up and spun her around. "You did it. You saved the day."

"Can I have my flowers now?"

Abby could ask for the world in that sweet voice, and he'd give her the moon and stars too. "You bet."

When they brought the flowers and cupcakes inside, Colt headed straight for the bedroom with Remi's bouquet. "I'll give these to Remi later tonight. Let's keep it a secret until then."

Ben popped open the cupcake container. "Can I have one?"

"Food first."

"What's for supper?"

Colt checked his watch. Remi wouldn't be home for another hour and a half at the earliest. "Let's have supper at the dining hall."

"Yay!" Abby threw her arms in the air and wrapped them around Colt. "I get to see Miss Vera!"

"Maybe she made her famous cobbler," Colt said as he flipped Abby over his shoulder.

Waiting for Remi to get home in the evening was torture. He'd be leaving for Newcastle in the morning, and the flowers were a pitiful substitution for the things he wanted to tell her.

Well, really only one thing–that he loved her. She'd freak out, but the truth was burning a hole in his chest. He wanted to tell her she was the reason he smiled. He wanted to tell her she was an amazing mom to the kids. He wanted to tell her that he didn't go a single waking hour without thinking of her.

But the flowers would have to do. She was bound to get squirrely when he finally told her the truth, and that wasn't the state they needed to be in when he'd be gone for the next seven days.

In truth, Remi was already struggling, and he couldn't add to the pressure. Her smiles came in short segments instead of extended periods of time. Sometimes, her smile was a second too late, almost like she hadn't understood the joke or the humor in the situation right away.

He pushed the worries away. She'd told him on Tuesday that she needed to take the afternoon to visit her therapist. It had been months since she'd gone, and the nagging fear that she was struggling because of him reared its ugly head. They'd been married for over two months, and the good days had outweighed the bad. Hadn't they?

After supper, he wrangled the kids back to the cabin where they started a card game. Abby was ready to play with her dolls after the first game, but Ben was determined to win a game before quitting.

Colt stared at the UNO! cards in his hand. The colors and numbers blurred. She was unhappy. She had to be. Why else would she need to talk to her therapist now?

"Hey, it's your turn," Ben said.

Colt checked the play card and then his hand before throwing down a blue eight.

The rumble of Remi's truck had Colt and Ben's heads rising in unison.

"She's home."

Colt pressed a finger to his lips, reminding Ben to keep quiet about the surprise. Abby had been playing in her room for over half an hour, and there was a chance she'd snuggled up with one of her dolls and fallen asleep.

Remi's footfalls thudded against the porch, and there was a moment of silence while she removed her boots before opening the door.

Colt stood and opened his arms. "Welcome home, princess."

Her shoulders sank, and her smile was tired but present. When she fell into his arms, the full weight of her exhaustion rested on his chest. He rubbed circles on her back and fought back the urge to ask how the session went. Was he allowed to ask that? Better safe than sorry.

Abby bolted out of her bedroom and pointed at Remi's bedroom door. "Uncle Colt has you flowers behind that door!"

Remi lifted her head from his chest and looked up at him with wide eyes. So much for sharing the surprise after the kids went to bed.

"Abby! Seriously? He told us not to tell."

Abby propped her hands on her hips and narrowed her eyes at her brother. "And Remi told us not to keep secrets from her."

Watching Remi, Colt waited for a reaction. Would she think he was pressuring her? Would she even like flowers? She never asked for anything that was just for looks, but was that because she didn't care about those things or because she couldn't afford them?

Remi knelt in front of Abby and took her hands. "I love that you don't keep secrets from me, but happy surprises are okay."

Abby bounced on her feet and pointed toward the kitchen. "There's mine."

"They're beautiful. Will you show me mine?"

Remi let Abby drag her to the bedroom where she emerged with the large vase of flowers. Her gaze locked on Colt immediately. "They're beautiful."

Colt rubbed his jaw. Remi usually brushed off his attempts at romance, but today, it seemed she'd graciously accept the gesture. "I thought you might need a reminder of me while I'm gone."

Remi rolled her eyes as she stepped toward him. "I don't need a reminder. I doubt I could ever forget you, considering you're the first person I see every morning."

Was she just pointing out a fact or begrudging the time they spent together? Maybe she needed some space. Was she tired of him?

Remi shouted over her shoulder as she put the vase on the kitchen table next to Abby's, "Kids! Get ready for bed!"

When the kids darted off to brush their teeth, Remi approached him.

His breaths deepened, and a chill rushed down his spine. Why was he nervous all of a sudden? The doubts had piled up, and he was second-guessing everything.

"Thanks for letting me go this afternoon. I know it was really out of the way, but I needed–"

"You don't have to explain to me. And I didn't *let* you go. You're free to go wherever you want."

"I know that, but we're a team now. I hate it when I'm not pulling my weight around here."

Colt placed his full hand over her mouth. "Shh. You pull more than your fair share. You're about to be doing it all by yourself for a week. You can take time for yourself and not feel guilty about it."

Her eyes glistened as she looked up at him, and the emotion that she kept so hidden was on full display.

"Do I need to cancel the trip? Say the word, and I'll do it. I won't go if you need me here."

Remi shook her head, and he lowered his hand. "No. You have to go."

"I don't have to do anything but take care of you and the kids. Whatever you need, just say it."

She leaned forward and rested her forehead

against his chest. "I need you to go. The stuff I'm struggling with has nothing to do with you or the kids. I can do this."

Colt wrapped his arms around her, wishing he could rip her sadness away and destroy it. "I know you can do anything, but you don't have to do it alone."

"We're ready for bed!" Abby shouted.

Colt held on to Remi, unwilling to let go yet. "I'm here if you need me, and I can make myself scarce if you need some time alone."

She shook her head. "Really, I'm having a tough time right now, but it's not because of you. Promise." She toyed with the top button of his shirt with her fingertips. "I'm gonna miss you."

"I'll miss you too. At the risk of sounding needy, will you call me? A lot?"

The transparent remark earned him a chuckle. "You've always been needy. No reason to change now."

"Uncle Colt! Aunt Remi! I need to take your blood temperature before bed!" Abby shouted.

Remi narrowed her eyes. "Blood temperature?"

"It's the new doctor set Stella gave her."

"Oh. Good. I haven't had my blood temperature checked in a while."

He released her and followed her into the kids' bedroom. Abby had her doctor tools spread out on the bed, and Colt let her check his ears, nose, throat, eyes, and chest. Abby was thorough and checked the same for Remi.

When the exams were over, Colt wasn't ready to leave. This was his last night with the kids for a while, and the urge to hold on to every moment had him lingering.

After songs and prayers, Remi bent to kiss Ben's forehead. She whispered something in his ear, and Ben's arms wrapped around Remi's neck.

"I love you too."

Colt gripped the blanket on Ben's bed. Love. He'd been telling the kids he loved them since day one, but Remi always skirted the word.

When she leaned over Abby, Colt listened close.

"I love you, sweetie."

Abby hugged Remi's neck. "Love you too." She placed a smacking kiss on Remi's cheek before letting go.

Colt took his turn saying good night to the kids and followed Remi out of the room.

She pulled the ponytail holder out of her hair, shaking down her long red locks. "Can we watch the Bama Georgia game?"

Leaving her in the morning would tear him up, but tonight, he'd hold her as long as she'd let him.

CHAPTER 25

REMI

Remi wrapped Colt's flannel shirt tighter around her middle as she stepped out of her bedroom. The snow outside and the dropping temps promised she'd be hard-pressed to find enough indoor activities to keep the kids occupied. She'd been given the week off while Colt was out of town, and after dropping Ben off at school, Abby and Remi would catch up with Hadley and the other kids on the ranch.

She padded lightly into the kitchen and flipped on the light. Colt's note lay folded beneath the two vases of flowers. She'd read it four times the day before. Could she lower that to three today? Probably not. She missed him so deeply that the warm fireplace hadn't been able to touch the cold void last night. Watching ball games wasn't nearly as fun without Colt.

The note was an anchor–a reminder that Colt still existed, even if she couldn't see him or hear his constant encouragement. She picked up the note and read it again.

I miss you already.
You're perfect.

How had he known? The therapy session had done her some good but not enough. The lines between truths and lies had been blurring in the last few weeks. Colt never missed a chance to remind her how much he appreciated her. He had an endless store of motivation and encouragement, but her old ways were fighting against him.

A lifetime of thinking she was a waste of space and too stupid to live didn't go away with a few sweet words. In fact, every sweet thing Colt said held a silent question behind it.

Can that be true?

And so began her tug-of-war. Who was right? Colt or her? And she was starting to become dependent on his regular pick-me-ups, so she'd seen the depression coming a mile away.

Hopefully, he'd have more news today after the

hearing and filings with the probate court. She was in need of good news.

But he could just as easily get bad news. The agency had run a background check on her–fingerprints and all–when they'd been in Newcastle two months ago, but it was only a matter of time before the agency had something to say about the tiny, crooked bricks in her past. They were there, plain as day and screwing up the entire foundation of her life. Their effects were still rippling through her life today.

The Justice family came to mind. The overwhelmed mother and oblivious father hadn't seen her coming until fourteen-year-old Remi had torn through their home. She'd been sure they wouldn't miss the vintage brooch she'd stolen from them, and she'd been right. Ten years later, she'd never heard another word about the family heirloom she'd traded for heroin.

Remi folded the letter and brushed the pads of her thumb over the paper. Just because she hadn't heard about it didn't mean the Justice family hadn't shared their suspicions with the case manager. That little tidbit could be sitting in a file with her name on it at the Weston County Department of Family Services right this minute.

There were other foster families, and some had noticed her thefts, though none were proven. Every home she passed through deemed her a miscreant, and the system was glad to be rid of her when she aged out.

All of those offenses liked to gang up and throw a party in her head. It was more like a bonfire that tended to get out of control. Those old ideas about her worth–or lack of–were beating her over the head, pounding her into the ground like a fence post.

How could she ever tell Colt about those things? He thought she was perfect, but he couldn't be more wrong. She was damaged. Tainted. Broken. Shattered.

A heart like that couldn't be mended. It was always a little bent, ready to sway a little further off course whenever the wind blew the right way. She hadn't reached the point of considering relapsing, and that was the reason the therapy session had been necessary. She couldn't ever let herself get to that point.

"Morning!" Abby sang as she bounced into the kitchen.

Remi laid the note on the table and opened her arms. "Morning, sweetie. You sleep okay?"

"Yep." She looked around, and her smile faded. "When is Uncle Colt coming back?"

"Only five days counting today. What would you like for breakfast?"

"Can we have bethel ham?"

Remi raised her eyebrows. "What is bethel

ham?"

"I don't know. They said it at church."

Remi slapped a hand over her mouth, giving her time to come up with a response.

"We always have bacon, but DJ said bethel ham sounds good."

DJ was a little boy in Abby's Sunday School class, so there must have been some pre-school talk going on about the pork options last Sunday.

"Well, there isn't a food called bethel ham, at least not that I know of. But Bethlehem is where Jesus was born."

"Oh! I knew that. I didn't know it was the same thing."

Ben stepped into the kitchen rubbing his eyes. "What's for breakfast?"

"I think Abby wants to switch things up. What about sausage?"

Ben shrugged. "Works for me."

Abby tugged on Remi's hand. "I'm hungry, and I'm about to get whiny."

Remi patted Abby's head. "Thanks for the warning. Get dressed, and I might have breakfast ready by the time you get done." Inevitably, it would take Abby ten minutes to get dressed. She could at least be close to having the eggs ready by that time.

She moved through the rest of the day on autopilot. Abby played, Remi helped Hadley with the kids, even though it was her day off, and Ben was full of pent-up energy when he got home from school.

When Ridge offered to take Ben for a riding lesson, Remi didn't resist. If Ben was off having fun, she could take Abby to the standing Tuesday night quilting circle at Stella and Vera's.

Remi and Abby arrived early, and Vera welcomed them with open arms.

With Abby wrapped up in her arms, Vera pointed to the jugs on the counter. "Will you help me make the drinks?"

Abby nodded. "Is that juice?"

"Apple juice. We'll mix in some mulling spices."

Abby's nose scrunched. "What's that?"

"Don't worry. We'll leave some plain for you. How does warm apple juice sound?"

"Yum!"

Remi left Abby in the kitchen and flopped onto the couch beside Cheyenne.

"You okay?" Cheyenne asked.

"I'm okay, but just barely. What about you?"

"Oh, just about to pull my hair out. I want the wedding to be small, but Linda and Everly have such amazing ideas that I want everything. That's stupid, right?"

Remi shrugged. "I don't know. I've never planned a wedding before. I've only attended like three."

"Including your own?" Cheyenne asked with a

bump of her shoulder.

"Including my own. It was nice. I definitely recommend the small, no-frills wedding."

Cheyenne turned her whole body to face Remi on the couch. "I have to ask you something, but I want you to know that it's okay to say no."

Remi rolled her eyes. "Duly noted. You know I'd do almost anything for you."

"Can Abby be my flower girl?"

"That's a big yes. She'd love it."

Cheyenne relaxed against the back of the couch and smiled. "Thanks. And can Ben be the ring bearer?"

"Also a big yes. And you can trust him to hang on to the rings."

"I know. And he really likes Ridge."

Remi patted Cheyenne's knee. "Are y'all thinking about having kids?"

"One step at a time, but yes. Ridge is so good with the kids."

Ava walked in and hefted a large tote onto the middle of the rug.

"You shouldn't be carrying anything heavy," Cheyenne said.

Ava stood and covered her mouth with a yawn. "It's not heavy, just bulky."

"You feeling better this week?" Remi asked.

"Much. I've only been sick twice this week."

"It's Tuesday," Cheyenne pointed out.

"But twice is an improvement." Ava flopped into the recliner. All of the ladies had unofficial assigned seats, and someone had even pulled Abby's toddler chair into the living room.

Abby walked slowly into the living room carrying a tray with two drinks on it. Her attention was so focused on the drinks that she almost walked into the couch.

"Who ordered drinks?" Cheyenne asked.

Abby stopped in front of the couch. "One for you, and one for you."

Remi and Cheyenne took their drinks. The amber liquid in the mason jar wasn't scalding, but it was warm enough that it tingled Remi's fingertips.

"I'll be right back with yours," Abby said over her shoulder to Ava.

Remi tugged Abby to her side. "Where'd you get this new apron?"

Abby lifted the skirt of the pink apron with lace trim. "Miss Ava gave it to me. It's beautiful."

Remi brushed her fingertips over the silky material. "It is."

Abby pressed a quick kiss to Remi's cheek and skipped back to the kitchen with the tray.

Remi's chest ached. She'd been at the ranch for years, and she still hadn't figured out how to react when the women did nice things for no reason.

When Abby was out of sight, Remi turned to Ava. "Thanks for that."

"No problem. One of the ladies at church makes them for her granddaughters, and she was happy to make one for Abby."

Fire rushed up Remi's throat, and something behind her nose tickled. Her eyes grew heavy, and she gripped the arm of the couch to keep from jumping to her feet and running away.

Abby returned with the tray and one more drink. She stopped in front of Ava, who made a huge show of gratitude.

When Abby turned to Remi, her smile fell. "You okay?"

Remi wiped her eyes. "I'm more than okay." The women at the ranch doted on Abby, essentially adopting her into their circle of happiness. If nothing else happened tonight, Abby would at least have a few hours when she could forget that Colt would be gone for the next few days.

"But you're crying."

Was she? Remi brushed her fingers over her cheek. Sure enough, the wetness was there. She didn't cry often, but it was always bound to happen when she was struggling to keep herself emotionally stable. It was a miracle she'd made it this long.

"They're happy tears," Remi said.

Abby tilted her head. "Happy tears?"

"Yeah. I'm just happy." It was true. Abby and Ben had everything Remi had always wished she'd had as a kid. Not only did the kids have a father and mother figure who loved them, but they had a group here who added extra love on a daily basis.

Stella stepped out of the hallway and halted when she spotted Remi. "What's wrong? Why are you leaking?"

Remi wiped the tears again. "I'm just happy." Everything had been numbed lately, but the tears were a sign that she was still alive and capable of loving and appreciating the good she'd stumbled into.

"Good. I'll grab my drink, and we'll get started."

Abby jumped up. "I'll get it!"

The rest of the evening passed with a note of happiness covering everything. Remi's breaths came easier than they had in over a week, and she slumped onto the couch when the kids were tucked into bed. She checked her phone, and a text waited from Colt.

Colt: Call me when you get the kids to bed.

Remi rested her head back against the couch, closed her eyes, and made the call.

"Hey, princess."

He could have said he'd rented a traveling circus, and she would have smiled. The ache of missing him ran deep.

"Hey, Walker."

"You know you're a Walker now too."

"Not officially. I haven't changed my name yet."

There was a beat of silence. "Are you going to? I

mean, it's okay if you don't want to. That's up to you. Just wondering."

She hummed and made a show of considering it. "I haven't made up my mind. Remi Walker doesn't really have a pop to it."

"Whatever. It sounds perfect."

Perfect. He obviously didn't understand the meaning of the word because he kept throwing it around when she was the subject of the conversation. If anything could throw up a red flag, it was "perfect" and "Remi" in the same chat.

Remi folded her legs beneath her and tugged a blanket over her lap. "How'd it go today?"

"Interesting, to say the least. The hearing went off without a hitch, but apparently Mark and Brittany had a will drawn up by a local attorney, naming me as the administrator of their estate."

"Did you expect them to have a will?"

"Not at all, but I figured if they did, I'd be the administrator. All that to say it makes it easier to get things done at the probate court."

"Awesome."

"No, what's awesome is that the will names me as their appointed guardian for the kids and names me as the executor of their trust."

"Trust?"

"Yeah. You're not gonna believe this, but Mark and Brittany received an inheritance from her grandfather earlier this year. They have zero debt except what they still owed on the house, and they ordered the remainder of their wealth to be compiled into a trust for the kids."

Remi sat up and gripped the arm of the couch. "Are you serious?"

"I can't make this up. I'll have access to the trust to use as needed to care for them, and they'll have access to the remainder when they turn eighteen."

"Wow." Remi stared at the fireplace, not seeing the flames that danced in the dim light.

"We don't know the total value, but there was an itemization with the will. It was dated this March, and the combined value of their accounts and assets was estimated at two hundred thousand."

"Two hundred thousand!" Remi slapped a hand over her mouth. There was a chance she'd just woken the kids.

"The car that was involved in the wreck has already been subtracted from that. Their auto insurance is refusing to pay out."

"Why?" The question was barely a whisper. She hadn't gathered her breath yet.

"I delivered the medical records to them today. Mark was over the blood alcohol limit."

Remi gripped her chest. The defeat and pain in Colt's voice was enough to rip her in two. "I'm sorry."

"Yeah, me too. I'd almost convinced myself he'd

beat it, but I guess you never really beat addiction."

Remi sank to the couch and gathered her shirt in her fist. How could she argue? He was right. She would be a grenade until her dying day–waiting for any unsuspecting moment to blow up and hurt anyone close to her.

"I'm sorry."

"It's not your fault."

It wasn't her fault that Colt's brother relapsed and paid the ultimate price, but it was her fault that she'd tied him to a sinking ship.

Colt sighed. "I can't believe any of this."

Remi swallowed and sat up straighter. "I imagine it's been a crazy day."

"Sorry to dish out that roller coaster of a day in one five-minute burst. It was a little easier for me to get the ups and downs over the course of twelve hours."

"Probably not."

"I still have to sell the house. I walked a realtor through it today. They're sending a photographer and videographer over tomorrow, so I've been cleaning for the last few hours."

The exhaustion in his voice drew her heart to him, begging to latch on and let him siphon out any comfort and joy she had left. She'd give it all to him. He deserved peace. She didn't.

"You there, princess?"

Remi nodded before remembering he couldn't

see her from the other side of the state. "Yeah. I'm here."

"This could change things for us."

"I don't want it to. I like what we have here." No, she loved their life. She wouldn't change a thing about it.

"We could have a bigger place. A little bit of land."

"We can, if that's what you want, but I'd rather save as much as we can for the kids. Making a living isn't getting any easier."

Colt chuckled. The deep rumble sent a chill down Remi's back. "That's what I wanted to hear."

"I don't want them to miss out on things, but—"

"We'll figure it out."

Remi released the hold she had on her shirt. Never in her wildest dreams could she have seen this coming. A husband, two kids, and a new cabin on a dude ranch. It was perfect. She understood the meaning of the word, even if Colt didn't.

"There is some bad news."

Remi tried to hold on to the perfect of the last few seconds, but it was already fading, being driven out and conquered by fear. "What kind of bad news?"

"This means Tasha is probably going to come out of the woodwork. She's a close enough relative that she has to sign a waiver before any funds can be released."

"What? Why?"

"I'm not sure. Camille said it could take a while, but she doesn't think this will be too big of a barrier. The will is solid, and it completely disinherits her by name."

"Really? You think Tasha will just sign away the rights to everything?" From what Colt had told Remi about Brittany's sister, the woman was a walking wrecking ball.

"If we can't find her after a certain amount of time, the probate judge will probably default. I don't know how all of this works, but she'll be notified. She'll also be able to contest guardianship."

Remi glanced at the kids' bedroom door. "She can't do that."

"Don't panic. No judge in their right mind would choose her over us. And she might want the trust, but she'd have to win guardianship and actually raise the kids to get it. That would be too much work for her."

"Are you sure?" *Please be sure. Please be sure.*

"I'm pretty sure. Really, don't worry about it. She'll never be the better choice for the kids. They have us."

Remi pushed a hand through her hair and sighed. There was no way on earth Tasha would take the kids away from them. Remi would fight to the death for Ben and Abby, and Colt would be right beside her through it all.

CHAPTER 26
COLT

The sun peeked over the horizon in his rear-view mirror as Colt pulled out onto the highway. The GPS said he'd be home just after noon, but he could probably beat that estimate. He gulped the coffee he'd picked up from a drive-through and turned on the radio. Where was the classic country station?

His phone rang in the console. He answered it and put it on speaker. "Good morning."

"Uncle Colt! Are you coming home?" Abby asked in greeting.

He'd always assumed hearing Remi's voice first thing in the morning would be the best way to start his days. Turned out, hearing Abby and Ben's was just as good.

"I'll be home today."

"We're gonna build a snowman in just a little

bit, but we'll build another one when you get home," Ben said.

"You build Remi, and I'll build mine. I don't trust her to get my figure right."

"I miss you," Abby said. The pout in her voice did strange things to Colt's chest.

"I miss you too, sweetie. And Ben."

"What about me?" Remi asked.

Colt wasn't seeing the road ahead anymore. In his mind, Remi stood with her hands on her hips and fire in her eyes.

He missed that fire so much it hurt.

"I miss you too, princess."

"Good to know 'cause I miss you too. Kids, breakfast will be ready in a minute. Say your good-byes to Uncle Colt and get your teeth brushed."

"Is it a short minute or a long minute?" Abby asked.

"All minutes are the same," Remi said.

"Nu-uh."

Colt was tempted to agree with Abby. Minutes seemed longer this past week. It had everything to do with missing the people he loved. "I'll be home right after you eat lunch."

"That means we have two meals to get through before he'll be here. Let's eat breakfast and build that snowman."

"Bye, Uncle Colt," Ben said. His voice faded away as he ran off.

"I miss you so much," Abby said.

"I miss you too." Good grief, this girl had a hold on him. No way was he getting choked up over a few little words.

"I love you from the top of my heart. And the bottom. My heart is so full!"

Okay, maybe there were going to be tears, but only because there was no one around to see. Who was he kidding? He was a total sap when it came to Abby.

"I love you too. See you lickety split."

"Bye!"

He reluctantly ended the call and gulped more coffee. It was a long drive back to Blackwater, but it might be five hours of quick minutes if he could find Tammy Wynette or Keith Whitley on the radio.

Colt rummaged through a hamper of clean laundry. Where were those slippers? After a day playing in the snow, Abby had her heart set on the pink-and-purple fuzzy slippers Vera had given her a few weeks ago.

"Are they in there?" Abby asked, clearly on the verge of tears.

"Found them!" He knelt to hold the slippers one by one as Abby put her little feet in them.

She wrapped her arms around his neck. "Thank you. I love you."

No one had ever told him love could hit like a kick to the chest. It knocked the breath out of him every time Abby or Ben uttered those little words.

"Colt!" Remi shouted.

He stepped out of the laundry room and bowed. "You rang, princess?"

She rolled her eyes, but a small grin told him she secretly enjoyed being regarded as royalty. "Camille just texted me. Asher and Hunter are playing at Barn Sour tonight." She turned her phone over in her hands. "Would you want to go?"

It had been months since they'd been to Barn Sour. They used to go at least once a month, but he'd completely forgotten that things like going dancing or listening to live music even existed. His new family had consumed his life so thoroughly that the old days had faded away.

"Really? What about the kids?"

Remi shrugged. "I was thinking maybe Stella could come over and put them to bed."

Colt rubbed his chin. "They'd like that. It sounds like fun. We can go if you want."

The growing smile on her face told him that was exactly what she wanted. "Great. I'll ask Stella now."

"I need to get a shower."

Remi already had the phone to her ear. "I'll let you know what she says."

After showering, he threw on a pearl snap shirt and a good pair of jeans. With his Sunday belt on and his hair combed, he rummaged in the cabinet under the sink, finally finding the cologne. He'd used the stuff a total of three times, and two were weddings.

When he stepped out of the bathroom, Stella sat on the couch already absorbed in a game of go fish with Ben.

Stella's brows jumped. "Lord, have mercy. You clean up nice."

Colt adjusted the cuffs of his sleeves. "You see me like this every Sunday."

Stella closed her eyes and inhaled a deep breath. "You don't smell like that on Sundays."

Remi's bedroom door opened, and she stepped out wearing a brown sweater and jeans that fit her curves. She pushed her hair over one shoulder, and his gaze landed on the smooth skin of her neck. She was killing him slowly, and he wasn't opposed to dying if it came at Remi's hands.

She slid her phone into her pocket and glanced at him before quickly looking away. "You ready?"

Ready for what? "Huh?"

She stopped in front of him. "To go. Are you ready to go?"

"Oh, yeah. I'm ready. Just need to get my boots."

Remi bent to kiss both of the kids while pulling one of his flannel shirts over her sweater. "Good night. Be good for Miss Stella."

"We will," Abby said as she laid her baby doll on the couch and adjusted a blanket over it.

Colt put on his boots and took his turn telling the kids good-bye. When they walked out of the cabin, the silent night hung in the air between them.

"Are we really doing this?" Remi asked on the way to the truck.

"I'm not sure, but I think it's happening. The kids didn't even try to talk us out of it."

"They love Stella, and she's just as energetic as they are. They know they'll have a good time."

Colt held the truck door open for Remi. "What about us? I'm not sure I remember how to have adult-only fun."

Remi patted his shoulder, then let her hand slide down his chest. "I think we'll remember."

His body definitely remembered how to send off all the alarms whenever Remi touched him. Sparks fired off all over his chest, and his mouth watered. If they spent the evening dancing, he might spontaneously combust.

Remi talked the whole way to Barn Sour. She filled him in on everything that had happened in the week he'd been gone. More than half the stories had her laughing as she told them, so that was a good sign.

When they pulled up at Barn Sour, Remi checked the clock on her phone. "What time are we planning to leave?"

"We just got here, and you're already planning to leave."

"I'm not planning to leave now."

"I think that's exactly what you're doing. Right now, you are planning when and how we will leave."

She huffed as she slid out of Colt's truck. He jogged a few steps to catch up to her, and she leaned into his side as he wrapped an arm around her.

"We'll leave whenever you're ready. Just give me the signal."

She looked up at him and tugged on her earlobe. They'd had a secret signal for years. It was their silent call for help if one of them needed saving from a conversation, but they'd used it as a signal when they were ready to leave wherever they were without announcing it to everyone.

Half a dozen people greeted them as soon as they stepped inside. Ridge and Cheyenne waved from a booth on the left, and Camille and three other Hardings waved from a table closer to the stage. Asher and Hunter were checking equipment and talking to Grady in his typical overalls and work boots.

Remi slid into the empty seat across from Ridge and Cheyenne. "Is this seat taken?"

"Now it is." Cheyenne scooted her water glass to the side. "We didn't know y'all were coming."

"We didn't either until half an hour ago," Remi said.

Colt punched Ridge's shoulder and sat beside Remi. "I haven't heard Asher and Hunter play in a while."

"I've missed this," Remi said. "I mean, I miss it, but I'm glad we have the kids. More than glad. They're definitely better than hanging out at a bar. You know what I mean?"

Colt wrapped an arm around her shoulders and pulled her in close. "We know what you mean. No need for all the rambling."

"Yeah. Parents need time to have fun on their own every once in a while. Who's keeping the kids?" Cheyenne asked.

"Stella," Remi and Colt said in unison.

Cheyenne waved a hand. "Oh, well you might as well stay out all night. The kids are entertained and cared for."

The waitress stopped at their table and propped her hands on the edge. "What can I get you?"

They both ordered water, and Colt stood to take off his coat. "You ready to get started?"

Remi laughed. "We just got here."

"I know, and I plan to take advantage of every second. On your feet, woman."

Remi scooted out of the bench seat and took off Colt's flannel shirt. "Geez. No one told me husbands were so bossy."

Colt picked up Remi's hand and threaded his fingers with hers. "I've been away for a week. That's seven whole days. Didn't you miss me?"

She followed him for a few seconds before racing ahead, leading him toward the dance floor. The upbeat country song vibrated in his veins, but the tingle where his palm touched Remi's overshadowed the sounds until all he heard was a dull roar.

As soon as she stepped onto the dance floor, she pulled him in, falling into a two-step. Apparently, dancing was like riding a bike because Remi hit every step he gave. The smile on her face grew until she laughed, throwing her head back and letting her hair tumble over her shoulders as they swayed. He pulled her closer with each song, and she didn't pull away. He always wished for more between them, but for once, she wasn't putting him in his place.

By the fifth song, she made the move and inched closer. If they kept this up, he'd burn alive before the night was over.

CHAPTER 27

REMI

R emi twirled into Colt's arms, landing securely against his chest as the song ended. Tilting her chin up, she halted as Colt's dark eyes raked over her face. The deep swells of his chest moved against her, and she fought to take in one decent breath.

She'd missed him, but absence wasn't enough to bring on the storm building inside her.

Colt slowly brushed a hand up her neck, trailing the pad of his thumb over her jaw. He held her gaze, and she forced a shallow breath. A staring contest. Now? She couldn't take it.

His fingers slid into her hair, and the intensity of his stare burned hotter.

The truth sucked out the last bit of air in her lungs. He was going to kiss her, and she'd never wanted anything like she wanted his lips on hers.

Not a drink, not a drug. Colt. She wanted Colt. She wanted him heart, body, and mind.

A choice stared her in the face: win the contest or take that first step toward a life with Colt.

She broke the stare and looked at his lips. She'd made her decision, and there were no regrets. She chose Colt and waited for him to make the next move.

Instead of kissing her, he tipped her chin up, bringing her gaze back up to his.

He brushed his thumb over her cheek, adoring her like they were the only people in the room. "I love you."

Remi's gasp could be heard over the shuffle of people as the dancers waited for the next song. Love. He loved her. She'd known it, but something inside her clicked into place.

He took a deep breath. "I love you, and I'm saying it in public because I'm hoping you won't make a scene."

She laughed. Laughed!

The color in Colt's face drained.

She grabbed his arm, pulling his hand from her hair. "Can we go home?"

Colt nodded and led the way back to the table where she gulped half the glass of water before grabbing Colt's flannel shirt. He held it while she slid her arms in.

When he waved at Ridge and Cheyenne on the

dance floor, Remi grabbed his other hand, squeezing it in hers.

Wait. Please wait for me. Could he feel her plea?

The ride home was quiet, but she kept her hand in his. Her firm grip begged him to hang on.

They quietly slipped into the cabin where Stella raised up from the couch where she'd been dozing.

She stretched and stood. "You're home early."

Remi shrugged. "It was fun, but I got homesick."

Stella patted Remi's shoulder as she headed toward the door to slip on her shoes. "Call me any time you want to go out. The kids are no problem at all."

"Thanks for coming over."

"It was my pleasure." Stella winked at Colt over her shoulder as she reached for the door.

"See you tomorrow," Colt said as he opened the door for Stella.

When the silence settled in the cabin, neither of them moved until the rumble of Stella's engine faded.

Colt kept his hand on the doorknob when he looked up at Remi. She'd taken a small step at Barn Sour, but he'd gone all in with a moon landing sized jump.

He loved her, and she could finally see the impact of that love. It had prompted her to announce their engagement, pushed her to marry him, and forced her to realize that he'd been silently showing her that love for years.

She pulled his flannel shirt tighter around her as she took one step toward him. "About what you said—"

"We don't have to talk about it," he whispered.

Remi shook her head. "I want to talk about it." She inhaled a shaky breath and took that big leap beside him. "Because I love you too."

There were two excruciating seconds before Colt stormed toward her. Her stomach tumbled as he lifted her into his arms. She hooked her legs around him only a moment before her back pressed against the wall. Her body was entwined with his—arms and legs wrapped around him as he stopped an inch from pressing his mouth to hers.

The dark of his eyes dilated until the brown disappeared. His deep voice shook as he whispered, "Remi, I love you so much it kills me."

She tightened her arms and legs around him. "Thank you."

A playful smile flashed on his face in the second before his mouth crashed into hers. She might have just made a joke about her terrible response to his incredibly sweet vows, but this kiss was nothing like the one that had sealed them as husband and wife.

No, Colt's kiss was a thunderstorm with no warning, ripping up the long-held roots of her inse-curities. One hand spread across the width of her back while the other pushed into her hair, cradling her face as he confessed his long-held desire. He'd been holding back this fire behind a wall the size of the Hoover Dam all these years, and she'd been missing out on this. *They* had been missing out on this.

When she couldn't gasp enough air, she pulled away, but Colt moved to her neck, placing soft kisses up the tender skin and over her jaw. The small brushes of his lips did nothing to help regain her breath.

After he'd kissed her enough to drive out all other thoughts, he locked his gaze with hers and breathed, "You. Are. Perfect."

They were the same words he'd written to her before he left town, but the full meaning seemed conceivable now. Whether she saw any good in herself or not, Colt saw it and believed it with his whole heart.

"Is this what it's like to be your wife?"

His mouth quirked up in a one-sided grin. "I tried to tell you I loved you years ago."

It was true. He'd loved her all this time, and she could see the truth now with a bittersweet longing for everything they'd missed out on. "I should have listened." She gasped. "Speaking of being your wife, I have a surprise for you."

His eyes widened, and he held her tighter. "What is it?"

"You have to let me go so I can get it."

He narrowed his eyes at her. "I'm torn. I want to know what the surprise is, but probably not enough to let you go."

She squirmed in his embrace. "Trust me, you want to see this."

He rested her on her feet, and she reluctantly left the warmth of his arms. In the bedroom, she rummaged in the old leather purse that she hardly carried. She pulled what she wanted out of the wallet and hid it behind her back as she jogged back into the living room.

"Close your eyes."

Colt did as he was instructed and held out his hands.

She pressed the card into his palms, and he opened his eyes.

"A card?" He held it up and read the first line. "Your social security card! It says Remington Walker!"

Remi slapped a hand over his mouth. She pushed thoughts of the way that mouth moved perfectly over hers from her mind. "Will you celebrate silently? You'll wake the kids."

His eyes were still comically wide as she let her hand fall from his mouth. She'd been hoping to surprise him, but his love declaration had already taken the spotlight this evening.

"You changed your name." He stared at the card

he held with gentle fingers. "You didn't have to do that."

"I wanted to. I'll be Remington Walker for the rest of my life. It was time to make it official."

He continued to stare at the card. Who could have guessed something so small could make him so happy?

"Your name is Remington Jo. Why have I not been calling you that all this time?"

Remi scrunched up her nose. "Because it sounds ridiculous."

He wrapped an arm around her waist and pulled her in. "Remi Jo Walker has a nice ring to it."

She playfully pushed at his chest. She'd never cared for her middle name, but Colt made it sound almost sweet.

Remi played with the cuff of the flannel shirt she wore. "I've been thinking about something else too, but it might be a little over-the-top for tonight."

Colt held up the card. "I'm not sure anything could top the L-word and this."

She tilted her head back and forth. To say it or not to say it?

"Come on. Spit it out. I can't take the suspense."

"Do you want to sleep in the bedroom?"

Colt adjusted the hold he had on her waist and lifted her into a football hold. She yelped and slapped a hand over her mouth.

"I was wrong. Official best day ever."

Remi pushed her hair out of her face and punched his leg. "Put me down. We have things to talk about."

He set her on her feet right inside the bedroom and tossed the social security card onto the dresser. "Yes. Talk. We should do that. You start."

Remi held up a warning finger. "Sleep. Nothing else."

Colt nodded, probably rattling his brain in his skull. "Got it. No touching."

"I'm serious, Colt."

His shoulders sank, but a grin spread on his mouth. "I know. I'm serious too. I can totally sleep next to you without ravishing you."

Remi narrowed her eyes at him. "I do love the new kissing development, but I'm not ready for...everything."

Colt wrapped his arms around her shoulders, squeezing her cheek to his warm chest. "I understand. I don't think we're ready either. Nothing has to be fast. We're already married, which means we have the rest of our lives together."

A quiet knock on the bedroom door had both of them turning their heads. Abby stood in the doorway, clutching Bun Bun to her chest.

Colt released his hold on her and crouched in front of Abby. "Hey, sweetie. What's wrong?"

The pitiful frown on Abby's face was enough to break Remi's heart. The nightmares had been less frequent lately. She opened her arms, and Abby stepped into the embrace.

"You know how you told me not to say hate anymore?"

"Yes." Abby's habit of hating everything that didn't go her way was getting out of hand.

Abby's chin quivered. "Well, I woke up because I had a nightmare, and I was talking to Bun Bun, and..."

"And what?" Colt asked, almost as impatient as Remi to hear what Abby had been discussing with Bun Bun in the middle of the night.

"And I told Bun Bun I hate mosquito bites." She wrapped her arm around Remi's neck. "I'm sorry!"

Remi pinched her lips between her teeth and looked over Abby's shoulder at Colt. Barely holding in the laughter, she whispered, "It's okay. It's okay."

Colt stood and walked out of the room, clearly about to burst.

"Abby, listen. You're not in trouble, but I do want you to stop hating so much. Maybe try to focus on the things you love, like Bun Bun."

"And you, and Uncle Colt, and Ben."

"Exactly." She rubbed Abby's back. "Actually, I think I need to learn the same lesson."

"Really?"

"Yep. I have trouble focusing on the good sometimes too. It's not easy, but you're doing a great job."

"Thanks." Abby rubbed the back of her hand over her eyes. "Can I sleep with you?"

"Well, Uncle Colt is going to be sleeping with me from now on, so how about I tuck you back in with Bun Bun?"

"That's okay. Bun Bun needs me to sleep with him anyway."

Remi and Abby passed Colt in the living room on their way to her bedroom. Remi gave him a warning glare, daring him to laugh in front of Abby.

He made a show of zipping his lips, but he looked like he was on the verge of bursting. At least Abby's appearance had moved the mood into safe territory before bed.

CHAPTER 28

COLT

"Let it snow! Let it snow! Let it snow!" Abby sang as she skipped toward the dining hall. Small flurries rained down to land on the foot of snow already on the ground.

Ben stepped up onto the porch, climbed onto the railing, and jumped off. His acrobatics were getting more daring by the minute.

Remi leaned closer to Colt as they walked. "I know I've seen you jump off that porch dozens of times, but I lose a year of life every time Ben does it."

Colt chuckled. He knew the feeling all too well. Who would have guessed they'd both be carefree in their early years only to be overly cautious with their kids?

Their kids. The thought never ceased to light a fire inside him. Happiness tingled from his toes to his nape.

"Are you saying you don't care as much about my welfare as you do Ben's, Mrs. Walker?"

She shoved his shoulder and huffed. "You know I don't mean it like that. He's just—"

"He's just going to have to figure out his boundaries on his own. I learned that from a parenting book."

Remi laughed so sharp and loud that it cut through the whipping wind. "I told you that years ago when you didn't want to take that one kid on a trail ride because he always got into trouble."

She had a good memory. Hopefully, she'd learn to overlook his faults. The thought of disappointing Remi was enough to keep him on the straight and narrow most of the time.

"Russell was the bane of my existence. He's nothing like Ben."

"Um, I remember he did a backflip off a boulder by the creek and spooked the horses. Sounds more like a daredevil than a menace."

Why did she have to be right all the time? "Yeah. Maybe I need to have a talk with Ben. If I've learned anything in my old age, it's that we only get one body, and if you abuse it, you have to lie in the bed you made."

Stella drove up and parked beside Colt's truck. Both of the kids retraced their steps to greet her with a hug.

"Those kids are good for all of us. I hope somebody loves me like that in my old age." Remi sighed, and the gentleness in her words was new. Becoming a guardian had no doubt softened her heart. Though, he'd suspected she'd always had a tender heart. She'd just worked non-stop to hide it.

Colt wrapped his arm around her shoulders. "The good news is we'll have someone to take care of us when we're old and grumpy."

"Are you bad-mouthing me, Mr. Walker?" Stella said as she walked up the porch steps.

"I wouldn't dare. I was talking about my retirement plan."

Stella let out one sharp laugh. "Retirement is overrated. What in the world would you do with all that time?"

Colt ran through a list of things he'd like to do instead of work. All of them included Remi and the kids. Going back to the rodeo wasn't even on the list. "You ever thought about retiring?" he asked Stella.

"Not once." She waved a hand in the air. "I never worked when Charles was alive. I did all my social calling in my younger years. Work here feels more like settling down."

Colt gently nudged Remi with his elbow. "You could take up dating. I've heard online dating is like a competitive sport these days."

"Pam Bruner has started one of those dating profiles, and her stories are always entertaining.

Maybe I'll pick it up just to make things interesting every once in a while."

Colt's phone buzzed in his pocket, and he pulled it out. "Hey, this is Camille." He jerked his head toward the front office, hoping Remi would follow him so they could talk to Camille together.

Remi turned to Stella and asked if she'd get the kids started on supper. By the time he answered the call, Remi was by his side.

"Hello."

"Hey, is this a good time?"

"Sure." He stepped to the side so Remi could enter the office, then shut the door behind her. "Remi's here too."

"Hey!" Remi wrapped his corduroy jacket tighter around her middle and tucked her hands under her arms. His clothes were ridiculously baggy on her, but they always looked better on her than they did on him.

"Good. Both of you need to hear this. We found Tasha."

Colt choked on air and sputtered for a few seconds. He prayed he was dreaming when the vise around his throat constricted. "Come again?"

"Tasha. And she made quite the entrance. The police just escorted her from my office."

"Nooo." Remi's eyes were wide and disbelieving as she stared up at Colt. "What happened?"

"She got our letter, and she wasn't too happy

about finding out about her sister's death months after the fact."

Colt tried to swallow, but nothing happened. The shock and grief had crippled him when he found out about Mark. If Tasha had a heart at all, she was feeling those same things now, and he wasn't sure if her grief would be as tempered as his had been.

"I'm sorry. You mean she didn't even know Mark and Brittany had died?" Remi asked.

"Seems so." The same confident bite Camille had used in the courtroom tinged her tone now. She'd probably given Tasha a run for her money.

Colt raised the hand not holding the phone in the air. "Don't look at me. I didn't know how to contact her. I haven't seen her in almost ten years." If he didn't see her for another twenty or thirty, it would be too soon.

"What is she doing in Blackwater?" Remi asked. A note of desperation tinged her words. "I thought Brittany was from Newcastle. I guess I just assumed Tasha lived somewhere around there."

"I didn't ask, but that's a really good question. She had the letter with my firm address on it, so I'm assuming that's what brought her here. We didn't get into pleasantries."

"And you had to call the police?" Colt asked. The skin on the back of his neck pricked, and a cold sweat beaded on his back. "I'm sorry you got caught in the middle of this."

"It comes with the job, unfortunately."

"What happened?" Remi asked. The hollow coldness of her voice had Colt reaching an arm around her.

"There was lots of yelling. She said she and Brittany had been working on making things right between them, and that Brittany had mentioned dividing their grandfather's inheritance with her if she got a steady job."

Colt huffed. "Sounds like she was dreaming. Last I heard, Brittany couldn't stand Tasha. They'd been rivals since they were kids."

"Tasha spun a sympathetic story at first. There were tears, but now I can see that it was all an act. When I told her Mark and Brittany's estates were to be settled per their wishes outlined in their Last Will and Testament, she dropped the act. That's when my assistant called the police."

Remi stared up at him and bit her lips between her teeth. He'd hoped to side-step the Tasha train wreck, but it seemed she was determined to barrel into their lives whether they liked it or not.

"Are you okay?" Remi asked.

"I'm fine, but a few office decorations didn't survive her visit. Her temper flipped on like a light, and she was still kicking and screaming when the police forcibly removed her from the premises."

Remi covered her mouth with a hand. Things had been going so well. It looked like it was Tasha's turn to throw a wrench in the plans.

"I should have given you more of a warning," Colt said.

"You did. I shouldn't have underestimated her. People lose their minds when large amounts of money are involved. Add in her obvious drug habits, and you have a recipe for disaster."

"Where is she now?" Remi asked.

"I'm not sure, but it would be wise to keep an ear to the ground. If she's in Blackwater, she might be looking for you two and the kids."

"You think?" Colt rubbed the back of his neck. He didn't want the kids within a hundred miles of Tasha, and not knowing where she was only turned his stomach.

Camille sighed. "There's more. She made some accusations while she was here."

"Accusations? Against you?" Remi asked, disbelieving.

"Not me. Colt."

Colt caught Remi's stare, and her face turned a sickly shade of white. His probably looked the same because the edges of his vision blurred and a chill raced down his spine.

"What?" Remi's question was barely a whisper.

"She claimed her using days were over, but she

said she first met Colt through Mark. She said they were affiliated with the same dealer."

"The same what?" Remi shouted. She tightened her hold on the coat she wore until her knuckles turned the same white as her face.

"She said Colt was a drug abuser. She didn't mention the time frame for the accusation, but she was adamant that you were a user."

Colt shook his head and stared at Remi. "I'm not. I've never touched a drug. I've never even smoked a cigarette."

"She said your dad was an alcoholic, and that you and Mark had followed in his footsteps."

When Colt pushed a hand through his hair, his cold fingertips left a trail of ice. His dad's curse was coming to bite him, and no amount of caution had done him any good. He'd been so careful. No, he'd been terrified to touch anything known for addictive tendencies. If addiction ran in the family the way it had with his dad and Mark, he didn't want to know if he'd been marked too.

Remi shuffled her feet. "She's right about them, but not Colt. He doesn't do any of that. I've known him for years, and I would swear to it before a judge."

Remi had always stood beside him, but was that faith fragile? Camille said Tasha was a force to be reckoned with. Would Remi ever side with someone over him?

"I don't think that will be necessary. She's pulling out all the stops, and I suspect she's trying to slander your name to disrupt the guardianship case."

"Can she do that?" Colt asked. "I mean, we have custody, but she can't reverse that, can she?"

"Custody can be modified if the circumstances are right."

"But it won't be. No one would give her custody, right?" The panic in Remi's voice reverberated through the small office and sank into Colt's skin.

Camille sighed. "She brought screenshots of text messages. Of course, these are inadmissible evidence since the name can easily be modified on the text string, and there are no timestamps, but–"

"But what? Text messages." Colt interrupted when the panic bubbled over the edges of his sanity. "I've never texted with Tasha in my life."

"What do the texts say?" Remi asked.

She wasn't looking at him. Why wasn't she looking at him? Why wasn't she screaming that all of this was stupid? She'd stood up for him a minute ago. Why not now?

"She claimed that she and Colt were once in a romantic relationship."

"No, no, no. No, we weren't. We definitely weren't." His words were hurried, pushed together by fear.

"Colt, prepare yourself for this one. She claims you were physically and verbally abusive."

"What?" His shout echoed through the small office, as Colt backed up until the cold, wooden wall was hard against his back. It was all lies. He'd never do that. No one would believe her.

Except, someone would. If Tasha screamed violence, the crime would sit on his shoulders and be branded into his skin for the rest of his life. Everyone would always wonder if she'd been the one telling the truth. And how could he prove his innocence?

He couldn't. The sad truth stared him in the face as Remi kept her gaze locked on the phone he held. He could see the wheels in her mind turning with every deep breath she inhaled.

"I didn't. I didn't." The feeble confession might as well have been steam, floating into the air and disappearing as if it had never existed.

"Don't panic, Colt. If I'm the only one she told, then the accusations won't go anywhere. If she told the police, that will be another story."

"The police she left with? Yeah, I'm not holding out hope that she suddenly forgot to tell the police about her lies."

He'd skipped breakfast, but acid bubbled in his gut. He was going to be sick, and something was bound to come up.

"Unless she's claiming these texts were sent and

received in this calendar year, I doubt there's a way to retrieve evidence. Cellular service providers can't retain text information that long. Not even a subpoena would help us."

Help. Camille was still willing to help, so that was something. But what about Remi? She stood in the middle of the room, hugging her middle, and looking as sick as he felt.

"Now that she's been vocal about her attacks, we can prepare to counter. Nothing is official yet, but—"

"But prepare for criminal charges? This is crazy. I wouldn't do that." Would his word be enough to save him? Probably not, but would her words be enough to condemn him?

"You're innocent until proven guilty. If there isn't any real proof, the charges could be dismissed. But remember, there are still no formal charges. Don't panic yet."

"Too late. She took the time to bring copies of forged text messages. She's serious. She planned it out." He clawed at the collar of his coat. His throat burned, and the edges of his vision were hazy as he kept his stare on Remi. She hadn't moved.

"I'll send you photos of the texts she brought. Read them carefully and let me know if any of the conversation is authentic."

"I can already tell you it isn't. I promise I've

never texted with her. I don't know her number. I never have."

"You still need to be aware of any and all information we can get our hands on. Read them and come see me. You can set up the appointment with my assistant."

Colt continued to stare at Remi. "You mean both of us, right?" They were a package deal now. At least, he hoped they were. Would she distance herself after this? He could already feel her pulling away, and the loss was cold and lonely.

He couldn't face this without her. He'd crumble. He would fight for her until his dying breath, but fighting for himself alone was an impossible task.

"Colt, I said don't worry until these things come to fruition. It's a moot point if she decides to leave and forget it."

"She won't." The things Camille warned of would come to the door of his home, and there was nothing he could do to stop it. Tasha wasn't afraid to attack her sister, and she sure wasn't afraid of Camille if she threw a fit worthy of law enforcement intervention at her office.

"As your attorney, I need to know the truth. Did you do any of the things she claimed?"

"No. None of them. I barely know her." He couldn't be any more honest than that. He really didn't know her other than what Mark and Brittany had told him. He'd seen the scene she'd made at

Mark and Brittany's wedding, but that was the extent of his knowledge of Tasha.

"Then we'll fight this. I believe you, and her actions prove her instability. She won't get away with this. Do you hear me?"

Colt shook his head. How could he believe her when no one knew for sure what would come of Tasha's accusations? "I hear you, but..."

"Then read the messages and set up an appointment to meet with me. We'll form a defense plan."

Colt swallowed the slicing blades that lined his throat. "Right. We'll do that." His use of the collective was all wishful thinking. Remi might not want to be a part of this. She was innocent, and he wouldn't bring her down with him.

"Good. I'll see you soon."

"Thanks," Remi whispered.

"Always happy to help."

Colt's own thanks died somewhere between his lungs and tongue. Camille ended the call, and he stood frozen, holding the phone that had relayed the end of his hope.

The office was cold and silent. Remi stared at the floor while she held his entire attention. Each vacant second hammered the nail into his coffin. Tasha wanted to bury him alive and take the perfect life he'd somehow stumbled into. And she would do it if he, Camille, and Remi didn't figure out a way to stop her.

"Remi, say something. Please."

She lifted her gaze to him, but her eyes didn't reflect an ounce of recognition. He was losing her, and he couldn't drag her back to the happy bubble of hope they'd been living in.

But he wouldn't give up. He'd hang on, kicking and screaming if necessary.

Colt's phone dinged, then dinged again. The texts from Camille came in, and he opened the photos. He stepped to Remi's side, showing her the images. He scanned the words, searching for any defense.

"I didn't send any of this." On the third photo, one word jumped out at him.

Princess.

Panic was a living, growing thing, pressing against the walls of his veins.

"Remi, I swear I didn't write that. You're the only woman I've ever called princess." He wrapped his hand around her arm, begging her to listen. Why were his words dying as soon as they hit the air? Why wasn't she hearing him?

She was as still as stone as she stared at the screen. That one word was enough to convict him, despite his innocence. How could Tasha have known about his nickname for Remi? She'd been planning this. Could she have found them already? Was she spying? How else could she have known?

Remi looked up at him, and any hope he might

have held on to was gone, snuffed out like a camp-fire doused with water. She looked at him like he was a complete stranger. No love, no gentleness, no kindness.

He released her arm and linked his fingers over his head. Think. Think. What could he say to prove his innocence?

He turned around and tried, "Remi, I–"

She bolted for the door, flinging it open and running toward the truck.

"Remi, stop!" He darted after her, but he wasn't quick enough to grab the door before she closed it behind her. He fumbled with the knob before throwing it open, leaving a wood-splitting thud behind him as he raced after her.

The hem of his jacket flared behind her like a cape as she leapt over the porch steps and into the parking area. He grabbed the porch railing and jumped over, landing hard and tucking into a roll in the snow-covered gravel. He was on his feet again without breaking momentum, but Remi had already made it to his truck.

"Remi, please." The rasp was desperate–a crip-pling plea. If she was having a level-ten freak-out, he couldn't let her sink too far into her own head.

She'd never had anyone in her life who loved her the way he did, and the same was true for him. No one in this world knew him the way Remi did, and if she doubted him, the whole world would crumble.

The truck door slammed the second before he crashed into it. He grappled for the door handle and jerked, but nothing moved.

"Remi, please. I swear it's not true." He pounded the side of his fist against the window. "Remi!"

Her auburn hair fell in a sheet beside her face, hiding her from his assessing stare. The screams burned his throat as she started the engine and shifted into reverse.

He held onto the door handle as the truck backed up. Remi jerked the vehicle in a hard left, and he lost the grip he had on the handle. She flipped into gear, sending the tires spinning as she headed down the trail. He ran beside the truck, but she easily left him behind. Panting, he looked around, searching for a way to follow her.

Vera stepped out of the dining hall, wiping her hands on her apron. "What's going on?"

He ran toward her. "Can I borrow your car?"

Vera shook her head, eyes wide and frightened. "I didn't drive today. Stella dropped me off this morning."

Colt pushed past her and burst through the double doors of the dining hall. Stella and the kids sat at a table closest to the door.

Her signature smile faded the moment she saw him. "What's going on? Where's Remi?"

"Can I borrow your car? She left, and I need to go after her."

"Remi left?" Abby asked.

Colt held out his hand. "Hurry. I need to go."

Stella snapped out of her shock and fumbled in her small bag. After what seemed like ten long minutes, she held up a key fob covered in purple sparkles and rhinestones.

"Where did she go?" Stella asked as she handed over the keys.

"I don't know. Can you watch the kids until I get back?"

"Uncle Colt, what's wrong?" It was Ben this time.

"I don't know." Colt pointed to the kids in turn as he backed toward the door. "Be good for Miss Stella."

He didn't wait for a response as he ran after Remi. She might be too far gone, but he wouldn't stop until he found her.

CHAPTER 29
REMI

Remi pushed the accelerator until Colt was only a speck in the rear-view mirror. The deep breath she'd been holding rushed out, coaxing tears in its wake. What was she doing? Where was she going? Stopping at the main road, she looked left and right. One led into town and the other led farther into the wild.

She pressed the heels of her hands into her eyes. *Think. Think.* The urge to bolt had smacked her in the face on a whim, and once she'd taken that first step, she had to commit.

Her mind had made itself up, hadn't it?

Obviously not, because she looked left and right again. Where was she going?

Away from Colt. That thought pierced her heart.

The moments alone forced her to really consider

her direction. She could still go back, but what would she say? What would he say? He'd tell her again that the simple word–that endearment that she held on to–was only hers. But did she believe it? He'd been calling her princess since the beginning. Had she always been one of many? She wanted to be special and worthy, just this once.

Everything inside her said Colt wasn't like that. He'd treated her like a prize, and while she'd been afraid to enjoy the attention, he'd always given it without pause.

Gripping the steering wheel, she recalled his kiss from earlier. He'd gotten up early to help Jess check the troughs and feed the horses. When he barreled back into the house later in the morning, he'd swept her up into a toe-curling kiss. The pounding of her pulse in her ears had been deafening as Colt's healing kiss swept over her. He'd been opening her heart over the last few months, and he'd painstakingly patched the wounds others had left behind. The chains around her heart were falling, one by one, taking with them the pain and scars of the past. It had all been erased in the wake of Colt's love.

The shock of Camille's call and the text messages after were enough to throw those walls back up, but a small, pleading part of her hoped it was all a misunderstanding. How could it be? The one endearment Colt held for her was sitting menacingly in the midst of those texts.

The old saying that it was better to have loved and lost than never loved at all was so wrong. She'd gone through life without opening herself up to hurt, and as a result, none of the things people had done to her in the past had hurt like this. The pain was shattering.

Remi rested her forehead against the steering wheel and closed her eyes. She needed to make a decision.

She whispered a prayer into the quiet cab. "God, please lead me. Help me see the truth. I don't know who to trust, and I'm lost." Lost was an understatement, but hopefully the Lord knew what was going on.

With a resigned breath, she lifted her head and pulled her phone from her back pocket. One name came to mind, and she pressed the button to call. It was a call for help. A call for wisdom and understanding.

"Hello."

"Hey, where are you?"

"I was just about to head home. Are you okay?" The friendly voice was a comfort and a reassurance that things might not be as bad as she feared.

"No. Can I come see you?" Remi's voice was as tender as a child's. She was seven again and hiding in the bathroom with her knees tucked close to her chest and her hands over her ears. The screaming on the other side of the door made it impossible to hear her own thoughts.

"Sure. I'll be here. See you in a bit."

Remi ended the call and turned left. With a destination in mind, she headed into town and parked in front of Camille's office. If Colt came looking for her, he'd spot his truck in plain sight, but she wanted at least a few minutes to meet with Camille alone.

Pushing open the door, Remi stepped into the vestibule. The old house had been converted into an office, and the former living room was welcoming.

Camille's assistant, Willa, stood from her desk. A strained grin was the focal point of her expression. "I figured we'd be seeing you today."

"At least one of us knew."

Willa jerked her head toward the hallway. "She's expecting you."

Remi nodded. She didn't have the energy for a proper greeting. Her thoughts were tangled up and tied in the current tug-of-war going on in her world.

The young woman waved Remi in. "Can I get you something to drink? Coffee?"

"No, thanks." Remi couldn't stomach a sip of water right now, much less coffee.

Willa knocked gently on Camille's open office door. "Remi is here."

When she stepped into the room, Camille stood and rounded the desk. "Let's go to the lounge."

Remi followed Camille back into the hallway and into a small sitting room. The whole place had the welcoming feeling of a home. Old bedrooms had been converted into offices and conference rooms, but the small touches of domestic life stripped the business of its cold intimidation.

Camille took a seat in a worn-in armchair and gestured for Remi to take the seat beside her. "Is this a business meeting or girl talk?"

"Girl talk," Remi said as she took her seat. Leaning forward, resting her elbows on her knees, she looked at the floor. "I read the texts."

"And what do you think?"

"I don't know. What do you think?"

"Which part makes you question Colt?"

Remi picked at her cuticles and debated. Emotion and her default logic swung through her mind like a pendulum. Which to trust? "Princess."

"I wondered about that part. It's not an overly common endearment, but the conversation around that word negated the sweetness. It seemed out of place."

Remi hadn't bothered to read the whole conversation carefully. The red flag spread over the entire thing, blocking out any rational thought.

"Do you think he had a relationship with her? Do you think he's lying?" Camille asked.

"I don't, but that would mean completely disregarding that word that Colt uses. It was the whole princess thing. He's always called me that."

Camille grinned. "You? A princess?"

Remi rolled her eyes. "I know. It's sarcastic, but I always thought it meant he was holding out hope that I could be something else."

"Like what?"

"Like the typical picture of a princess. The quiet kindness, the selflessness, the honor–I'm so far from those things. I thought it was special. When I saw it in the messages Tasha gave you, it felt like she'd ripped something good away from the happy life we're trying to build."

"It sounds like that's exactly what she wants. Do you really think Colt could call someone else his princess?"

"No. Not really. But is that just because I don't want to believe this?"

"I'm not sure. Colt knows you're really not a fairytale princess. He knows your heart, and though you're not as innocent as a fairytale princess, he sees those gentle traits in you. I don't think that's something he would share with someone like Tasha."

Remi rested her forehead in her hands. "It's so stupid, but Colt is so over-the-top."

Camille laughed. "He's pretty extra, isn't he?"

"You have no idea! He's so caring and soft. He's all the things I should be. But I'm the hardened one."

"It's okay to be different from society's picture-perfect couple. I think the two of you balance out well. I've seen you with the kids. I've seen you working as a team to help others." Camille rested a hand on Remi's shoulder. "I've seen you give up the safe and secure life you had to take in children who were strangers. If that's not selfless and kind, I don't know what is."

"Anyone would have done that."

Camille shook her head. "That's not true at all. You forget that I work in family law. I see the worst of people daily. The injustice is crippling. Parents don't care about their kids. Parents don't give their kids basic needs. Parents neglect them and abuse them, and I get a front-row seat to that painful circus. You and Colt have been a bright light in my career. You took those kids in before you knew about the money. You stopped your lives and jobs in a heartbeat to help Ben and Abby."

There was a moment of silence, and Remi looked up. Tears shone in Camille's eyes, reddening the edges.

"It gave me hope. You gave me hope that I'm not alone in this mission to help families."

Remi swallowed. If only someone like Camille

had been around to fight for Remi in those early years. She hadn't met a single person who cared the way Camille did. "You're doing a great job. I can't imagine how hard it is to see those things over and over again."

Camille tilted her head. "But you did, didn't you?"

Remi looked away, unable to face the full reminder of those hard years. "I deserved it. I asked for a lot of that mess. I ruined my own life."

"You didn't know any better."

"How much do you know about all that? We haven't talked about it, but I've been expecting it to come back to bite me."

"I know enough, but this isn't about you. It's about your trust. I've known Colt for a long time, and he's always been a good guy. I know people can hide their worst from the world, but I don't think the man we know would abuse a woman. People don't change that much."

"But they do. I did!" Remi pointed at her chest. "I was ten times worse than whatever you read in my file. If you can think of something terrible, I probably did it. Except murder. I didn't do that. But I stole, cheated, lied, and hurt people. I did it all on purpose. I was walking destruction, and at the time, I didn't care who I hurt. Colt could have been the same, and I would never be the wiser."

"Have you ever felt like his past didn't add up?

Has he ever told you things that seemed disjointed?"

"No, it's actually the opposite. I believed him whole-heartedly."

"And do you think he's a good enough actor to keep that up for years? Even when you've been married since September?"

Remi sighed. "No. I don't think that."

"What about now? What are *you* like now? I think that's important."

"Now, I'm different. I care too much, and I'm scared to admit it." Remi pushed the heels of her hands into her eyes. "I was Tasha. I was headed down all the wrong roads, mostly the one that led straight away from Heaven. I overdosed. I should have died."

Camille rubbed her hand over Remi's shoulder blade, soothing a hurt so deep that no one had touched it before. "God was saving you for later."

Remi looked up, daring to hope that the words were true. Kendra had saved her, Mr. Chambers had saved her, the kids had saved her.

And Colt. He'd saved her too. Was this all a part of God's plan? It had to be. Nothing else could have put these opportunities in her path.

"I guess you could say that. After the overdose and the rehab, I saw a light at the end of the tunnel. I saw a chance to have some good in my life instead of bad on top of bad on top of bad. And I took it. I held on so tight that nothing mattered more than walking the new path I was desperate to keep." She looked up at Camille. "I'm still not sure it's going to stick. After this, I don't know which way is up."

"We've all been through trauma," Camille said.

"Even you?"

"Even me. I was in a car wreck, and I lost my memories. I didn't know who to trust. I didn't know who was manipulating me into being the person they wanted instead of who I was. I didn't even know who I was, but everyone was trying to tell me."

"Now, that's an identity crisis," Remi admitted.

"It was! I finally realized who I could trust."

"Your husband?"

Camille nodded, and a genuine smile spread over her face. "Noah. He's always been special, and even though I literally forgot him, he helped me remember all of the wonderful times we'd had. We were best friends most of our lives, and he never gave up on me. When I thought he was a stranger, I knew in my heart that he wasn't really."

"I think I know what you mean. Colt has always been the same. He's been there for me since day one, and he hasn't asked for..."

She recalled his vows. He promised never to ask for more than she was willing to give. That vow must have crushed him when he wasn't sure if she would eventually love him or not. Yet he'd been a constant rock in her life.

"Remi, the terrible childhood you went through was more than a kid should ever have to endure. From what I've heard, Colt didn't grow up in a stable home either."

"No, his mom left, and his dad is still an alcoholic." Even though she'd known about his parents, she always imagined a kid version of Colt with a happy-go-lucky smile. Now, she could see that her idea was probably not the reality.

"We all handle things differently. We never want to talk about the things that hurt us. We're always pushing back against it. But the one thing we all want to know is how to overcome it. How to deal with it in our daily life. Sometimes, that means forgiving when it seems unforgivable. Sometimes, that means forgiving yourself."

Remi bit the inside of her cheek. She hadn't forgiven herself because the blame she'd always held was still there. Knowing about forgiveness and putting it into action were two completely different things.

"I thought I was getting better. Moving on. But–"

"But it doesn't seem like you've even learned how to manage the hurt you think you caused yourself. Forgiving your dad for not being around. Forgiving your mom for neglecting you. Forgiving yourself for screwing up as a teenager. All of those things will have to happen before you can make the decision to love yourself the way the Lord loves you. Unconditionally, with and without flaws."

Guilt and shame were ganging up to kick her in the behind, and she deserved it. She'd promised to follow Christ, but she still wasn't living like Christ wanted. She wasn't being good to herself or the people He had put in her life to guide her.

Camille sat up straighter. "And remember, those text messages could have been fabricated a million different ways. She could have changed the name on a number who had really sent her those texts talking about how she deserved to be hit, and she'd be lucky if he took the time to dig a grave when he finally did her in."

Remi flinched. "Okay, I may have skimmed over that part. Colt would never say that, and he would never hit a woman. I know that."

"Princess could have been edited in. If Tasha is here in town, she probably already knows where you and Colt are. Please be vigilant. She could have overheard him call you that out in public. I'm telling you, there are pages of her offenses in the judicial system since the time she claimed Colt said and did this to her."

Remi covered her mouth. How could she have doubted him? How could she have abandoned him when he needed her most? He had to be losing his mind over this. And if Tasha knew where they were, she and Colt needed to be a united front to protect the kids. The thought of that sack of crazy getting anywhere near her family turned her stomach.

"Do some thinking on your own and pray. Please pray for wisdom and understanding. We might not know the answers, but I have no doubt that the truth will come out in time."

Remi nodded. "Thank you. I'm sorry to lay more drama on you after you had to deal with Tasha earlier."

Camille slapped her hands on her thighs and stood. "You're a walk in the park compared to her. A ray of sunshine."

Remi stood, wiping her eyes. "Said no one ever."

"Well, I'm saying it today, and I'm not in the business of lying." Camille wrapped her arms around Remi.

This. This was the kind of truth talk she'd needed. She needed friends who would tell her when she was being stupid. "Thanks again. You probably saved my marriage."

Camille pulled back and laughed. "You have no idea how good it is to hear that."

Remi glanced at the door. "I need to go."

Camille was already pushing Remi toward the door. "Don't wait to be excused. Go find your man and work this out. I'll be fighting for you two from afar, but I'm just a phone call away if you need me."

Remi smiled as she looked over her shoulder. "I'll remember that." She picked up the pace as she neared the door, and practically jogged by Willa at the front desk. Skipping the steps off the porch, she jumped into Colt's truck. She had to hope he'd forgive her for leaving.

CHAPTER 30

COLT

Colt gripped the steering wheel, twisting it in his hands. Remi had only been gone for half an hour, but the minutes had been long and torturous.

She doesn't want to be found.

But she doesn't know the truth.

She doesn't care about the truth.

She doesn't care about you.

Scanning every vehicle on the streets of downtown Blackwater, the last bit of his hope died. Would she have even come into town? What if she went to Jess's? Jess was at the ranch, so that didn't make sense.

Nothing made sense, and that was the bottom line. Tasha was getting her way, even if it was all a lie.

Colt's phone rang, and he answered on the first ring. "Any news?"

"Sorry. She didn't answer my calls either," Jess said. Her usual matter-of-fact tone held a hint of concern, which only managed to level up Colt's worry.

"Thanks. Keep trying. Any ideas about where she would have run off to?"

"I'll let you know if I think of something. My neighbor said Remi hasn't shown up at my place."

Colt scrubbed a hand over his face. She was slip-ping through every crack, falling through his fingers like water. "Thanks."

Jess ended the call, and he dropped the phone into the cupholder of Stella's car. Remi had left the ranch, so she had to be in town somewhere. Maybe she went to the church. The doors were locked, but driving by was worth a shot. He headed out of town, back toward the ranch. The small church was covered in a white layer of snow, and there wasn't a single tire track in the snow-covered parking lot.

The steeple jutted into the blue sky, reminding Colt to ask for help when things looked darkest. He turned the car toward the ranch and prayed as he drove. The helplessness that vibrated under his skin diminished centimeter by centimeter. He wasn't any closer to finding Remi, but the Lord seemed to be telling him to sit tight.

His phone dinged with a message as he turned

back into the ranch.

Camille: She's on her way home.

Colt let out a rough sigh. She'd been with Camille. What did that mean? The heads-up implied at least a little trust from Camille, but did that extend to Remi too?

Where would she go when she got back to the ranch? She'd left him at the dining hall, so maybe she'd expect him to still be there considering she ran off in his truck.

He huffed. His truck. Since they'd been married, he'd started thinking of everything he owned to be hers too. *He* was hers. Now, all of those carefully tied connections had been undone like slipknots.

He parked in front of the dining hall and trudged inside. The large room was nearly empty. The summer crowds were gone, and only the year-round workers remained. No sign of Stella and the kids, but Brett, Jameson, and Ava sat at a table near the serving bar.

Ava stood. "Did you find her?"

Colt tossed his hat onto the table and sat beside Brett. "She's on her way."

"Where'd she go?" Brett asked.

"To talk to Camille."

"What happened?" Ava's soft question held a dozen more. Remi was known to make quick decisions, but she stuck to them. If she wanted to leave, she was long gone.

"Where to start? I told you about Brittany's crazy sister, Tasha? Well, she's here, and she knows about Mark and Brittany's inheritance. She showed up at Camille's office and threw a fit. Then she accused me of..." The blood in Colt's veins burned hotter. He'd been so worried about Remi's mad dash that he hadn't stopped to let his anger at Tasha fester. "She said we used to date and that I abused her."

"That's a load of crap," Brett said around a mouthful of bread.

"Thanks for the quick support, but Remi wasn't so convinced."

Ava sat slowly. "She couldn't really think you'd do that, right?"

"She seemed like she didn't believe it. But Tasha showed up with some screenshots of text messages she said I sent. They're terrible, and completely fake."

"So, Remi had to know they were fake," Jameson said.

Colt held up a finger. "You'd think, but somewhere in that long string of lies, Tasha added in a landmine. Princess."

"Nooo," Ava said. "How?"

"Beats me!" Colt scratched furiously at his head. "I have no idea! Remi has always been my princess, and no one else. Tasha either got lucky with that nickname or she's been watching us."

"You said she's here in Blackwater?" All of the color had drained from Ava's face.

Colt looked from Jameson to Ava, remembering the times when their home had been in danger. "Yeah, and I know that means the ranch might not be safe. I had no idea until today, but I won't blame you if you want us to leave until this is sorted out."

Ava shook her head. "No, we've dealt with threats before. We'll keep our eyes open."

Colt hung his head. "Where are the kids?"

"With Stella and Vera at their place," Ava said.

"I bet they were scared."

Ava's soft hand rested on his shoulder. "They were, but I'm sure Stella and Vera are keeping them occupied."

Brett waved a roll in the air. "Tell me more about this dumpster fire."

"Tasha. She's a piece of work. She found out that Mark and Brittany weren't actually living in eternal debt, and she wants a piece of the pie. Or all of it. I'm sure she wants all of it."

"Wait, I thought Mark and Brittany were broke too," Brett said.

"Welcome to the club. I only found out a couple of weeks ago that they'd gotten an inheritance from Brittany's grandparents earlier this year."

"Plot twist!" Brett shouted. "So, the kids got that money?"

"Yep. Remi and I already decided not to touch it

unless we have to. We'd rather save it for them, you know?"

"That's great," Ava said. "But people are greedy, so I can see why Tasha is causing trouble."

"Brittany always said her sister was a druggy. It seems Tasha doesn't like change."

"Unless it comes with money," Brett added.

"She didn't even know her sister had died. For months!" Colt hadn't talked to his brother every day or even every week, but it wouldn't have taken him months to find out his brother had died.

Brett slapped a hand on Colt's shoulder. "You're a good brother. I mean, I would know if something happened to Jess, but anyone else in my family, I probably wouldn't get the memo if one of them kicked the bucket."

"Brett!" Ava gasped. "You don't talk to your family?"

"Nope. Just Jess."

"And Jess doesn't either?" Colt was suddenly shocked out of his own problem by Brett's confession. Colt and Remi weren't the only ones with parent problems.

"Jess doesn't either. They're different. Living in a different world. Jess and I keep our distance for the good of all."

Ava shook her head. She'd dealt with her fair share of family problems, including a father she hadn't known about until only a few years ago. "Families. I love mine, but the secrets..."

"Addiction," Colt added.

"Neglect," Jameson said.

"Murder."

Everyone stopped and looked at Brett.

Brett shrugged. "I'm sorry. Murders. Plural."

Colt pinched the bridge of his nose. "I'm sorry. I don't think I can comprehend your family problems right now."

Ava spread her hands on the table. "Why are people so cruel?"

"Beats me," Brett said.

"But you and Jess are so normal," Colt said.

Brett forked the last piece of chicken on his plate. "I'll take that as a compliment."

"I guess it shows that people can hide a lot of hurts," Ava said.

Colt checked his phone. How long would it take Remi to get here? "Remi's one of those, but I'm hoping her story doesn't include murder."

The dining hall door opened, and Colt turned around. Remi stood framed in the doorway wearing his flannel shirt.

Every nerve ending in his body stood at attention. He rose to his feet and fisted his hands at his side. He wanted to grab her and kiss her senseless. He wanted to beg her to stay, beg her to listen.

But she'd left, and that meant she probably

didn't want any of those things, no matter how much it hurt him.

"Where have you been, young lady?" Brett shouted and pointed a finger at Remi. "Don't look at me in that tone of voice."

Ignoring Brett's attempt to diffuse the tension, Remi let her hand fall from the doorknob and took one step into the dining hall. Colt moved to meet her, but it wasn't the furious rush he wanted. He closed the distance between them in slow, careful steps, afraid she'd run away like a scared animal again.

When he stopped in front of her, she glanced up at him before looking back at the floor. She bit the side of her bottom lip and pulled his shirt tighter around her.

The hurt of her retreat. The sting of her rejection. The anger of her dismissal. Every bit of it hit hard and all at once.

But the tears in her eyes said there was something he didn't understand, and he wouldn't find out if he lashed out at her.

"I looked everywhere for you," he whispered.

She looked up at him again and let out a deep exhale. "Can we talk?"

Colt reached for her hand, desperate for a link and an anchor. He brushed the pad of his thumb over her soft skin and nodded. "I thought you'd never ask."

CHAPTER 31

REMI

Remi stalked into the silent cabin, walked straight to the far wall, and turned around to pace the length again. The ride to the cabin had been quiet, but everything bubbled and boiled beneath the surface, threatening to erupt like a destructive and messy volcano.

She stopped in front of Colt, handed him the keys to his truck, and turned to pace again. He was waiting. She had to say something. Why were the words building and clogging in her throat?

Colt tossed the keys onto a table beside the couch and sat down. With his elbows propped on his knees, he rested his forehead in his hands.

Okay, so he wasn't going to rush her. Good, because she hadn't figured out where to start. She moved her pacing to the living room and tracked back and forth in front of the fireplace.

Colt didn't move. Why wasn't he panicking like she was?

Camille's words came back to her.

We've all been through trauma.

We all handle things differently.

Remi stopped and looked at Colt. He raised his head, and for the first time, she got a look at the pain he was hiding. The happiness she'd known and loved for so many years was gone, replaced by a haunted stranger. And she'd been the cause of at least a part of the hurt.

She opened her mouth to speak, but the words didn't come out. She tried a second time, and the attempt wasn't much better.

"I...I know you didn't do it." The heaviness behind her eyes seeped out, and her chin quivered. "I know you didn't do what she said you did."

Colt looked down, only marginally relieved by her words. The wound ran deeper than she'd expected.

She twisted her ring around her finger. "I know you wouldn't hurt anyone. Not on purpose. You're not capable of hurting a spider, much less a person."

He lifted his head again and glanced up at her before turning his attention to the cold fireplace. "I didn't do any of it. I didn't have a relationship with her. I didn't text her. I didn't hurt her. I most definitely didn't call her princess."

Remi nodded, sure that he was telling the truth.

"I believe you. And I'm so sorry I didn't stay and tell you that from the start."

"I don't know how she knows what I call you, but I swear I never said it to her or anyone else."

Remi sucked in a shaky breath, fighting with everything she had not to turn into a blubbering, sobbing idiot at his feet. She sat beside him, leaving a safe distance between them, and directed her thoughts toward the things she needed to say.

"I don't trust a lot of people. And that's silly because I'm the one who shouldn't be trusted."

Colt turned to look at her. "I've always trusted you."

"I know. That was stupid on your part."

Colt huffed and turned his attention back to the floor. "I still do."

She tried to swallow, but the knot in her throat was unmoving. "Maybe that means I still have a shot."

"A shot at what?"

"Being honest with you. I haven't done that before—not really."

Colt waved a hand in the air. "Be my guest."

She scooted back on the couch, turned to face him, and tucked her feet under her. "Here it goes. I was born in Idaho. I don't even know where. I've just seen my birth certificate. I don't remember my dad. I don't remember when he left. All I know is that mom told me once that he has kids all over the

country, and he doesn't care about any of them."
Remi shrugged. "I was about ten when she told me
that, and I still don't know what to think of it. On
one hand, it validated my theory that no one cared
about me. It almost made it the norm."

"When you say 'On one hand,' it implies there's
another hand."

"If no one cared about me, then it was strange
when someone *did* care."

Colt's brow furrowed. "I care."

"I know. I just couldn't understand why." She
waved a hand in the air, trying to get back to the
part she needed to tell. "My mom had a revolving
door of men in her life. They weren't all terrible
guys, but things never lasted long with any of them.
My mom was a charmer. Men fell at her feet, and
they fell hard. But Mom's attention always ran out,
and the fallout was always epic."

"You sure she was your mom? You have none of
that thirst for drama."

Remi huffed. "Like I said, it's on the birth certificate, or I would have questioned it myself. Anyway,
some of them were bad. Not just a little bit bad.
They were terrible, and the fights with Mom usually
got physical."

Colt reached out his big hand and squeezed her
knee.

"Some of them hit me." Remi wiped her eyes on
the sleeve of Colt's shirt she wore.

Colt pulled her closer to him, wrapping his arms around her. "Remi, I–"

"I don't want to talk about it. At least not in detail. I don't think any good could come from that."

He nodded. "Okay."

Remi pulled back a little, determined to do exactly what she'd said she'd do and open up to him. "Basically, Mom's main focus was her dating life. She loved men a lot, and she didn't care about me all that much. I got special attention when she wanted to show her current boyfriend that she was the perfect mom, but she didn't do much for me. I had to learn to do things on my own, and I did. The state took me from her when I was eleven, and she never tried to get me back."

"Remi, I'm sorry."

She shook her head. "It was actually a relief. I didn't have to worry about trying to please her anymore. The pretending was over. I'd been pretending to be the quiet, content daughter I thought she wanted, and I didn't have to do that anymore. From then on, I did everything wrong."

Colt chuckled. "Everything? Maybe you are dramatic."

Remi ticked off the list on her fingers. "Lying, sneaking out, drinking, smoking, stealing, vandalizing, influencing the other kids to do the terrible things I did. I was awful."

"You know, you told me that stuff before we got married, but I still can't believe it."

Remi shrugged. "Believe it, because it's true. I wasn't ever arrested, but I should have been. I stole from foster families all the time. I never saw anything formally documented, but it happened. Some of the families were nice, but that didn't stop me from causing trouble."

"Maybe I should have been calling you trouble instead of princess."

"It would have been more accurate, that's for sure." The truth hurt, but it was her own fault. She'd made a bed, and now she had to lie in it.

Colt squeezed her knee again. "I told you none of that matters to me."

"I know you said that, but it should matter. I bet you've always been a straight edge, but I haven't. What could you possibly want with me?"

Colt sat up straighter. "Everything. A life, love, kids, the works. I want everything with you."

"That's insane, Colt. Do you hear yourself?"

"I do. I haven't always been a good guy, but just because I haven't stolen or cheated doesn't mean you're worse than me. I'm not perfect, and neither are you. We're the same."

"We are not the same."

"We're the same, whether you want to accept it or not."

Remi stared at Colt. His words were so final and full of truth. He really believed they were equal.

"I overdosed." She hesitated, letting the confession sink in. "I almost died. I should have died."

"No."

Colt's sharp retort didn't phase her.

"Yes. I could have. I was supposed to come that close to death to see what could happen." She stood and threw her hands in the air. "I could have died without knowing God. I could have died before I had another chance to make things right."

Colt stood, squaring up with her. "You just said you had another chance to make things right. Why can't you believe that it's already happened?"

She looked up at him, and the fire left her. "I do. It just took a lot of convincing, I guess." She took a few steps away and fought to sort out her racing thoughts. "When I woke up from the overdose, a woman was there. Kendra. She kept coming by my room, and she was so unbelievably nice! I hated it at first. Then, I wanted it to be real. She said the nicest things, and she asked me how I was doing. She seemed to really care."

"And did she?" Colt asked.

"She did. She told me she didn't have anything better to do than talk to me, but I found out later that she had a husband and kids who were about to give her grandbabies. She had a job. She had a life! And she was still hanging out with me."

Colt rubbed a hand over his jaw. "Kendra from Deano's Diner?"

"Yep. I found out later that she used to be me. She'd almost lost her life to drugs, but she turned things around. And I selfishly wanted that. She helped me get into a rehab, and by the time I got out, I believed I could beat it. That I could be like her."

"I had no idea. She's worked at the diner for as long as I can remember. She goes to church with Grady. Her kids are older than us."

"She's been clean for over thirty years."

"And you?"

"Four. I'm still not convinced this dream life is going to stick."

"That's up to you. But the dream life is always there."

"I get that now. Kendra read the Bible to me. Over and over. And it all went over my head at first. Then I started asking questions, and all of it seemed too good to be true. I'd never heard of any of it before. Forgiveness? Washing away my sins? Nothing could do that."

"Except Jesus."

"Except Jesus," Remi repeated. "I know He forgave me for all that stuff, but I still forget sometimes. After all that praying Kendra did for me, I still stumble. A lot."

"Welcome to the club," Colt joked.

Remi rolled her eyes. "You always do the right thing. You have no room to talk."

"The fact that you think I'm infallible is ridiculous."

"I want you to do something wrong for once just so I can know you're human."

Colt shook his head. "Give me time. I'm bound to screw up."

"Screwing up is *my* job."

Colt pulled her into his arms, and she rested her cheek against his chest. The comfort of this home–where her body and soul belonged–soothed all of the old wounds.

"If we mess up, we mess up together," Colt whispered.

"I guess so."

"I know so."

Remi lifted her head and wiped her face. "After the rehab, Kendra got me a job here. She got me in touch with a good therapist–someone who truly cared. She got me into church, and I gave my life to Christ." She paused as the truth hit her. "I'm not doing a very good job of being a good Christian."

"Stop that. Everyone has moments of weakness. Everyone backslides."

"I know I'm not that person I used to be anymore, but those mistakes still haunt me. That's what happened today. I know you're a good man, but I was afraid you'd lived a double life like I had–

one bad and one spent making up for the bad. So this is all part of my grand apology for running out on you today when you needed me most."

"Why didn't you tell me all of this?"

"Because you would never look at me the same way again. Don't you see? I'm scared of ghosts. All the people who should have cared about me, they left me. And they left me a little more broken. Then, I was just a mess of what they'd left. The parts they didn't want. That's why I couldn't open my heart and give myself to someone like you. Because I'm garbage–the trash other people left behind."

He pulled her back to him. "Stop. I won't let anyone talk about you like that, including you. You're not those things." He lifted her chin until she was looking straight up into his eyes. "Don't you get it? I want your mind, body, heart, and soul. My life is better with you in it, and I'd take a lifetime of torture over a day without you."

His words sank into her skin, wrapped their letters around her heart, and filled her with the truth of his love. She smiled, feeling the ease of their friendship seep back into the conversation. "That's very poetic of you."

He slid his hand up the side of her neck, trailing his thumb over her cheek. His touch was as soft and gentle as a warm breeze. "I love you more than I love breathing. I don't need air. I need you. My love is unconditional. You need to accept that. I'm not going anywhere."

Remi bit her lips between her teeth. How could she accept something she didn't understand?

But she did understand it. Or she was trying to. The Lord loved her despite her faults, and Colt was telling her he could do that too. It pressed against the old ideas she'd held about love and devotion, but maybe it was as real as Colt thought it was. There were many forms of forgiveness and grace that she'd never understand, but Colt was showing her that he could give her the family she never had growing up. He was giving her a do-over but better.

Colt wrapped an arm around her waist and pulled her in closer. "You're perfect. I've meant that every time I've said it, but it doesn't mean you don't have faults. It means you're perfect for me. It means you're perfect for Ben and Abby. It means you're a crucial part of this family, and we're not whole and perfect without you."

She let her forehead rest against his chest. "I'm so sorry I left today. I left when you needed me most."

His heavy hand rubbed a circle on her back, soothing the ache of her mistakes. "You came back. That's all that matters."

Remi lifted her head. "No. I'm going to keep standing by you through this. I'll make up for what I did."

"I can't tell you what that means to me. It makes me sick to think about hurting a woman, even if it's Tasha. I want to punch a tree every time I hear her name."

"Same. She's trying to take the kids from us, and I just can't–"

"No. We're not losing the kids," Colt interrupted. "Never. You can mark it in stone. We'll never lose Ben and Abby."

Remi took the first full breath since the phone call with Camille earlier. Her determination was renewed, standing at attention on the front lines.

They knew what was coming next. Colt might not have seen it before, but Remi had. "We'll have to fight to keep them."

Colt smiled down at her, fiery resolve burning in his eyes. "Then we'll fight together."

She reached up and wrapped her arms around his neck. "I hoped you'd say that."

CHAPTER 32

REMI

Remi stepped out of Colt's truck and opened the back door. Abby lifted her arms, allowing Remi to unbuckle the car seat.

"Can I get a sucker?" Abby asked.

"Me too!" Ben shouted from the other side of the truck.

"We'll see." Remi looked at her watch. "It'll be lunchtime soon, so maybe we can get one and save it until after."

"I want purple," Abby said as she climbed out of the truck.

"Ben."

Colt's authoritative tone caught Remi's attention.

Ben sulked. "Do I have to?" Colt held out his hand, and Ben took it. "I'm too old to be holding hands."

Abby reached for Remi's hand. The gesture was second nature. At least one of the kids cooperated with the hold hands in parking lots rule.

"You're eight and a flight risk. You'll be holding my hand when you're sixteen at this rate," Colt said.

Abby skipped beside Remi. "I'll hold your hand forever. And when I get old, I want to build another house beside ours and connect the porches."

Remi held in a laugh. "I'm not sure your husband will agree to that."

"I'm not sure I'll agree to it," Colt whispered.

Remi elbowed him in the side. They'd recently taken their marriage to the next level, and Colt had started pushing for more adult alone time. She understood exactly where he was coming from. She and Colt had settled into the newlywed stage, and they had a lot of lost time to make up for. The kids had spent more than a handful of evenings with Stella and Vera over the last month.

"If I have a husband, he can live in the old cabins like Mister Brett and Mister Lincoln and Mister Paul."

Colt sucked in a breath through his teeth. "Maybe we need to table this conversation. I'm not ready to hear about you getting married."

"Me either. Who do you think I'll marry?" Abby asked.

Remi forced a smile and waved at Hudson, one of the teens who helped out at Grady's Feed and

Seed, as they walked in. "You probably haven't met him yet."

"How do I know when I meet him?"

What a question. If only God gave a clear sign for those kinds of things. Remi could have saved a few years of pushing Colt into a safe zone.

Before she could think of a good answer, Colt spoke up. "You'll just know."

"How did you know you wanted to marry Remi?"

Colt waved his hands in the air. "It was like lightning. Everything else stopped, and I knew she was the one as soon as I saw her."

"What a load of..." Better to not finish that thought. "It wasn't anything like that."

"How do you know?" The confident tone in Colt's question might have made her think twice.

"I was there."

"Well, you're a little dense about these things."

"I am not!"

She definitely was, but she didn't like being told so. And why was he telling the kids that the decision on who to marry was as cut and dry as lightning and time stopping? Maybe it had been for him, but it wasn't like that for everyone, including her.

Colt stopped in front of the first aisle and turned to them. "Okay, let's split up. Remi and Abby, you're looking for a shovel and outdoor spout covers. Ben and I will get the horse feed."

Ben stood tall and gave a dramatic salute. "Sir, yes, sir."

"Can we get suckers too?" Abby asked.

"Those are at the checkout counter," Remi reminded her.

"Okay. Let's go." Abby tugged on Remi's hand.

Gently pulling Abby the opposite direction, Remi pointed toward the garden section. "We'll meet you at the checkout counter."

Colt and Ben raced toward the warehouse, and Remi rolled her eyes. What was the protocol when she needed to chastise her kid *and* husband for running in a store?

Abby held onto Remi's hand as they turned down the aisle with hoses and attachments. There were six options at the end of the row, and Remi scanned the tags and information on each. She narrowed it down to two, holding one in each hand and comparing.

"Abby, white or gray?" The color seemed to be the only difference between the two.

When Abby didn't answer, Remi looked up. "Abby?" The aisle was empty.

"Abby!" She knew better than to get out of Remi's sight. Shoving the spout covers back onto the shelf, Remi rounded the end of the shelving and looked up the next aisle. "Abby!"

Remi's breaths came in shallow draws as she checked the aisle on the other side. "Abby!" The call had turned into a full-on yell as she ran along the end of the aisles. No sign of Abby, and her heart rate grew with each empty aisle.

Running out of the garden section toward the front of the store, Remi kept shouting for Abby. She scanned the store, looking left and right fast enough to check the aisles on both sides.

"Ben!"

Colt's shout drew her attention, and she ran toward his voice. She met him at the entrance to the warehouse, and the look on his face told her all she needed to know.

"Have you seen Ben?"

She sucked in a breath that did nothing to ease the panic building inside her. "Have you seen Abby?"

All color drained out of Colt's face. "Abby too?"

"She was right beside me. I let go of her hand to... What do we do?"

"Colt!"

They both turned at Colt's name. Grady jogged toward them holding Abby against his chest and over his shoulder. The older man wasn't used to any physical exertion, and his face was turning red.

"Abby!" Remi ran to meet him. She pushed Abby's dark hair from her face. She clung to Grady as tears streamed down her face. As soon as she spotted Remi, she reached out her arms. Remi hugged the little girl to her, clinging tight. "What happened?"

"A woman was carrying her toward the door," Grady said. "I saw that it was Abby, and I confronted her. She dropped Abby and ran. I caught her just before she hit the ground."

Tasha. It had to be Tasha. If Remi ever got her hands on that woman...

"The woman. Did anyone catch her?" Colt asked quickly.

"No. Cathy ran after her, but she got away."

"Did she have Ben too?" Remi asked, praying the answer was the one she wanted–needed–to hear.

Grady's eyes widened. "No. Is he here too?"

Colt grabbed Remi's shoulder. "I'll check the warehouse exit. You check the other door." He pointed toward the exit on the far side of the garden section.

"I'll keep Abby," Grady said, reaching out his arms.

The last thing she wanted to do was let go of Abby, but Ben needed her more. "Stay with Mister Grady, sweetie. I'll be back soon."

Abby transferred her intense grip back to Grady, who wrapped his plump arms around her. He tipped his chin toward the exit. "Go."

Remi ran her fingers over Abby's hair. "I'll be back." She turned and ran for the exit before she had time to debate. Ben needed her, and the thought of losing him was like a giant claw digging out her chest.

Tasha. Remi was going to burn the world to the ground to get to that evil woman. Nothing would stop her from destroying Tasha if she hurt one of the kids. She was a full-on lunatic. There was no telling what she would do if given the chance.

Remi pulled out her phone as she ran and quickly dialed 911. A feminine voice greeted her.

"What is your emergency?"

"Someone took my son. We're at Grady's Feed and Seed. She tried to take my daughter, but we can't find my son."

"What is your name?"

"Remi Walker." She panted as her legs pushed harder. Almost to the door, and still no sign of Ben.

"Is your daughter safe?"

"Yes."

"Does she need medical assistance?"

"I don't know. I don't think so."

"I'm putting the police department on the line. Please don't hang up."

"Okay." Remi skidded to a stop at the door. She turned left and right before running outside. No sign of anyone. There were a few cars parked in the side lot, but no sign of movement.

"Miss Walker, I have Officer Keller on the line."

"I'm at Grady's. How soon can you get here? I think my son was taken!" She ran back into the store, looking left and right. Her mouth was dry, and the edges of her vision started to blur.

"Remi? I'm on my way. Sit tight."

The familiar voice tugged her into the present. "Dawson?" She went to church with Dawson Keller, and having a friend on the line brought a small kindling of hope.

"Asa is with me. He's setting up roadblocks. Don't worry. We'll find him."

Tears rushed down her cheeks in an instant. "Thank you." Her words were ragged and hoarse. She quickly brushed the back of her arm over her face as she ran through the store.

"How many abductors were there?"

"Probably two. A woman tried to take Abby, but I don't know about Ben yet."

Remi had run all the way back to Grady and Abby with no sign of Ben. She laid a hand on Abby's back and bent at the waist. What little breakfast she had left was about to make a reappearance.

"Stay on the line with me. We're about two minutes out. Paramedics are on their way."

"Thank you." She gasped for air, unsure if the words were an appreciation or a prayer.

She looked up at Abby, who still clung to Grady. Pulling the sucker from her mouth, she offered it to Remi. "Are you okay? Do you want some of my sucker?"

Abby had no idea what was going on, and

thankfully, that was partially because she was unharmed. Had Ben fared as well?

"No, thank you, baby. I need to find your brother."

A woman who worked at the feed and seed ran up and handed a bottle of water to Remi. "Are you okay?"

Remi took the water and drank. "I'm fine. Where is Colt?"

The woman pointed toward the warehouse. "He just ran out into the parking lot."

"Thanks. Grady—"

"Go. We're fine here." He still had a firm hold on Abby, who seemed pleased with the attention.

"I'll be back soon." She held onto the bottle of water and ran toward the warehouse. Ben had to be okay. She couldn't comprehend anything else. They couldn't lose him.

The sun blinded her as she jogged into the parking lot, and the exploding sound of a gunshot stopped her in her tracks. Time stood still as the gray edges of her vision drowned out the daylight.

CHAPTER 33
COLT

Colt almost ran into Hudson. The teenager skidded to a stop when he saw Colt. "I tried to stop him!"

"Which way did he go?" Hudson knew Ben. The two talked about football and dirt bikes every time they were in the store.

Hudson pointed to the bay doors. "That way."

Colt pushed his run to the max. If they got out of the parking lot, their chances of finding him would diminish. The midday sun was blinding, but an older black car pulling out of a parking space caught his attention. The vehicle backed out fast, and Colt's assurance that the kidnapper was attempting an escape ticked up. He almost reached the vehicle before it shifted into drive. He called on a speed he hadn't used in years, but the car was too fast. It sped through the parking lot toward the main road, leaving Colt behind.

He couldn't catch it on foot, and he couldn't let them get away. Where had he parked the truck?

Tires screeched, and Colt looked toward the end of the parking lot. A red Ford F-150 blocked the road leading from the parking lot to the main road.

Colt kept running. If he was lucky, this would stall the car enough to let him catch up.

As soon as the hopeful thought entered his mind, the reverse lights lit up on the black car.

Uh-oh. Colt stopped running, stared at the blacked-out tag, and waited to see which way the car would go. A second later, it started backing up, headed straight toward Colt.

Fight or flight? He definitely wasn't running away if Ben was in that car. The guy would have to run him over first.

And it looked like getting run over was a possibility as the car sped toward him. Colt stretched out his hands and braced his feet for impact, hoping the guy driving wasn't too keen about committing vehicular manslaughter today.

A louder engine roared, and a blue pickup sped across the parking lot. The truck pulled into the row thirty feet in front of Colt just before the car slammed into its passenger side.

"Hudson!" The kid wasn't old enough for a

license, but his quick thinking might have saved Ben.

Colt ran to the truck and knocked on the window. "You okay?"

Hudson gave him a nod and a thumbs up.

Colt ran around the truck and jerked open the back passenger door of the car. Ben had his head tucked between his knees and his hands over his ears.

"Ben! Are you okay?" Colt wanted to drag Ben out of the car, but the fear of injuries stopped him.

Ben nodded, still crying.

The man in the front seat groaned and opened the driver's side door. His dark, shaggy hair fell over one eye, and his coat hung loose over his skeletal frame.

"Don't move!" Colt shouted. There was no way that guy was getting away after trying to take Ben.

Colt ran his hand over Ben's head, shoulder, and arm. "You okay?"

"Yeah. I'm okay," Ben sputtered through tears, and his shoulders shook.

"Stop!"

Colt looked up and out the windshield at the man's shout. Noah and Camille Harding raced toward them. Colt should have recognized that red truck.

Camille would know what was happening, and

no doubt Noah would already be running to catch the man.

Wrapping his arms gently around Ben, he whispered, "I'm so glad you're okay."

"That man wouldn't let me go!" Ben shouted.

"You're safe now."

Camille's quick footsteps came to a stop behind Colt. "Are you okay?"

"He had Ben. We already got Abby away from Tasha." Well, he assumed it was Tasha. He hadn't seen the woman who'd tried to kidnap Abby, but he'd bet his life savings on Tasha.

Camille looked over the car, drawing Colt's attention that way. "Noah went after him." Fear shook her voice, and understanding had Colt's stomach dropping.

"Can you stay with Ben?" He didn't want to leave, but he trusted Camille, and at this point, Noah was in more danger than Ben.

"Yes. Go!" She waved her hands, shooing him out of the back seat.

Colt turned to Ben. "I'll be right back."

Ben nodded and glanced up at Camille. "Okay."

Colt slid out of the car and scanned the parking lot for Noah and the man. "Call the police."

"Already on it," Camille said.

Colt rounded the car and pushed into a run, glancing from one end of the parking lot to the other. It wasn't a big area, but it connected to the restaurant parking lot next door. The guy had plenty of asphalt to cover.

He slid in between two trucks and caught a glimpse of Noah's dark hair. Seconds later, Colt spotted the man. Noah had almost caught up to him.

Pushing into a quicker run with a target in sight, Colt darted through another row of vehicles. The wail of a siren split the quiet streets, urging Colt into another burst of speed.

The man reached the end of the restaurant parking lot and stopped. A row of abandoned shops blocked his path. Instead of changing course or running around the buildings, he stopped and rounded on Noah. The man raised his arms and steadied a gun at eye level.

"No!" Colt's shout did nothing. The desperate scream was drowned out by the deafening pop of the gun and the high-pitched shattering of glass as the bullet cut its way through the parking lot.

The split-second of panic eased when Noah rose from a crouch and dove for the man. He'd ducked just in time. Colt wouldn't have believed it if he hadn't witnessed it with his own eyes.

The impact threw the man to the ground, and the gun went flying. Noah fought to restrain the man while dodging elbows and the frantic man's snapping jaws. With his hands tied, the guy bit at

Noah's arms until Noah flipped him onto his stomach with his hands secured behind his back.

Colt skidded to a stop and crouched beside Noah. "Thanks for going after him." There wasn't a doubt in Colt's mind that the guy would have gotten away if Noah hadn't been so quick on his feet.

"Get his shoulders," Noah growled. Holding the man down was a constant fight.

Colt leaned his weight onto the man's shoulders, pressing the guy's cheek flat against the sidewalk.

Quick steps drew Colt's attention, and he glanced over his shoulder. Jerry Lawrence panted as he approached them at a slow run.

"You okay?"

"No injuries," Colt said as he rustled against the man's squirming. "Can you guard the gun?" He jerked his head toward the black pistol on the sidewalk about ten feet away.

Jerry headed straight for the weapon. Colt took stock of the situation and inhaled a deep breath. He'd never been so thankful for friends as in that moment. No doubt the Lord had sent helpers. He trusted Noah Harding and Jerry Lawrence with his life, and the men had come through in Colt's time of need despite the danger to themselves.

"I think the law is here," Jerry said.

Blue lights flashed closer to the feed and seed,

and Colt said a thankful prayer. They had Abby and Ben, and no one had been hurt. Their lives could have changed in the blink of an eye. Despite his and Remi's best efforts, Tasha had almost succeeded in taking the kids. The thought of what she might have done if given the chance had bile rising in his throat.

Two police officers ran toward them across the parking lot. Asa and Dawson kept the same, quick speed while keeping one hand over their weapons.

Jerry raised his hands, taking one small step away from the pistol. Colt and Noah kept their hold on the man, but his squirming and shouting increased.

Colt shoved harder into the guy's shoulders. "Give it up. You'll never walk free again after this."

"Everyone, put your hands where I can see them!" Asa shouted.

Colt glanced back and forth between Asa and the restrained man. If he let go, the guy would run again. Noah slowly lifted his hands, but Colt kept his grip.

"Do it, Colt," Dawson said.

Colt had known Asa and Dawson since he came to Blackwater. They were good guys, and as much as he wanted to trust that they could do their job, he didn't see the sense in letting the guy who had tried to take Ben get one inch of freedom.

Despite the screaming in his head, Colt loosened his hold. As soon as his hands lifted, the man scrambled to his knees. Colt reached for him again before Asa shouted.

"Get back, Colt!"

Dawson had the guy whipped back to the ground within seconds.

Okay, so they *could* do their job. It didn't help the tingling in Colt's fingers as he fisted and flexed them at his sides. He'd never been a violent man, but the fear of Ben and Abby being taken had ignited a protector instinct he couldn't shake. Fire and carnage filled his thoughts as he kept his stare on the man he wanted to rip apart.

Three more police officers joined Asa and Dawson as they wrestled with the man. The kicking and screaming had to be considered resisting arrest. Maybe he'd rack up a lengthy list of offenses and rot in prison for the rest of his life. Colt intended to do whatever it took to help that happen.

Jennifer Freeman approached Colt, Noah, and Jerry. "You men okay?"

Colt had met Jennifer a few times but never in uniform. Her blonde hair was pulled back into a tight bun, and her stern expression was focused on the men.

"We're fine," Colt said. "Are the kids okay?"

Jennifer nodded and pulled out a small notepad. "They're both being checked out by the paramedics, but they seemed to be fine."

No one would be *fine* after this. Colt would be sleeping with the lights on until further notice.

"It's my understanding there were two suspects," Jennifer said.

"Yeah, a woman had Abby. Probably Tasha White."

"Colt!"

Remi ran toward him. Her red hair streamed behind her, as she pumped her arms at her sides. A police officer reached out his hands to keep Remi back, but she twisted out of his grasp.

"That's my husband!"

Boy, did it feel good to hear her call him her husband. The kick in the gut pulled him out of the adrenaline of the struggle.

He turned to meet her. The tears streaming down her cheeks hit him hard, and he opened his arms as she barreled into him. He wrapped her up and held her tight, hoping to temper her sobs. The sound gutted him as she sank into his chest.

"I heard the shot, and I thought..."

Colt brushed a hand over her hair. "That's what you get for thinking."

She punched his side before letting her arm slip back around him. "Colt Walker, I'm so mad at—"

Colt pressed his lips against hers, cutting her off. Her kiss was hard and fierce until she pushed him away.

She lifted her head long enough to shout. "You scared me!"

Colt swallowed hard, painfully aware of his own fear. "You scared me too."

Remi buried her face back in his chest. "I'm so glad we're all okay."

"The kids?" Colt asked.

Remi looked over her left shoulder and pointed to the sidewalk near the restaurant. The parking lot was bustling with law enforcement and bystanders now, but Colt had no trouble finding Ben and Abby in the crowd.

"They're with Grady and Camille. I was afraid to bring them over here now in case..."

Good. Two people he trusted. "He's gone. I still don't know who it is, but Asa and Dawson just loaded him into the patrol car." He raised a finger to Jennifer, then jerked a thumb toward the kids on the sidewalk. "Can I?"

Jennifer jerked her chin. "I'll come get you in a minute for a statement. Just don't leave."

"We won't," Remi answered as she took his hand and followed him toward the sidewalk where the kids waited.

Abby spotted them first, and her eyes widened at the same time she pushed out of Grady's arms. She ran straight to Remi, and Colt made a beeline for Ben. Wrapping the little boy in his arms, he inhaled a deep breath as he buried his face in the crook of Ben's neck. "I'm so glad you're okay."

"Thanks to you! Hudson told me you chased that guy down!"

Colt shook his head and let his gaze run over Ben's face and arms, checking for injuries. "I would never let you go without a fight." Colt wrapped Ben in a tight hug, wishing he could hold on forever. "I love you, bud."

"Love you too," Ben whispered back.

Jennifer shouted behind them. "Hey!"

Colt turned but kept his hold on Ben.

Jennifer pointed to the feed and seed. "You can wait inside. I'll come get you in about ten minutes."

Colt hadn't noticed, but fluffy flakes of snow drifted slowly over the parking lot. Ben shivered in his arms. "Let's get you warm."

"Uncle Colt!"

Abby reached her arms up to him, and he set Ben on his feet to wrap Abby in the same, rib-crushing hug as Ben. "Hey, sweetie."

"I love you," Abby whispered.

"I love you too. You have no idea how much I love you."

Abby snuggled closer to him. "I do."

Remi's soft voice shook behind him. "I'm so sorry," she told Ben. "I love you, and I'll never let you out of my sight again."

"Does this mean I don't have to go to school?" Ben asked.

Remi looked up at Colt in the same moment her tears returned. "Don't judge me if I turn into a hover-mom after this."

Colt stood to his feet, pulling Abby up with him on his hip. Remi stood with Ben, and Colt wrapped his arms around the three people he loved most. "I think you still have to go to school, but I might try to bribe the school resource officer to keep you in his sight all day."

"Aw, man," Ben groaned.

Remi brushed a hand over Ben's hair. "I'll do anything to make sure you're safe."

Colt stared at the woman who'd made good on her vow to fight by his side. There wasn't a better woman out there for him, and he'd be thanking God day and night for sending Remi into his life.

She looked up at him, and he brushed a thumb over her cheek. "I love you."

Remi blinked misty eyes and smiled. "I love you too, Walker."

"Me and you against the world?"

Remi slid a hand behind his neck and pulled him down to her, pressing her lips against his in a sweet, short kiss. "Until the very end."

CHAPTER 34

REMI

A bby whined and squirmed in her car seat. "I don't like these shoes. They hurt my feet."

Remi opened the glove compartment in Colt's truck as he parked beside the Weston County Courthouse. "I know we have bandages in here."

Colt sucked in a breath through his teeth. "I may have used them all."

Remi stopped rummaging to glare at him. "And you didn't replace them? You're officially fired."

"Can I take this jacket thing off?" Ben whined.

Pinching the bridge of her nose, Remi took a deep breath. "Can we just make it through this hearing? This is important, guys." She turned to the kids in the back seat. "Eyes on the prize. Today's the big day."

"Apopshun!" Abby shouted.

"Adoption," Colt said slowly.

Remi bit her lips as she turned her attention to the first aid kit. The whole thing was a mess with empty bandage wrappers and ointment with the lid half screwed on.

Ben tugged at the lapels of his jacket. "How long until I can take this off?"

"I have no idea how long this will take." Colt pointed across the street. "Focus on the ice cream waiting for you when this is over."

When this is over. How could they blame the kids for being antsy? Remi was wishing the hours away herself. But the end of the hearing was only the beginning. If the judge approved the adoption, they'd walk out of the courthouse as an official family.

"Found it." Remi held up the bandages.

Abby tugged off her patent leather shoes and extended her foot to Remi between the seats. Remi pulled down the back of the frilly sock and secured the bandage to Abby's tiny heel. As soon as she pulled the sock back up, Colt grabbed Abby's ankle and tickled the bottom of her foot.

"Ahh!" Abby screamed, laughing loud enough that two men in suits walking in front of the parked truck stared as they passed.

"Other foot," Remi said. She focused on the task, trying her best to stop the shaking in her hands.

Camille was pretty positive the judge would grant the adoption. Everything had gone smoothly over the last few months, barring Tasha's intervention, but they hadn't heard a word about her since the incident at Grady's Feed and Seed.

No news was good news, except when a woman who wanted to hurt your kids was on the loose. Remi lived in a constant state of anxiety, looking twice and three times. Checking locks she'd already checked. Watching over the kids like a hawk. The vigilance was exhausting, but the consequences of a lapse in awareness was unacceptable.

Colt had changed too, and there wasn't much either of them could do about it. The fear of losing the kids hung over them like a cloud. Thankfully, the kids had recovered and seemed as happy as ever.

The sheriff's department had gathered a little bit of information from the man who'd worked with Tasha. He'd confirmed her identity and explained their ridiculous plan to take the kids, drop them off somewhere nearby, and report Colt and Remi for negligence. In their hair-brained scheme, they thought kidnapping kids would be overlooked as misplacing children as if the two were interchangeable.

Remi pressed the second bandage to Abby's heel. "Done. We'll change into comfy shoes as soon as we get back to the hotel."

Mark and Brittany's house had sold a few weeks ago, and while Remi had feared the kids would miss staying at their house on the trip to Newcastle, the excitement of staying in a hotel overshadowed any sadness.

Ben leaned forward, grabbing onto the back of Remi's seat. "Can we go to the gym when we get back to the hotel?"

Remi lifted her brows and looked at Colt. "That's all you."

"Oh, come on. You don't want to hit the weights?" Colt practically laughed behind the words.

"Are you saying I need to work out?" Remi glanced at Ben in the back seat and shot him a wink.

"No, you're perfect. But I wouldn't mind seeing you running on a treadmill like a Baywatch lifeguard." Colt narrowed his eyes, almost challenging her.

And that intense stare? She might be convinced to do crazy things if he kept looking at her like that. "Nice try, but if you see me running, you better start running too."

"Why?" Abby asked.

"Because someone is probably chasing me." Remi locked up the first aid kit and shoved it back into the glove compartment. "Everyone ready to do this?"

Colt's large hand rested gently on her arm. "Let's say a prayer first."

Remi was all for prayer–with reason and without–but the mention evoked a spark of fear. They'd been praying for months about this. Did they need extra prayers? Was this hearing not a shoo-in like she'd expected?

"Yeah." The word was tentative as she opened her hand to him.

Colt slid his calloused hand against her smoother palm and bowed his head. "Father, this hearing will be a big moment for our family, and we ask that You go with us into the courtroom. We pray that You calm our unease and give us peace. We pray that the judge sees our family for what it is–already perfect and complete. God, we thank You again for bringing us together when we needed each other the most. Keep us strong and united. Thank you, Father. Amen."

"Amen!" Ben shouted. "Let's do this."

Remi's phone dinged with a message. "It's Camille. She's waiting inside near the judge's chambers."

Remi stepped out of the truck and reached for Ben's hand while Colt unstrapped Abby from her seat. They met at the front of the truck, and Colt slipped his hand into hers as they walked. With Ben on one side and Colt and Abby on the other, the link was complete. Touch was one thing that calmed the anxiety. If she was holding on to the things she loved most, no one could take them from her.

They walked up the stone steps and passed through the old wooden doors. The metal detector remained silent as they entered the main lobby. The clink of Remi's heels echoed off the tile walls, reminding her of the suit jacket and pencil skirt she wore. She could count on one hand the times she'd worn business attire, and Ben's restlessness in the formal clothing was all too understandable.

They turned a corner and spotted Camille chatting with a middle-aged woman at the end of the hallway. A few other smartly dressed men passed them carrying briefcases and shucks of files.

"There she is!" Abby shouted as she pointed at Camille.

Camille turned, and a smile broadened on her face as she spotted them. She waved them over, turning back to the woman for a few more seconds.

Abby wiggled out of Colt's arms and ran to meet Camille. The pitter-patter of her little shoes lightened Remi's heart. The kids were happiness in human form. How did she ever end up with so much pure joy in her life?

Camille hugged both of the kids before standing and straightening her skirt. "Everyone ready?"

"Yes!" Abby and Ben shouted at the same time.

"Shh," Remi whispered with a finger in front of her lips. "You're gonna get us kicked out before we can get the final order."

"This won't take long. It's our turn next." Camille looked at her watch. "You'll be out in time to get that ice cream well before lunch."

Remi worked to control her breathing. Was the air getting thicker, or was it just hot in here?

"Colt?"

Camille's questioning word pulled Remi out of her panic. She looked up at Colt to find him jerking his head back toward them.

"Yeah." The color had drained from his face, leaving a strained expression.

"You okay?" Camille asked.

Colt turned to look back down the hallway toward the intersection that led to the main exit. When he looked back at them, Remi recognized the fear on his face. "Yeah. I'm fine." He stretched his neck to one side, then the other. "Just nervous."

"Don't be nervous. This is going to be easy," Camille said.

Remi slipped her arm under his, wrapping her hand around the crook of his elbow. "I'm nervous too, but it'll all be over soon."

He slid his hand over hers. "I know. I'm just ready to get out of here."

"I know what you mean." They still didn't know where Tasha was, and despite confirming her identity on the security footage at the feed and seed after she tried to take Abby, she was still on the loose. Newcastle had been her home once, and it might still be, and any connection to Tasha left all of them on high alert.

The doors to the judge's chambers opened, and

a man and woman stepped out. They wore the basic black suits that dotted the hallways of the courthouse, and their conversation was still on the hearing they'd just wrapped up. Behind them, another group of four people stepped out carrying briefcases. One pulled a small, wheeled bag behind her.

A white-haired man wearing a suit the color of sand peeked his head out into the hallway. "Y'all can come on in."

"Show time," Ben said as he darted around them to be the first into the courtroom.

Remi, Colt, and Camille stopped to shake the man's hand, and Camille pointed out where they would sit. A few other people Remi didn't know entered the outdated courtroom over the next few minutes. The kids sat in old wooden chairs beside her. Ben was drawing on one of Camille's extra legal pads, and Abby sat right up against him, watching every move he made.

Colt wrapped his arm around her shoulders, and she sank into his embrace. She had so much to lose now. Before the day was over, the legal equivalent of cement would bind her family together.

"I love you," Colt whispered.

"I love you too."

The steady hum of the conversation in the courtroom hushed in an instant as the judge stepped out of a back room and walked behind the desk. It wasn't as stately as the high seats she'd seen on TV, but it was at the head of the room.

Everyone stood, and Remi waved at the kids to do the same. They scrambled to put the writing pad and pencil behind them as they got to their feet.

The judge waved a hand, and Camille nodded for them to sit. The formalities of the judicial system were a mystery to Remi, but thankfully, Camille stopped to explain things as often as necessary.

The heavy wooden door of the courtroom squeaked, and Remi turned around. The man in the sand suit was heading toward the entrance, but someone slipped in just before he could close the door.

Remi grabbed Colt's sleeve as the pounding in her ears grew into a roar. Tasha strutted straight past the man as he began speaking to her. She didn't slow down or give him a shred of attention.

Colt pushed his chair back and stood, blocking Remi's view of the woman she'd hoped to never see again. Remi's grip tightened on Colt's arm as Tasha walked straight up to the judge's desk.

"Your Honor, this is a closed hearing," Camille said as she stood to her feet.

While Camille looked completely unfazed, Remi's panic skyrocketed, leaving her with chest pain and blurry vision.

Abby patted Remi's shoulder. "That's the woman!"

"I know, sweetie," she whispered back. Her own words sounded muffled as she kept her gaze on Tasha. She wore light-wash jeans, an off-white baggy sweater, and tennis shoes that had seen better days. Her brown hair was pulled back into a messy ponytail, but she held her chin high as she halted in front of the judge's desk. A police officer was already making his way toward her.

"Judge, those kids are my sister's, and that man isn't fit to take care of them." She pointed behind her at the table where Remi and Colt sat with the kids and Camille. Tasha's speech had a lazy twang and the words were drawn out too long. Abby was easier to understand in most cases.

"Who are you?" the judge asked.

"Tasha White," she spat back.

"This is my courtroom, and you are speaking out of turn."

The police officer inched closer to her, ready to move at the judge's order.

"If you had objection to the matters involved in this hearing, you should have filed a motion in my court," the judge said. "If you are a named party or a family relation, you can have a seat. Otherwise, leave."

Tasha crossed her arms. "I am a family member, and–"

The judge stood in a flash, and Remi jolted. His

peaceful expression from a few minutes ago was gone, replaced by a reddening anger.

"Leave this courtroom. You have no business here, and you're hindering the judicial process."

"I have every right to be here, and I won't leave because–"

The judge gave the officer a nod. "You will leave. I won't have this in my courtroom."

Tasha jerked her arm away from the officer. "He hit me! He tried to strangle me! He tried to kill me!" she yelled and pointed at Colt.

Remi's mouth opened as the anger brewing inside her threatened to boil over, but Camille reached across Abby to grip Remi's shoulder with a firm hand.

The judge rested his hands on the desk and leaned forward. "This isn't criminal court, and we have rules and appointments for a reason." He waved his hand at the officer. "Get her out of here."

The officer wrapped his hand around Tasha's upper arm, but she pulled back. Another officer ran into the courtroom just as she swung her elbow at the officer trying to restrain her. She barely missed the man's head, and the second officer didn't hesitate to tackle her to the ground.

Remi stood, scooting the wooden legs of her chair against the tile floor, and grabbed for Abby. Tasha and the officers rolled on the floor, moving closer and closer to Remi, Colt, Camille, and the kids.

Amidst shouts and thuds, Remi and Colt moved the kids back. Remi held Abby to her chest, hoping to block out some of what was going on. The last thing the kids needed to see were supposed adults fighting, especially with law enforcement officers.

It was still hard to believe Tasha had strolled into the courtroom with confidence and confronted the judge. Maybe she hadn't gotten word about the warrant out for her arrest after what happened back in Blackwater, or maybe this was her last-ditch effort in her attempts to get custody of the kids and the trust that came with that role.

Remi had never had money, but she was seeing with her own eyes that people would do desperate things for a dollar. She clung to Abby and kept an eye on Tasha as she resisted arrest.

"I thought I saw her in the hallway earlier," Colt whispered.

"And you didn't say anything?" Remi asked.

"I thought I was just being paranoid!" Colt raised his voice to be heard above the scuffling.

Two other officers ran in to help, and minutes later, Tasha was handcuffed. Two officers kept their hands on her as she shoved her shoulders and pushed against them, yelling the entire time. She kicked to the side, landing a blow to the side of the officer's knee.

"She's lost her mind," Remi whispered.

"A long time ago," Colt said.

A hush fell over the courtroom as the doors closed behind the officers escorting Tasha out. The echoes of her shouts were muffled in the hallway.

The judge took his seat and opened a file on his desk. "Mrs. Harding, I appreciate your warning about Miss White."

Camille nodded once. "You're welcome, Your Honor."

The judge shuffled through a few of the papers on his desk. "Now that we've been hindered enough, let's do what we came here to do."

Half an hour later, the judge approved the adoptions of Benjamin and Abigail Walker to be filed in the Weston County Circuit Court by order before the end of business hours.

Colt wrapped Ben in his arms and shook him. "We did it."

Abby threw her hands in the air. "Yay!"

Remi reached for Abby and squeezed the little girl's shoulders. The rush of the win filled her lungs and left her feeling dizzy.

Remi was a mom. Abby and Ben would forever be her children in the eyes of God and the law. Despite the safe life she'd thought she wanted months ago, this was her calling. She was a parent, a wife, and a saved child of the Lord.

She picked up Abby and turned to Colt. No one

had ever looked at her the way Colt did with love in his eyes. He wrapped her in his arms and pressed his lips to her cheek.

"I love you so much."

"I love you too."

Camille hugged Ben and reached for Abby. "This is a huge win, guys. You think you can take care of Uncle Colt and Aunt Remi for the rest of their lives?"

"Oh yeah," Ben said. "I'll even feed them and water them every day."

Everyone burst into laughter, and Remi gasped for air. No one had told her to expect dreams to come true that she'd never hoped to ask for. No one had told her that love like this existed. But most of all, no one could take this away from her. Not anymore.

CHAPTER 35

COLT

The church parking lot was packed, and the bright-green wreaths with red bows stood out on the front doors amidst the snow-covered landscape. With Christmas coming next week, the hum of excitement buzzed in every moment.

Their first Christmas with Ben and Abby would be a highlight Colt would never forget. Remi had bought most of the gifts, but Colt had a few surprises up his sleeve. Every Christmas event brought them closer to the big day.

Colt opened the back door of the truck, and Abby shivered.

"Hurry. Hurry," she said through chattering teeth.

"You got it." Colt made quick work of the car seat straps and hefted her out onto her feet.

Abby ran to Remi's side, bundling her coat around her. "Can I play with baby Jesus?"

Remi chuckled. "You have to take turns with the other girls."

He'd already had his questioning moment about baby Jesus after last week's Christmas program practice. Remi said the girls had fought over who got to hold the doll that would represent Jesus in the play. They'd been forced to come up with clear-lined rules for playing with baby Jesus.

One more thing to add to the list of problems he never expected to encounter.

Inside, the church was bustling. Almost every person wore some shade of red, green, gold, or silver, and the angel tree stood brightly lit in the front of the sanctuary.

Remi ushered the kids into their usual pew. "We have a few songs and announcements before we can go get ready."

"Can I have the gold crown with the red diamonds?" Ben asked.

"I guess so," Remi said.

Stella and Vera were already seated, and Abby ran to greet her friends with a hug. Remi scooted in beside her, and Colt and Ben rounded out the end of the pew.

Abby was engrossed in a conversation with Stella when the music started, and Ben kicked his church boots against the back of the pew in front of them. The kid usually didn't have trouble paying attention, but everywhere Colt looked, even adults were squirming in their seats. The excitement of the Christmas play was alive in the air.

When the song was over, the preacher took his place at the front.

"Good morning, and Merry Christmas!"

The congregation responded with their own greeting, with kids shouting at the top of their lungs.

"That's the kind of excitement I want to see in the Lord's house this morning! Let me go over a few upcoming things to remember, then we'll dismiss the youngsters to get ready to take the stage."

Colt scanned the room. There weren't many empty seats, and he spotted a dozen faces he hadn't seen in a while.

"Shh!" Remi whispered.

Abby and Stella jerked into silence. Stella made a gesture of zipping her lips, but Abby just giggled.

A smile spread over Colt's face. Never had he imagined having a ready-made family, but his had truly fallen into place like the pieces of a perfect puzzle.

"That'll do it for today. Kids and anyone who was brave enough to volunteer to help out with the play, you're dismissed."

Remi and the kids shuffled out of the pew, and Colt scooted down to sit next to Stella.

"Ten bucks says a kid goes AWOL," Colt whispered as the pianist played the first notes of "Silent Night."

Stella looked up at him and swatted his arm. "I will not make that bet with you. But really, we should be praying the kids don't put up a big fight. They're a big group."

Remi had been telling him about the antics the kids got into during practices, and even she wasn't optimistic about the play going off without a few hiccups. "At least we'll be entertained."

Three songs later, the music director nodded at the signal. "It looks like our little ones are ready to show us a thing or two. Without further ado, I'll hand things over to Lauren."

Lauren was the head of the children's education department, and she never batted an eye when kids threw her for a loop. Colt had seen that kind of steadfast patience in Remi a lot recently, and he was beginning to understand the fortitude necessary to keep a smile on when kids were tearing down the walls.

She accepted the microphone from the music director and shook her hair off her shoulders. "Good morning. We have a beautiful program to share with you today. These kids have worked so hard, and I'm proud of all of them for being brave enough to stand up here in front of you and tell the story of Christ's birth. We have so many blessings to celebrate, but the birth of our Savior is at the top of that list."

A loud thud sounded from behind the wall on the left side of the sanctuary, and Lauren paused.

"And I think we're ready to begin."

The lights dimmed just as the blood-chilling scream filled the room. "I didn't do it!" a young boy yelled.

"Uh-oh," Stella whispered beside Colt.

"I think that's Sawyer," he whispered back.

There was a ruckus in the lobby, and everyone turned to look over their shoulders to the open double doors leading to the vestibule.

Sure enough, Sawyer Henson was wrestling against his dad. When the kid caught sight of the whole congregation watching them, he took the opportunity to call out, "Y'all pray for me!"

Colt burst into laughter, though he tried to cover his mouth. Stella grabbed a hold of his arm and rested her forehead against it as her shoulders shook with laughter.

A second later, another boy, Abel Nicks, darted out of a side door toward the front of the sanctuary wearing a velvet cape and a gold crown. He propped his hands on his hips and stuck out his chest before shouting, "I'm impossible!"

The same moment Abel finished his declaration, Remi caught up with him and gently herded him backstage. She gave everyone a cheerful wave and a smile as she pushed Abel along.

Laughter rang out in the church louder than any song he'd ever heard, and Colt couldn't stop laughing. Stella wrapped her arms around her middle. When she straightened, she wiped tears from her eyes, but it was no good. She fell into another fit, and the tears started up again.

Lauren quieted her own chuckles and announced, "Okay. Let's start over. *Now*, we would like to bring you the story of Jesus's birth."

There were still some random laughs when a kid dressed as an angel entered from stage right. Within minutes, Ben was on the stage dressed as a shepherd, and Abby stood with a group of girls as angels. Despite a few boys using the shepherd's hooks as swords and one kid picking his nose the whole time, the whole play was perfect. It took Colt a second to understand how young kids could understand the birth of the Savior enough to teach adults the significance of every event, but they'd done it. Watching Abby shout "Hallelujah!" and Ben's bow before the manger would be forever seared in Colt's memory.

Stella bumped him with her elbow. "You did well," she whispered.

"Me? Remi and the kids did all this."

Stella shook her head and grinned up at him. The shallow wrinkles around her eyes grew deeper as her cheeks lifted. "No, you did well." She pointed to the front of the church. "Look how happy they are."

All of the kids held hands and bowed as the church applauded as one. Remi stood to the side with a goofy grin on her face. He'd never seen her so radiant, and he'd never been so thankful to belong to her. She fought against his dream of a home and a family for so long, but he knew without a doubt that she didn't regret the push that brought them together. God's love and grace had smiled down on him in more ways than he could count.

He caught Remi watching him and shot her a wink. Her shoulders pulled in as her smile grew. She'd started blushing lately, and it was his favorite thing about her. If he loved her well enough, she'd be this happy in his arms forever.

CHAPTER 36

REMI

Remi's eyes slowly blinked open. Rolling onto her back, she rubbed one eye and then the other. The sky outside the bedroom window was dark, but a faint light bloomed at the windowsill.

She turned to look at the clock. It was just before six in the morning, and the kids weren't rustling yet.

On her other side, Colt lay on his stomach with both hands tucked under his pillow. His dark hair stuck out in all directions, and the peaceful expression on his face reminded her that this home–this family–was real.

Remi turned to look up at the ceiling and closed her eyes. She repeated the same prayer in her mind every morning, but the words never lost their power.

Thank You for this happiness.

It was one sentence, but it held reverence for

every joy and every blessing the Lord had given her, even some new ones lately. It held the promise of forgiveness for all those years she spent running. It held a faithfulness that she'd had to learn through trials. It held an assurance in the Lord's perfect plan for her.

She opened her eyes and slowly lifted the blankets. Colt stretched beside her and groaned.

When she looked at him, his morning smile stopped her short. It was like an explosion in her heart. This man loved her, and he loved her with a resolve she'd never believed in before seeing it and experiencing it for herself.

"Morning, princess."

The endearment had her head spinning. She'd worried that Tasha's spying would ruin it, but after the investigation showed she'd been following them for days before showing up at Camille's office, her attempt to steal something precious and private had backfired.

Remi was still his princess, and she knew without a doubt that she was the only one.

"Morning. I'll get the coffee started."

Colt threw a heavy arm over her and pulled her close. The force of his capture stole her breath.

But when he snuggled close to her, she relaxed against his warmth.

"I can't believe the kids aren't up yet," he whispered.

"I bet they stayed up late hoping to catch Santa in the act."

"I don't even care if it means we get to stay right here for a few more minutes."

Remi rested her head against his chest and draped a leg over his. The old question threatened to derail her good morning.

Could she have had this happiness with him sooner?

Maybe. Maybe not. She'd never know. It was possible she needed to have faith in God's love before she could understand unselfish human love, and she didn't regret that life lesson. Colt had been patient about knocking sense into her, and he still put a quick end to those intrusive thoughts when the old guilt tried to creep back in. He'd been a good model of unfaltering love, and if Colt could love her–faults and all–then God would certainly have no problem doing the same.

There wasn't a question about it anymore. Every time she wondered how Colt or her Heavenly Father could possibly love her, the thought expired almost on arrival. It had been proven and written in stone.

A door opened and closed seconds before Abby gasped and screamed, "Everybody get up! Santa came!"

Remi moved to get up, but Colt tightened his hold. "Don't move. Maybe she'll go back to sleep if we stay quiet."

Remi wiggled in his arms. "Yeah, right. Abby will have hers and Ben's gifts opened before we get out there if you don't let me go in the next two seconds."

Colt groaned and lifted his arm. He rolled onto his back and rubbed his hands over his face. "All right. I'm up. Let's do this." In one swift move, he was on his feet and reaching for his T-shirt.

"I don't know how you do that," Remi whispered.

"What?"

"You wake up so fast! I need at least ten minutes to stretch and yawn before I'm ready to face the day."

Colt tugged on his shirt. "If you woke up next to a beautiful woman every day, you wouldn't have trouble either."

Remi swatted his chest as she walked by. "Give it up, Romeo."

"I'm serious. You're the most gorgeous woman I've ever seen."

Remi rolled her eyes as she stepped out of the bedroom, but a rush of heat covered her face. "Merry Christmas!"

Abby launched into Remi's arms. "Merry Christmas! Santa came, and he ate the cookies!"

Under the tree, the plate where the cookies had been held only a few crumbs. "Looks like it. First things first. Everyone, brush your teeth. Then, meet me at the couch."

Ben stepped out of the bedroom looking bright-eyed. "Merry Christmas!"

Remi leaned down and pressed a kiss to his forehead. "Merry Christmas."

Colt headed to the kitchen to start the coffee, and Remi rearranged some of the presents under the tree. Would the kids like them? She had no idea what they were used to, but she'd wanted to give them things they would love and things they could enjoy together.

"Done!" Abby shouted as she flew out of the bathroom and jumped onto the couch.

"Stay right there until Colt and I get our teeth brushed and get back in here."

Ben took his place on the couch too. When everyone was back in the living room, Colt picked up his Bible on the way to the recliner. "Everybody ready to hear the story?"

"What story?" Ben asked.

Colt opened the Bible to the page he'd marked. "Luke chapter two."

"I already know this story!" Abby said.

"Me too," Ben added.

"You're gonna hear it again this morning, so sit tight," Colt said as he got comfortable in the recliner.

Remi sat between the kids as Colt read. She'd

heard the story before too. In fact, they'd all heard it many times this month alone, but there was something special about Colt's steady voice reminding them of the reason they celebrated Christmas.

When he finished, he closed the Bible. "And that's just the beginning."

"Now presents!" Abby said.

"I want to pray!" Ben shouted.

Colt opened his hand to Ben, gesturing for him to go ahead.

"God, thank You for Colt and Remi. I love living here, and I love Christmas. Thanks for all the presents and everything. Amen."

Colt stood and clapped once. "And go."

"Wait!" Remi said.

"I can't wait!" Abby said.

Remi reached for the five matching boxes. "Open these first." She handed one to Colt, Ben, and Abby, and kept two for herself.

"Why do you get two?" Colt asked.

"Because. Just worry about yours," Remi said.

"Ready, set, go," Colt said quickly before tearing into the wrapping paper.

Ben was the first to get the box opened. "It's pajamas."

Colt pulled his out, and his eyes widened. "They match."

Abby's mouth formed a perfect O. "Family

jammies!" She rubbed her hand over the night-gown. "This is the softest thing in my life."

Remi held hers up too. "What do you think?"

Colt stood. "I didn't take you for a matching pajama kind of mom, but I'm here for it. I'm wearing this all day."

Abby struggled to her feet. "Me too. Me too."

"There's another one." Remi held up the smaller package and shook it in one hand.

"Who's it for?" Ben asked.

"All of us. Open it." Remi placed it in the middle of the room, and Ben and Abby descended upon it, ripping and tearing until the box was torn open.

Ben held up the tiny onesie that matched the other pajamas. "What's this?"

"That's not gonna fit any of us," Abby said.

Colt dropped the clothes in his hands and stared at the onesie in Ben's hand. When Colt turned to look at Remi, recognition lit up in his eyes. "Are you serious?" he shouted.

Tears filled Remi's vision. The hormones were already working overtime. "Yeah." The word came out shaky, but it was news she was happy to deliver.

Ben looked over his shoulder at Colt. "What's she crying about?"

Abby's chin quivered. "Are you okay?"

"I'm great," Remi said. "I'm happy."

"We're having a baby!" Colt shouted. He bent

over, grabbed Ben under the arms, and hoisted him into the air. "We're having a baby!"

"A baby!" Abby shouted. "Are you sure? How do you know? Where are we going to get it?"

Remi covered her face when the tears kept coming. She'd been thrilled when she realized what was happening, but Colt's excitement was unfiltered joy, and he'd shared that happiness with her.

When she lifted her head and lowered her hands, Colt knelt in front of her. His fingers threaded into her hair as he pulled her in for a kiss. The press of his lips against hers was hard and fierce, strong and sure like his love.

Ben and Abby cheered and jumped around the living room, but Colt's smile held Remi's attention.

Oh, good grief. His eyes were all shimmery, and if he cried, she would just lose it all and fall into sobs. The emotions were in full control, and she couldn't do anything to stop herself.

"I love you," he whispered.

"I love you too," she whispered back.

"My present for you is officially outdated."

Remi chuckled and rubbed her eyes. "Why is that?"

He stood and reached for an ornament on the tree–the only one that the kids hadn't made out of paper or popsicle sticks. He put it in Remi's hand. It was an interlocking set of four horseshoes. Each had a name on it, and a banner at the bottom said "The Walkers."

Remi threw her head back and laughed. "It's perfect. We'll have something to remember our first and only Christmas as a family of four."

Abby and Ben launched themselves at Remi from both sides, and she wrapped her hand around the ornament, protecting the gift Colt had given her.

"Easy. Easy." Colt pushed a hand through his hair. "Son of a biscuit. I'm gonna be one of those crazy hover husbands."

Remi reached around Abby to wipe her face again. "That's only news to you. I've been expecting it since I found out."

Colt stared at her and shook his head slowly. "I make no apologies."

Remi tightened her arms around the kids. "Me either."

"We have something for you too!" Abby said as she shuffled out of Remi's lap.

Ben ran into his and Abby's bedroom and came back out a second later with two pieces of construction paper. He handed a pink one to Abby and kept a green one in his hands. Ben counted to three, and the kids offered the pages to Colt and Remi.

Remi took hers and opened it. Inside the folded page, a drawing took up the left side. What looked to be a boy knelt on the right, and a woman wearing a crown and a dress that flowed out at the bottom wide enough to cover the width of the page. A big ring with a scribbly jewel was drawn between them.

The right side of the page read, "Can we call you mommy?"

Remi jumped up and gasped. "Really?"

"Woo-hoo!" Colt hollered. "You bet you can!"

Ben punched a fist in the air. "Yes!"

Colt pointed to the drawing in his card. "I have to ask. What is up with my hands?"

Remi peeked at the picture to see a drawing of what was supposed to be Colt with big, clawed hands.

"Those are your tickle hands," Abby said.

Colt looked at the drawing again. "Oh, they look deceptively creepy. Anyway, you can officially call us Mom and Dad."

Remi's excitement dimmed when she thought about Mark and Brittany. "Are you sure?" she asked the kids.

Abby nodded vigorously. "We're sure."

"Yeah, we haven't forgotten Mom and Dad because you talk about them a lot, but we're really glad you let us come live with you." Ben's voice started to shake. "And we need a mom and dad."

Colt wrapped Ben up in a hug. "We get it. You can call us Mom and Dad, and you'll always be our kids."

"Like the new baby?" Abby asked.

"Just like the new baby," Remi said quickly.

Colt stood and propped his hands on his hips as he paced the living room. "Whew. Anyone else need to run around the house a few times?"

"I want to put my new jammies on!" Abby said.

Colt grabbed his pajamas and darted around the tree, leaping over presents. "I'll get mine on first."

"Nu-uh!" Ben said, right on Colt's tail.

Within seconds, Remi was left alone and laughing in the living room. She walked to the bedroom and closed the door behind her. Colt was pulling the shirt over his head and struggling. "Come on. We have to beat them."

Remi tugged the hem of his shirt down and leaned in close. Colt's frenzy subsided, and she wrapped her arms around his waist. She lifted onto her toes and met him in a kiss. His hands found a home on her waist, pulling her close as he brushed his lips slowly over hers.

When the kids' hurried footsteps echoed through the house, Colt broke the kiss.

"Can we do more of that later?" he whispered. "I'm so happy I can't stay still."

"Anytime." Remi looked up at him. "I've been thinking about something lately. Would you like to renew our vows?"

Colt laughed. "You mean renew *your* vows?" He stood up straight and nodded once, mocking her pitiful excuse of vows at their wedding as he said, "Thank you."

Remi swatted his chest. "I was nervous!"

"You were something because who says 'Thank you?'"

"I really want another chance to tell you how much I love you. And I want to do it in front of our friends, family, and God."

"Next Saturday work for you?" Colt asked.

"I don't care when it is, but I want this. I want you."

His intense stare sent a shiver over her skin as he locked eyes with her. "You have me. You have all of me. My whole heart for my whole life."

Remi smiled. "Same."

"Let me see your drawing," Colt said as he grabbed for the paper she held. He studied it for a second before waving it in the air. "You look great. I look like Edward Scissorhands."

"I even have a crown," Remi pointed out.

Colt looked at the drawing again. "You know, I think you need a promotion." He slid his arms back around her. "How does queen sound?"

"Queen?"

"My queen. Queen of this home. Queen of this kingdom we're building."

Remi swallowed hard and whispered, "I like that." Colt had changed her in ways she never thought possible, and it was all for the good. She would be honored to spend the rest of her life leading their home beside him.

Colt glanced at the door where the kids could be heard rustling around in the living room. His shoulders sank an inch. "I really wanted to win."

Remi looked up at her best friend and whispered, "We've already won."

EPILOGUE

C olt rocked back and forth in his boots. They weren't his worn-in ranch boots, but at least he'd been able to come to a compromise with Everly. She'd wanted him to wear dress shoes.

A shudder raced up his spine. Dress shoes sounded as appealing as wearing a monkey suit. At least his Sunday boots were comfortable.

Glancing at the door to the music minister's office, he stretched his neck to one side and then the other. Brett had about two minutes before Colt took matters into his own hands.

The door opened, and Brett stuck his head in. "The coast is clear. Operation Waverly is a go."

Colt didn't waste a second. He rushed into the back hallway of the church and counted the steps to the nursery. The whole day had been a series of slow minutes, as Abby called them. If only time would stretch out this far for the rest of his life. Those were the minutes and seconds he wanted to savor.

He rounded the corner, and the nursery came into view. Colt checked both ways before slipping into the room. He closed the door behind him and set his eyes on the prize.

Remi raised her arms, covering very little of the front of the white dress she wore. "Colt Walker! Get out!"

"No way. I worked too hard to get in here. I'm not leaving yet."

"You're not supposed to see the bride before the wedding. And as much as I think that's the stupidest thing I've ever heard, Everly said I would regret it if I gave in."

Colt took two steps, clearing the distance between them. "Then, I'll make sure you don't regret it."

Remi opened her mouth to speak, but Colt sealed his lips to hers. Breathing in the fire she ignited, he slid his hands over the smooth fabric of the dress at her waist and pulled her to him. With each move of her mouth against his, the space between them melted away, leaving only one person, one heart, and one mind.

She was a part of him—now and forever. He hadn't been fully himself since the day he met her. She'd changed him, and only for the better.

Remi's arms wrapped around his neck, and her

fingers slid into his hair. Every kiss, every touch between them contained pieces of the desire he'd hidden for years. All of it belonged to Remi, and he'd spend the rest of his life showing her and their family the extent of his love.

When he pulled away, Remi's eyes slowly fluttered open.

Victory. Pure, sweet victory.

"That was nice," she whispered. "Definitely no regrets about the pre-wedding rendezvous."

"Since Everly said I should be respectful and not ravage you in front of everyone, I wanted to get that off my chest before the super classy wedding we're having."

"Vow renewal. You've already sealed the deal."

"You better believe I did, and it wasn't even my idea. Either time."

Remi's mouth opened wide, and her eyebrows shot up. "Are you kidding me?"

"Nope. It was your idea. Both times."

"Colt! I–"

He cut her off with another kiss. They both knew he'd wanted to do the proposing, but he was having too much fun giving her a hard time about proposing to let it slide.

The door opened, and Remi pushed against his chest, taking two big steps back.

"Remi!" Everly's voice might have been a little

high, but the smile on her face said she was more amused than disappointed.

Remi pointed to him. "He started it."

"I did, and I have no regrets," Colt said.

Everly jerked her head toward the hallway. "Will you get to the altar? We're about to start."

Colt turned back to Remi and gave her a wink before following Everly. His second wedding to Remi was as casual as the first. Dozens of their friends filled the pews the way they did every Sunday, and Colt stopped to say hey to a few people on his way to take his position at the front of the sanctuary next to Brother Higgins.

A few minutes later, the music started, and the doors at the front of the church opened. Abby stepped into the large room with a smile that gathered all of the attention.

Who knew a little girl could completely steal his heart? Abby had, and Colt planned to continue to spoil her rotten every chance he got.

When she reached the altar, Colt met her and swept her into his arms. She giggled in his ear, and he whispered, "I love you."

"Love you too." She kissed his cheek sweetly before he set her on her feet. She took her place on the other side of the pastor with confidence and waited until Ben walked down the aisle.

Ben watched the toes of his boots as he walked a

little too quickly to the front of the church. He marched up the step to stand next to Colt.

Colt leaned over. "Psst."

Ben looked up.

"Thanks for being my best man."

Ben held up a fist for Colt to bump, and they both turned toward the doors where Remi would hopefully appear soon.

And appear she did. Wow. Colt had seen her less than ten minutes ago, but Remi knew how to make an entrance. Her auburn hair was a little wavy, and her dress showed off the figure that would soon be changing with the pregnancy.

Remi was an amazing mom, and a montage of the perfect months they'd spent together as a family flashed through his mind. There had been a point in time when she'd sworn she wasn't made for motherhood. She'd thought she wouldn't be a good wife.

Oh, how wrong she'd been. The woman knew how to set her mind to something and excel.

Remi's smile beamed, and he swallowed the rising emotions. He needed to make it through the vows without blubbering like a baby.

When Remi stopped in front of him, he offered her his hand. She took it, but it wasn't the graceful, soft motion of a princess or a queen. She took his hand the way she'd taken his heart–with assurance and determination.

Unable to resist, he pulled her in for a hug.

Unable to speak, he just held her for uncounted seconds. If their friendship had been strong before, it was unbreakable now.

They took their places in front of Brother Higgins and faced each other hand in hand.

"We're gathered together to witness the renewal of vows between Colt and Remi Walker. They have pledged their devotion before God, but it is my understanding that Remi wanted a do-over."

Their friends laughed. Most of them had heard of Remi's "Thank you" vows. She turned and grinned at them, comfortable laughing at herself.

When it was Colt's turn to recite his vows, he squeezed Remi's hands.

"I stand by my original promises to you. I intend to love you and care for you until the day I die. In sickness, health, joy, and sadness, I'll be right beside you. Remi, I've loved you since day one. How could I see you every day and be with you all the time and not be completely head over heels for you?"

Remi bowed her head and laughed, but they both knew it was the truth. He'd decided a long time ago that Remi was his other half–crafted by the great Creator to be his partner in life.

He looked down at their joined hands. "I knew you would break me before I could earn your love, but you were worth all the waiting. I love you, and I'm grateful to be your husband. I give you and our family my loyalty forever."

Remi's shoulders tensed, and she bit her lips between her teeth. She was holding back tears, and it was nice to know Colt wasn't the only one overwhelmed by the ceremony.

Brother Higgins gave Remi the go-ahead, and she nodded, still staring at Colt.

She released a deep breath and whispered, "Hey."

"Hey," Colt whispered back.

"I love you."

Her words were still quiet, so Colt adopted the same tone. "I love you too."

When she spoke again, her volume was bolder. "I'm late to the game, but I know where I'm meant to be now. You showed me how to love myself, and through that, I knew I loved you too. Thank you for loving me patiently and giving me the room to grow in my own time."

Her shoulders swelled with a gasping breath, and she let it out through rounded lips. "I'm hard to love, but you didn't give up on me. My trust was broken by others, and you paid the price for that. I shouldn't have done that to you, but if trust is earned, you've earned mine a hundred times over. I give you my trust, my heart, and my devotion. I'll gladly stand beside you for the rest of my life." Her chin shook as she let out a ragged breath. "Thank you for giving me the love and family I never thought I would have."

Colt wrapped her in his arms and let her cry on his chest. She was everything he'd hoped for and more. His life wasn't complete–they still had a baby on the way and who knew what else–but he was whole, and he always would be.

Brother Higgins rushed through the rest of his planned service. "You may now kiss the bride."

The small crowd erupted in cheers as Colt sealed his lips with Remi's. The salt of her tears remained on his lips as the kiss ended.

"I'm pleased to reintroduce Mr. and Mrs. Colton Walker!"

The cheers rose as the congregation stood to their feet. The guys from the ranch hooted, and every woman in the room wiped their eyes.

Colt swept Remi and her flowing dress into his arms and carried her down the aisle, ready to love her and their family with everything he had for the rest of his life.

BONUS EPILOGUE
BRETT

Brett sipped punch out of the teensy clear plastic cup. The reception was cool and all, but would it kill them to use bigger cups? He'd refilled the squatty little thing a dozen times already. Half of his dinner had been spent running back and forth to the refreshments bar.

"Brett."

He turned at the call and tipped his kiddie cup to Everly. "Hey, nice party."

She tilted her head and gave him a proud grin. "Thanks. Would you mind helping out? I need someone to help load the gifts into Colt's truck."

The punch slid down the wrong pipe in his throat, and he coughed. "Were we supposed to bring gifts?"

Everly waved her hand. "Not really. The invitation said that the couple were already established in their marriage and didn't need gifts, but a few of the church friends wanted to give something anyway."

"Whew. That's a relief. Yeah, I'll help out. Lead the way."

Brett chucked his trusty cup in the trash as he followed Everly to one of the Sunday School classrooms. Everly's description of "a few" might differ from Brett's. There were no less than twenty bulky gifts on the long table.

Everly picked up one of the bigger ones. "Hold out your arms."

Brett did as he was told as Everly stacked the presents.

"Okay. That's enough for this load." She picked up a few of the medium-sized gifts and a jingling set of keys. "I'll go first and get the doors."

Brett followed her out the side door of the church to where Colt's truck was parked. Darkness had fallen, and a light layer of snow covered everything in sight. Everly clicked the key fob and opened the back door of the truck.

"You just stand there, and I'll load them in," Everly said.

He handed over the last one. "I think we can fit the others in here."

"If not, we can use Blake's truck too."

The loud rumble of an engine interrupted the quiet night, and they both turned as headlights shone their way.

The truck sped up the road and jerked to turn into the church parking lot. Rubber burned and snow flew as the driver locked the brakes. The vehicle shook to a stop, and the passenger door opened. A thin woman fell out onto the gravel pavement, not even trying to brace for the impact.

Brett was running before the truck peeled back out onto the road. "Get Jameson!" he shouted over his shoulder at Everly. Brett had watched the woman's head bounce off the pavement, and the foreman had been an EMT in his former life. If the woman needed medical help, Jameson was the closest, fastest option.

Brett slid to the ground beside the limp body. Dark blood tangled in her hair, and she lay limp on her side.

Brushing the hair from her face, he shouted, "Ma'am? Ma'am?" The silence turned his stomach as he cradled her head to roll her over. She fell lifeless into his waiting arms, and he pressed his fingers to her neck, searching and praying for a pulse.

His own heart was beating loud enough to pound in his ears, and he closed his eyes to focus on the feel of her skin beneath his fingertips. Finally, the small flutter of her heartbeat allowed him to breathe. He leaned his ear to her mouth and closed his eyes to focus again. He couldn't hear breathing.

Frantic, he pushed the matted hair from her

face. The pounding and crunching of quick foot-steps in the thin snow behind him should have calmed his panic, but it didn't. Blood was every-where, and he was powerless to help.

One last brush of her hair, and he could see her face.

He couldn't hear the running footsteps anymore. Couldn't breathe. Couldn't think. Couldn't see anything but the familiar face in the dim moonlight. Even swollen and bloody, he'd always recognize the face that haunted his dreams.

"Thea."

OTHER BOOKS BY MANDI BLAKE

ABOUT THE AUTHOR

Mandi Blake was born and raised in Alabama where she lives with her husband and daughter, but her southern heart loves to travel. Reading has been her favorite hobby for as long as she can remember, but writing is her passion. She loves a good happily ever after in her sweet Christian romance books and loves to see her characters' relationships grow closer to God and each other.

ACKNOWLEDGMENTS

This book brought me through a tough time in my life, and there were moments when I didn't think I would finish it. Despite the difficulties, I think this book helped me grow more than any other. I poured my heart into the story. It was my reminder to hope. If Colt and Remi could overcome their obstacles, I could be strong enough to hold my head up when the world was against me. Because we're warned that the world will try to break us down. We're also reminded to look to the Father for guidance and acceptance, not the world.

First, I want to thank the friends who have encouraged me through the writing of this book and so many others. Stephanie Martin and Hannah Jo Abbott reminded me daily to keep my focus on the Lord's work. They supported me and cheered me on when I didn't know how to write anymore. Best of all, they prayed for me. They prayed over my family, my heart, and my work. Those prayers were answered, and I never forgot that the Lord was with me. I never felt alone.

I have one major piece of advice for you. If you don't have friends who will pray for you, find some. If you can't find anyone, come to me. I'm pretty easy to reach on social media, and I will stop what I'm doing to pray for you in that moment. I believe in the power of prayer, and I'll also remind you that you're never alone.

Next, I have to thank my beta readers. They give me the best advice, and I trust them to be honest with me at all times. They certainly made this book and all of the others better. I'm blessed to have a group of women who support me so wholeheartedly. Trudy Cordle, Demi Abrahamson, Tanya Smith, Ginny Roberts, Laura De La Torre, Haley Powell, Natasha Wall, Stephanie Taylor, Vicci Lucas, Pam Humphrey, and Jenna Eleam, thank you so much for your friendship and guidance.

I'm always thankful for my cover designer, Amanda Walker, and my editor, Brandi Aquino. They polish everything I do and make it into a beautiful, finished piece.

I never have dedications in my books, but consider this one dedicated to my husband. He's the one who showed me how we could do things better together. He's the one who cheers me on and encourages me when I'm tired or losing sight of my purpose. He's the one who prays with me and points me to the Lord. He's the reason I was able to finish this book.

Last, but never least. Thank you for reading and taking a chance on this book. I know there are millions of things in this world we can turn to when we want entertainment, and it means a lot to me that you chose to take the time to read this book. I wrote it with you in mind. Every word was meant for you, and I hope this story touched your heart the way it did mine.

THE OTHER SIDE

WOLF CREEK RANCH BOOK 5

They fell in love before their families hated each other. Will their love be enough to mend fences?

Thea Howard skipped town ten years ago after a tragic accident. She left behind the man she loved along with the grief and anger that consumed their lives.

Brett Patton never expected to see Thea again. When he finds her injured on a snowy night, he sees his second chance with the one who got away.

Despite the years, distance, and obstacles between them, Brett helps her hide at the ranch where he works, but his attempts to convince her that things could work out between them this time come to a screeching halt when she disappears.

Brett won't stop until he finds the woman he never stopped loving. Can he find her in time to get their second chance? Or will their feuding families once again rip them apart?

Made in the USA
Coppell, TX
18 February 2025

46079155R00260